COLOR ME PRETTY

B. CELESTE

COLOR

ME

PRETTY

B. CELESTE

color me pretty

b. celeste

This Book is sold subject to the condition that it shall not, by way of trade or otherwise, be lent, re-sold, duplicated, hired out, or otherwise circulated without the publisher's prior written consent in any form of binding or cover other than that in which it is published and without similar condition including this condition being imposed on the subsequent purchaser.

Color Me Pretty

Copyright © 2020 by B. Celeste

This is a work of fiction. Names, characters, businesses, places, events and incidents are either the products of the author's imagination or used in a fictitious manner. Any resemblance to actual persons, living or dead, or actual events is purely coincidental.

Cover Artist: RBA Designs

Interior by: Micalea Smeltzer

Published by: B. Celeste

All rights reserved.

No part of this book may be reproduced or transmitted in any form or by any means without written permission of the author

dedication

To everyone who asked for a father's best friend
romance from me. This one is for you.

playlist

"Nobody" – Selena Gomez
"Skyscraper" – Demi Lovato
"Colors (Stripped)" – Halsey
"Stay with Me" – Sam Smith
"Try" – Colbie Caillat
"Nightmare" – Halsey
"Never Enough" – Loren Allred
"Unsteady" – X Ambassadors
"Never Be the Same" – Camila Cabello
"Say Something" – A Great Big World
"Try" – Colbie Caillat

prologue

DELLA

A PLUME of cigarette smoke was the only indication that I wasn't alone in the brisk night, shadowed by the few lights in the alleyway. I wasn't walking away from the thrumming music because of the overwhelming scene inside the normally barren warehouse, I was doing it for the man I'd seen sneak out the emergency exit. He looked more uncomfortable than I did, suffocating in dark dress clothes and putting on a good face to appease the people for the sake of his best friend.

Pushing myself off the brick wall that vibrated my chest with every pump of the slow bass, I found myself drawn to the smell of tobacco, my nude heels clicking over the cracked pavement until my eyes were welcomed by expensive polished Tom Ford dress shoes and pressed dress slacks, perfectly tailored to the tall six-five figure encompassed by them, until my gaze drifted over the tight white silk pulled over taut muscles and olive skin with the sleeves rolled up to his elbows, showcasing bulging veins in his forearms, despite it being forty degrees tonight.

I knew the brand of the shoes he wore because I'd once used them to stand on during a dance very similar to the one we walked out on only moments ago. My feet were too tiny to keep up with the slow melody that he set for us at the time. *Stand on my feet, little Della.* I knew they must have been expensive because the blonde woman who'd been wrapped around his arm that night had all but gasped at me using them as a platform. I didn't like her because she smelled too much like alcohol and something strong and floral that made my eyes itch. More than that, my dislike stemmed from her taking up all his time and attention if I wasn't plastered on his feet.

But Theodore West and I danced like that, my tiny feet on his large shoes as he took lead, for as long as I wanted, which was much longer than a man like Theo would typically grant anybody. Even the blonde. Perhaps the kindness he offered me then was why I followed him into the dark, letting the secondhand smoke absorb into my lungs with every inhale I forced myself to take.

I hated smoking, and always wanted to scold him for doing it when he knew my grandfather had died of lung cancer. I may not have known my grandparents, but that didn't make the outcome of their demise any less important when the man I grew up adoring sucked in nicotine like it was his favorite flavor.

"You shouldn't be out here." His gruff voice penetrated the silence, making my leather covered arms pebble with goosebumps.

Tightening my jacket over the skin exposed from the deep V of my black cocktail dress, I hugged myself for warmth. "You shouldn't be either, especially without a jacket on. It's cold."

"I'm fine." He took another drag of his cigarette, still not looking at me. His focus was on the empty road, dimly lit by broken streetlights. My father had loved this section of the city despite it being worn down and half abandoned. He hated me coming here alone, forbidding it on more than one occasion, no matter his soft spot for the warehouse that he met my mother in when they were younger.

"You left," I noted idiotically, shifting on my feet. They ached from the four-inch platform heels I subjected them too, but they made my legs look good, longer, which my five-two height needed to pull off the longer dress. It was my mother's favorite item of clothing and seemed fitting for tonight's "celebration" of my father's life.

He finally turned his head, his dark blue eyes piercing mine until I shrunk back. "What are you doing out here, Adele?"

Adele. Not Della. He called me that when he was

3

upset. Not always at me, just life. It made sense considering we were saying goodbye to a man we both mutually cared about. Swallowing past the lump in my throat, I swiped a palm down the side of my thigh. "Checking on you. You were quiet all night and looked like you wanted to murder everybody who came up to you."

"I'm not a fan of the socialites who decided to come," he remarked coolly. "Your father kept them in his good graces out of civility, but even he thought they were pompous assholes. We both know who his true friends were when shit hit the fan. Where were they then? Don't get me started on their comments on the reception like it should have been held at the fucking Ritz or some shit."

I used to hate it when he swore. His brow would twitch, and his fists would clench if he got really angry, and I always itched to comfort him, to make him feel better. But Theo was not the kind of man you controlled, least of all when he was worked up. He was the man you let control you, and you did it with a smile. It was understandable that he was agitated tonight. He was right about the people in attendance—they sucked up to my father because of the power he held as the governor of New York but talked behind his back the second he turned away. I was surprised that so many people showed up since the scandal broke leading to the Saint James family downfall.

He dropped the half-smoked cigarette onto the ground, damp from the earlier rain showers, and extinguished with the tip of his shoe. "Go back inside, Della."

The nickname I preferred to be called eased the tightness that had formed in my chest since the night began. There was only so much smiling and thanking people I could do while listening to their empty condolences as if they cared my father was dead. They didn't care when he was arrested. Why start now that he was buried next to my mother six feet under? "What about you?"

He looked me over, his eyes roaming over my covered form, the familiar black leather jacket cradling my body for warmth, before letting his eyes drift back up to mine. The slight shadow lining his square jaw was unlike him. He preferred to be clean-shaven, business called for as much. *"Presentation is everything, Adele,"* his ex-wife Mariska would always remind me whenever I told him I liked the stubble. It made him look as tough as his personality. No nonsense. Free. I used to think he shaved for her, but even after their divorce over four years ago, he kept up with the façade. Until now, I supposed.

"I'm going home. I did my part." His pause, heavy sigh, and shifted weight made me wonder if he was reconsidering. He'd stayed almost all day to help set up since the people Aunt Sophie hired had bailed, something she'd been rambling on about when she called freaking out that she'd have to reschedule. I didn't blame him for wanting to go, I just wished he didn't. I wanted him to stay. For me. He asked, "Are you going to be okay? You got a ride back to your place?"

I nodded slowly, moving my wavy platinum blonde tresses out of my face. I'd dyed my normally light brown hair two months ago and was met by mixed reactions. But Theo told me he liked it, told me to ignore the "other assholes" who thought otherwise because their opinion didn't matter. He of all people knew their opinions mattered to me too much. They always had growing up. I'd just wanted to pretend to be somebody else for a while—somebody blonde who had fun with little care. Maybe a piece of me even thought the hair color would appeal to Theo more than my natural did. Turned out, hair dye didn't have magical powers.

"Aunt Lydia said she'd give me a ride back after cleanup. Are you...Will you be okay?" I knew how much he cared about my father. They were friends for a long time, most of their lives, having shared the most important milestones together every step of the way. When news broke that Anthony Saint James had been involved in a money laundering scandal that took funds from the state *and* people close to him who had invested in his endeavors, things had gotten bad. Theo was questioned because my father had once been a partner in his growing business, and he hadn't been hit by the economic fraud my father was committing unlike others close in his circle. The investigators were sure they'd find him as guilty as my father, but there was never any evidence indicating as much. And Theo...he never left my side through it all. Not once during the trials or

6

media blasts did he consider for a second abandoning me to the vultures that New York City, and my father, had fed me to.

His eyes closed momentarily. "I'm supposed to ask you that considering whose funeral we're at."

I let my shoulders lift, giving him the best smile I could under the circumstances. "We all lost somebody."

"He was your father."

Taking a daring step closer, I inhaled the strong cologne and tobacco mixture wafting from him. He was all man, all the time, in the way he smelled, acted, and carried himself. His blue eyes could see through me, and his smile, on the rare occurrence he gave one, melted the skin right off me.

"He was your friend," I added softly.

The way he watched me, looked down at me with such intensity, had me shivering. "Are you cold?"

Slowly, I shook my head. Rising on my toes, I brushed my lips on the underside of his jaw, causing him to lock up. It was only a tiny caress, but his reaction made it seem like more. It always did when we got close. And we did. Often.

"Della."

"Don't worry." I stepped away before he could say anything more or move from me first. That kind of rejection on a night like this was one I wouldn't be able to walk away from without another piece of my heart shattering. "It was a goodnight kiss. Nothing more."

His voice was rough, cracked. "It can't be anything more, not even now. Never again. Do you understand?"

I blinked, noting the faint mark of pink lipstick on his skin where my lips rested for a microscopic moment. "I told you I understood when you left my apartment that morning."

Theo knew which morning I meant. It still hurt to think about even all this time later. To think he believed I would pounce on another opportunity to be in bed with him just because my father was gone made my stomach ache. I might not have been on the best terms with my father after what he'd done, but that didn't mean I was going to use his death as an excuse.

I didn't want Theo's pity.

I wanted his love.

"His death changes nothing," Theo added.

His death changes everything. Just not what he was insinuating. Deep down, I knew he was trying to get a reaction out of me. Maybe even hurt me in order to distance us. He'd done that plenty since the morning he left my apartment in a hurry like I'd threatened him. As if waking up beside me in our state of undress was that unappealing to him when he was the one who showed up and initiated our actions that night to begin with. Hurt laced into my being, squeezing my heart to the point of physical pain, but I held my head up high and pretended it didn't bother me, no matter how much I clung to the possibilities that involved the man in front of me.

He was good at hurting people. That man was skilled at putting others in their place when it benefited him, but never me. Never his little Della. It made me wonder who he'd become now that his oldest friend was truly gone. Not just off to prison, to Rikers Island, but gone.

Who will you become now? I wanted so badly to ask him.

Theodore Bennett West. My father's best friend. The man I've loved ever since I knew what love was, even when I shouldn't have.

During a very drunken binge when his guard was down, he made it feel like maybe those feelings were reciprocated. Except he woke up in a tangle of my cheap clearance sheets, half naked, with a mask of regret and disgust on his face when he saw me in nothing more than a matching pink panty set beside him after he'd stripped me of my normal pajamas. He'd barged his way in smelling like his liquor cabinet, touched me in ways I'd never been touched by him before, and made me feel…whole.

I could still taste the whiskey on his breath, the tobacco on his tongue, and the desperation in his words as he told me he needed one night. Just one.

"Just one night, Della. That's all I need to…"

I didn't know what he needed the one night for, but it was clear something had happened. It didn't take my body long to cooperate as he pinned me against the wall with his hips, pressing his hard erection against me to show me what exactly he needed. The way he ground into my softest spot and touched me in my most sensitive area with those rough fingers made the spark I'd suspected we'd had since I was old enough to know what that felt like, come to life. There was a fire in us that night as he kept me against that wall and made me come using just his hand while his mouth had devoured mine like he needed more.

Though we hadn't gone as far as I would have liked before he passed out from who knew how much alcohol he'd consumed, the moments we shared were permanently tattooed on my flawed skin for the world to see. I didn't hide it.

"As I said," I replied instead, voice skillfully calm, "I understand just fine, Theo. Please drive safe."

He stared at me for a moment too long before swiping his large palm through his longer-than-normal tussled brown hair and turned on his heels. No jacket, and not another word.

And I watched him walk away.

Again.

chapter one

DELLA

TURNING the page of sheet music, I settled back onto the bench and straightened my spine before placing my fingers onto the ivory just as Aunt Sophie showed me.

"I'm not sure I'm getting this," I admitted, trying to remember which keys were which.

The pristine middle-aged woman sitting in an elegant red armchair beside the window scoffed. "You just need to keep practicing as we discussed. Your mother should have taught you how to play years ago."

Fighting the frown that always came with the conversation, I rolled my shoulders and pressed down on the keys until an ungodly noise came from the pianoforte. There was no doubt in my mind I'd gotten it wrong, mixed up the keys for the umpteenth time no matter Sophie's insistence that I'd get it. My mother hadn't taught me how to play because I never showed interest, and she never liked forcing me into things that wouldn't make me happy. That was why Sophie disliked her.

"She needs to be pushed, Elizabeth. What better way to discipline her?" Not long after that exchange, I'd started ballet. Sure, my mother had suggested it, but it wasn't like she'd twisted my arm to get me to go. I liked the pretty leotards and all the pink we'd worn—the bows, the tutus, the uncomfortable pointe shoes I learned to love with time. Ballet became a way my mother and I grew close, and it appeased Sophie in some ways because she saw how I excelled at it.

"You have the fingers for it," she kept going, waving her hand at me absentmindedly as she flipped through some feminine magazine. It was the same one I'd seen my mother look at and begged to read to me.

"You're too young to learn what's in these, my sweet Adele. When you're older," my mother would promise.

But the day never came because breast cancer took her from us mere months after she was diagnosed. It was fast, aggressive, and ugly. My father had never been quite right after her passing, but he tried for me. For our family. Considering I was only twelve at the time, he did what he could with what knowledge he had having two little sisters—Sophie and Lydia. Plus, they'd both offered to help whenever he needed it. As always, my father had been too proud. It was a trait I got from him.

"My fingers seem to disagree," I murmured, dropping my hands into my lap and sighing to myself. "Perhaps another instrument?" *Please say no.* When I gave up dance after circumstances became too much, Sophie insisted I needed something in my life. Even though I'd long since found joy in painting, Sophie told me the hobby I invested in had to be something "appropriate" for young women because getting paint under my nails wasn't that. It still made me want to roll my eyes, but I relented and tried what she wanted me to. I owed her that much. She did a lot for me after my mother died, starting Sunday brunches so I'd have an excuse to leave the house for a while, and giving me old albums of photos from my father's childhood, including some of his teenage years that had my mother in them.

"Piano is classy, Adele." I'd gotten her full attention now, the magazine forgotten on her skirt-covered lap. She wore her usual attire—a tight pencil skirt with a button-up tucked into the waist that showed off her sleek curves. She garnered every straight male's attention with the swivel of her hips no matter where we were. But she never flaunted, flirted, or gave any of them a hint of hope. "How are you going to get a man otherwise? Most men of prestige expect their women to have talents that go beyond the kitchen."

My face instantly contorted with disbelief. "Maybe

with my fast wit and brain? It isn't the fifties anymore, Sophie. Women can be individuals."

Her eyes rolled, something she did often when I opened my mouth to point out how derogatory she was to her own sex. "Trust me, darling, men don't want wit."

"On the contrary," a new voice cut in from the door-way. Looking over my shoulder, I smiled wide at Lawrence McKinley's casual stance against the door-frame of the parlor.

"Oh, hush." Aunt Sophie stood, a smile on her own face that contradicted her tone. "I wish you wouldn't encourage Adele on her silly thoughts. Come, give me a hug."

Lawrence was a friend since we were in diapers. We did everything together from bathing to schooling. We fought like siblings growing up, but things changed during our experimental pre-teen phases, which lead to us being each other's first everything a few years later. Too young, I realized now, but I didn't regret it. Even though we were still good friends, we never turned into more for a lot of reasons. Mainly because of his obses-sion with his male teammates, and mine with a certain forty-year-old business mogul.

My best friend wrapped Sophie in his freakishly long arms that were muscular from the sports he played. Football was his favorite, but baseball was what he was best at, which was what he got a scholar-ship for at Bentley University, a private school in the city. "I find Adele's thoughts anything but silly. You should see the way men look at her on campus. I doubt they'd care if she couldn't play the piano to save her life."

"Hey!" He wasn't wrong, but I couldn't help but frown over his bluntness.

He walked over to me and pressed a kiss to my temple like he always did in greeting. If it weren't that, he'd pick me up and spin me around until I got dizzy. "You know I love you, Della, but you're not a musician. Never were."

Standing, I playfully shoved him away. "I know that but you're my friend. You're supposed to lie and tell me how talented I am."

His laugh was deep, rumbling his broad shoulders until I couldn't help but join in. "As your *best* friend I'm obligated to tell you the truth. You suck. Now painting? You're better than anybody at that. Have you seen her work, Sophie?"

"I have. Don't get me wrong, they're good. But—" I tuned her out while she explained why painting wasn't classy, clean, or good enough for me to do. It didn't matter what she thought. I found painting relaxing. Like dance was, once upon a time. I'd only just started listening again when Sophie shook her head at us. "I never understood how you two never dated. We all thought you'd be engaged by now."

Perhaps Lawrence's bisexuality wasn't obvious to those who didn't spend enough time around him, but to me it was plain as day. It didn't matter who a person was, he had eyes for anyone good looking. That had been me once, but even after our teenage transgressions

15

we knew it wasn't enough. He was my friend, the very best, but nothing more. He'd asked me if it was because of Theo, how I looked at my father's friend, because even he knew it was more than a crush.

"Now who's silly," I replied softly, looking at Sophie. "We're still young. Just because you were married at my age doesn't mean I want to be, and I doubt Ren does either."

"That's because you haven't even tried."

Ren dropped an arm around my shoulders, tugging me into his side. "I tried setting her up with one of my teammates, but she said he wasn't her type."

"Alec spends more time talking about himself than anything else. Do you really blame me for not wanting to be subjected to that?"

Sophie waved her hand in the air. "You don't want to be with a college boy anyway. They're too immature. It'd suit you better to be with somebody older."

My mind instantly went to Theo, and Ren must have known it based on the way his lips quirked up at the corners. He used to tease me about my "stupid girly crush" when I admitted that I liked Theo West. As time went on and I got older, we both realized it was more than that. He was older than my twenty-two years, but he was a few years younger than my father. I'd kept that in mind whenever my conscience told me it wouldn't work. I'd seen how his eyes wandered over the past few years like they never had before, and if the early morning he'd stormed into my apartment so long ago now wasn't an indication, he'd certainly felt *something* for me that I held onto no matter what he told me. "I'm not dating right now. I've only got a semester left of school. I want that to be my focus."

"Of course," my knowing best friend played along, causing me to elbow his stomach. He moved his arm and winked. "We should probably go. Or did you forget you agreed to go to the house with me tonight?"

Sophie frowned at him. "That frat you're part of? I'm not sure Adele should go there after the brawl that happened last time."

"It was hardly a brawl," I argued lightly. Two guys were arguing over a girl and it got a bit messy. Beer went everywhere, including all over me. I'd broken a heel. Somebody accidently yanked my hair trying to catch themselves when the men bumped into the crowd. It was an interesting night to say the least.

"She'll be safe, Sophie. I promise."

"I feel like I need to protect her now…"

That my father couldn't. My father might not have been fond of me going to these "social events" with Lawrence, but he knew I'd be smart and cared for. I was never one to make reckless decisions, especially if it meant risking my father's reputation. Not that it mattered. He did that just fine himself.

"I've got her back, Soph." Ren was the only one who could call her that. My aunt always had wandering eyes whenever he was around, which was more times than not. I found it more amusing than weird, because neither one would do a thing about it. Ren was a smooth talker most of the time, so Sophie had a sweet spot for him.

We walked out shortly after I changed into something more "frat appropriate" which, in Lawrence's mind, was a yellow sundress that hit mid-thigh, strappy heels, and a layer of makeup that I only applied whenever I went out to college events. While I normally preferred clothes that covered me, bare feet, and little to no makeup, it was fun to put on a front that I could wash off as soon as I locked myself away at night.

The drive to the frat house was short, only ten minutes. As soon as Lawrence pulled his Jeep into his usual parking spot in the back, he jumped out and jogged around to my side and opened the door with a grin on his face. "My lady."

Rolling my eyes, I got out and adjusted my dress. "You're in a much better mood than last time I agreed to one of these. Did you finally get laid?"

He gasped, his palm flattening against his chest in mock offense. "That isn't a very ladylike question, Adele. I thought Sophie taught you better than that."

The smile on my face grew over his theatrics as he guided us into the house, our arms linked as people greeted us in the packed hallway as soon as we stepped through the door. He waved, slapped a few people on the back, and grabbed a beer that was extended to him before passing it to me.

Shaking my head, I look around the room to find other familiar faces. "I don't want to drink today. Is

Jase here? Wasn't he the one who begged for this party?"

"*Social gathering*," a husky voice corrected from behind me before two arms wrapped around my waist and picked me up. I squealed in Jase's arms as he spun us, narrowly missing a few innocent bystanders.

"Ah, that's right. You could get shut down if the college finds out about any potential parties."

He set me down with a boyish grin on his not-so-boyish face. Unlike Ren's boy next door look, Jason, his frat brother, was more matured. In looks, that was. He was the prankster, the guy that got them into trouble nine times out of ten. Even Lawrence was surprised he hadn't been booted yet. I liked him though. He was fun and could get me out of my head even when I was stuck in there for a while.

"Good to see you, Della." He bent down and pecked my cheek before shoving Lawrence's shoulder. "I thought you said you wouldn't be here. Something about 'duty calls elsewhere.' Unless our resident blonde was the duty?" His eyebrows wiggled making me laugh. Even he suspected we were more than friends. I didn't come to the frat often because I was busy with school, painting, and spending time with Sophie and Theo when I could. When I did make an appearance, it was always with Ren, Jase, and whoever their flavor of the month was. In fact, it was not so long ago I learned the redhead I'd been talking to was sleeping with both...at the same time. It'd made me uncomfortable to know what Ren was up to, but I never judged.

Shortly after that discovery, Jase had admitted that he would have made a move on me if it weren't for Ren's territorial nature. Even though I set the record straight, for what felt like the millionth time, Jase told me he wouldn't make a move anyway because Ren was his brother. Maybe not by blood, but by bond. I could respect that. Plus, I didn't want Jase as more than a friend to hang out with when I was around anyway. He was nice but knowing what he enjoyed was a little too much for me. It made me wonder what Ren had thought about our few times together. We hadn't done a lot more than was I assumed was common—traditional even. Looking back now at my lack of sex experience, I wasn't sure what other kinds there were which made me feel like such a prude. A feeling I hated.

Snapping out of the thought, I grinned at Jase and said, "He had to come to my house and insult my piano playing skills first."

His face twisted. "You're learning to play piano? Boring." He dropped an arm over my shoulders but had to bend slightly because of our height difference. He was well over six feet tall, probably close to six-three. "Let me guess. Your aunt? The one that looks like there's something shoved up her—"

"Yep, that'd be the one."

He chuckled. "Want me to tell her what men really want? I could probably show her a thing or too so she could get a good visual."

Unlike Lawrence, I had no doubt that Jason *would*

try to hook up with my aunt. "I don't need therapy, but thanks."

Ren shoved his friend away and stole my arm again. "Come on. I want us to hang out downstairs. I challenged Rita and her latest boy toy to beer pong and need a partner."

As he dragged me toward the basement stairs off the kitchen, I couldn't help but tease him. "Is this the same boy toy you've been going after since you had that sociology class together?"

"Perhaps." Translation: yes.

"You're hopeless."

"Hopelessly infatuated," he corrected before shooting me another wink. As soon as he walked into the open living area where a pool table, flat screen, and few couches were set up, we got loud cheers from some of the other guests. There weren't many people lingering down here because it was typically for "VIP" guests only, usually girlfriends of the fraternity, or whoever they were hooking up with at the time. Then there was me, the perpetual best friend slash third wheel. I was okay with it though because it meant I didn't have to suffocate in the crowd of people upstairs.

I spotted Lawrence's crush instantly hanging around Rita Malcom. She was a sweet girl that ran in a similar social circle as us. Her father worked with Theo as some investor—they might even be friends or something close to it if memory served. Rita and her father both showed up to the funeral where she'd given me a hug and her father gave me his apologies. For once, I'd believed somebody had actually felt bad that my father was killed. I didn't talk to Rita much other than the occasional greeting in passing or during these where we were typically partnered up for whatever Ren forced me to take part of, but I could see her being a friend. An ally.

As always, I didn't get a choice before I was teamed up with Rita to go against Lawrence and Ben. He was cute, around the same height as Ren, and the kind of preppy, clean-shaven guy that my best friend usually went for. He was on the lacrosse team at school, something Rita told me a while back when they first started hanging out. Like a lot of women who hung around this house, she was into any sports team and loved the attention from the players. She was sweet, but knew how to play the field, so to speak.

We lost horribly after forty-five minutes, and I downed one too many sour beers despite telling Lawrence I didn't want to drink. I usually opted against alcohol because of the medication I was on for anxiety, something my therapist had prescribed a few years ago. I didn't take them on days I knew I was going out because there was a chance this would happen. Truthfully, I wasn't even sure if they worked that well. I had good and bad days where I felt more anxious than not. It wasn't as debilitating as it used to be when I went out because media wasn't parked in front of my building trying to get an interview. There weren't paparazzi following me and snapping pictures from shrubbery or calling out my name to get an ugly photo that would be on every gossip site known to man. It was because of them that I got worse. Not just my anxiety, but...

Blowing out a breath, I cradled my stomach where a pink scar rested. How many times did TMZ make comments on my appearance? *She's gained weight. Stress eating is a sign of guilt. I thought she was a dancer?* The comments on my thighs, the way I filled out my leggings on the way to practice, the tint of my skin or how and if I wore makeup, all came back to one thing: I was a Saint James, which meant I was guilty. Guilty of pretending I didn't care about what my father had done to people or how he abused his power. Guilty of not caring about the state of the New York after my father was arrested. They crucified me in every way possible until I hated myself more than I already did. Because I did gain weight from stress eating. I did stop trying at ballet. I did stop caring. Not about others. About me.

I just...stopped.

My mood swings then had gotten me in trouble with Judith, our ballet teacher, when I stopped being able to do the routines as easily as before. She'd berated me for gaining weight and demanded I go on a special diet, making me see a dietary specialist to help me cut out the food I was "poisoning" my body with. Then there were the stretch marks. The little reminders on my stomach and thighs that told me I'd lost control when the trial began. It was televised. There were reporters every-where. I'd snuck food everywhere I went with me to ease the pain, in the form of chocolate, carbs, and anything in between. I'd damaged the body that had once been naturally thin, and my metabolism did nothing to stop the transition that would send me into a downward spiral every time I stepped in front of those studio mirrors.

"Again, Adele!"

"Higher! If you didn't eat that, you'd get a better jump!"

"What was that? Can you not bend further because of the extra padding?"

On and on it went until one day I'd broken down after practice. I'd waited until all the girls left before I realized what I needed to do. So, when I got home, I threw out all the junk food, got rid of anything that wasn't appropriate for my diet, and...stopped eating altogether. When my father looked, I was nibbling here and there to disregard any growing suspicion he might have had. That was when I discovered purging.

The anxiety medication might have helped more than I gave it credit for, but there was no medication from the level of self-hate a person had for themselves. There wasn't a pill to swallow to make people love themselves. No injection could make self-worth higher than self-consciousness on a whim. It would always be a fight for me to eat without sticking a finger down my throat or finding new methods of starving myself when nobody was looking. There were always going to be days when I wished my weight was as low as my self-esteem.

But I was better.

Be better.

Those words were a chant in my head, a soft-spoken

demand that was not pointed at me, but one I took as a sign that I needed to listen.

"Be better," my mother had said.

It was about two hours into the party when I stumbled toward the little kitchen downstairs off the main room and grabbed a bottle of water from the fridge. Ren was flirting with Ben, Rita was hanging around a frat boy who looked new to the scene, so I stayed in the corner and tried sobering up.

After about ten minutes, the water was gone, and I was tired of watching everybody couple up. Throwing the bottle into the recyclables, I pushed away from the wall on slightly unsteady feet and started walking toward Lawrence until an arm hooked around my waist from behind.

Nearly falling from the jerked motion, I groaned. "Jase, I'm not—"

"Not Jase." A pair of hot lips found the back of my neck, making me lock up. My elbow instinctively jabbed the unknown person who was giving me unwanted attention but he barely budged. "Relax, babe. I'm just playing around. You looked lonely."

I managed to turn, glaring at the idiot who smelled like cheap beer and even cheaper perfume of whoever he was mauling last. It shouldn't have surprised me to see Evan Wallace there, grinning at me half-baked like the stoner he was. "Seriously, Evan?"

"What? Lawrence is busy so I figured I'd keep you company." He hated Ren and I didn't know why, but worse, he disliked me. I barely knew him but his actions

25

toward me since we first met had been nothing but annoying. He'd made comments, catcalled, and tried getting me to go to his attic loft with him. It didn't matter how many people told him to stop, Evan was determined to do what he wanted, and it gave me a bad feeling every time.

"I don't want you to," I stated firmly.

"Aw, don't be like that, babe."

"Don't call me that." How many times had I told him that? It was impossible to tell at that point, that was how many.

His arm went back to my waist, hooking it around me and tugging me into his chest. The smell coming from his breath was nauseating, so I held my breath. It didn't help that I felt off, tired, draggy, and realized I'd drank too much to be wandering about. "You always play hard to get. We both know you're not with McKinley even if you've fooled others into believing it."

"That doesn't mean I want you." Shoving him away with what little energy I had, he stumbled into a group of girls who all complained when beer spilled onto the hardwood. It wouldn't be the worst thing the floors had seen. I was sure of it.

The water might not have helped all that much because my legs felt funny, but Evan's persistence was definitely doing something to keep me hyperaware if not semi-sober. Blinking back the heaviness of my eyes, I backed up and made my way toward Lawrence.

Except he disappeared.

"Shit," I grumbled, wincing at myself. I normally

didn't swear unless my filter was off. That usually only happened when I was pissed, tired, impatient, or a little of all three. I guessed drunk could be added to that list.

Rita saddled up beside me. "He and Ben went upstairs. Said something about fresh air, but I think we both know that's a lie."

I rubbed my temples. "Doesn't that bother you?" I loved Lawrence, but he didn't care if the people he chased were with somebody else. If he was interested, he went for it. Shameless flirting usually led to more with him if he set his sights on somebody. It was sort of impressive how bold he was, even if I didn't agree with his tactic.

Rita shrugged. "Ben and I were having fun, but I think he was using me as a beard because of his dad. His family is old school if you know what I mean." Ben's family wasn't one I knew, but it was upsetting if that was the case. I didn't know many people who were against that kind of relationship, but I wasn't naïve to think they didn't exist. Ren's parents played dumb, but I was almost positive they knew of their son's interests and just chose not to intervene.

"That sucks."

"What about you? Not strung out for your best friend. He's cute. You'd make an adorable couple, and unlike Ben, it looks like Lawrence swings both ways."

Instantly, my head shook. It was instinctive at that point because I'd had the conversations plenty of times. "That won't be happening in this lifetime. We're just friends. Although, I'd be tempted to question that since he ditched me."

She giggled, flipping her hair over her shoulder. "I'm sure they'll be back down soon enough. Want to grab a drink with me?"

I wanted to be nice and say yes, but my head was already light and fuzzy, and all I wanted was to go home and sleep tonight off. If Ren was busy with Ben, that meant heaving to find somebody else to get me home, maybe Dallas, a driver Sophie hired for me when the one my father employed was let go right after the arrest was made. "I really shouldn't. I'm going to find Ren. I kind of want to head out."

"You just got here!" She normally stayed until the middle of the night, but that wasn't me. Not even on the days I was sober, maybe especially then. Seeing what the people here did without a care in the world made me realize how much I didn't fit into their crowd. Or any crowd, it seemed. Plus, there were still people who gave me one look and started whispering. Probably about the scandal and my father, maybe about the articles online on me. That was when the tingling started, the itch of anxiety creeping up the back of my neck like prickles of heat sent to taunt me as they watched me.

I waved despite Rita's protest and gave her an apologetic smile. Evan's eyes were still on me like a hawk, following me as I weaved through the crowd. They were narrowed and it made my skin crawl, so I stayed vigilant of the way he moved a few feet behind me like he didn't want me knowing he was but was too smashed to be as stealthy as he wanted. Even a few of his frat brothers had talked about the growing difference in him over the past year. He was always annoying, but then he turned into a drunken stoner who acted out like he had nothing left to lose. Maybe if he wasn't such a pest to me, I'd find it in me to care, even be concerned.

My hand found the phone in my dress pocket, speed dialing Lawrence by muscle memory as I pulled it out. He didn't pick up, making me wonder just how busy he got with Ben as soon as they'd found a place. There was a chance they'd gone to his room, but there were too many other ones in the house for me to check and the stairs were packed full of people already.

Blinking back exhaustion, I stumbled into a few partygoers when my legs became like jelly beneath me. I murmured an apology that a few people brushed off, while a guy I recognized as Ren's teammate looked me over with concern from where he was talking to somebody by the refreshment table. I thought his name started with J. Jamie? Jacob? It didn't matter.

I dragged my hand along the wall until I made it outside, my fingers dialing a different number as my feet became heavier.

He picked up after one ring. "S-Something's wrong," I slurred, dropping onto an abandoned beach chair outside the house. There were a few people mingling, one couple making out on the lawn, and empty cans and red cups littering the freshly mowed grass.

"Where are you?" His voice was clipped, but there was enough worry etched in it to make me think it wasn't because I called. At least, I hoped it wasn't.

I was pretty sure I gave him the address, but my brain shut off somewhere between sitting down and saying anything to him. My phone was on my lap, my eyelids blinking heavily, and my mouth like lead to the point I couldn't move it. A voice in my head told me to stay awake, but it was hard to listen.

It was sometime later when I heard my name being called before familiar hands found my arms. His deep voice barked at somebody before I was being lifted.

"Della?" A new voice said from close by. "Jesus Christ, what happened?"

"What happened," the man holding me spat, "was that you left her alone at an STD fest. What the fuck did you think would happen?"

My eyes cracked open slightly to see Theo's hard face glaring over me. I didn't turn my head, but I recognized my best friend's voice as he replied, "I'm sorry. Shit, I was just—"

"Does it look like I give a shit what you were doing?" Theo snapped, his grip tightening around me. His head shook as he carefully adjusted me in his arms so one of them was perched behind my knees and the other supporting my back.

"I'm sorry. As soon as my buddy noticed she was acting off, I came as soon as I could."

Theo didn't grace Lawrence with a reply before turning. His eyes found mine as we walked, the cold air making my overheated body feel better despite the goosebumps that formed from the way his gaze bored into me. "What did I tell you about drinking at these?"

I couldn't answer him. He swore again.

I tried saying something, but he just quieted me, yanking open a door before carefully draping me on cool leather seats. I didn't remember what happened after that except drifting off to the familiar and easing scent of tobacco and cologne.

chapter two

THEO

THE LAST THING my dick should have done was get hard when I stepped back from pulling my comforter over Della's sleeping form, but it became suffocated behind the zipper of my slacks as soon as I saw her curl into my sheets, knowing she'd smell like me.

"Fuck," I grumbled, closing the door behind me. As much as I wanted to make sure she was okay, I didn't need to watch her sleep before going to the fucking master bathroom and rubbing out a permanent hard on that appeared whenever she was around.

Dropping into the leather chair in my home office on the other end of the house I won during my divorce, I scrubbed a palm down my face and eyed the tumbler of amber liquid left abandoned when I got the call. I wanted to drain it, pour another one, and dive back into the work still sprawled across my otherwise organized desk. Unfortunately, the reason why that was a bad idea was sleeping in my bed.

Somebody had drugged her drink, I was sure of it. And her own friend, the one she told me countless times always protected her when they were out, couldn't even keep his dick in his pants long enough to make sure she was good. Blood boiled under my skin thinking about the pretty boy who she shared a past with—one I wasn't stupid enough to believe was just platonic. I'd seen the way he stared at her ass when she swiveled those goddamn hips she grew into. She didn't seem to know people like him watched, but they did. It wasn't always because of her past like she assumed, it was out of desire and it pissed me off.

She'd denied ever getting involved with Pretty Boy, the McKinley kid, for years. I'd known better than to believe it because they were always pushed together by Sophie. I didn't give a shit if she thought they made a cute couple, it was only a matter of time before the kid wanted to start pushing his luck with her. I was a teenage boy once too and knew what my dick wanted. Anybody with eyes could see that would happen between them at some point.

"Fuck," I repeated, gripping the nearest manilla folder and studying the contents to shove the thought out of my head. I didn't want to think about who Della had been involved with in the past. I knew for a fact it wasn't many people at all. Pretty Boy was definitely one, and maybe the Phelps kid who hung around her a few summers before her father's arrest. The only good thing that came from that was the Phelps family and their kid, who I didn't care enough about to remember the name of, left Della alone when news broke because they didn't want to be involved with anybody that had the Saint James last name. I'd seen what it did to Della, but I couldn't get myself to care because it meant I didn't have to threaten some asshole over how they treated her.

Focusing on work helped, it always did. Not just because of Della, but life. The divorce. The drama. The gossip. Then the trial. I dove into what I did best— making money. I hardly made friends in my line of work because that wasn't what I set out to do. Most people I encountered only wanted to use me for my bank account anyway, so it wasn't worth it. Anthony had been the only true friend I trusted, and not even what he'd done wavered that.

Work was the same bullshit, different day as I stared at the files. Numbers in black that had more zeros than most people saw in their lifetime and names of millionaires attached that I knew for a fact were too full of themselves for their own good. Most days, I liked my job. The business world was one where I got to get shit done in my own way, at my own pace. Typically, it was straight to the point without the bullshit attached.

Before Anthony Saint James became governor, he'd once been a partner in my consulting firm that I started shortly after acquiring my master's in business from NYU. He had set his sights on something else, something bigger, while I was content staying on the sidelines and watching him get everything he wanted. In fact, I encouraged him. That was what friends did and I was happy to see him achieve whatever the hell he put his mind to because it meant something to him.

I was far from a jealous man. Possessive, perhaps, but not jealous. Everything Anthony worked hard for was well earned—the job, the title, the family. He loved Elizabeth and Adele with everything he had, even more than his job. There wasn't anything he did that he wasn't good at; being a loving father and husband and governing an entire state. He'd had bad days, some worse than others, and I wasn't sure Della knew when their parents' marriage was rocky, and he stayed with me for a week. I was under the impression he guised it as a trip for work. She had no reason to believe otherwise because her parents had the kind of sickening love that people envied. Me though? Not so much. Not until I saw what her death did to him. He was ripped apart, like a piece of him was suddenly missing, and I didn't realize until then, that it was the kind of love worth envying. Something I didn't have with my wife at the time.

I worked until the early hours of the morning before dumping out the warm alcohol that taunted me and heading to my bedroom upstairs—right next to the one I used to share with my ex. There were plenty of other rooms in the house, but I favored the downstairs one since it was close to the office, kitchen, and gym. I rarely went anywhere else on the second floor unless there were guests over and that was rare considering the few that stopped by shared a bed with me only until they left in the morning like agreed upon.

Maybe it was knowing that Della was downstairs after what had happened that left me restless, maybe it was the stiffness in my boxer briefs that I refused to relieve no matter how painful it got, but I gave up sleeping more than four hours and found myself in the kitchen just as the sun rose.

I heard the light footsteps before seeing her from my peripheral, her body leaning against the archway leading into the kitchen. She was still wearing the same dress from last night even though I set clothes on the end of the bed for her to change into. Then again, who knew if she even saw them or wanted to wear something that wouldn't even fit.

"How are you feeling?"

She straightened at my question, pushing herself away from the wall when I held out the cup of coffee I was originally going to down myself.

Her long fingers wrapped around the steaming mug. "Tired," she croaked, clearing her throat and giving me a timid smile. "I, uh, talked to Lawrence and he told me—"

Cutting her off with a glare wasn't what she expected, but her lips pressed together when I said, "I don't want to hear about that piece of shit right now. He knew better than to leave you alone there."

"He's not a piece of…" Her voice was quiet, hurt by my words. She cared about him. I knew it. Didn't like it, but I understood. Della got her loyalty from her father. "He isn't my babysitter, Theo. It was a frat party and he deserved to have fun. I should have known better than to drink so much, and —"

"Is that what you think happened?"

She frowned.

"You were fucking drugged. Slurring your words, hardly able to stand or open your eyes. It wasn't from drinking too much. I know for a fact you can hold your own. *That* you get from your mother and Sophie." Her cheeks tinted pink, but I ignored the embarrassment. "I never liked you going to those. You're a target to people. Especially now."

"I am not!"

I eyed her, then turned my back to prepare a second cup of coffee. "Don't act stupid, Adele. It doesn't look good on you."

"What the hell is your problem?" I knew I hit a nerve when she started swearing, and I hid the twitch of my lips as I grabbed creamer from the fridge.

"Careful, Della, or you'll have to put a dollar in the swear jar."

"I'm not five anymore," she pointed out as if I hadn't figured it out for myself. I rolled my eyes and walked over to the table, setting my coffee down before pulling a chair out.

"I've noticed." The words probably shouldn't have slipped, but they did.

She was quiet.

Clearing my throat, I took a sip of my coffee before gesturing toward one of the open spots around the large oak table. It was always too big for me and Mariska, especially because kids were never in the future for us. "Might as well sit down. You want me to make you something for breakfast?"

Her lips twitched slightly, and I could only imagine what the sudden amusement was for. I wasn't a bad cook, but I was out of practice considering how much I ordered takeout or delivery to the office in the center of the city. Compared to her, who I knew enjoyed being in the kitchen and experimenting on new recipes, I looked like one of those amateurs in those shows she enjoyed watching on Food Network. There were a few she'd all but force me to watch with her that I didn't mind so much, and one that made me feel like a Michelin chef based on the appropriately titled *Worst Cooks in America*.

Della finally walked over, dropping into the seat directly beside mine. "If I opened your refrigerator, I'd probably find it empty."

My brow quirked. "Is that so?"

She gave me a challenging stare. "Am I wrong? You're never here. People talk, Theo. You live at your office."

"Not much for me here," was all I graced her with, lifting my mug to my lips again.

Her shoulders lifted. "I just think it's sad. Your home is beautiful, you know I've always thought so. But it's barely ever used." I had known that. When I bought it, Mariska was at some art show in a different state, so Della tagged along. She was a moody pre-teen, but somehow, I always got her to calm down. When the agent had walked into the kitchen, Della had all but drooled over what she saw. If memory served right, she'd even picked out her own room upstairs. The real estate agent, an older gentleman, had smiled at me when Della was exploring the second floor and said, *"Your daughter reminds me so much of my own."*

If I didn't bulk at his statement, it was a miracle. The more I thought about it, the more I realized he wasn't wrong. I'd spent a lot of time with her, teaching her things, just like a father figure would. When the man had seen my expression, he just chuckled. I wasn't sure why, but he did. I wasn't about to explain I didn't have kids and never thought about it either, because what did that say about me toting around a young girl that wasn't mine?

I couldn't help but lean toward Della, my eyes pinning hers until she squirmed. "Tell me, Della, how would you use my house?"

She visibly swallowed, her eyes going to my lips for a microsecond longer than normal. Whatever thoughts were crossing her mind were dangerous because her cheeks darkened right before she averted her eyes. "Your kitchen," she whispered. I blinked, not all that surprised by her answer. "It's too pretty not to be used," she continued, looking over her shoulder at the marble countertops and stainless-steel appliances.

Out of everything her active imagination could

probably conjure I couldn't help but tease. "You'd...cook?"

"Sure. Why not?"

It was hard not to grin. "Two minutes ago, you were swearing at me for calling your friend an asshole."

"You called him a piece of shit," she corrected instantly.

"Same difference."

Her eyebrow twitched, a telling sign that I was getting under her skin. The chuckle escaped me before I could stop it, breaking her irritation and making her stare instead. "I've gotten better at cooking over the years," she diverted. "Breakfast is my favorite to cook, though, so I prefer learning how to make different things. Even though Sophie told me I could just hire somebody to do it. She forgets I don't live like her anymore."

I was surprised by a lot of things she said at times, but now it was namely that her Aunt Sophie would even suggest she use money to hire somebody for a skill that women were supposedly meant to master. I was glad Della didn't let her aunt brainwash her into believing anything. Sophie had an abundance of money because of her husband, and before that was well-off because of her family. She didn't know a time when you couldn't shake a Benjamin at somebody to get them to do work where she could have done it herself. Shit, I'd bet the money in my wallet that she didn't even know how to boil water. "Why breakfast?"

Her eyes returned to me, bright blue like her

father's—almost cerulean. I'd remembered when she was little how much she complained about not having her mother's eyes because she loved the gray color. I had to admit, Elizabeth's eyes were unique. Like melted silver. Della wouldn't be herself without her soulful baby blues though. "You can do a lot of different things. Eggs, pancakes, waffles. I prefer making sweeter things, like dessert plates. Remember those salted caramel pancakes I got during the trip me, you, and Dad took? We went to—"

"Denny's," I mused in fond remembrance. I'd had a similar stack that were meant to taste like cinnamon buns after she convinced me to order them just in case she hated hers. The ones I'd gotten were her favorite, but she wanted to branch out and was afraid she wouldn't like the ones she opted to try. As always, I caved and agreed while Anthony shook his head at us. It never took much to be persuaded by the innocent-eyed doe when she wanted something. "Sophie had a conniption when you told her how excited you were to go there."

She sighed lightly, a wavering smile on her lips. "I never understood why Aunt Sophie was so against going to places like that. It's my personal favorite when I'm hungo—" Her words abruptly stop, like she realized what she was saying wouldn't be something I approved of.

"When what?" I questioned slowly.

Her bottom lip drew into her mouth as she avoided my gaze. I knew the answer though. It wasn't like I didn't have eyes and ears on her. She went out, not frequently, but enough. She drank, again not often, but sometimes she'd walk away with a hangover and wind up at Denny's to cure it at two in the morning with her friends.

"Please, do finish," I prodded, setting my coffee down and cocking my head.

She managed to stifle a sigh, brushing her fingers through her long hair that rested in tangles past her breasts. "Like you don't know. You were the one who told me greasy food helped hangovers."

"And coffee," I pointed out with a grin.

"Anyway, I like Denny's. We should go there sometime since you spend most of your time eating out anyway."

Her words went straight to my cock, making me bite back a groan when my mind took me to a place it shouldn't have, one that involved the spot between those thighs of hers. There was no way to adjust myself without her noticing my hand disappearing under the table, so I shifted in my chair and cleared my throat to try focusing on anything else. "I do cook, you know."

"With what food?"

Grumbling, I finished off my coffee and pushed the cup away. "What are you planning to do today? You're going back to school on Monday, correct?"

Her eyes stayed locked on her coffee. "Yes. My professors are all expecting me bright and early. I've caught up on most homework, so it shouldn't be so bad."

Studying her while she stared off, I tried figuring out if she was as all right as she pretended to be. She was always too strong, too stubborn, for her own good. "It's okay not to be okay, Della. Your professors won't fault you for holding off considering the loss. The entire state is grieving. You can too."

Her nose twitched, probably thinking the same thing I was about just how much the state was mourning the loss of her father. Maybe if he had made better choices, the statement would be accurate. "I need to go back. School keeps me busy, and I'm almost done. Dad wouldn't have wanted me to take a leave of absence. We had...*I* had everything planned out perfectly."

We. Anthony talked about her future more than she did. Her degree started in business just like ours, but her heart wasn't invested. She loved to paint, to draw, to be creative. Once upon a time, she danced—the very thing that got her into Bentley U. Everything about her was about the creation of something beautiful. It was webbed into her existence for everybody to see it in how she walked, talked, and acted. The business world would eat her alive the second she stepped into it regardless of who she was related to—or exactly because of it. Tight skirts, high heels, and cleavage-revealing shirts wouldn't save her from that scrutiny like it did for some successful women because her blood was considered tainted from the scandal.

"Perhaps it's a good idea to start planning what would make you happy instead."

Her eyes narrowed in on me. "What is that supposed to mean?"

Standing, once I knew my dick wasn't tenting my pants, I grabbed my empty coffee mug and brought it to the sink. "Nothing, Della. I just know what you want to do, and it's nothing you planned with your father."

"That isn't true."

I simply hummed, not offering a verbal reply. Her chair scraped back, and she appeared next to me, her lips pinched down. "It's not true," she repeated.

One of my shoulders lifted. "Fine. It isn't true then. What do I know? I only spend nearly every day with you." There was an edge to my tone that passed disbelief, which I knew she could pinpoint easily.

"I get it, okay?" Her tone was softer, quieter than mine. "You're trying to make a point. I get it. That doesn't mean I want to believe it."

Which point, little Della? my eyes asked hers when I turned my head.

The one we both avoid, hers said back.

I straightened when she set her full cup next to me. "Thank you for the coffee, but I should get back to my place."

Rolling my neck, I reached for my phone to call Dallas, only for her to shake her head. "I already texted Ren. He'll be here in a few minutes."

My nostrils flared.

"Don't start," she whispered. "He's all I have, Theo, whether you like it or not. He's a good person."

My open glare wasn't lost on her.

I wanted to tell her she was wrong. She had me too, we both knew it. But the second those words left my mouth it would change everything. It'd mean more than an innocent declaration of family — of familiarity that we were accustomed to over the years.

She didn't need that.

I didn't either.

Not after what I did a year ago.

So, I let her leave.

chapter three

DELLA

THE MIRROR IS NOT the enemy.

I repeated that to myself at least three more times before walking over to the shower and turning it on. The steam would do its job with time, fogging the glass before I peeled off the clothes that hid what I struggled seeing. Some days were better than others, but I could feel the edge of a relapse forming as anxiety bubbled in the pit of my stomach. Truth was, I didn't hate my body. Not anymore. I learned to like it with time and therapy, but it didn't change the days that made me see my imperfections highlighted in my reflection whenever I passed it.

It took months after starting therapy before I could

turn my head when walking past storefronts to see what graced the windows staring back. A girl too thin who felt too large, worried about what the media would say when pictures floated around, or when people would turn and whisper at formal events. I would never be cured from the thoughts that plagued my mind whenever I went clothes shopping and found clothing too snug or too loose. There would always be faults—cellulite and stretch marks and things my eyes narrowed in on with an embarrassing amount of obsession. There would be days when I couldn't fight the urge to loathe a piece of me that didn't deserve the kind of self-hate I'd inflicted when counting my calories, then eventually my ribs when they showed because of how badly I treated myself.

But I tried and that was what mattered.

Running my hand on the piece of ripped paper with elegant scroll I'd taped onto the edge of the mirror, I took a deep breath and forced my gaze on my almost naked complexion, half hidden by the steam on the glass. *Be better.*

The shower I took was longer than normal, and I knew my aunt would be displeased considering I'd be undoubtedly late for our Sunday brunch. I, however, didn't have enough energy to care. I knew my limits and needed the time to myself to prepare for everything that came with the outing. Sophie would gossip about her so-called friends and their families, making believe that she and Andrew were far better than the scandals that happened in her social circle, and belittle me for my posture, what I put onto my plate, and how I didn't call her back when she called yesterday.

She was the last person I wanted to talk to after getting home from Theo's house. If he were anybody else, I'd have to worry about her chastising me about what happened at the party. Thankfully, he wasn't the kind of person to rat you out. At least, not when things like this occurred. There were few times he spoke up about what I did in my life. The only time he chose to intervene, when I wished he hadn't, had left us with a wedge between whatever friendship we'd formed over the years. Though Sophie, and many other family members, had told me I was silly to even call it that.

"Don't be naïve, Adele. Theo is not your friend. He's your father's. A man like that has no use of a girl your age."

Perhaps it was those words that left me huddled in my room for days after he told my father that I'd been starving myself—that I'd been purging, exercising too much, moody beyond help. If what my aunt said were true, Theo wouldn't have even bothered to tell my father of my choices he disapproved of. Looking back now, I saw that wasn't true. He cared, perhaps more than anybody, considering nobody else was willing to speak up about what I was doing.

The missed meals.

The extra hours of exercise.

The covered mirrors.

Throat thickening, I looked at the pricks on the wall where tacks held a sheet over the large vanity mirror once upon a time. Theo had done me a favor by telling my father, but that didn't mean it hadn't hurt.

"What are you doing, Della?"

"Are you out of your mind, Della?"

"You could kill yourself, Della!"

I could have. Theo was right. And while that was never my end game, it was a very likely possibility when I finally looked at myself in the mirror after he'd torn the sheet off in his rampage from weeks of me shutting him out.

"Tell me what you see," he'd demanded. When I didn't offer him a reply, he turned to me, spine straightened to full height, and told me what he saw instead. "I see a girl who has fallen too many times to the predators of the world who want nothing more than to tear her apart, but I know that girl is much stronger than she believes. One day, that girl will become a woman who wears her confidence proudly. Want to know why, Della?"

I'd known he was going to tell me why regardless of if I wanted him to or not, because those dark blue eyes were fierce with an intensity that racked my soul as I stood in front of him and the mirror in nothing but pajama shorts and a tank top that had emphasized just how little remained of my body.

"You will fall, fail, and break over and over in this world. But you will also rise, succeed, and put yourself back together because only you can. That doesn't mean there aren't people here who want to help—who aren't willing to make a few threats to those worthy of the breath. Understand, Della?"

What I'd understood that day was that he wanted me to fight—for me, my father, and even for him. He would never say those words though because he knew better than anybody that I wouldn't be able to love myself if I didn't try for my own wellbeing. The important thing was that he wanted me to do my best, to fight, and I did.

I did, over and over, and fell just as he said. I failed. I thought negative things, found myself counting my calories, and skipping meals then saying I'd "forgotten" because I'd been busy. Sometimes it wasn't even a lie. I'd be in the studio painting and would lose track of time until somebody found me. That was when I'd realized I'd lost a day in the kind of art I felt comfortable in.

My own.

Unlike my skin, my art was something I found unconditional love in. I could express myself in the way I captured silhouettes on canvas and paper exactly how I wanted, but never wishing I could be who I created. Ripley, my therapist, always told me she was worried I'd lose myself in temptation again, wanting to be the things I made of acrylic and oil, but that was never the case.

My art was an escape I so desperately needed, but one I found reality in through the soft curves of fuller thighs and blemished skin of reddened faces. What I brought to life was salvation, society needed to know it wasn't alone in a fight so many fought against themselves.

Flaws.

Imperfections.

But it was easier to tell my peers that they shouldn't

judge themselves for eating too much or too little when my own demons picked apart my every move.

Blowing out a timid breath, I walked to the mirror with a white towel wrapped around me tightly and raised my palm to the fogged glass. I counted to three before swiping away until my bare skin greeted me, my hair falling in tangled waves past my shoulders and over my average B-cup breasts.

When I wiped away the steam to reveal the rest of my body, I froze…

Then dropped the towel.

That doesn't mean there aren't people here who want to help —who aren't willing to make a few threats to those worthy of the breath. Understand, Della?

I whispered, "I understand" to my naked reflection.

MY LIPS PINCHED at the hour mark of brunch, my plate half-full and my tea untouched. It smelled like lavender, Sophie's favorite but not mine. I hated tea but she insisted I just hadn't gotten the taste for it yet. Something told me that wouldn't happen anytime soon.

"…when you were going to start dancing again. I told her that surely you'd do it by the next recital in the fall. You were the top of your class, after all."

Eyes widening over the conversation I had tuned back into, I gripped the fork in my hand a little too tightly, until the silver stung my fingers, as I poked at the quiche on my plate. "You know I don't dance anymore, Sophie. It wouldn't be a good idea for... obvious reasons."

Her manicured hand waved in the air as if I were simply joking. "Jamie isn't nearly half as talented as you are, but her mother insists that she's getting there. Same with that Atwell girl. What was her name again? Lauren?"

Clearing my throat, I dropped my fork onto the tablecloth. "Good for them. Jamie is a sweet girl and Lauren is...talented. Just because you don't like their mothers doesn't mean you need to wish for either of them to fail."

The way she blinked at me made me want to squirm, but I held my ground. Chin tipped up I locked our gazes until she looked away first. "I mean no harm by stating facts, of course. You know how much your mother always loved going to see you perform. I just think it'd be a good idea to at least try getting back out there."

She made ballet seem like dating, and I couldn't stop the snort from escaping me in time. Her eyes narrowed at the unladylike sound, but she didn't call me out on it like normal. Even she knew that bringing up my biggest trigger was risky. "I danced because she wanted me to, but I know myself well enough to know I'm not strong enough anymore. Maybe it would have been different if she were around, but it's not."

"We'll get you a trainer—"

"Sophie." I sighed, shaking my head. I wished Aunt Lydia were here to be the voice of reason, but she always had other places to be for these brunches. Lucky woman. "I wasn't talking about physical strength. You can't use my mother every time you want to get your way either. It isn't fair."

Offense took over her face, her hand going to the expensive gold chain around her neck that Andrew bought her for her birthday last year. I was sure she'd actually gotten it for herself using his credit card like she normally did. "I wasn't doing that at all. I simply want what's best for you. You can't stop doing what you love just because…"

My brows raised, waiting for her to finish the sentence. When her painted lips remained closed, I was tempted to text Ren and see if he could pick me up like he had at Theo's. Then again, I was still a little upset with him over what happened at his frat. It wasn't his fault, but he could have told me where he was going before ditching me that way I knew where to look. Plus, he'd admitted that Evan had a bad reputation around the house but wouldn't go into further detail. It didn't take a rocket scientist to see whatever rep wasn't just some bad boy thing based on the way Ren had gripped the steering wheel of his Jeep.

It didn't help matters either when I felt Theo's anger like radiation being absorbed into my skin. It wasn't like I thought his agitation was unprecedented, I just didn't want him thinking ill of Ren because of one night. There wasn't even proof that I'd been drugged because nobody had taken me to the hospital, not that I would have wanted them to. The only alcohol I'd drank was from the game I'd played, and anybody could have drunk it, and one and a half beers that Ren himself had given me after I sobered a little. Had I set it down? It was possible, which meant I was at fault too.

"Because what?" I pressed lightly, curious as to what she'd say. It wasn't like my condition was a secret. It certainly circulated around the people who Sophie hung out with. They wanted the details, the reasons I'd starved myself to the point my body was shutting down. Some of them were bold enough to ask why any young girl would want to look so frail and broken. That one still got to me. I wished she'd replied, *"Maybe some of them want to reflect what they feel like on the inside"* but I knew Sophie had kept quiet and pretended like I wasn't sick and struggling. Did she even know that was how I'd felt inside? I doubted it.

While I also wasn't nearly as physically strong, it was my mental and emotional health I'd be more concerned about with standing in front of the mirrors while stretched over the barre, being trained rigorously and told what to eat and what not to again. My diet was restrictive, the training during practice and off the floor intense, and the critique on the dancers' bodies demeaning. I couldn't put myself through that and believe I'd make it out without failing again. Only the next time might be harder to come out of.

I used to love dancing because it felt like flying and freedom and peace. I loved it even more because my mother's face lit up every time she saw me glide across the floor. I'd been called graceful once upon a time.

That was, until everything the trainers said got to my head, until the press told me I'd been too bulky to make it big.

The way I'd watch myself in the mirrors, the frailty of my skin, the amount of times I stumbled during practice because I hadn't eaten enough for the amount I was burning, especially during recital season, was like a warning sign flashing. Nobody saw it. I ignored it. I was killing myself for everybody else's approval. Sophie said I was fine, that all the girls had to change their lifestyles in order to be the top of the top and I doubted any of her friends believed her. Did they call her out? No. That wasn't the way things were and we both knew it.

All that mattered now was that the love I'd grown for the sport my mother and I shared had dwindled as time went on and disappeared altogether when we laid her to rest. My passion had been buried in the coffin alongside her, never to be seen again. I'd forced myself to continue until I was nineteen, told myself she would have wanted me to, guilted myself into thinking it was the best option. It was Theo who told me I could find passion in other things, things that were safer and less triggering when I'd finally agreed to get help. Because of Theo, I'd found art.

I'd been saved.

Sophie's voice pulled me from the potentially dangerous train of thought. "You know I love you, Adele. It's just sad to see such talent wasted. But your health means more."

My health means more because it causes less gossip for you to hide from.

My aunt loved to spread gossip but loathed being the center of it. Once my eating disorder came to light, she was swarmed by people who wanted to hear every-thing. Paired with the flare of my father's incarceration? She didn't know what to do besides lie to everybody, chastise me, and save face for her friends as if the Saint James' were just that. Saintly.

Maybe people sympathized with me, but I was sure many more had judged. Theo refused to fill me in on the city gossip, and I knew he was always in-the-know even if he didn't want to be. Like Sophie, he heard who cheated, who broke up, and who was in love. He just didn't care, especially if talk involved me or my family.

I believe the words he always used were, *"Why would I give a rat's ass what people do with their lives?"*

He had a point.

"Your concern for my talent is noted," I told her calmly, a smile tilting my lips as I was trained. However, the following words were not in the social etiquette handbook I'd gotten lectured on time and time again. "However, what I do with my life is of no concern to you. Just be happy I'm still breathing."

"I *am* happy you're still breathing. What kind of comment is that?"

"One that's justified," a husky and low voice butted in. I couldn't help but smile at Theo's appearance in the doorway.

Sophie turned to him, surprise clear on her face.

"What on earth are you doing here? You haven't come to brunch in months."

"Della and I have plans." His eyes turned to me with an eyebrow quirked. "Unless you forgot? I know how much these brunches mean to you, spending quality time with your aunt."

It took everything in me not to waver a smile, which would have given away his sarcasm. He delivered it so smoothly, so carefully, most people wouldn't know it at all. It was how he got away with so much in conversation. Unlike those people, I knew better.

"Our plans." I shook my head, dropping my napkin on the table. "I can't believe I forgot about them." My eyes turned to my aunt, who was frowning. "I'm sorry, Sophie. I need to go."

She stood when I did, her palms flattening her typical Sunday best. The attire was flashy and bold but fitting for her personality. "Don't think I don't know what you two are up to. I'm not stupid."

For a split second, my mind took me back to the night Theo stumbled into my flat and pressed me against the wall. Heat gathered between my thighs just remembering how hard he was everywhere, especially where he'd ground against me with his hips like he was trying to prove how much he needed an escape.

"I don't know what you mean," I managed, feigning innocence.

Sophie's eyes rolled as a small sigh escaped her lips. "I know I'm not your favorite, but you didn't need to plan an escape route. You could have simply said you didn't want to come."

She knew I'd never do that though without a good reason.

Theo appeared beside me, a palm going to my lower back. It wasn't unusual, but the flutters in my stomach were a new occurrence since the night my mind liked taking me back to. Maybe he didn't realize it, but Theo found ways to touch me every time we saw each other now. Our hands would brush, our shoulders, some part of him always needed that contact and I never shied away from it because I'd all but beckoned him to make those moves. "We really do have plans, Sophie. She goes back to school tomorrow."

My aunt's eyes widened. "I forgot all about that. Are you sure—"

"I'm sure." I didn't mean to cut her off, but I didn't want to discuss this further. Whatever her opinion was, it was probably going to upset me more than I already was.

"Fine. Just think about what I said, okay? I spoke to Judith and she'd love to have you back. They'd be fools not to know you were the reason people came to the recitals before."

I could feel Theo tense next to me, but he remained silent until we said our goodbyes. I promised Sophie nothing, knowing I wouldn't break a vow or lead her astray. My mind was set.

When we were safely outside, Theo chose to speak. "She was trying to get you to dance." It wasn't a question, so I considered not answering. I knew Theo wouldn't relent though.

"Yes. I told her no."

There was a stretch of silence. "You're smart, Della. You know your limits. She may not say it, but I will. I'm proud of you. Your father would be too."

Tears burned the back of my eyes, but I refused to let them fall. I simply said, "Thank you" and climbed into the car that Dallas usually drove us around in.

Once we were both buckled, he turned to me with a small smirk gracing his sculpted face. I knew by the glint in his eyes he was up to something. "Want to go to Denny's?"

Part of me wanted to tell him no. It was rare I told him that though. I loved spending time with him, especially one-on-one. But that nagging feeling cemented in the bottom of my stomach, the one that made me want to curl up in bed and not come out for days, resurfaced.

It told me not to eat my favorite pancakes or be with my favorite person or do anything other than sulk until every one of my defenses I'd custom built had fallen again.

I wanted to tell him no so bad.

But I didn't. "I'd love that."

THE WAREHOUSE WAS MUSTY, but it was my favorite place to go to think, which wasn't often. Usually I avoided my thoughts, but sometimes they were unavoidable, and I had to accept that. That was why I was sitting on an old crate in the middle of the empty room with a sketch pad on my lap of a new project I'd been wanting to draw ever since it popped into my head one night when I'd been too restless to sleep.

A pencil outline of two faceless people took up most of the white sheet. Running a finger over the lines, I traced the larger hand that raised to the much smaller face. I'd pictured it a gentle touch, one of longing. That was what my mind conjured in the middle of the night on repeat. I figured if I could draw it, paint it, something, it'd free my conscious of the taunting memory of what it felt like that night.

Sighing, I looked up when a flutter came from the rafters. Birds got in all the time and hung out with me while I wallowed. Sometimes I drew, sometimes I'd just sit around and listen to the silence. This side of the city didn't have a lot of traffic. It felt forgotten, almost like it was mine and mine alone now that my father was gone. I'd seen pictures of it in better shape when my parents were younger. It'd made sense why they liked sneaking away, having parties, breaking the rules like two people in love.

Part of me had been jealous of their tale, like I wouldn't get that feeling. Not as easily as they did. Both my mother and father came from wealthy backgrounds. My father's family was always in politics, and my mother's from law. It made sense that they'd meet considering the mutual events held for the two groups of people. I'd been to my fair share of black-tie formals where I watched my father mingle among the best the city had to offer. When I was younger, I'd usually have somebody watch me while my parents went to them, but my father took me when I was fifteen and let me pick out a fancy silver dress that flitted to the floor gracefully and hung off one of my shoulders. I'd felt beautiful then and hadn't hated the way people complimented me. I should have, but I'd been too distracted.

I wasn't even sure what the event was for—some charity, I believed. What I knew for sure was that Theo West would be there because my father told me he'd donated a mass sum of money to the cause. He'd looked uncomfortable when I finally laid eyes on him, across from the large ballroom everybody mingled about in, until he saw us. My chest had warmed when he made his way over, greeting my father with a typical handshake and me with a kiss on the cheek.

You look beautiful, Della. Maybe it was those words that had cemented the thought I'd already made myself before being dropped off at the doors that night. The dress was gorgeous and fit my body perfectly, my hair was styled in a skillfully curled updo, and I'd put makeup on that made me look older. I realized the moment I'd captured Theo's attention that I subconsciously did it on purpose. I wanted to catch his eye and see his reaction and wasn't disappointed.

Lifting fingers to the cheek he often kissed, I found myself smiling. From somewhere in the distance, music thumped loudly. Nothing I knew, but the bass was evident from whatever place it traveled from. A car maybe? One of the rundown apartment buildings a block away? Whatever song it was shifted to something slower, and I found my head swinging in a slow melody, my feet moving to the new beat, muscle memory taking over.

I wasn't sure when it happened, but my sketchpad was set on the crate and I was on my feet swaying. Eyes closed, I turned to the beat and found my feet gliding me across the floor as I hummed to myself.

Getting lost in the old me as my feet swept across the cement, I gasped when an arm hooked around me, and familiar spicy cologne took over my senses. Before I opened my eyes, the hardened body against mine pressed us closer together as he took lead. One rough palm held mine while the other rested on my waist as he led us in a slow dance.

Cracking my eyelids open, I saw the fitted light blue button down against a bulky body wrapped in earned muscle before drifting my gaze upward to light scruff, full pink lips, and up to dark blue eyes gazing down at me.

"You don't smell like tobacco today," was the brilliant greeting I gave him as he turned us. If I looked down, I'd see Tom Ford shoes, polished, stepping to the practically non-existent music.

He grumbled, "Trying to quit."

My brows drew up. "Really?"

One head nod was all I got in return as he tightened his grip on my hand and waist. "You were dancing."

Swallowing, I rested my cheek against his chest and listened to the thrum of his heartbeat as my body eased into him. "Not really. Just…playing more than anything."

He hummed.

"What are you doing here?" I asked, changing the topic to something lighter.

"Dallas called."

Pressing my eyes closed, I nodded against him. It made sense, I guessed. Dallas was striking up conversation the whole way he drove me here, something he did more times than he probably liked. I enjoyed the thirty-something-year-old's company. We had light conversations and he seemed to genuinely care. Plus, he knew my mother. Not well, he admitted, but enough to tell me on occasion how much I reminded him of her. It always made me smile when I heard those words.

"You shouldn't be out here by yourself," Theo scolded quietly, his chin resting on the top of my head. "We've been over this."

I couldn't help but roll my eyes, something he would have given me grief over if he'd seen me do it. "I'm not alone. Dallas is lurking outside pretending not to be."

His silence told me I was right.

"Plus," I added softly, "you're here."

Another hum.

We danced liked that for a moment longer, our breathing on the foreground of sound that took over the warehouse. I found myself remembering all the times I'd begged him to do this with me when I was younger. Sometimes it called for dancing when we were at events —other times it was in the living room of my parents' house when he visited, and I clung to him until he caved. It never took much.

I found myself softly laughing over the fond memory. It seemed like so long ago. I wasn't sure what it was like to be as innocent as I was back then. "Remember when I used to stand on your shoes while we danced like this? Where were we when that woman, the blonde, had a fit when I stood on top of those fancy Fords you had on?"

My smile widened when his deep chuckle vibrated against me. "Arabella. I remember well. She reprimanded me all night until I finally told her to leave."

I hadn't known that. "Oh."

"She was a bit much," he admitted. "I needed a date and your mother insisted…" Ah. My mother always meant well, but I'd heard my father and Theo talking about her matchmaking skills. Or lack thereof. I loved her, but I agreed with the men. I didn't like anybody with him, though I tolerated Mariska because I had no other option when they'd gotten married. If he'd found somebody he cared for, who was I to stop him? I was raised to be proper and civil, and that was what I was. Sometimes, I even liked Mariska, even if I was a little moody toward her because she got to spend so much time with Theo.

"I'm surprised you didn't get sick of me always bugging you to dance then." I'd been relentless and he always did as I asked. My father joked I'd had him wrapped around my finger, a place I wanted him to always remain, even if that was selfish.

"I didn't mind."

"You never used to—" I squealed when he lifted me up and guided my feet to his shoes where they rested as soon as he dropped me back down, then started laughing when he kept dancing just like that. Like the old times.

"I enjoyed those days, Della," he told me honestly, his face drawing back ever so slightly until his breath caressed the side of my face.

"You did?"

Half his lips quirked up. "I did. Those were simpler times when there was nothing heavy to worry about."

I licked my lips as his nose grazed mine. My heart sped in my chest as I closed my eyes again and willed him to close the gap between our lips, but it never came. So I said, "Things now are certainly complicated because of my father…"

His sigh was felt in my soul, heavy and burdened, and I wanted to know his thoughts. "It isn't just your father that makes things complicated now."

"It isn't?"

A pause. "No, Della, it isn't."

We kept dancing like that, my feet on top of his, without another word spoken between us. I wanted to push him for more, for whatever he wasn't saying, but I opted to soak in the moment instead because I knew it'd have to end.

I wrapped my arms around him and used his chest as a pillow as he moved us in a slow circle. My only hope was that he didn't end it too soon.

chapter four

THEO

ANOTHER CURSE SLIPPED past my lips as I read through the emails crammed into my inbox from over the weekend. It wasn't like I hadn't known they were there considering I'd logged on one too many times, even after Friday night. I'd just tried taking advice a long time ago from somebody who knew what he was talking about.

"Work can't be everything, Theo."

Anthony made the choice to leave work behind after hours because he had a life to go home to. Even when Mariska was in mine, it was never a clear decision I got to make. While she was with her girlfriends, the studio, and who knew where else, I was pulling overtime to sort through the mess Interactive Marketing had surrounding it when stock nosedived, or investors dropped for one reason or another. My money was tied up in IM because nobody else's was, so I saw no point in listening to him when he told me to go home to my wife when the weekend came around.

Blowing out a breath, I noted the numbers on the second monitor screen and realized the stress wasn't worth my time. We were doing fine, better than. So, I got through the emails that mattered and ignored the rest, making a note for Abigail, the secretary, to finish going through non-essentials another time when she wasn't busy doing paperwork.

When my phone rang as I logged off for the day, I was tempted to ignore the name across the screen but thought better of it. It wasn't often that Sophie Vasquez called me, but it was always interesting when it happened.

"To what do I owe this pleasure," I greeted, voice as leveled as it could be. Once upon a time I had no problem with Sophie besides the slight irritation over how she treated Della like a child no matter how old she was. I'd gotten over it because I knew Della could handle herself, and she usually did. There were times, though, when Sophie pushed too far, and I couldn't help but want to rip into her knowing her niece wouldn't.

That, however, wasn't the reason I regarded her with caution. When things got rocky with Mariska, she was the first to take note. I wasn't surprised when she'd shown up at my office and closed the door behind her.

What had taken me off guard was how easy it was for her to forget she had a husband when she'd locked the door and propositioned me as if cheating were the answer for her unhappiness.

"Cut the pleasantries," was her response. It'd taken one firm rejection that day for her to remember her place. Sophie wasn't the kind of woman who enjoyed being refused more than once considering her pride was what she put before anything else. Including family, given the circumstance of the call. "Adele listens to you, so you need to help me."

My laugh was as dry as my tone. "Do I, now? Why would I help you?"

"You've always cared for her." Shoulders stiffening as I sat up in my chair, I swiped at my freshly shaven jaw and waited for her to continue without saying a word. "Don't try to pretend otherwise, you've been protective since day one. Even Anthony told me he saw how you were there for her. That means something."

"And that matters how?"

"She cares about what you think."

My teeth ground together. "Is this about her dancing? She seemed clear on her answer. You need to—"

"Adele is throwing her life away because she's afraid. You and I both know that her mother would have wanted her to keep going."

I stood, impatient with this conversation and wanting it to end. "Not at the cost of her life. I know you were never a fan of Elizabeth, but you can't take that

68

out on Adele." The beef she had with her brother's wife was beyond me. Elizabeth was a kind woman who loved Anthony and Adele as much as he loved them. They were a perfect fit in every way, so I couldn't figure out why Sophie disapproved so much. It'd remain a mystery because I couldn't find myself caring enough to ask.

"I am doing no such thing."

"You're trying to make sure Della doesn't make the same mistakes you and your brother did." It was clear as day whether she confirmed it or not. "If there's one thing you're right about, Sophie, it's that she listens to me. So, if I tell her about what happened at my office when you visited me, I'm sure she'd look at you much differently than she does now."

Her silence was telling. I wasn't going to tell her that I'd caught Della dancing at the warehouse, or that I suspected she danced more often than she would admit. It wasn't anybody's business but Della's, especially where Sophie was concerned.

I kept going, not willing to allow Sophie to get a word in edge wise until my point was made clear between us. "She would also listen to my opinion that she dances *only* if she were ever ready to, but never for anybody else. I'm sure that wouldn't go over well with you, would it? You'd rather force her hand."

"You would really risk her future like that? She was given the lead role in Swan Lake and had a fair shot at being part of the international competition and *winning*. Don't act like you're not disappointed she gave up. I saw it in your eyes when she announced she wasn't going back."

Had I been disappointed? Yes. But only because Della felt connected to her mother through ballet. Her father and I wanted what was best for her, and she was killing herself slowly by being part of that world. It seemed like the easiest choice to support after what the media had driven her to.

"I believe this conversation is over," I all but spit, about to hang up when she stopped me.

"You can think badly of me all you want. Half of what you already assume is most likely true, but I loved my brother dearly. I may not agree with his choices in a wife, but I've always looked up to him and loved Della like a daughter." Her words made little sense to me, especially because Sophie was not a maternal figure. She'd stepped in when time allowed and I respected her for it, but she was no mother to Della even if she tried to be.

"Why are you telling me this?"

Her sigh was light but burdened. "I have made many decisions in my life that I'm sure my brother didn't approve of as well, but the one I never did was trying to be part of Adele's life. She's pulling away and I don't want to lose her too. We both know Andrew is hardly around. Seeing her is what I look forward to."

"It doesn't feel good, does it?"

There was a pause. "What?"

"Being coerced into doing something that leaves you miserable," I stated casually. She was roped into her marriage because of Andrew Vasquez's status as top District Attorney. He came from old money that he inherited and was set for life. It was clear to anybody who saw them that they regretted the decision. He spent more time with his mistress across the city than he did with her, probably with a kid or two if rumors were true. Did I pity her? No. She walked in a willing participant and was trying to put Adele in the same situation.

"Remind me, Sophie, how *is* Andrew? Still warming his secretary's pussy or is it his law partner he spends his nights with these days?"

It was a low blow and I knew it, but it got the desired response. "Fuck you, Theodore. You're no better off considering Mariska found somebody who wasn't you to share her body with. Just because it was after your separation doesn't mean the desire wasn't there before it was made final. What does that say about you? So, excuse me for being stupid enough to believe we could help each other. Or that you'd, at the very least, be willing to help the girl you say you care about."

My chuckle was low and dark, building as my head shook at her ruse. "You're lucky, Sophie. Adele is still in your life in some form despite the bullshit you spew at her. I'd suggest stopping while you're ahead before you lose her for good. She won't need my help making that decision if you keep it up."

Her breathing halts for a split second.

"And Sophie?"

"What, Theo?"

"Don't waste my time with your false concern. You

never wanted to help me, you simply wanted to claim what you couldn't have to get back at your husband. I'm no pawn."

Before she replied, I hung up and blew out an irritated breath. Who the fuck did she think she was? She was no more than a sad middle-aged housewife who threw away any future picked out for her by someone else. I'd raise hell if anybody pushed that on Della. She deserved more. Anthony knew it. Elizabeth knew it. Everyone but Sophie, who did whatever she pleased despite her brother's wishes.

I dropped back into my chair. "I need a fucking smoke."

I was staring at the desk when I heard, "I thought you were going to quit." Without even looking up I knew who the feather-light voice belonged to.

"Shouldn't you be at school?" As soon as I looked up, I took in her outfit and fought back a smile. Her white shorts were a little too short on her long legs, but they didn't cling to her smooth skin. They were high-waisted like she preferred wearing and loose, with a striped shirt tucked into them and an oversized white blazer over top, left unbuttoned. She always dressed to impress, which made her parents happy. I knew when she wasn't out, she was in paint-stained overalls, pajamas with ridiculous fucking pictures on them, or workout pants with knee-high socks featuring obnoxious patterns.

Della was always eccentric in her style preferences

when she had nobody to dazzle, and that was what impressed me most about her.

She walked in, the heels of her shoes clicking against the floor as she stopped in front of my desk. "It's almost five thirty. I don't have anywhere to be since…"

Since she stopped dancing. I knew that. It wasn't like she'd stopped recently—it'd been years. But that didn't mean it wasn't hard to see her lingering when she was normally elsewhere doing something that she loved a long time ago.

Her throat cleared. "I was going to head back to my place and work on some projects a little, but I figured you'd still be here."

While my building was on her way home from campus, it didn't make sense why she'd come. "Something I can do for you?"

Her lips twitched, tilting downward like the question hurt her. I wasn't trying to play coy, or even play it off, but I was no stranger to the way her eyes lingered on me. It was the same way mine did on her, I was just better at hiding it. "I was checking in, I guess. I…" I wanted to kick myself knowing she was hesitating because I made her feel unwelcome. She brushed it off. "Can I make you dinner?"

I blinked. "Come again?"

She stood tall, nodding once. Her hair was pulled back in some kind of twisted updo, but a thick strand fell loose and caressed her cheek. The same one that was tinted pink at her own words as she waited for my response. "I want to make you dinner. I have something in mind that I think you'd like. You can't go wrong with a homecooked meal, right?"

The chair creaked under my weight as I leaned back with my hands folded on my stomach. "Depends what it is." That was a lie. I'd be happy with anything that I didn't have to take out of a container, especially if she were the one cooking it.

It wouldn't be the first time she made me food. There were times in the past I let her experiment on me with meals she wanted to create that her father wouldn't eat. He'd either be too busy or too tired by the time he'd gotten home. There were days when she'd admitted that she hadn't even bothered making more than necessary because it just went to waste.

"Chicken alfredo with garlic bread."

My stomach reacted instantly, but it wasn't loud enough for her to know I was all in. Instead, I studied her for a moment until she shifted in uncertainty before giving her a light smile. "I need to lock up since Abigail left. Did you take a cab here?"

"Uber."

"What did I tell you about those?"

Her blue eyes rolled, lined with thick black lashes, and a brightness in them that always made her look happy even when she wasn't. "Like taxis are any better? Plus, they're practically the same thing."

I couldn't argue with her, but that didn't stop my deadpanned expression from crossing my features. "You have a driver."

"That I hate using," she replied instantly.

"You like Dallas."

"Yes, I do like Dallas." Her agreement was light, making my lips waver upward over her gentleness. She liked everybody, that was the problem. "But that doesn't mean I like using his services when I'm capable of getting myself places other ways. Not to mention, Dallas's wife just had a baby and it wouldn't be fair for me to call him away while he enjoys Cody."

"Cody?"

"The baby."

"Ah." I flattened my palm against my dress shirt, today's choice charcoal gray that hid a stain I'd accidently gotten on it during lunch, before grabbing my jacket from where it hung by the door. "I still don't want you using Uber."

"You're being silly."

"I'm being practical." I wasn't and we both knew it, but I liked our banter. "You could call me if necessary."

"I wanted to surprise you."

And surprise you did, little Della. But capturing the sight of her bare thighs and the way they were shaped from years of dance, even after her extensive weight loss, made me realize just how much I needed to stop calling her that. I rarely did it aloud anymore because it felt inappropriate, like an insult somehow. Adele was no longer the little girl who begged to dance while standing on my shoes, but a grown woman capable of pulling any man to the floor and demanding they dance with her. That didn't stop me from dancing with her over the weekend, relishing in an old memory that calmed us both down, when I found her moving by herself. I wanted to give her peace of mind, something to hold onto that would never change. We'd always have the past.

Not only that, I supposed, but words could be triggering for her. I'd done the research after her official diagnosis, even asking a therapist who'd specialized in eating disorders what I could do to help because I was desperate to be somebody she could lean on if she needed. Della, no matter what she believed, didn't need anybody. She was stronger than she gave herself credit for. That didn't mean I wasn't going to try avoiding terms or affirmations that put her in the place she fought a long time to get out of.

"You're doing it again. Being all overprotective for no reason. I told you last time we talked about this that I would be fine. Look, I haven't been kidnapped yet."

I eyed her. "You do realize you just jinxed yourself, right? Your father will haunt me when news breaks that former Governor Saint James's daughter went missing after hailing a taxi all on her lonesome."

I didn't miss the way her lips pressed together, and eyes dulled at the statement, causing me to rethink what I'd said. Sighing, I walked over and waited for her to look at me. The tips of our shoes touched we were so close, and I saw the pink painted on her toenails from where they peeked out the front of her heels. "I'm sorry. I know you don't like people referring to you like that. It just slipped out."

She hesitated for a moment before lifting her gaze to

meet mine, looking at me through her lashes. "It's stupid, right? He was my father and I loved him so much. It shouldn't irritate me when people call me that."

"But you're your own person. I get it." I didn't think Anthony ever saw how much Della would flinch whenever she was asked questions about him or addressed by anything except her name. It was always as Governor Saint James's daughter, or some other association that made her less of an individual. I understood why it ate at her. "You'll always be Della to me," I whispered despite my better judgement. My fingers itched to reach out and cup her jaw, to brush the full bottom lip of hers, but I forced them to remain by my sides.

"Your little Della, you mean," she teased, her eyes lighting back up to their natural color.

Slowly, I shook my head. "Not anymore." She frowned at that, but I didn't let her get into her head to dissect it because I knew whatever conclusion she'd come up with wouldn't be a good one. "You're too old for that now. It would be an injustice to the woman you've become, to your character."

Her face flushed, the pink in her cheeks deepening and making me want to touch her that much more, to feel the heat blossoming beneath my fingertips. "You're too nice to me."

"I'm telling the truth. That's all."

She stood back first, putting distance between us that I should have done. It made me realize just how closely we stood, and I hadn't given a shit. "So, chicken alfredo?"

Not able to stop the amused laugh from bursting past my pressed lips, I buttoned my suit jacket and shook my head. "I'd never say no to you, Della."

She gave me a long look and I realized my mistake once the words were out, but it was too late to fix it. So, we let it be.

THE HOUSE SMELLED like garlic by the time I'd made it downstairs after a quick shower and change of clothes. Della had taken off her blazer, draping it across the kitchen table as she focused on stirring something on the stove. Even with her back to me, I knew her tongue was sticking out slightly in concentration, something she'd done ever since she was little. I'd always found it cute, endearing even, because she had no idea she did it. It allowed me to hold onto something that didn't change with her as time passed. It was always going to be something that made Della...Della.

"I can feel you staring," she told me, looking over her shoulder with a bright smile and catching me with my own stretching my lips. I walked in, unfazed by being caught, though I should have been.

"It smells good." I stopped beside her, looking into the large pot, a sauté pan according to her, with noodles, chicken, and white sauce mixed together.

"I'd hope so, I followed the recipe closely to make sure it came out perfect."

I reached above her to grab a glass from the cupboard, my side brushing against her back, and felt her lean into me before realizing what she was doing. My lips twitched at her body's reaction. It was an instinct I clung to, welcomed.

"Even if you didn't follow it, it'd come out perfect. There's nothing you do that is anything less."

She froze, her hand white knuckling the wooden spoon that I wasn't sure was mine or something she brought with her. "We both know that isn't true."

Instantly, my gaze snapped to her face which was keen on avoiding me. "Don't fucking do that, Adele."

She flinched.

"Don't put yourself down."

"Theo, I'm —"

"No." My voice was hard, causing her lips to snap shut hearing my impatience. "I will not let you do that to yourself. You've come so far. Don't go back now."

I heard the soft, slow exhale she took and watched her body loosen from the tension building. "I'm not, Theo. Promise. But we can't pretend that I didn't have a...a moment when things weren't good. Ripley told me I'm always going to have days where I have to fight a little harder and that it's good I can acknowledge the moments when they arrive. And, if I'm being honest, I'm okay with admitting I'm not perfect. I tried too hard to be my whole life and that was what hurt me the most."

This was the reason I admired her. Even though she was supposed to look up to people like me, older, wiser, with more life experience, it was me who looked up to this twenty-two-year-old. And I gave no fucks about it even at my forty years of age.

"You never cease to amaze me, you know that? It doesn't matter what happens, your strength is blinding. I know people who have lost far less, been through things that don't even compare, and have a bigger reaction to them. But not you. That's inspiring."

She stopped stirring again to turn and glance up at me, her eyes searching mine for a long moment like she was trying to find something. "That means a lot coming from you, but I'm not so sure I can accept the compliment. Especially because there are people who will always have it better than me and those who have it worse. I don't like considering my circumstances to be a reason that puts me above or below others."

Shaking my head, I turned to the faucet and filled the cup with water.

"What?" she doubted.

"Nothing, Della."

Her palm brushed my arm, causing me to look over my shoulder at her curious gaze. "No, I want to know what you're thinking."

"I already said what I thought, you just emphasized it by saying what you did. You are, and always will be, beyond your years. I'm not sure if that's a good thing or not."

"Why wouldn't it be?"

My dick was willing to answer that when it strained against the denim it was trapped in. She didn't grasp how sexy it was that she was strong and humble. "Because experience ages people, and normally not the good kind."

Her frown was instant. "It isn't like I had a bad life, Theo. You know that better than anybody. I just had moments that weren't as stellar as others. And before you scold me for pointing that out, I'm just stating facts. Overall, I've lived a good life that I'm grateful for. Loss and all."

I watched her for a moment, water forgotten in my hand, before smiling. "Like I said. Wise beyond your years."

She just shrugged.

After food was plated sometime later, we sat down beside each other at the table. Even though I'd offered to eat in the living room and watch TV, something I knew she did more times than not at her place, she insisted she wanted a normal dinner because she only ate on the couch at home because she had nobody else to talk to.

There were more times than I liked to admit where my mind wandered to her when I was alone. Not in a sexual way, usually, but more with concern. I knew she lived alone and didn't have people over often. Not even Pretty Boy. She spent a lot of time in her spare room turned studio, painting and getting lost in whatever project she had going. But there were days when I couldn't help but wonder if she ever felt lonely, isolated, like she didn't have a choice but to accept dinners in front of the television, probably watching some historical documentary or food competition, or if she hardly thought of it at all.

"Theo?" Snapping out of the thought, I realized I was staring at my plate in silence. "Does it not taste good? I could make you something else if you—"

"It's fine." To prove it, I dipped my fork into the pasta and wound it around the silver prongs before taking a hearty bite. She watched me like she was waiting for me to spit it out. Once I swallowed, I said, "I mean it, Della. It's great."

"You were staring at it like you found a hair or something."

Chuckling, I looked at the full head of hair that she'd let loose as soon as she walked into the house. I preferred it down. It made me think of all the times she'd ask me or her father to brush it out for her because her arms were too short to detangle it after baths. The one summer Elizabeth had convinced her to get it cut so she'd be cooler, she ended up sobbing while clinging to my legs, and not even my promise that she looked cute, which she had, could calm her down.

It'd been in a few fantasies I tried keeping locked up as well, where a fistful was wound around my hand as I pulled her head back and kissed the fuck out of her while I thrusted inside her pussy. I didn't allow myself to think about that often though.

"Lost in thought," was the only information I offered her.

Her bottom lip stuck out, making me smirk, but I hid it by eating more so she couldn't think I was lying.

"I've gotten better," she admitted, picking at her own food. Her garlic bread was almost half eaten, though the small portion on her plate was barely touched. I'd wanted to tell her to eat, to put more on the plate, but I held myself back because it wouldn't have done any good. At least she was eating something. "So, stop looking at my food like you're going to lecture me."

"I wasn't," I assured half-heartedly.

"Mmhmm."

I grinned. "I was just thinking about how well your cooking skills have gotten."

"I'd hope so," she mused, twirling her fork around some pasta before stabbing a piece of chicken with it. "I've come a long way over the years considering my only other options were finding new Pop-Tarts and Healthy Choice meals to try."

She had people to cook for her, but she never used them. When her mother was alive, she'd cook all the time for the family, but then she became busy with the charities she helped with and the events she'd gone to constantly with Anthony. They did everything for their family, for Adele, but their daughter was on her own more than I liked. It was why I'd stepped in so much, brought Della with me various places, that way she wasn't always alone with the hired help.

Being the stubborn child that she was, she always insisted on eating premade meals, things she could make easily without anybody else's help. When Elizabeth passed, her father tried to take up cooking and meal prep, so Della had something to eat that wasn't loaded with sugar, especially considering Adele had become hyperaware of what she was eating, no thanks to the expectations that came with being a dancer and the way the tabloids came at her when she put on weight from the lack of proper nutrition. It hadn't mattered that she burnt twice as many calories from her routines, she struggled with her body image because of everything in her life. I'd read that it was common for adolescents to have those challenges, but Della was a special case. She spiraled with the stress of her loss, in how swiftly everything changed for her because of her parents.

"I still have a long way to go considering I nearly burnt down my father's house trying to prepare Christmas dinner that one year. I'm still afraid to do anything with turkey."

I couldn't help but laugh. "If it makes you feel better, I can help you this year. Can't just give up because of one incident."

My mind went to my conversation with Sophie about her dancing, but the words didn't feel the same. "You're right, but do you really want to risk your kitchen getting burnt to a crisp?"

I shrugged. "I have the money to fix it."

"Very encouraging."

"I do my best."

Her phone chirped from somewhere in the kitchen, causing her to look behind her. I frowned when she got up and dug through the purse that she'd draped on the island next to the empty fruit bowl. The sigh escaping her lips made my brows pinch. "Trouble?"

"It's nothing."

"Della."

She walked back over, dropping into her chair with her phone still in hand. "My professor emailed me about an opportunity that she'd brought up months ago. The deadline is this weekend and she needs an answer."

"What is the opportunity?"

"An art class."

I waited for her to enlighten me.

She set her phone down. "It's an art class I've been wanting to be part of since sophomore year when the school started offering it. It's not a regular class, it's more like an invite-only event that only happens every two years and lasts for a week. They select students based on submissions throughout the year and apparently mine was one of them."

Pride swept through me. "That's great, Della. Why do you seem upset by it if you've wanted to do it for two years?"

"I just..." She licked her lips, her eyes darting to the phone. "I haven't been very inspired since Dad passed away. I'm afraid if I go that they'll be disappointed with what I produce. They bring top artists to evaluate and offer guidance. It'd be embarrassing if they felt they wasted a spot on me."

"What did I tell you about putting yourself down?"

"You don't get it, Theo."

I learned toward her, my food forgotten along with hers. "Then make me."

She met my gaze. "It's simple. I don't feel as though I'm good enough. I mean, my art. I don't think my *art* is good enough."

But that wasn't what she meant at all. "I know you better than that, Della. Don't try to bullshit me again."

She said nothing.

We returned to our food, clearing off our plates in silence. It wasn't uncomfortable, but thick. I knew she wanted to say something but wouldn't let herself.

"You going to tell me what's on your mind? Can't say I like seeing the way your brows pinch. The crease is back." The crease was a tell that something bothered her.

"You don't want to hear it, Theo."

I crossed my arms over my chest, eyeing her in disbelief. "Try me."

"I was thinking that you're a good man, and that I'm glad you're in my life." Her delivery was soft as she looked up at me, her lips neutral as we locked eyes. "I owe you a lot for what you've done for me all these years."

This time, it was me who remained silent.

"That's all," she whispered.

chapter five

DELLA

As soon as the door opened from the crowded hallway to the side stairwell, I inhaled a breath of fresh air that wasn't littered with Chanel perfume, marijuana, or some other odor. Rounding the corner that lead to the first floor of the Freidman Art Center, I stopped in my tracks when three familiar faces appeared directly in my path and blocking me from passing.

"Adele," Lauren Atwell greeted with the usual tight smile she'd give competition. I used to think it was genuine, but I'd learned better over the years from dancing alongside her.

Jamie Miller and Ophelia Wright were directly

beside her, both looking less intimating and more welcoming than their pack leader. I gave them both small smiles, but only Jamie returned it. "Hey, Della."

Lauren all but glared at Jamie's kind response. I barely refrained from rolling my eyes before she caught me. "We've missed you at practice. There was talk that you may even be coming back."

Talk that started because of Sophie, no doubt, but I didn't call her out on it. "I heard the new girls are doing well. Sounds like there's a lot of competition this year."

Ophelia opened her mouth to speak, but Lauren cut her off. "They're okay, but obviously not as good as the seasoned dancers. So, is it true? Are you coming back?"

Sighing, I adjusted the floral bag draped around my arm. It wasn't as big as most backpacks I'd seen others have but held what little materials I needed for the semester. "No, it isn't. If you don't mind, I really need to get going."

"Ah, yes. To the art department." The way she said it made my eye want to twitch, but I held back. Her tone was no different than Sophie's, and it bothered me more than I liked it to. Lauren's opinion shouldn't matter. Sophie was family, so the bubble of disappointment that appeared when I saw disapproval in her eye made sense. Lauren was just somebody who loved getting under my skin, and I hated that I let her so easily. "I heard you were honing your talents elsewhere. It's a shame. I liked having actual competition."

Jamie and Ophelia's frowns were evident to everybody but Lauren. I was tempted to say that she had competition standing right beside her, which wouldn't have been untrue. I did hear that Jamie had begun training harder to earn a better spot in recitals, and Ophelia always had the kind of natural talent that would take her far if she really wanted it to. Their mothers never pushed them as hard as Lauren's did with her, so their training wasn't as vigorous.

"Like I said," I told her quietly, "I need to go. It was good seeing you guys." I made a point to look at Jamie and Ophelia when I said that, giving them smiles that they both returned with head bobs.

When I sidestepped Jamie and escaped, I heard Lauren snap at them. I felt bad, but Jamie and Ophelia were old enough to decide who they wanted to be friends with. Once I stepped into the open first floor, I was immediately pulled into a hard side that smelled like lemon drops and mischief. I eyed my best friend as he grinned at me like he was innocent. "I was going to rescue you when I saw the shark enter, but Lauren scares me, and I got a papercut earlier, so she'd be able to smell my fear like blood."

I playfully elbowed him, but he didn't seem to care. "You fed me to her willingly then? Some friend you are."

"Did I mention I'm sorry about the party and tell you how much I love you?"

"Yes, to both. Multiple times." He had apologized profusely about what had happened. I told him what

89

Theo said about being drugged, and the look on his face
had told me he came to the same conclusion. One other
girl had been taken to the hospital when her friends
found her acting strange. Thankfully, nobody was hurt,
but it made the school open an investigation that shut
down the fraternity temporarily. Between the third
strike they had for even throwing a party and the alle-
gations somebody roofied drinks, it didn't look good for
them. I wasn't sure I felt bad for them though. Jase
knew they'd been warned but he held the party anyway,
and even though it wasn't his fault someone was trying
to hurt women, it still happened and could have turned
out way worse than it did.

"You're also pretty," he added, batting his lashes,
and making me snort.

We walked side by side down the less packed first
floor hallway, which had more room for students to mill
about while they waited for classrooms to empty.

"In hindsight, I'm lucky to even be alive after the
way your guard dog snapped at me. I deserved it, but I
feared for my life. Definitely would rather face off with
Lauren."

"Would you stop calling Theo that?" I huffed,
eyeing him for the millionth time. "It's bad enough I
kept having to defend you to him when I woke up at his
place. I already told you both that you're forgiven, and
it wasn't your fault."

"But he still hates me, doesn't he?"

"Theo is..."

"I get it, Del. I do. He's the father figure you

needed, so he wants you to be safe. I know that you care about him...a lot. And no matter what you say, I'm always going to feel bad about what happened. About what *could* have happened. Listen, word got around that it might have been Evan who drugged a few drinks that night. There's been talk he's done it before but..."

"He's never gotten caught." My stomach dropped over what that probably meant. I told him I'd suspected him considering he was following me after I turned him away. And Evan...there was something off about him that went beyond his distaste for me. "They have to kick him out, Ren. Please tell me there's at least a hearing or something with the council or whatever it's called?"

"They're voting at next week's meeting."

I blew out a breath. That was something. I wasn't sure why it was taking them so long. Nobody really liked Evan from what I could tell. How hard was it to secure a vote that made sure he wouldn't harm people?

"But." My body froze as we stopped at the double doors that led to my salvation in form of paint fumes. "It doesn't mean anything will happen. Talk is talk."

"What if there was proof?"

"There isn't. We know it. He knows it."

I shook my head, anger boiling my blood. People like Evan got away with too much. I would know, I'd seen it happen countless times. Who was I to talk though? It was no secret that my father hadn't gotten away with things, which should have been prime reason for people not to think their money could protect them. "He deserves to be kicked out of the frat whether there's clear evidence or not. If plenty of people are talking about it, obviously there's a reason."

He dropped his arm and turned to me, his light eyes dulled. "I agree with you, but it's not that easy. We'll deal with him eventually, okay? You don't need to worry about it."

"How can I not? You know better than anybody that Evan hates me already." I frowned, blinking at my friend with genuine concern. "There are innocent people he probably hurt, and even more he hasn't had a chance to if nothing is done."

"We don't know for sure he hates you. Why would he? You've done nothing to him, Del. And what happens to other people isn't on you," he reminded me. We'd had similar conversation before, so I knew where the conversation was going. "You need to stop trying to fix the world's problems and focus on you and yours."

"I didn't realize I had problems."

He eyed me skeptically.

"Whatever," I grumbled, pushing hair behind my ear. "Was it at least worth it?"

He blinked.

"Ben."

A slow grin tilted his lips. "If that's your way of asking if he's a good kisser, I never kiss and tell."

I smacked his arm. "Liar!"

He laughed. "Nothing is worth you getting hurt, but I know what you're really asking. I had fun. Ben is nice. But would I date him? Maybe, but he isn't out. So, I suppose the answer to your question is leaning towards no."

Wrapping my arms around his midsection for a quick hug, I squeezed him before stepping back. "You really love me, huh?"

"Like you had any doubt."

I smiled and reached for the door handle, but he beat me to it and opened the door. He bowed and gestured for me to enter, making me giggle. "See you later? Coffee at the Hut?"

"You're not going to stay late here?"

I looked in the empty art room before turning back to him. "My project is almost done and I'm not sure I'll start another. Text me when you're done with the guys?"

The flicker of amusement told me I said the wrong thing. "I didn't think you wanted the dirty details, Della. Naughty little vixen."

I blushed. "I meant with practice and you know it. I heard Tommy say Coach has been rough on you guys."

One of his shoulders lifted. "He doesn't want to lose another game. Can't say I blame the guy. We were horrible last season and practice this season hasn't been much better."

"Then don't hold back," I told him knowingly. He hated attention but loved the game enough. In fact, he was the best one on the team, not that he'd admit it. "You've got what it takes to make it big even if that's not what you want."

He didn't say anything right away. "I'll text you

later, okay? If you still want to go to the Hut, then you know I'll be there."

I turned to walk in when he called out my name, causing me to glance back at him. His lips wavered as he watched me for a moment. "I'd go against Lauren, Evan, and whoever else I needed to if it meant you were okay. You know that, right?"

"Of course." Why would he even ask that? Just because the frat party happened, didn't mean I blamed him. I wasn't even mad anymore because rationality overtook any irritation I had for him disappearing.

Ren nodded once.

"Theo knows it too," I added, though unconvincingly. Theo *did* know Lawrence would do anything to make sure I was okay. He just refused to admit it because he preferred hating on Ren instead.

His lips pinched. "I doubt that, Del, but thanks for trying to make me feel better."

I gave him a small smile, one of reassurance even though he didn't need it. "He trusts my judgment even when he shouldn't. If I say you are good people, he knows it. As for fighting people for me..." The laugh couldn't be stopped at the sight of him facing off Lauren. Ren had muscles, but he just didn't have the vigor that Lauren did when she meant business. "I don't doubt you could take Evan, but Lauren..."

He flinched. "Go get creative, Del."

I stuck my tongue out at him before disappearing into my happy place. The door clicked behind me, letting me exhale the breath I'd been holding knowing I was on my turf. Nobody could take this away from me, judge me, or tell me I didn't look right while doing what I loved.

The canvas I was met with had an acrylic version of the sketch I'd been working on at the warehouse, but it shifted. The two faceless figures were intertwined in a warm embrace, ballet flats on polished dress shoes, with their arms around each other. It was soft, the colors muted, but the tone something far louder.

I called it "Safe Space" because that was exactly where I was when I was in Theo's arms.

MARCH PASSED in a blur of monotony that I welcomed. Classes flew by, the work wasn't hard to complete, and nobody said anything about my father. The silence was what I needed.

It was the beginning of April when the rain showers hit, and normally I liked watching from the living room window, but my mood had dulled over the past week considering it was the three-month anniversary of my father's death. I went on with my life as I should have, but closed myself away because pretending all day was too tiring. Ren understood to some degree, only checking in on me occasionally after I left campus, and never asked me to go to parties because he knew what I'd say.

I was curled on the couch with a throw over my bare legs and the History Channel on the television screen when my phone rang. A clap of thunder rattled the windows, causing my focus to go to the glass to watch lightning strike and light the darkening sky. When my cell rang again, I pulled my gaze away from the downpour and back to the screen to see Theo's name flashing across it.

He started in as soon as I hit accept. "You didn't go to Sophie's."

"Most people start a conversation with *hello* and *how are you*," I pointed out tiredly, laying back down on my side.

He didn't hesitate. "You always go to her house on Sunday, and I know what today is. Even if she were on your last nerves you wouldn't leave her on her own to handle things."

Closing my eyes, I shifted my knees up until they were tucked by my chest, so I was balled up. Of course, I'd felt bad leaving Sophie alone, but I knew she'd be okay. She'd have brunch, day drink, and drown herself in town gossip by phoning her friends. If I honestly thought she'd need me, I would have sucked it up and went. "I don't feel well, that's all."

"Do you need to go to the doctor?" The alarm in his voice warmed my chest, but also burned my cheeks considering what I had wasn't some contagious illness he needed to fret about.

"No, it's nothing serious. Just, uh…" Biting into my lip, I winced and tried figuring out how to explain that it was just my period sucking the life out of me one cramp at a time. The stress of Dad's death anniversary only fed the typical migraine that accompanied my menstrual cycle, so I'd been drugged up in the dark all day trying to get rid of it while listening to whatever was on TV.

"Ah." His throat cleared, seemingly in understanding. "Are you all right?"

"It's not the end of the world, Theo."

"You didn't answer my question."

"I'll call Sophie later to see how she's doing, but I'm fine. It's been a hard week. I won't act like I was okay throughout it."

He mumbled a curse. "I should have made time to check in on you. I knew—"

"I'm not your responsibility," I cut him off, even though I knew he'd argue. He made it his responsibility to worry, and sometimes I enjoyed it. It made me feel like I was on his mind, but not in the way I wanted.

"Since when?"

I thought to all the times he'd taken care of me when my parents were busy saving the world and building a future for us. I looked up to them and all they did for others, but there were times I wish they'd done more for me in their time on earth. It never hit me until I had to see them both buried, hearing hundreds of people give their condolences and assuring me what amazing people they were as if I needed to hear that. I knew it. I'd witnessed them make a difference every single day. But that didn't dissipate the envy that grew despite all the good they did—even after Dad's one poor decision that changed everything.

"Like I said, I'm fine," I repeated. My tone was

muffled by the hand I scrubbed down my achy, over-heated face.

"Christ." His hard tone confused me. "I'll be there in thirty. Maybe forty." Before I could tell him that wasn't necessary, he hung up on me.

I sat up, staring at the background of my phone which had a picture of my favorite painting filling the space. Had he really just done that? Anger settled in the pit of my stomach. I wanted to turn off my cell and fall asleep like I'd begged my body to do all day, but there was too much weighing on my mind to get comfortable enough to slip into unconsciousness. Between that and the cramps, I'd watched TV all day instead, forcing myself to eat whatever was premade in my refrigerator even though I had no appetite.

It wasn't that long of me absentmindedly watching a documentary on Egypt when the knock came at the door. Peeling myself off the couch, I didn't think twice before answering in my frumpy pajamas that were loose, torn, and stained, but soft and comfortable, before opening the door and finding Theo. He was holding a paper bag that was filled to the top with items, leaving me staring in confusion.

He walked past me, breaking my focus. I slowly closed the door as he walked into the open kitchen and set the bag down on the closest counter. "You need to look before you answer the door, Della. We've gone over this."

"How do you know I didn't?"

"You say that every time."

"Because you're not Superman. You don't have x-ray vision that clearly proves I didn't check before answering."

He stared at me.

My nose twitched. "Fine, but you were the only person I was expecting."

"Another thing you say every time."

Padding over, I looked in the bag and gaped at the feminine products, chocolate, and medicine resting on the top. He didn't look away when I moved my eyes to him. "You bought me this stuff?"

He acted like it was no big deal. "I wasn't sure what you needed, and I know you tend not to eat when you're on your period. Better to eat something even if it isn't a full meal. Though—" He pulled something out of the very bottom and passed it to me. "—I also bought this since I know you like it."

It was a container of potato soup, my favorite go-to when I didn't feel well. My mother used to make it from scratch which beat any other version I tried, but I couldn't perfect the recipe because she'd done it all from her head.

"Want me to heat it up?" he asked.

"You bought me Tampons."

"Yes, I did."

I blinked, staring at him like he was some foreign entity gracing me with his presence. "I'm sorry, it's just unexpected. Nobody has bought me stuff like this before besides my mom, and most guys wouldn't be caught dead shopping in that aisle."

"Well I'm not just some little boy like the people you hang around," he pointed out matter-of-factly. And he wasn't wrong. I'd tried getting Ren to make me an emergency run to the campus store when I was out and the school bathroom dispenser was empty, or even just to ask any girl he passed who probably had something tucked away in their bags, but he was too embarrassed. I'd held a grudge against him for weeks because I'd had to wrap toilet paper around my underwear to make sure I'd be safe enough until I found something better.

I emptied the bag and smiled at the selections of products. He'd gotten different kinds of pads and Tampons, all making my smile grow wider on my lips. "Thank you." Reaching for the dark chocolate and soup container, I walked over to the microwave and began preparing the soup.

"I can do that for you," he offered, walking up behind me until his chest brushed against the entire backside of me. His arm reached out and plucked the sizeable plastic container away from my capable hands and began taking over.

Realistically, I should have moved. But he could have too, and he remained pressed against me invading my space. I absorbed his body heat, the warmth he offered, and stared at the chocolate bar resting in front of me on the marble countertop. That annoying voice in my head told me not to open it—to throw it away when he left so he thought I ate it. But my mouth watered over my favorite snack with the little almond pieces mixed in and I was sick of fighting myself. I knew the thoughts were purely because of the bloat that made my stomach look like I'd gained weight and that it'd go away in a few days, but that didn't silence the demon that demanded I do something about it. "You didn't have to do any of this, Theo."

"I know."

"I was okay on my own."

"I know."

Hesitating, I leaned backward ever so slightly so my back rested on his front. He froze for a moment, then eased. "But I'm glad that I'm not alone because...I needed somebody." It was hard to admit that aloud, but I'd been thinking it all day. I'd considered calling Theo mid-afternoon to ask him to come over and watch TV with me but refrained. He had his own life that didn't involve me.

The soup was set on the counter beside my hand before I felt his hot breath against my cheek just before his lips pressed against the flush of my cheekbone. "I know you did, Della. That's why I'm here."

I couldn't fight the grin. "You mean you didn't just feel like shopping for Tampons? I'm shocked, Theo."

His deep chuckle vibrated against my back. "You always were sassy when you wanted to be, little Della."

My tongue swiped across my bottom lip over the name, one I'd found endearing. But now it felt different, like I wanted to be called something else. "I'm not so little anymore."

I felt his nose brush against my ear as he whispered,

"No, you're not. And unfortunately, I'm not the only one who's noticed."

A shiver raked down my spine, but he still didn't move. I was glad because I meant what I said. I needed somebody here.

I needed Theo West.

chapter six

DELLA

I'M REACHING for the last fruit cup when a manicured hand snatched it just before I could. I looked over to see Katrina Murphy smiling with her typical bright green eye shadow and heavy black liner that looked model perfect. She rocked anything she wore, no matter how crazy.

"I thought you were Lauren," I said as she pulled me into a hug. She moved back with an offended look pinching her face, but the amusement told me she didn't really feel it.

"Watch it, Saint James."

I grinned, stepping back as she passed me the fruit cup. "In my defense, she has it out for me. Two weeks ago, she took the last chef salad and the week before that—"

"Yeah, yeah. She's a bitch." Her neutral painted lips twitched at the corners. "So, did you miss me, you beautiful bitch?"

Snickering, I reached for her free hand and squeezed it. I told her when we video chatted a few months ago, but she looked great. Skinnier, not that she needed it, but she didn't look unhealthy like my version of skinny had been. "I did. But why are you back early? I thought you were traveling."

Katrina was on a European vacation over winter break when she decided to extend her stay into the new semester. She'd let me know over a two-minute phone call that she'd be back during the summer, and I knew the call was cut short over a guy because of the baritone voice in the background that day demanding she come back to bed.

"Mikel is married." Her pause was thoughtful. "Or *was*. I'm pretty sure his wife was throwing his belongings out the window of their house when we talked last."

She didn't even sound sorry about it. "I thought you said he was divorced."

She gave me a timid smile. "I thought he was. For a while. Then things started clicking together and I realized he lied."

I gaped, walking us over to the register and paying for the fruit. "And you stayed with him? You deserve better than that, Kat."

Her eyes rolled. "We both know I'm no saint, Della. When I first found out I was angry he lied, but I liked Mikel. Plus, the sex was phenomenal. Why would I give that up?"

The woman working the cash register froze for a moment, her lips twitching upward at the conversation between me and my eccentric, wild at heart friend. I met Katrina when we were little, and we couldn't be more opposite to this day, but it worked for us. She loved parties, which she dragged me to if Ren didn't, sleeping around with as many guys as possible, which I'd always envied, and doing whatever she wanted without consequences. I loved Kat because she was herself no matter what people thought of her, but sometimes I wondered if it got old. The wild child thing. Then again, her family didn't seem to care what she did because they never stopped her, so why should I question it?

Once outside the campus store, we found a free picnic table to occupy while the sun was still out. "Did they let you re-enroll? The semester is half over."

"Nah. I was visiting a couple friends in Humphrey when I saw you walk in. I know I should have reached out sooner about your father, but..."

I waved her off, not wanting to talk about it. There was no point bringing up the past. Neither of us could change what our fathers did, and it took a lot not to think about the implications that hers might have been more involved than was let on. Considering he was free and roaming, I guessed that wasn't the case. But still...

"My dad still asks me about you," she said softly, watching me peel open my fruit cup and stab at a piece with the plastic fork I snatched. "He wanted me to tell you he was sorry he couldn't be at the funeral."

It hurt to swallow. "Well, tell him thanks."

"Della—"

"No, it's fine." Clearing my throat, I focused solely on the food in front of me. Unable to do more than stare, I poked around to find the different types in the fruit juice.

"Are you okay? Like, really okay?"

I knew what she was asking. "Yes, Kat. I told you when we talked last that I was better. Nothing has changed."

"A lot has changed. Your dad—"

"I know about my dad," I snapped. I rarely did that, lost my temper. As much as I loved Katrina for her strong personality, there were moments I wish she'd drop something. She knew my father was a sore subject, but not as much as my disorder was. Blowing out a deep breath, I set the fruit down on the table. "I told you I'm fine. I didn't lie. So just…"

She shifted uncomfortably because she wasn't used to being yelled at. People were intimidated by her and her own father rarely ever raised his voice when she was involved. She had him wrapped around her finger. "I'm sorry, Del. I just care about you. I know how hard things were for you and how much stress could make it worse."

I felt bad, so my shoulders dropped. "I didn't mean

106

to get angry. I just don't want to talk about this. Tell me about what you're doing now that you're back."

Her dulled expression changed in a millisecond, becoming much more chipper as she perked up. "I'm renovating the guest house to move in to before my classes start this summer. In fact, Sam and Gina said they'd help."

Ah. Sam and Gina used to dance with us once upon a time. Their mothers were friends with our mothers, so we'd all hung out quite a bit growing up. I never liked them because they were into things that I didn't like being part of. Sam almost got arrested for shoplifting when we were sixteen, but her father got her out of trouble. I was certain they still participated in the hobby because I saw Gina's mugshot in the New York Daily only months ago for stealing liquor.

"Get that sour look off your face. They're not that bad," she scoffed knowingly.

I tried my best to act unfazed. "I didn't know you hung out with them still. I heard that Sam got into some trouble at some high-end party last year." Theo had been at that party because it was for some investor who put a lot of money in Interactive Marketing. Sam's father had made it no secret he wanted in, so he was there to try talking with Theo when Sam showed up drunk before causing a scene. I wasn't sure what happened with the potential business Theo could have drummed up from it because I heard Sam's dad was a strong-willed man.

"They like to party. So what?"

I didn't say anything.

Kat sighed. "You need to lighten up. Why don't you come over to my place tonight? They'll be there and they mentioned how much they've wanted to reconnect. They feel bad about…things."

I held my tongue, knowing it was better not to say a word about what those things were. Reminding myself that they weren't their fathers usually helped, but it would be easier if they didn't act like they didn't have a foot in the door of the family business they should have been avoiding altogether if they were smart.

"I have a lot of homework," I told her quietly, picking up my fruit again.

She grabbed it from me. "You're lying. I know you, Della. You're bad at it. My place. Eight. I'll tell them to be on their best behavior."

It didn't matter what she told them, they marched to the beat of their own drum. I used to wish I could be like them. Free. Willing to take risks. But the risks they took weren't the same kinds I wanted to.

I knew Kat though. She wouldn't take no for an answer, which meant one way or another I'd wind up at her house. If she was moving into the guest house out back by their large pool, who knew what I'd be walking into.

She took a piece of fruit and winked. "I see the wheels turning. Live dangerously for once, Del. You know you want to." Passing me back my food, she grabbed her purse and shot me a wink. "I've missed you."

Why didn't I believe her though?

THE MUSIC WAS LOUD, vibrating the ground as I walked toward the white house that was larger than my flat. I heard laughter, something crash, then more laughter following. Hesitating at the double glass doors that were wide open, I glanced into the building to see white everywhere inside too—carpet, walls, furniture. Except the expensive sofa that looked nearly identical to the Adriana Royal living room set that we had in our living room growing up had a bright red stain in the middle of it now.

Sam stared from her empty glass to the cushion, looking too amused over the wine stain. It was probably Cabernet, Screaming Eagle if I knew Kat. Her father loved the expensive stuff and had a cellar full of various wines he collected for garden parties they held on their estate.

"You made it!" Kat greeted me as soon as she stepped into the living room. Her arms wrapped around me as she squeezed me tightly to her, my lips weighing into a frown at the alcohol stench radiating from her.

It wasn't quite eight yet because I knew if I were even a minute late, she'd blow up my phone and then hunt me down. Getting noise complaints from my neighbors again because of her loud entrance in my building was the last thing I needed when I wanted to lay low.

I pulled away first, keeping her at arm's length as I

watched Gina and Sam dance in the corner of the room. There was something off about them, but I couldn't put my finger on it. I didn't see them often enough to know exactly what. "This place has changed," I noted, examining the fur rug under the glass table perched between the furniture and the cobblestone fireplace that was lit despite it being warm out.

"I told you I was renovating," she sang, looping an arm around my waist. "Want something to drink? I took out that nasty white wine you love so much."

"Lame!" Gina called out from where the two of them danced.

I refrained from rolling my eyes, but the blush from her comment couldn't be hidden on my face. "I'm driving home later, so I'll pass." I paused. "But thank you."

Kat snorted. "Always so polite." She unwound herself from me and grabbed a glass of red wine for herself to drink, stumbling slightly while doing it. "I obviously don't need to introduce any of you, but how nice is it that we're all together again?"

I wasn't sure that was the word I'd use, but the other two cheered. Although, I was certain they'd cheer over anything right now based on the empty bottle of wine on the floor and the half-empty one on the table. "What are you guys planning on doing tonight?" I asked, walking over to the armchair, and sitting.

Kat gestured toward her wine. "Drink?"

That made Sam laugh. "What else is there to do on this fine Wednesday night?"

My lips twitched. "You mentioned renovating. How many rooms have you done so far?" I knew the guest house had three bedrooms and two and a half baths. We'd spent a lot of time here when we were younger having sleepovers and gossiping about boys we liked. It was in this same house that Kat admitted she had a crush on Lawrence, and Gina insisted she was going to tell. To my knowledge, Ren had no clue Kat had a thing for him, but what did I know? The only thing I was sure about was that old crush was long gone considering Kat's adventures with other men who were the exact opposite of my best friend.

"I've only done the living room." She dropped onto the couch, staring down at the stain beside her. "Though it looks like I'll need a new couch thanks to *someone*." Another laugh from the girls. "But I want to do my room next. It sees a lot of visitors, after all."

I couldn't help but smile. "What were you thinking?"

Before she could speak, Sam all but crashed into Kat on the couch. "Who cares about all that? It's boring. We need to have fun."

I frowned. "I actually like—"

Sam groaned. "Yeah, we know. You like all the artsy stuff. Your mom did too, right? She was an interior designer or something?"

I didn't realize she remembered. "Yes, she loved what she did. So, I don't find it boring at all. I thought that was why I was here."

Kat frowned. "You're here to hang out with your

friends. Don't think I haven't heard the way you hole up in your apartment or visit your aunt when you're not in school. Or go to that creepy ass warehouse your dad was always obsessed with. No offense, but Sophie is the last person I'd want to be around, and that warehouse is shady. You need to live your life, Del."

"And not be a buzzkill," Sam added.

Kat cut her a look that made Sam roll her eyes before returning to Gina. "Ignore her, she's a mean drunk."

"How'd you know I visit the warehouse?" It wasn't somewhere I'd ever taken her. I felt like it was my spot alone—something I shared with my parents even if they weren't around. My father hated when I snuck away to it on my own, but when he'd find me there, tell me stories about Mom, and everything would seem okay.

Gina snorted. "Kat is very familiar with that side of town. Aren't you, Kat?" The girls all exchanged a look that I couldn't decipher in time before Kat glanced at me.

"I've seen you around. Know some people who've seen you pass through. You used to tell us about it, remember? Not hard to figure out where you go."

That wasn't the place anybody should go, I knew that. So why was Kat there? It didn't make any sense.

She changed the subject. "Remember when I wanted to get my room decorated to look like what I imagined the inside of a princess's castle looked like?" She giggled, looking at me with a wide smile on her face. "I'm glad my father suggested we wait because all that pink would have made me throw up now."

I didn't want to let go of the last conversation, but I saw she wasn't going to have it. So, I laughed at the memory. "He did buy you that pretty canopy bed though with the pink tulle curtains. We used to pretend we were royalty."

"We are."

I shook my head. "No, but it was fun to pretend for a little while. Everything was so much easier back then when school was fun and dance was enjoyable." It made me think of what Theo told me in the warehouse when we danced. It really was easier when we were younger. Naïve. I understood now more than ever why ignorance was bliss.

"And our families weren't caught up in corruption," she added, downing the rest of her drink in one long swallow. "Enough of that. Memory lane is officially closed. We can be whatever the fuck we want now that we're adults. Screw our families."

My stomach churned. "I don't know about—"

Sam and Gina walked over with mischievous looks on their faces. It was Gina who said, "I heard y'all wanted to start having fun. Lucky for you, I can help with that."

Reaching for a black leather bag with a designer emblem on the front clasp, she dug through a side pocket until she produced something small. The grin she shot us wasn't what made me dread what was coming next, it the wink as she set the tiny bag of white powder down onto the table.

"What...?" My voice cracked. I knew what it was. I'd never seen any in person before, but I'd heard it'd been circulating again. Dallas was listening to the news one day when we were in the car and I'd heard that laced cocaine was going around, and death tolls were increasing from overdoses.

"Shame, isn't it?" Dallas asked, shaking his head as the reporter read statistics from the city. I'd told him it was, half out of it and wondering why anybody would risk their lives like that. When I realized I had no right to judge, I'd tuned out the radio.

"Don't be a buzzkill," Sam said again.

My eye twitched.

Kat grabbed my hand and squeezed. "It's not so bad, Del. I've done it a couple times and it makes you feel good. Promise."

She promised? "Are you kidding me, Katrina? That's *cocaine!*" I hissed the last word as if there were people around to catch us. I didn't want to be anywhere near this if something bad happened.

The two other girls laughed like it was the funniest thing they'd heard in a long time, and I wondered how much of the substance was already in their system on top of the alcohol.

Kat squeezed my fingers again. "Come on, Del. Would I ever lead you astray? Remember all the fun times we had? Our parents always said we brought the good out in each other, challenged each other."

My heart raced in my chest as I looked at the three of them one by one. My eyes finding Kat's again, I shook my head. "This isn't good though. I didn't even know you were into this kind of stuff. You weren't before you left."

It was Gina who cackled. "Oh, please. She was the one who got us into it. Kat was always the wild one out of all of us. Why do you think she's on the same side of town your little warehouse is?"

I stared at my friend who was a ghost of the person I'd spent so much time with. At least I got the answer to my question from earlier. All the times we laughed, cried, gossiped, played, and everything in between seemed like nothing but a distant memory that might not have even been real because I didn't know this version of Kat at all.

"Kat?" I wanted her to deny it, but she didn't. Instead, she sat there looking at me for a microsecond before her gaze traveled to the powder now spread in lines on the table. Whispering her name again, I realized it was pointless. How long had she been doing drugs? Something told me the 'couple times' she'd mentioned was more than that.

Sam spoke up. "You of all people should really consider this, Adele. I mean, I lost twenty pounds between this and heroin. It's not all bad, even if you hear the worst of it."

My stomach bottomed out. The version of me who'd researched ways to lose weight would waken if tempted, and I didn't want that. "I should go."

Kat stood when I did, her eyes widening like she was afraid of something. I realized when she spoke that she was scared I'd rat them out. "I want you to stay. I miss my best friend. If you don't want to do it, you don't have to. But…"

But don't tell anybody.

Jaw ticking, I reached for my bag and set it on my shoulder. "I missed you when you were away," I admitted, ignoring the lingering gazes of the other two. "I'd felt bad when I pulled back after things with my father happened. I figured you traveling was better than being around everything that was going on here. Like maybe one of us could get out and have fun. But this? This is dangerous, Kat."

I heard it before I saw it, but from the corner of my eye I noticed half of the first line gone with Gina hovering over the table. My eyes widened.

"If you really cared you would have reached out and acted like a friend," Kat snapped, taking me off guard. "But you didn't. You were stuck in your perfect little world here acting better than everybody else with Theodore West just like always. Stop pretending to be an angel, Adele."

Eyes stinging with oncoming tears, I brushed them off and realized it was more than likely the drugs talking. It didn't make it hurt any less. "If I didn't care, I wouldn't ask you to stop."

She rolled her eyes before reaching into Gina's purse and grabbing another clear bag from it. She held my wrist and pried open my palm to drop the bag into it. "Remember when you told me I looked good back in December? It wasn't because I was hiking. Sam's right. You lose weight *and* have energy. You could start dancing again without being critiqued by Instructor Satan."

I hated that she called Judith that. Even on the days she made me feel like trash, I respected her. She was good at what she did, even if she was harsh sometimes.

She bent my fingers around the drugs until I cradled it in my palm. "I just think it's time you took back your life now that you don't have people around to control it."

My nostrils flared. How could she talk about my dead parents that way? Hers were still alive and kicking —her father managing to get the best lawyer that obviously proved all the rumors false. Her mother was still part of the same social circles that looked down on everybody else, especially my family. Even with controlling parents, she did whatever she wanted without a second thought. She wasn't trapped, so I wasn't sure why she felt like she could tell me to escape my cage as if she had a clue what being in one was like in the first place.

"I don't know who you are anymore," I told her quietly.

She grinned. "I'm Katrina Murphy. But better. And if you listen to me like you used to, you could be the best Adele Saint James that New York City has ever seen."

"If she gets that stick out of her ass," Sam commented from behind Kat.

Gina just laughed and finished doing her line, her body swaying backward when she sat up. I saw the rolled money she was using and knew without a doubt it was a counterfeit bill. Like father like daughter.

I looked back at Kat. She said, "I'm just trying to help you out. Judge me all you want, but you won't get rid of that and you'll keep asking yourself why as each day passes until you cave. Want to know why? Because I know you, and you want an escape, but you've been too chicken to take one."

Silence was what greeted her.

And when I walked out with them throwing comments at me the entire way, I gripped the bag in my hands and heard her words on repeat. I told myself I'd flush it, dump it, throw it away when I got home.

But when I got there…

It remained hidden in my purse.

chapter seven

THEO

"DOES it sound like I give a fuck?" I demanded over the phone, grabbing a few folders to bring home with me.

"Now, Theo—"

"Don't." My warning shut Richard, or The Dick as I liked calling him, up quickly. "I've had enough of your bullshit. You've been hounding me for too long and my answer has not, and will never, change. Do you need me to draw you a picture? Hire a fucking sky writer?"

His huffed murmur wasn't understandable, irritating me more as I locked up my office. "I'm sorry, what was that?"

Silence.

I grinned knowing he wasn't the kind of man to speak up when asked. He liked to talk shit behind everybody's backs like his wife, like half the women in the goddamn city, acting like he had more courage than he did. "I don't know if you remember, Richard, but I've been doing just fine without you and your check-book and I'll continue to do so. Whatever shit you got yourself into can stay far away from me. Understood?"

His breath caught, leading to a husky laugh. "I seem to recall an investigation following the arrest of one Anthony Saint James. He was your partner at one point, correct?"

My jaw ticked as I stopped at the elevator, waiting for the doors to open. "If you followed the news so closely, you'll know that my business had nothing to do with what he was involved in. He gave up his partner-ship long before that point, so the feds had no damn reason to crucify me."

"Which is why I'm offering my services."

His "services" were shit to me. If there was one person I knew not to trust, it was Richard Pratt. He only did things for his own benefit, and I didn't want to know why he wanted to partner and invest with me. The whole thing was shady.

"Pass." When the door finally opened, I walked in and debated hanging up. But he'd call. Again. For the third time this week. I wasn't sure why the sudden need to get involved with Interactive Marketing, but there had to be one. He'd hounded me in the past about it, but never like he did now. "If you know me at all, you'd know that I would have given you an answer by now if I was interested."

My reputation didn't say a lot of great things about me on a lot of fronts, especially being associated with Anthony. Despite not participating in his extra curriculars, people thought what they thought. To them, I was the cruel businessman who refused to help his lifelong friend when he needed it most. Did I have moments when that guilt plagued me? Yes. I spent too many sleepless nights considering what I could have done differently. I could have lied for him. Had his back. But I'd had his back, his entire family's back, for too long. I wasn't going to lose everything because of his choices. I wouldn't go down with him over things I didn't know. And I'd like to think he wouldn't want me to. Not after he talked to me about Adele.

"Somebody needs to be there for her, Theo. I'm glad it's you." But I doubted he knew the kind of ways I wanted to be there for her when she turned eighteen. It wasn't like a switch flipped when I realized she was officially legal. There were consequences no matter how old she got, even without the obstacles that would normally be in people's ways when it came to the fragile situation. It was the way she carried herself when she realized what power she held. Her movements became confident, her eyes lingering bravely, and her words —

Fuck.

The sass in her replies were why I became infatuated with the woman she became. And did I hate myself for it? Yes. Did that make me stop thinking about her in every way I shouldn't have? No. It made it worse. Like the forbidden fruit I wanted to pick and keep for myself.

"Perhaps," he agreed casually. "But I have a feeling you'll change your mind. You can only handle so much. You're only one person with limited power."

"Are you trying to tell me something?" It was a nicer way of asking if he was threatening me. Even I had my limits on how to go about conversations with assholes like The Dick. He got his way by waving his money around and talking smack. He was the kind of guy who could charm anybody if he wanted to, so people listened. That left me at a disadvantage if he decided to go that route, which I had a feeling he would.

"I'm just making a point, Theo. Nothing to get upset about. We'll talk another day. Maybe over lunch. My treat."

His treat, my ass. People refused to let him pay wherever he went. I'd heard the rumors. He had enough dirt on people to get his way. It was how he played dirty. The more scandal he could collect, the likelier he won at whatever endeavor he went after. I just needed to know what his intentions were with me because it certainly wasn't innocent.

"You still look after the Saint James girl, don't you?"

My phone cracked when I tightened my grip around it. "Watch yourself, Pratt."

The fucker chuckled. "Relax. I happen to know

she's still friends with my youngest. Samantha. Remember? They'd play together all the time when they were younger thanks to the wives."

The wives. I remembered everybody Della was around, and I never did like that little girl with half the fucker's DNA. Samantha Pratt always got into trouble. She was just like her mother and wanted to be the center of attention. I didn't doubt she picked up a few traits from her father too. Whichever they were, I highly doubted they were good.

"I recall," I said dryly.

"Considering their friendship, we'll be in each other's lives one way or another. I have it on very good authority they've rekindled their friendship quite recently. I'm just saying, we might as well make the most of it." His *or else* lingered in the dead air between us. I wasn't stupid enough to believe he brought up Adele out of genuine curiosity. Hell, last I heard he didn't even like the family he was stuck with because his daughter could cost him his reputation and his wife was no better with the amount of money she spent and men she tried roping in.

My lack of response fueled his amusement, but it was better than me feeding him anything else. He wanted a reaction and I wouldn't give him one.

"You have a good night, Theo."

If I ground my teeth any harder, I'd need to get them fixed. "You too." *Jackass.* "Tell your wife I said hello. I'm sure she'd be happy to know I'm thinking about her."

The disgruntled noise he made was satisfying right before I hung up. I didn't know his wife well, but that didn't mean she didn't know me. She tried to get me in her good graces years ago for her own benefit. What that was, I didn't care enough to think about, but from what I heard, it involved a lot less clothing.

When I arrived on the ground floor, I said my usual goodbyes to the employees who worked the front desk and doors with the tip of my head and decided tonight was a good night to bust out the good whiskey while I finished up some work at home. A nagging feeling told me to be cautious because whatever Richard referred to was going to involve more than just me if he didn't get his way.

Like it did too often, my mind drifted to Della.

A FEW DAYS into the new week, I decided to stop holing myself up between my offices. It wasn't a surprise that I found myself at the high-rise apartment complex that a certain blonde was living in, five floors up. It'd been a while since I checked in and I never liked texting her if I could see her instead. She couldn't bullshit me face to face like she could on a screen.

I wasn't expecting the muffled sound of something sounding oddly like a dog on the other side of the door when I knocked. I paused when I heard it, whatever the hell it was, and convinced myself it had to be the TV. Some sort of documentary.

But then I heard, "Shh! You're going to get me in

trouble." That was undoubtedly Della's voice, which wasn't as quiet as I bet she'd hoped. It made a grin tug at the corners of my lips, but as soon as a door closed inside, I wiped it away in time for the front one to open.

Della peeked her head through the slit and straightened as soon as she saw me. I was about to reprimand her on not checking the peephole first when I realized how pointless it'd be considering it was the same conversation every time I showed up. Which, admittingly, was too many times as it was.

I shouldered my way in, listening to her close the door behind me before she walked over to where I stood and crossed her arms over the ridiculous overall shorts she wore. They were spattered in paint, blues, reds, and yellows coating the front of her, and I couldn't help but chuckle. The outfit was the same one her mother used to like dressing her up in and I always wondered if she was paying homage to the woman that I knew she loved so much.

My eyes found a large bag of dry dog food resting against the kitchen counter before an eyebrow quirked at a yapping noise coming from behind the door of her bedroom.

She winced at the deadpanned expression I gave her. "Before you say anything —"

"You know animals aren't allowed in the building, Della," I told her anyway.

Her frown was instant as she toed the floor with her bare foot. "They technically allow fish and small cats. I figured I could convince them that a small dog was no different."

The yapping got louder.

Walking over to her bedroom, I opened the door and watched a tiny blur of brown dart out. I turned and watched whatever it was spin around in the open area between the kitchen and living room, chasing its tail. "What the hell is that thing?"

"He's a mutt. Be nice!"

"They're not going to care what size it is, there's a reason dogs aren't allowed." I pointed to where the fluffball growled at the bag of food like it was offending him somehow. "They're loud, for one. I have no doubt the pretentious assholes who live on your floor will complain. Then there's the fact you live on the fifth floor. They need to be trained, taken out, and what if it has an accident?"

"I'll clean it up." I hated the way her voice sounded so small, but I was only trying to make a point. She bent down and scooped up the dog, letting it lick her jaw. "He's kind of cute, don't you think? There's no collar and he's way too skinny to have a home. I found him going through some garbage outside the building."

I cursed. "You picked up a dog from the side of the road?"

"It's not like I picked up a human off the streets, Theo." I had no doubt she'd do that too if she felt the person needed help. "How could you even question this cute little face? He's got nowhere else to go."

Her theatrics didn't work on me. "I'm trying to get

you to see the facts before you get too attached. You can't help everybody that needs your generosity. There are shelters for strays around the city."

To nobody's surprise, she held the dog closer to her body in protection, like I'd snatch him up and run. "Some of the shelters euthanize innocent animals for no good reason other than limited space. At least if I keep him, I know he'll be safe."

I blinked. "You didn't name it, did you?"

She gave me a timid smile.

"Della," I chastised, pinching the bridge of my nose as the dog barked again.

"His name is Ramsay. Like Gordon Ramsay because his hair reminds of the chef's."

I blinked again. Twice. Slowly.

Her teeth bit into her bottom lip. "I'm going to train him, so he doesn't make noise, and most of the apartment is hardwood or tile flooring so it wouldn't be a huge hassle to clean up."

"And smuggling him in and out to go to the bathroom?" I questioned, eyeing her skeptically.

Her face contorted to one of deep thought, but I could tell she was coming up blank based on the pleading look in her eyes. "I'll figure it out, Theo. Promise."

I'd heard those words before. It'd been a long time, but a much younger version of Della had delivered them when she tried convincing me that she could raise a cat without anybody noticing. Her mother was allergic though, and even if she weren't, she probably would have had a heart attack over the fur that'd be everywhere. She was OCD and needed everything to be clean and precise.

"I'll figure it out, Theo. I promise. Mom won't even know there's a cat in here. It'll live in my room and I'll feed it and bathe it and play with it and everything will be okay."

The thought made me smile, just a tiny one that I doubted Della could even see. It eased the tightness in my chest that'd lasted the work week so far in the slightest way. Della always did that, even if she didn't realize it. "I don't see how this is going to work in your favor."

"But…?" she hedged, eyes widening.

I blew out a breath and shook my head. "I don't have anything else to say. You're old enough to make your own decisions, I'm just here to tell you that they're not the smartest."

Her shoulders dropped. "Gee, thanks."

I simply shrugged. "Speaking of bad decisions, you need to be careful around Samantha Pratt."

"What?" I didn't miss the way her face paled at the name.

"Samantha Pratt," I repeated.

"I heard the name just fine the first time, but I don't understand—"

"She comes from a family you don't want to get twisted up in. I know you two used to play when you were younger, but it's better if you steered clear now."

Della frowned. "It's not like Sam and I are friends,

Theo. I saw her once last week, and that was the first time in years."

Good. "Better to keep it that way."

Her frown deepened. "You know, people say that about me too. They think it's best to stay away from the Saint James' because we're all bad people thanks to Dad."

"Della—"

"I'm just saying. I have no intention of hanging out with Sam, or the others, like we used to when we were younger. I'm not stupid. Things have changed with all of us. We've grown up. I just don't like thinking that families are all alike because they share the same blood. That's all."

My sigh was heavy. "You're right."

She set the dog, Ramsay, down and it began circling around her. "What if he lived with you?"

"Excuse me?"

She beamed. "It's perfect!"

"No."

My answer didn't deter her. "Come on, Theo. Ramsay is some sort of Pomeranian mix. It isn't like he'll get much bigger which means he won't take up much space in that big old house of yours. *And* it'd be good for you."

"How do you reason that?"

"You're by yourself. A dog would be perfect company. Plus, I'll come by and take care of him. I'll buy him food, a bed, toys, everything he'll need. You'll just maybe need to take him outside occasionally."

"Della—"

She latched onto my arm, her eyes widening into those goddamn puppy dog ones she used to shoot me with when she was little. It got me then and it still did now.

Son of a bitch.

The dog was ugly. Whatever it was mixed with didn't do it any favors, and Della was right. It was too skinny. The ribs were evident through the patches of fur missing, but it seemed to be in good spirits despite its poor nutrition. But did I want a dog? No. Once upon a time I'd considered it, but a bigger one. One that could hold down the house when I was away, so people knew not to fuck with me. Whatever ran around our feet was no more than the size of a rodent. I'd seen bigger cats.

I cursed again when I met Della's eyes. I knew better than to believe she'd relent. The idea was set in her head, so the chances of the dog showing up at my house when I was at work was more than likely.

Sighing, I stared down at the dog. "Is it house-broken at all?"

"Well..." Before she could answer, the fucker started peeing right there in front of us.

"Ramsay!" Della chided, frantically looking around. She ran into the kitchen and grabbed paper towels from the counter and frowned when Ramsay ran into her room.

She looked at me. "So, he needs some work, but I

can handle it. I'll get him a crate while he's being trained. It'll all work out."

I didn't believe it, but I played along while she told me all about how much she wanted a pet. As if I didn't know. As if I hadn't almost caved hundreds of times and surprised her with a damn kitten, bunny, puppy, anything she wanted.

But I didn't.

And now?

Fuck me.

I had a damn dog for a roommate.

"Do you want anything to eat?" It was the third time Della had asked within a two-hour period and I hadn't meant to snap at her, but I'd had a bad day and didn't want to be bothered. I'd told her to leave me alone and get her fucking dog away from me because it'd been driving me nuts all day demanding attention.

Truthfully, he hadn't been that bad. He'd had an accident in the morning, and I'd caught him gnawing on one of the kitchen chairs. Did I care? Hardly. I cleaned up his mess, scolded him, and gave him a toy to chew on instead. But the day had been trying with clients that continuously pissed me off and another email had dropped about a different partnership with somebody even less enthusing than Richard Pratt.

I could have apologized to her sooner, but I knew it would be better to put space between us. She cooked something for herself based on the smell of spice wafting into my office, and I was sure she'd gone to walk the dog when the door opened and closed sometime later. Now? The quiet hum of the television greeted me as I walked into the den to see her cross-legged on the couch with a sketchpad on her lap, the dog by her side, and a show about aliens on the TV screen.

Immediately, she looked up at me. "I'm sorry if Ramsay shouldn't be on the furniture, but he seemed a little off and he calmed right down when he settled there."

Of course, he would. Anybody would if they got to be next to her for even a second. I didn't relay that information to her though. "It doesn't matter to me." If I'd still had the leather couch that Mariska bought, maybe I would have given a shit given how hyper the dog was. Then again, would I have really cared if he ripped the cushions? No. Not if it meant pissing my ex-wife off in some way. Not that it mattered, considering she'd taken the furniture set that she was adamant about picking out when we moved in, along with a few other pieces—art, mostly. It was the only way she and Della had gotten along. They both enjoyed going to exhibits in the city, especially new ones that were limited time, so they could talk about whatever the hell method was used or where they felt something would go in the house.

"You're angry," she murmured, moving the pad off her lap. Today she donned basic jeans and a gray shirt that's collar showed a little too much cleavage from the deep V.

"I'm not."

"You're glowering." Was I?

"Thinking about Mariska." It was all it took for understanding to cross her face. She reached over and ran a hand down the dog's back. Ramsay stretched out beside her in satisfaction.

"Did she call you?"

"What?"

Her brows went up. "Did you hear from Mariska? I mean, it'd make sense if that's why you're in a bad mood. If I were in your shoes, I probably would be too."

Rounding the couch, I sighed as I dropped onto a cushion opposite of her. The dog was in the middle, acting as a barrier to leave plenty of space between us. "I hope you never have to be in my shoes someday to understand."

"How so?"

The chuckle escaped me quietly. "Being divorced and bitter doesn't exactly make people want to be around you."

"Do you *want* people to be around you?"

I turned my head to look at her, her eyes trained on me like she was trying to figure out my answer before I said it. "Most days? No."

Her lips twitched.

"But even assholes like me enjoy having company

from time to time," I added, voice even. I didn't tell her what company I wanted, but she seemed to draw her own conclusions with a muffled noise climbing from her throat.

"Is that your way of apologizing?"

I lifted a shoulder.

"I didn't mean to upset you," she said next, making me sigh again. Before I could tell her she didn't, she added, "Are you lonely? Is that why you want company?"

The way her words rushed past her lips made me think she hadn't really wanted to ask but needed an answer. It was endearing in a possessive kind of way and I shouldn't have liked her needing to know but did. "What's it to you, Della? I'm a grown man. I need specific company I doubt you'd get."

She scoffed this time, her legs uncrossing as she shifted her body towards me. Ramsay was startled and jumped off the couch, curling up on the floor under the aged wood coffee table. "You said the other day that I was a grown woman, so how would I not know what kind of company adults like to keep?"

Eye twitching, I ground out, "You better not know."

Amusement flickering across her face made me realize my mistake instantly. She'd gotten to me and she knew it. There were days I bet she even planned as much, just like when she was little and demanded my attention, and my attention alone.

I swiped a palm across my stubbled jaw, knowing I needed to shave again soon. I'd been too busy to care, staying home more than not until the running rodent was better trained and could be trusted alone while I was out. "You are an adult. Doesn't mean I have to like it or what the implications are."

Her laugh was soft, cut short as she scooted over to me. My body tensed as she put a palm on my knee, not moving or gripping or kneading which would have driven my cock to harden even more than it already was. Della was innocent in the way she touched me right now, but when I met her eyes…

"Don't look at me like that."

"Like what?" She batted her lashes.

I moved her hand away. "Sometimes I think there's evil under that good girl smile of yours."

Her eyes dulled as she pulled back. "Why do people keep calling me that? Just because I follow the rules doesn't mean I'm some goody-two-shoes."

"Whoa." I studied her. "What was that about? Who's been calling you that?"

She grumbled out something I couldn't understand before scooting back to her side.

"Della."

"Theo."

I dropped my head on the back of couch and closed my eyes for a second. "We both know that whatever was happening couldn't. That's all. I'm sorry if I offended you."

"You didn't," she snapped.

I eyed her knowingly.

"I'm just sick of people telling me what I am all the time." Her admission made me tense, because I knew it meant she'd been going through shit that she hadn't said a word about. When had she stopped coming to me about things that upset her? "You know how I mentioned I'd seen Sam for the first time in years? Well, it was when I went to see Katrina. Sam and Gina were there making comments. It just…I'm not that innocent and they act like who I am is some boring, too good saint."

I hated they made her feel like being good, being pure in her truest form, was a bad thing. "Those girls have always been bad for you. It shouldn't matter what they think. We've been over this."

"And we'll keep going over it. You'll tell me that, my therapist will tell me that, Lawrence will tell me—" She took a deep breath and shook her head. "It doesn't matter how many times I hear it, Theo. My brain is wired to care, just like it's wired to follow the rules like I was always taught. How hypocritical is that? It wasn't like my father could do the same. Who knows what Mom knew about? Probably everything."

Brows drawing up over the sudden change in conversation, I'd watched her unload years of pent up frustration that she'd never once talked about. It didn't matter how many times I asked her if she was okay, if she wanted to talk about her parents, she refused. I only hoped she was at least talking to her therapist about it, but I never asked because the sessions were between them. "You're not your parents, but that doesn't mean you can't look up to them and their values."

She snorted.

I corrected myself. "The values they taught you, that is. We both know they weren't bad people. Your father just got in too deep with the wrong people, but he wanted to make it right. That counts for something, doesn't it?"

Nothing.

"They loved you."

Silence.

I did what I told myself not to. I grabbed her arm gently and slid her body over to me, ignoring the surprised gasp when I positioned her on her side so her head was on my thigh using it as a pillow. Brushing loose strands of hair out of her face, I looked down at the rest that billowed over my lap and couch. "I don't expect you to forgive him, and neither does the world."

It was a moment before she said, "I'm angry, Theo. So angry. I feel like I don't have a right to because…"

Because they were her parents.

I kept combing my fingers through her hair until her body eased. She always loved this when her mother did it.

Telling her she had every right to be angry wouldn't have made a difference. She'd feel bad about feeling any negative way no matter what I, or anybody else, told her. She'd bottle it up until she burst—until she broke down and shattered for the world to see. And the cruel world we lived in was waiting for it to happen. I knew it, she knew it, and that was why she tried to fight it. But fighting didn't do a lick of good when she didn't find a reason to.

So, my hands faltered behind her ear where I brushed more strands. "Do it for me, Della. If nobody else, remember that I was always here rooting for you. All I want is for you to fight. Can you do that?"

The quiet I was given in return sliced through me thick and deep and I wasn't sure I'd get a response as the minutes passed. It was the deep sigh, the relenting exhale, that gave me hope that she'd do as I asked. It wasn't because she felt she owed me for the years I'd helped raise her, dedicated to her when she needed me most. It was the unspeakable understanding we had. The one we'd always had that eased her parents knowing I was there for her.

I just needed her to be there for herself, never letting the world beat her down like it so often wanted.

"Sometimes I wish that night between us never happened, because it wouldn't hurt so bad knowing that there are limits to this," she whispered, catching me off guard. My hand stopped moving over her scalp completely, stilling as she added, "But maybe it's better that way. How it ended. We ended."

How it ended.

She didn't know the truth about that night though. I'd been too drunk, barely remembering half of what I'd done. Waking up in bed next to her and being pissed off over the prior night's transgressions hadn't been the reason I'd stormed out after telling her it was a mistake.

It was knowing that, if something happened between us, I wanted to absorb every single moment. How she panted. If she yelled. The way her nails dug

138

into my flesh as she begged for more. I wanted to know every freckle on her body, memorize her taste, and ink the sounds she made when she said my name into my skin.

I wanted it all

But I didn't want it like that, with me fucking drunk and only remembering bits and pieces. Neither of us deserved that, especially not her.

"That's where you're wrong, Della." The words were heavy between us when I paused, her body tensing where it laid beside me. "It didn't end. That's the fucking problem."

"I don't see the problem in that at all."

I chuckled. "I'm sure you wouldn't."

A long moment passed between us before, "Theo?"

I hummed out a reply.

When she didn't say anything, I looked down to see her eyes had closed. The soft snores came shortly after, and I wondered what she was planning to say.

Maybe it was better not to know.

chapter eight

DELLA

DEEP BREATH IN. Deep breath out. Bending as I stretched into downward dog, I listened to the instructor call out another vinyasa that would normally be easy for me if I'd kept up on my regular routines. I'd slacked off on just about everything having to do with exercise because I hated how people looked at me, waiting for me to relapse as if running a mile or two would suddenly lead to me sticking a finger down my throat as soon as I got home.

Forcing the thought away, I wobbled into the next position and watched the bare feet of the older woman who taught the class come closer, stopping just in front of my purple mat. "Mind if I help a little?"

I heard snickering coming from a few familiar people surrounding me as I nodded, feeling her gentle hands get me in the proper form so I didn't hurt myself. Once upon a time I'd been complimented in every class for my fluid movements and flexibility. I still had some of both, but it was harder after years. People commented on the way I walked with grace like any dancer did no matter how long it'd been since they last practiced, but my abdominal muscles weren't as strong, and neither were my arms. I'd lost obvious definition that used to help me which was why I'd convinced myself that yoga was a safe bet if no other workouts appealed to me.

The problem was, I knew people were right to worry about what exercises I did. It was more than just Ripley asking me what I did to stay physically active or asking if I counted calories again. Other people were waiting for me to fail, watching me carefully, too carefully, and they had no reason to. It pissed me off. A lot.

After another twenty minutes, we ended with the typical namaste before rolling our mats up and preparing to leave. The center I went to for these classes shared rooms with other instructors, so we could never stay longer than a few minutes before the next course started.

"Bye, Adele," one of my other classmates said, giving me a wave before walking out with her mat tucked under her arm. Her name was Brielle and if I had to guess I'd say she was mid-thirties. Quiet, but sweet. She greeted everybody even if they never offered her so much as a wave in return, but I always smiled and spoke to her if I had the time. She was one of the few people who didn't pester me about personal things when everybody else liked talking behind my back.

Speaking of. "I was wondering if you'd come back," Tiffany Anderson commented, stopping beside me. Her silvery blonde hair took a lot of money to keep up because she always hated the dark brown it was naturally. She kept it in a tight bun during yoga, just like she did during dance. "The girls and I were talking about reaching out to you to see if you wanted to join us again."

I doubted that, but I smiled anyway. "It was time to try rejoining. I need some work, obviously."

Her smile wasn't as tight as I would have expected. "You'll get there, especially if you expect to compete again. I noticed that your arms barely held you up and your legs shook when we did the balance series."

My eye twitched despite trying to hold it back. I wasn't sure why everybody thought I was coming back. Aunt Sophie had to be the reason speculation stirred. It didn't matter how hard I tried squashing it, rumors spread like wildfire, especially when it came to dance. Spots were always limited, and it was only the best of the best who were offered a chance to prove themselves worthy of the title.

"I don't plan on competing again, Tiffany. Whatever people are saying is just because my aunt is trying to get me to change my mind, but I won't."

Tiffany, who'd always been one of my biggest

competitors next to Lauren, looked disappointed. Normally people were happy to know they didn't have to worry about peers taking their spot. Not her based on the pinch of her lips. "You don't have to compete. It's just... Can I be honest with you? I don't understand why you're set on quitting. I mean, I get things were... hard for you. I'm not that much of a bitch to brush off what you've gone through the past couple of years. You're talented though and it would suck to win at something because there isn't enough worthy competition. We both know Lauren thinks she's got every lead spot in the bag since you walked away, but everybody else knows that there are a lot of other people vying for the same roles. And that still isn't good enough. Not when people know there's a possibility you're coming back."

I stared at her blankly.

She sighed. "I get it, okay? You probably don't care because we're not friends. We barely got along when we danced together. But that doesn't mean I want to get handed things without proving that I worked my ass off for them. The only way I can feel that way is if you were back."

Again. I blinked.

"And because I hate Lauren," she added, grinning. There was no stopping the matching grin on my face, causing us both to laugh. She had a point and I wasn't going to ignore that. But I knew whatever her understanding of my condition was, it was not on the same level of mine.

People knew all about me. But they didn't really know me at all. Things got bad fast and it only got worse when the media began picking me apart like they had the right to. It stopped being about the talent everybody said I had and about how I'd gotten there, as if my father had paid off people to let me participate in recitals, awards, and gain the recognition I deserved. Nobody saw the way I worked every single day, multiple times a day, or how much sleep I lost trying to perfect one single move at a time. They couldn't see how little I put on my plate because I knew I couldn't afford to gain weight or else I'd hear about how bloated I was, or how full I'd gotten, or how I wasn't doing something right because I'd lost control.

So, no, she didn't understand what it was like even if she tried to. I didn't think she was pretending because Tiffany was a lot of things, but fake wasn't one of them. She said how it was, even if it hurt. She'd been blunt her whole life, some would say a fault of hers, but I admired it even if I was on the receiving end. And I was. Often.

While most of that had been to my face, I knew what she said behind my back to the small group of friends she had. Some dancers, most not. It was hard to keep friends who you competed against because no matter how strong you thought your friendship was, you were going to go head to head with them at some point. Some people, like Lauren, were sore losers. Others like Tiffany said a few harsh words and moved on. Trained harder. Ate better. Worked at it until there was no reason to be beaten.

I could picture us being friends if we didn't have dance between us. But even now, without me competing, I knew it wouldn't happen. I'd be the threat that always taunted her, the person she'd made comments about when she thought I wasn't listening.

Sighing, I managed a nod. "I get what you're saying, but I can't picture myself ever going back. Competing or not. Plus, I hear Lauren has gotten better. Maybe she's competition after all." I hated to think that some girls were so unworthy of not being deemed competition, but there were always people who were better or worse. That was life. Did I flaunt it? Comment on it? No. That wasn't my place.

Tiffany hefted a sigh before looking toward the door where more people exited. "For the record, I think you're making a huge mistake. But I'm not shocked to hear your choice. I knew Sophie was full of it when she told the ladies at the club."

I closed my eyes for a split second. Of course, she was still running her mouth about it like gossip could change my mind. "When did she do that?"

"A week ago? A week and a half?"

I wet my bottom lip and looked at her again, tipping my head. "Thanks for letting me know. And I'm...sorry if you're disappointed. I just can't do that to myself."

"Ladies," the instructor said from where she was putting her bag over her shoulder. "We need to clear out now. You can continue your conversation outside."

Tiffany and I walked side by side toward the door, her shoulder bumping into mine as we entered the hallway. "What if I helped you? You don't want to come back, fine. But that doesn't mean you should stop dancing. Not unless you never liked it, and let's be real, there's no way you would have stuck it out if you hated it. We all saw the way you moved, Adele. It was flawless. We were all sure nobody would ever be able to compare."

That was the thing nobody got. Being so high on the pedestal meant the fall would hurt that much more. "I didn't hate it," I confirmed, adjusting my mat perched in the crook of my armpit. "It was something I started because of my mom and what I found passion in for a long time. But that turned into critique and then into something darker. I don't know how you could help with something like that, Tiffany."

She stopped by the front doors leading into the sunny day outside. People milled about, walking around us, and talking about whatever. Classes. The weather. Exercise. But Tiffany and I stared at each other like it was a competition in itself. Except, I was trying to figure out her motive. Why would she help me at all? It didn't make sense. We weren't friends, like she'd pointed out, which was why it seemed strange she was willing to help me get over whatever I feared. Which was a lot.

"I've got a private studio I work out in," she told me casually. "It's not as nice as the one we used to practice at, but it works. Why don't you give me your number and I'll text you the address? You can choose to show up or not. No pressure."

"Why?"

She shrugged. "Why not?"

Unable to fathom an answer, I found myself typing my number into her phone. She didn't look cocky about it when she slipped it into the mesh pocket of her yoga pants.

"Think about it," was all she said before waving me off. I stayed standing where I was, watching her walk away in awe.

"Stop! You can't do that, Ramsay!" I tried running but got tripped up in the red leash he'd managed to wrap around my shins. I caught myself before faceplanting into the grass while he ran after some invisible animal. Flopping onto my back, I let the sun absorb into my already overheated skin and listened to the loud yaps that came from the corner of the yard.

"Why are you laying on the ground?" A shadow eclipsed over me, allowing me to open my eyes without wincing at the sunlight.

"Our dog tripped me."

One of his brows went up.

"My dog," I corrected. I knew better, though. Theo totally loved Ramsay, he was just pretending not to. I saw them cuddling on more than one occasion, and Theo always talked to him like he was another person. He *did* enjoy having a dog around, and it was mutual.

Ramsay completely ignored me when Theo was in the same room. I might have rescued him, but he wasn't mine anymore.

He reached out, wiggling his fingers for me to take his hand. I stared at it for a moment and debated staying where I was. When I'd woken up on his lap over a week ago, I hadn't known what to say. He was sleeping, his cheek against the back of the couch cushion, with an arm draped over my side. I knew if he woke up, he'd make a big deal out of it, say something, so I snuck out before he could with nothing more than a note that I'd be back to take care of Ramsay after classes.

He hadn't said a word about it, so I didn't either. We moved on with our lives like we'd been doing since the night I found out what it was like to kiss a man like Theo West. I never let myself linger there long because it hurt too much to come back to reality knowing that he'd walked away without one look back at me the morning after.

"Christ, Adele, that was a fucking mistake."

"Take my hand, Della," he commanded.

"I'm good."

He sighed and squatted beside me. "Is there a reason you're being more stubborn than usual today?"

"No."

The way he eyed me called me out on my bullshit without so much as a word.

I palmed my lids and exhaled softly. I'd gotten a few hours of sleep but was stressed about exams and a final project for Contemporary Art I still hadn't started. All those things were weeks away, but professors were keen on reminding us that they lingered.

"School," I admitted. *Life. Dancing. Art.*

He moved his pantlegs up before sitting down with his knees bent and arms resting on top of them. "What about it?"

I blinked at the expensive light-colored gray pants he adorned before meeting his gaze. "You're going to get grass stains."

"So are you."

Glancing down at the cheap tee and denim shorts I wore I shook my head. "My stuff doesn't cost as much as yours. Plus, most of my clothes are stained anyway."

He didn't say anything. Instead, he waited for me to indulge him on my problems. Why did I always do that? Theo should be sick of me by now considering how much of his life I've taken up with my burdens.

They're not all yours, a small voice reminded me. I flicked it away.

"I haven't been able to paint much, that's all. It's not a big deal, except I've got a big project due that happens to be a large chunk of my grade. I've stayed up late trying to come up with ideas, but nothing helps. I start something that I love, then lose all interest in it."

It didn't help that I'd been getting minimal sleep at night. There were times when that happened more often than not, and I'd cave and take a sleeping pill that Ripley prescribed me. Considering the bottle was nearly full, I didn't do it often. I had hoped if I got a full night's rest, I'd be inspired the next day. It didn't happen, though. Instead, I felt the nagging feeling in my gut telling me to do anything but paint. Run. Bike. Dance until I sweat through my clothes. Whenever my mind conjured ways to exhaust itself, I had to pull back and remember why that wasn't a good idea.

The soft hum that came from him had me turning to study his face. He looked off in the distance, his eyes seemingly following the running puppy. According to the vet I'd taken him to, Ramsay was only eight months old. Since I took him in, he'd gained a few much-needed pounds and had more energy than I knew what to do with. He was happy, though, so I was too.

"Did you talk to your professor about it?"

No, I hadn't. I knew what Professor Ambrose would say. It was the same thing she told everybody. *You're blocked.* But that didn't help figure out why. What was causing me to lose the one thing I got to control? The one thing I was able to do to take my mind off everything else? I didn't need to run, bike, dance, or exercise my thoughts away. I could do that with paint, and it was like my mind was setting me up to walk down the only other path I knew to take when I needed an escape.

"I'll take that as a no," he said.

"She would have told me to meditate or do yoga or something," I grumbled, sitting up. I brushed some grass shavings off my arm. "Which, I am. I joined yoga again and it has relaxed me. I just need to find inspiration."

150

"How can I help?"

His question shouldn't have thrown me, but it did. I stared at him in all his genuine six-foot-five glory and acted like he'd never offered me help before. It was a ridiculous reaction considering all the times he'd done just that, but he limited those moment now.

"Uh…I'm not sure."

Head cocking, he watched me carefully before his eyes went back to Ramsay. The dog was laying in the middle of the yard like he'd run himself right out of energy. Maybe he'd take a long nap so I could go home and try working on my project, which would equal hours of staring blankly at a canvas and screaming into a pillow afterward in defeat when the image that came into my head didn't transfer onto the canvas.

It was always the same one. A ballerina whose body was too little, too brittle, too…dead.

"Come on." He stood, offering me his hand again. That time, I took it. It was hesitant, but I was curious as to what he was doing.

I followed him inside, with Ramsay close behind us when Theo whistled for him and walked up the stairs to a room I hadn't been in, in a long time. It looked like storage now, but once it had housed his ex-wife's art collection from over the years.

"What are we doing in here?"

He ignored me and opened a closet, rifling through something before pulling out a covered canvas. Setting it against the wall, he carefully pulled the sheet off and stepped back. I stared at the colored lines and paint splattered piece with parted lips. My eyes went to the corner to see a signature. MM was etched into the bottom right, pinching my brows.

I hadn't gone to many exhibits with her, but usually I knew which pieces she had in her collection because she let me study them. She loved an artist from further upstate, River Tucker, who I became obsessed with as well. It was how we bonded because I knew that was important to Theo. He'd always said he wanted his *two favorite women to get along.* Maybe it was how he referenced me as a woman and not a little girl that made the tingles shoot down my arms or the flutters settle into my stomach, but it made me want to please him. It wasn't hard to do considering Mariska wasn't that bad of a person. Her personality wasn't the friendliest, but she didn't set out to be mean on purpose, least of all to me. Then again, she probably knew Theo would never allow it.

"Who is MM?"

"Mariska Maase," he answered calmly.

My brows went up.

"Her maiden name," he explained, fingering the edge of the painting. "She commissioned these under that even after our wedding. That alone should have been enough of a clue that it wouldn't last. Wishful thinking, I suppose."

I stared harder at the painting knowing she'd created it, in awe over the harsh brushstrokes, long lines, and darker colors. It was moody, like she was trying to set the tone. Was it about how she felt? There was no date like some artists put next to their initials, which meant I couldn't be sure if it was during the rough patch of their marriage. It wasn't exactly something I could ask Theo considering there had to be ill feelings toward the subject matter. From what I remembered, it wasn't a drama-packed separation. They both seemed to want it, but they still had years of history between them.

"It's beautiful." It wasn't a lie. Mariska had talent and I'd known it from the start. I rarely saw paintings she made, but she would sometimes share tips and tricks with me on my own if she were around when I worked on my pieces.

"It is." He stuffed his hands in his pockets and cocked his head. "She told me to keep it and I could never figure out why until I stared at it for a solid hour one night. It's us. Or, who we became. Dark. Distant. Angry. I was never good at reading paintings like you two could, but she wouldn't have given it to me if she didn't want to make a point. We became strangers in our own home, and she told me the only way she could."

I swallowed, sad for him but knowing words wouldn't help. We both stared at the painting, and I could see it. The lines were in dark blue and black, distanced but nearly touching. They could easily be silhouettes of people, a couple. The somber mood certainly called for what he analyzed, so I couldn't argue with his summary.

All I said was, "I'm sorry, Theo." But I wasn't sure

what I was sorry for. For Mariska leaving? For her giving him this? Both of those things? It was hard to tell. I cared for Theo, that much was sure. I didn't want to see him hurt, and even though he looked fine now, he had to have felt a certain way about it.

As expected, he gave me a terse shrug. "I didn't show you for pity. But I thought maybe it would spark something. She used her experience, her feelings, to make something that told a story. So, what's yours?"

I blinked. "My story?"

A nod.

"I…" I nibbled my lip. My story wasn't pretty, certainly not beautiful. Mariska had the kind of ability to turn something sad gorgeous. A lot of artists did. But what would mine turn out to be? A black canvas. White paint? That was what my world had become. Black and white. Nothing more or less—nothing technicolor and hopeful like I wanted. "I don't think I have one worth channeling. Not one I'd want people to critique any more than they already have."

My past was no secret. In fact, it was broadcasted for everybody to see. It took my father dying brutally in prison before the media decided to act like they felt bad about what had happened rather than insisting me and my family deserved the kind of pain that we'd all suffered since the scandal broke.

"Bullshit."

I drew back. "What?"

He crossed his arms over his chest, the button down he wore stretching over his broad muscles. "That's bullshit and you know it. You're scared of opening yourself up to what you've shut away, but maybe that's the problem. People can only take so much, Della, even you."

I said nothing. All I could do was stare, not sure if I was offended or just irritated that he was right. Maybe a little of both. I mean, he wasn't wrong. I knew there'd be a day in the not so distant future that I broke from keeping it together. I just figured I'd shut myself in my apartment to do it and ignore the rest of the world. What was wrong with that?

"Do you really think Mariska wanted to paint something like this?" The *yes* was at the tip of my tongue, but I held it back. He must have sensed that because he shook his head. "She was a lot of things, but she wouldn't have put herself out there like this unless she felt a reason to. And you know what? If I think hard enough, I can probably remember the day she finished this. Not long before she left, she looked lighter. Like a weight had been lifted. The truth, I suppose."

"The world already knows my truth."

"*You* are the only one who knows your truth," was his argument. His voice was hard, not willing to give me room to disagree. "You told me how angry you were, but it isn't for the same reasons people probably think. Paint that. Hell, Della. Paint whatever makes you feel something."

I looked at him for a long moment, knowing what was about to pass my lips was pushing the boundaries he'd drawn. "What if what makes me feel something involves you? Us?"

He didn't even pause. "Then paint us how you see us. Scarred. Broken. Beautiful. Make it real, because reality fucking hurts, Della."

"Is that…how *you* see us?"

That time, there was hesitation. "I see two people who have seen what the world can do to those less deserving of its wrath."

It became hard to swallow as I absorbed his words. Did he think we somehow deserved what was coming to us? What had happened? That wasn't normally how he spoke, not about anything I'd endured.

"I see." Forcing out the words through my tight lips, I brushed off the hurt and stepped away from him.

He cursed when he realized what he said, reaching out to cup my arm just above my elbow. I stared at the contact, waiting for him to draw back like he normally did. "I didn't mean it like that. How many times have I told you that you were never at fault for what's happened? It's me, Della, that the world would punish in a heartbeat. It's gone after people who didn't warrant that type of treatment, but me? It's only a matter of time before shit hits the fan and I'm not taking you down with me when it does."

"Why?"

He scoffed. "What do you mean 'why'?"

"Why would you assume the world is after you when you've been nothing but kind? You took care of a child that wasn't yours. You sacrificed your time to a person you didn't need to. Pretend you're some ruthless businessman, but that isn't who you are to me. If I don't deserve being treated like shit because of things I couldn't control, you shouldn't either."

"That's your viewpoint, little Della."

"Stop." Abandoning the naivety that told me to flee the room, I opted to crowd him where he stood by his ex's painting instead. "You no longer get to act like I'm too young. I can't handle the hot and cold from you. One second, I'm an adult and the next, when it's convenient for you, I'm little Della again. I know what you're doing, and it won't work."

His features hardened, not in offense but something else. Caution. Jaw ticking, he remained silent on his own accord which only fueled my agitation further.

"You can't have this both ways, Theo. I won't play a part in your life as anybody but me. Adele Maria Saint James. Twenty-two. The little girl you taught to slow dance, to ride a bike, the one you learned to braid hair for, she's gone. She grew up. *She* is standing right here waiting for the man she adores more than anything in this world to see her for what she is instead of what he pretends to view her as for his own protection. You want to be the big man on the block—the person the world should fear and punish? Then own up to it for once."

The low growl that rose from his throat should have told me to back down, especially when he closed the gap between us and towered over me. I kept my head held high just like he always told me to do. It was that moment when he knew he'd raised me to be his biggest downfall, I could see it in his wavering demeanor. His walls were crumbling. All. Because. Of me.

What did he expect? We'd been circling around this pent-up frustration for over a year. Longer, even before he stormed into my apartment and made the first move. I'd crushed on Theo West ever since I knew what that was, and whether he knew it or not, it'd been brewing to this inevitable outcome since.

"Fuck," he rumbled, before his hand gripped my jaw and tipped my head to meet his dark gaze. "Are you trying to ruin this?"

I took a deep breath. "Maybe I'm doing the exact opposite. Pretend all you want, but even if we are scarred and broken, that doesn't mean we aren't deserving of some good in our lives."

His fingers tightened but not enough to hurt. We stared at each other like that, his eyes piercing mine, refusing to blink. The first one who did would lose, and we were both too prideful for that. He wasn't the only one pretending to be somebody else, after all. I was selfish. I've wanted Theo West for most of my life in any way I could have him. I wanted all his attention, affection, and time. I got along with his wife for him, his "friends" who I learned were no more than associates as I'd gotten older, and anyone else I knew was important. All for me, so I could call him mine.

"I'm not the one who showed up drunk at your house," I reminded him breathily. Maybe I shouldn't have, but that would be backing down. We never talked about it because I'd been too afraid. But in moments like this, with his hands on me, I felt confident.

"Don't," he warned.

"I'm not the one," I said despite his protesting, "who made the first move. Who begged you to kiss me. To touch me. To lick me because I needed you to know what I tasted like. That was you, Theo. All of it. That doesn't mean I didn't want it or that I don't think about it. I do. A lot. Especially knowing that you made the choice to push me against that wall and—"

He cursed again before his mouth was on mine and my back was pushed against the wall similarly to how this unraveled the first time. I knew the painting was still there, pressing against the back of my calves, and I didn't care. What I cared about was barely recognizable because his lips and teeth and tongue were dominating my mouth until all thoughts were hazy at best.

Grip tightening on my jaw, I winced as he rolled his hips into mine to pin me there. He was hard, and heat instantly pooled between my legs when I tried getting the friction I needed to get myself off, but he refused to let me move. One of his hands trailed down my side and grabbed my hip, kneading the muscle as his tongue twisted with mine and his teeth nicked my bottom lip. He wasn't too rough, but he wasn't gentle either. It was a combination I wouldn't expect any differently from a man like him.

Just as I started lifting my leg to wrap it around him, he pulled back and slammed a fist into the wall. I flinched at the abrupt change as he backed away, his fingers going to his hair. What I didn't expect was the harsh glare that he gave me, like I was somehow to blame for him kissing me. *Again.* Had I egged him on? Yes. But he was a grown man who made his own decisions.

"Don't you dare say it," I warned, trying to hold back the sting of tears. My nose burned as I watched his jaw lock. He was in his head, thinking, overanalyzing, and all I wanted him to do was stop. *"Christ, Adele, that was a mistake."*

Those words *hurt* even still.

"Maybe you'll have some inspiration now," was what he said instead, walking to the door.

What. The. *Fuck.* "Is that what we're going to pretend that was? You helping me find some sort of emotion to use for my project?"

He paused by the door. "That was me giving you what you wanted, but stopping it before I couldn't take it back."

I wasn't going to pretend that wasn't a firm kick to the chest. So, instead of telling him as much, I stared at his tense back and walked toward the door. He blocked my way, so I brushed past him just barely touching his shoulder with mine and jerked away when he reached out.

Turning to look at him, I met his distant eyes and said, "For the record, *you* are the one who ruined this. Not me."

"Della—" He murmured. I heard the guilt in his tone, the regret. But I refused to figure out if it was genuine or not because it was hard to tell with him sometimes. He was more than just hot and cold. Moments ago, he'd burned me, and I welcomed it freely. But now? Now I felt the ice take over my veins because it was the only way to simmer the boiling blood that came with seeing his mask slip back into place. The one he wore when he realized he saw me as more than little Della.

"If you really want to help me, figure out what you want without destroying everybody else. Okay?"

I was proud for walking away. For not looking back. I wouldn't let him tell me it was a mistake or that he regretted anything. Once was enough. Twice? I knew I wouldn't handle it well. Not that the first time was anything I wanted to remember. I'd cried for a week remembering how he looked at me. That wouldn't be now.

And when a day passed and I heard nothing from him, I didn't think about it.

Or when another came and went.

I took care of Ramsay after smuggling him back into my apartment, went to classes, and hung out with Ren like I was fine. Was I? No. But just like Theodore West, I was great at pretending.

chapter nine

DELLA

THE STRONG ARMS came from nowhere and threw me over a broad shoulder before I knew what was happening. Yelping, I grabbed onto a white t-shirt, probably with some sports logo on it, and tried balancing myself while the strong scent of lemon drops suddenly hit me.

"Lawrence!"

His laugh was deep as he spun us around. I was glad I opted not to wear a dress today like I had planned considering the heatwave we'd been experiencing as spring hit. It wouldn't have stopped him from flashing my panties to everybody around us though.

"Ren," I complained, smacking my fists into his back. He only laughed louder and returned the favor.

On my ass. Rolling my eyes as he set me down, I ignored the catcalls from people walking past us on the quad, recognizing some of his frat buddies and teammates. "Was that necessary?"

"You ask that every time and the answer never changes," he mused, pecking my cheek.

He offered me his arm like nothing happened and I took it without second guessing it. "The Hut?"

"Sure."

We walked side by side, weaving past groups of people who were talking in the middle of the sidewalk. "You've been unusually quiet lately. Don't think I haven't noticed just because I've been busy with practice."

"And Ben," I teased.

He knocked my shoulder with his. "He might be another distraction, but Coach is being his usual self to get us ready for the big game. You're going right?"

I snorted unattractively. "Don't I always?"

"You've been staying in a lot."

The pause was there, other people's conversations filling in the temporary silence between us. I was about to come up with an excuse, one he'd probably see right through, when Tiffany appeared a few feet away as we neared the building housing our favorite hangout.

My feet stopped, jerking Ren to a halt too. He looked at me with pinched brows, seeing my gaze on the blonde who was looking back. To my surprise, she lifted a hand and waved.

"Who's that?" Ren asked quietly, interest high in his

tone. I didn't miss the way his eyes checked her out in the tight leggings and shirt she wore, showing off her athletic body.

"Someone I used to dance with."

His "ah" wasn't as quiet as he looked her over again. Her eyes darted between us, but she didn't walk over. I was glad there was no pressure to reach out to her. She was letting it be my choice just like she said, but that didn't mean I didn't feel a little guilty about it since she was being kind.

"Want to go say hi?" he asked next. We started walking slowly in that direction.

Tiffany looked over her shoulder like somebody was calling her, so she lifted a finger and glanced back our way. I nibbled my lip and debated on what to say. *Hi* was usually a good place to start, but I knew Tiffany long enough to figure out she'd want to talk about more than the weather and how classes were going.

She made the decision for me, backing toward the group of girls who must have been waiting for her. When her back turned, I realized my face must have given away anything I had to say. Which was little.

Ren murmured, "Or not."

"It's my fault. She was being nice to me last week and I didn't reach out to her."

"Why not?"

"She offered to help me with something."

"Dance?" he guessed.

I eyed him.

"You evade everything that involves it," he said,

164

chuckling over my expression. "I may not be the one with a perfect grade point average, but I'm not a total moron. It's like anyone says the five-letter word and your eyes glaze over. Kind of like mine do when I see someone hot. Not like how we both look in math class."

That made me roll my eyes. I used to be a straight A student, but I fell behind when I took a few weeks off after news of my father hit. I hadn't found the energy to study as much I used to. The look he was referring to wasn't the first time I'd been told I had it. Judith had said I reminded her of herself because there was a longing in my eyes for dance, but since I'd walked away from it that longing had shifted. It wasn't like I hated the profession. I respected people who trained hard and worked their asses off, and sometimes even envied them for doing it. "I'm still considering her offer. That's all. I'm not sure I even have the time."

He opened the doors to the Hut and hauled me in with a chortle. "That's the lamest excuse you've made yet, but I still love you. I can see you miss it. People should make time for the things they love."

I eyed him as he greeted a few of his friends who were already sitting off to the side. We'd probably wind up next to them where I had to listen to baseball stats, how much they hated their coach that day, and which parties they were going to next. I'd smile, nod, and laugh when I felt it was necessary while Ren stared at me knowingly. I never left though because, like he said, it was important to make time for things you loved. That included him.

He squeezed my hand which I didn't realize I'd slipped into his. "Your normal? Or are you feeling adventurous today?"

"Your version of adventurous scares me, especially food related." My nose scrunched over the thought of the food combinations he'd consumed. For years, it only took some silly dare before he'd eat something disgusting that churned my stomach.

"Boring," he teased, letting go of my hand to put in an order for us. I waited by the pickup counter while he flirted with the girl working the register. It made me shake my head because he'd been rejected by her twice already, but he didn't care. I was pretty sure the other girl working was her girlfriend, so it was all innocent enough. A typical day in the life of Ren.

I pulled out my phone to check a few emails while we waited only to find a text from Theo. Opening it, I couldn't help but smile over the picture of Ramsay sitting obediently and staring up at the camera. There were no words that accompanied it, which only made the smile grow.

Ren walked up beside me, looking down at the screen. "Why haven't I met your dog yet? Who gets to see him?" Without asking, he plucked the phone from me and studied the sender before groaning. "I thought we were mad at Theo."

"*We're* not mad at him. *I* am."

"Which means I am by default."

"You never liked him," I countered.

"Because I see how you look at each other. It just weirds me out a little considering the age difference."

Heat blasted over my face. "Not again. He isn't *that* much older than me."

He raised his hand. "Eighteen years. But hey. Whatever, Del. I've done weirder things with people older than me. I just want to make sure you're okay, and whatever went down with him upset you."

"I'm fine," I told him for the hundredth time. How many times did I have to tell him before he was convinced? I wasn't going to explain that I had the most intense kiss of my life thanks to my father's best friend and how I'd gone home that night and slipped a hand between my thighs to relieve the pressure he'd left, even though I was pissed at him for backing away. If it was like before, we'd be the same. Tiptoeing around each other until the frustration built again. It was a cycle I wanted nothing more than to break.

"Which definitely means you're not." His tone was casual as he called me out, but there was a hint of amusement tilting his lips upward. "I thought you said you weren't talking to him. By the way, you still haven't told me why."

I snatched my phone back and hip bumped him. "Stop pouting. I don't want to talk about why. And he's watching Ramsay because the owner of my building almost caught me when I was taking him out to go to the bathroom. Or he did. I'm not sure. I dropped Ramsay off at Theo's house yesterday morning after he went to work then texted him because I was afraid if I did get caught, Ramsay would get taken away while I was here."

He gaped at me. "Dude."

I winced. "I didn't want to actually *see* Theo. Don't judge. You just said you've done worse, so don't hate on me."

He parted his lips before realizing he couldn't argue. Shrugging, he nodded. "Fair. But I still want to know why you're angry at him. My imagination has gone wild, so it's better to just tell me."

He wasn't wrong, but that didn't mean he was getting anything from me. Whatever he was imagining was probably way dirtier than what had happened, but I wasn't caving. "You could meet Ramsay if you want. I never told you that you couldn't."

"Uh, at *his* house?"

I gave him a "duh" stare.

"Pass."

"Coward."

"I'm not denying it." He walked up when the cute raven-haired girl called out to him. I was sure he winked, and she blushed, which made me question my previous assumption over her dating status. Maybe she was like Ren. They'd be cute together. Then again, a lot of people would look good with my best friend. It was like he fit everywhere.

It made me wonder if I did. I couldn't picture myself with him when the opportunity struck, and I never saw myself with anybody else either. Lawrence had told me it was because I was infatuated with Theo for so long, I couldn't get my mind to let it go. I wasn't so sure it was that simple though. If I wanted to, I could at least try being around other people. Guys my age. Maybe some a few years older. It just didn't feel...right. Not because I was obligated or owed anything to Theo, but because he was the only person who truly understood me. Who made the flutters appear in my stomach with a single side-smirk. Theo was just...my person.

We walked over to Ren's friends as expected. I was glad to have the distraction because as soon as he sat down, his friends started in on him. The ragging lasted long enough for me to finish my drink and check my school email. One of them was from my art professor who wanted to meet with me before I left campus for the day. After replying with an agreed time, I hovered over Theo's name until Ren decided to pay attention to me.

"No."

"No, what?"

He grabbed my phone and turned the screen off before shoving it into his pocket. "If you're angry with him, you'll be angrier that you texted first. Remember all the times you tried stopping me from making stupid choices?"

I deadpanned. "It didn't stop you."

One of his friends snorted. "She's got you there. You cave in seconds when chicks are pissed at you." Men too, but I didn't say that aloud.

A girlfriend of one of his teammates leaned over and grinned at me. "Are you having boy troubles? The chase always worked for me, girl. I'm just saying. Play hard to get and he'll be eating out of the palm of your hand in no time."

The blush was unstoppable. "It isn't boy trouble. It's complicated."

Ren laughed, the fire in his eyes mischievous as ever. "More like daddy issues."

Everybody got quiet in a second. Ren stiffened beside me before his wide eyes found mine. The mischief extinguished when guilt flooded them.

Clearing my throat, I squirmed and looked down at the folded hands in my lap to avoid the pitied glances cast in my direction from the people surrounding us.

"Shit, Del. I'm so—"

"It's okay," I whispered, voice cracking. I knew he didn't mean it like that. Ren was being...Ren. Dirty-minded. And he wasn't wrong to make the joke. Maybe if it were a year or two later considering what happened to my actual father, people would have laughed.

"Can I have my phone back? I should get going to get some work done. Plus, I need to meet with Professor Ambrose."

He passed it to me but didn't let me just take it right away. "Are you really leaving? We can head out and maybe go to—"

I patted his leg with a soft smile. At least, what I hoped looked like one. "It's okay. Really. I still have that project due, and Ramsay needs to be taken care of." I was aware people were still watching, though some pretended not to be. Badly. "I'll text you later?"

He just frowned but nodded.

I pecked his cheek. "Love you."

His voice was full of sympathy. "Love you too. If you need anything, let me know." He knew I wouldn't, but he always made it a point to say so.

I waved at everybody else and walked out without looking back. Pulling out my phone, I typed out a text to Theo and hesitated to send it. When I realized it wasn't what I wanted, I sighed and turned it off, so I wasn't tempted. Ren was right, I would have been angry at myself to reach out even when part of me was still irritated.

It didn't take long to make it to the Friedman Art Center where Professor Ambrose's office was perched in the art department wing of the building. I always loved seeing her there because her shelves were full of her favorite self-made pieces—paintings, pottery, any kind of medium that she felt invested in at the time.

My knock on her door was light, but she immediately looked up with a big smile on her aged face like always. "Adele! Come in, come in, dear. I was happy you could see me on such short notice."

I entered and dropped into the seat across from her. "It's no problem. Is everything okay?"

She waved her hand. "Of course. I didn't mean to scare you by asking to come talk. It's about the figure drawing class you got accepted into this summer with Kolinsky. I was ecstatic when you finally let me know you were going to take the spot offered."

I'd only accepted the offer after talking to Theo

about it. I wasn't sure if I should have considering my doubt, but it was too good to pass up since it was the one type of drawing I knew would benefit my work most. "What about it?"

"There's something I want you to consider," she propositioned, the smile still spread across her lips. "I know it may seem like a ridiculous notion, but it's one I truly want you to think about without giving me an answer now. Okay? Can you do that?"

I blinked. "Uh..."

"I think it'll help you."

"What will?"

When she explained it, my eyes widened, and I was pretty sure my heart stopped too. She delivered the idea so casually that it seemed like we were having a chat about the weather. Not...*that*.

After she finished her spiel, all I could do was stare at her with parted lips. My fingers had curled together on my lap as I soaked in every word. I knew why she suggested it, why she told me it could help me. But...

"I don't know, Professor Ambrose."

"I know." She stood and walked around her desk, sitting in the chair directly next to mine and reaching for my hand. "I've noticed how hesitant you are lately. You never used to be so in your head, and I know there's a lot to think about. Why not do something about it? Take control."

Swallowing, I shook my head. I confided in her some time ago that I felt I'd lost control of my life, which was why I nosedived into rock bottom and done what I did. She'd known me since freshman year, seen my struggles, and was always willing to help. "I've been trying to get past the block, but—"

"Have you though, Adele? I know you, dear. You've always been dedicated no matter the situation. What you went through, what you're still going through, is a lot. It will always feel like somebody is holding you down because they want to see you fail. But it's up to you to push back and find your place in the world again however you can. I know a lot of students, and nobody else here at Bentley has the strength and perseverance to get through the magnitude of horrors like you can."

"I don't see how your suggestion helps do that," I admitted honestly.

She patted my arm. "If you agree, you'd be putting yourself out there for yourself. Not for anybody else in that room. It'd be about accepting that you're worthy of that kind of attention. You'd be fighting what your brain wants you to drown in. And you know what else? You'd be *living* the very art you create. Remember the piece you submitted to the Bentley Art Journal? It was of the girl posing in front of a mirror, but she was—"

"Faceless," I whispered. I'd called the piece "Curvy" and it was no more than a few outlines of a woman being judged by the crowd.

"All your pieces are faceless," she noted pointedly. "Perhaps it's time to put a face on your paintings, dear. Really put yourself in the art that so many people stop and stare at. Because it isn't the last name they see when something of yours is displayed. It's the meaning."

Inhaling slowly, I locked eyes on the floor and tried sorting out my thoughts. Even if I wanted to say no to her offer right then and there, she wouldn't accept the answer. She was right. I needed to think about it. As for my art... "I feel like faceless creations are what I'm known for. It wouldn't feel like me if suddenly I started painting people who were..."

"Complete?" she offered. "Have you considered the reason for that is because you're afraid of what the faces would look like?"

I swallowed.

"They're you. Each one. Aren't they?"

I said nothing. "May I suggest something else?" she asked, squeezing my arm.

I nodded.

"Do something crazy. Something spontaneous that you've always wanted to do but were too afraid of. I've found that facing those fears, no matter how big or small, helps when it comes to chipping away at what the conscious might not tell you the real problem is."

My lips parted to speak but closed when one image came to mind. One person. One thought that I'd had thousands of times. It sent sparks down my body, fire forming in the back of my neck, and my heartrate skyrocketing.

I thought about Theo.

"Sounds like you know what you're talking about from personal experience," I managed to say.

Her laugh was light. "And by the flush in your cheeks, it looks like you have a pretty decent idea of where to start. Take my advice, Adele, and truly consider what's being offered. I know it won't be easy, but I assure you it will be worth it without a doubt in my mind."

I knew she was right, but it didn't stop every internal response in me to argue against it. I'd been judged on far less things but putting myself out there like she was insisting would be the same as opening me up to free fire on a battlefield.

The only difference was that I'd welcome it, *choose* it, which meant I could anticipate everybody else's next moves. Maybe that was better, because it meant I'd be the one to move the pawns and take back the control I felt was stolen from me for so long.

"I'll think about it," I offered quietly.

When we bid goodbye, all I could think about were her words. But they weren't the only thing lingering in my head. And when I showed up at my apartment, I couldn't help but stare at the man, and dog, sitting on the couch waiting for me like fate was offering me a hand.

I'd made my decision.

chapter ten

THEO

HER UNBLINKING EYES traveled from me to the television where Animal Planet was showing something about dog breeds. Hell if I knew why she loved watching it, but there were seventeen episodes recorded, so I figured it had to be interesting enough.

"I prefer the serial killer documentaries you make me watch," I noted, grabbing the remote and turning it off.

My words snapped her out of whatever train of thought she was having. She set her belongings down on the counter and crossed her arms over her chest. "It's for Ramsay."

"The murder shows?"

"Animal Planet."

I blinked, noting the pink settling into her cheeks as she reached down and pet the dog in question. "It calms him down if the TV is left on for him, especially that channel."

"You leave your television on for your dog? Do you know how much that racks up the bill, Della?"

I knew immediately it was a stupid thing to say because her face drained of the surprise that I'd bestowed on her by being here, and anger took its place. "What is with people being assholes to me lately? I'm aware of what it costs, Theo. I pay the bills. *All* of them. Remember?"

Sighing, I tried backtracking because I knew the topic was sensitive to her. "I didn't mean to—"

"Of course, you didn't! You never mean to do anything that would upset me, right? Not that you'd ever admit. But, rest assured, I know what money I'm forking over every month because I work my ass off to make sure I can keep a roof over my head, the lights on, and my stomach fed without any help. But thanks for the reminder."

I waited until she was done because I knew trying to reason with her would be pointless otherwise. Though, the pinched expression on her face and the way the crease formed between her brows told me I was in the doghouse regardless. Metaphorically speaking.

"What are you doing here?" she asked, tone softer now that she took a moment to breathe.

"I'm proud of you."

177

Her lips parted.

Standing, I walked around the couch with my hands stuffed in my front pockets. "I know the past few years haven't been easy for you, but you've always held your head up high. You've made it through. Look at this place." I did just that, studying the bright colors, wide open space, and smiled at the modern style that screamed Della. A few walls were aged white brick, the windows were large and feeding the room with natural light, and everything she furnished inside matched her personality to a 'T'. "It's yours. Not your father's, not your mother's, or anyone else's. You made yourself a home and proved to everybody that you didn't need your family's money."

If she were raised any other way, she would have been screwed. When the scandal broke and her father went away, they seized all assets, including properties. She was allowed two bags worth of belongings out of everything she'd once called her own, the rest was taken away. That didn't stop her from pushing forward. Even though there was room at my house, she refused to accept any help. It took her an additional three months to save up the money she needed to secure this place through commissioned art, and a few odds and ends jobs around campus.

"So, I know that you know how much it costs. I didn't mean anything bad by it. In fact, it shouldn't surprise me that you'd leave the television on just so your dog doesn't get lonely."

"A lot of dogs have separation anxiety and need to

feel secure when their owners are gone," was her defense.

My head cocked. "And how do you know he has separation anxiety?"

Her bottom lip drew into her mouth as she looked at Ramsay. "He destroyed your armchair and favorite pair of shoes. Plus, he peed on everything even though he hadn't done that in a while since we trained him to go out. I read up on it and vets say that it's probably anxiety. Since I started leaving Animal Planet on, he hasn't done anything bad."

I did love the shoes that I found chewed up without an ounce of hope they could be fixed. I threw them out as soon as I saw them and simply told Della rather than showing her the mess he'd made. It was bad enough she wanted to buy me a new chair, but the shoes would have made her feel worse had she seen the state they were in. They were one of Tom Ford's most expensive designs.

"I'm here," I continued, "because I needed to make sure you were okay. Plus, I knew you were probably missing your demon dog."

"You're not mad I left him at your house?"

"I told you that you could." Hell, I liked the little bastard. He got on my nerves when he wanted attention, but I'd even found myself missing him when I realized she'd taken him back after leaving the other day.

"But we're fighting," she stated quietly.

That was where she was wrong. I stepped up to her, moving a piece of curled blonde hair behind her ear.

"This isn't fighting. We were both upset, and things got out of hand." She flinched, and I knew she was thinking worst case scenario. "Get out of that head of yours. I didn't mean because of what happened. I meant after."

"When you basically said it was a mistake again?"

"I didn't—"

"You can't keep kissing me and pretending like it was an accident. People don't just fall onto other people's mouths. That was what pissed me off the most and you didn't even seem to care that it did."

"Because I didn't chase after you?" The scoff came out of me before I could stop it, fueling the fire that didn't need any help growing.

"It's not about the chase!" she yelled, her fists clenching at her sides. She shook her head and walked away from me, peeling off her mesh sweater and draping it on the back of the kitchen chair she passed. Her white tank top was practically see-through thanks to the cheap material and the darker bra visible underneath.

"What was it about then?"

She gave me her back as she washed her hands in the sink before toweling them off and pouring herself a glass of water. "Listen, I want to work on my project tonight. Ramsay can stay here if you don't want to take him back with you. I'll figure it out."

"No."

She froze halfway to her bedroom before slowly turning on her heels. "What?"

"I let you walk away because I knew it wouldn't do

either of us good if I did chase after you. We were angry. Tensions were high. Things would have been said that couldn't be taken back. So, yes. I watched you walk out."

To that, she had no reply.

Walking over, I stopped just in front of her and watched the way her body leaned into me. It was a natural response that I lived for. Always had. When she was little, it made me feel like she knew I'd protect her. But now? Now it was different. That need to protect her was tenfold even though I'd learned a long time ago she could look out for herself.

"This time we're talking it out because we *are* both adults whether I like to admit it or not. And I don't, you're right. I hate that you're not little Della anymore because that means the world can get you and I can't do a fucking thing about it. That doesn't mean I'm not going to try like hell even if it pisses you off."

"By making me angry and calling me a child? How does that help anybody?"

It helps me. "Are you going to work on your project?"

"You're changing the topic?"

"Technically, it all ties in. Thought maybe you found some inspiration after the conversation we had before you stormed out."

"Our argument," she corrected.

All I did was shrug.

"You're impossible, you know that?"

I didn't deny it.

"I'm going to try getting the project started. Sometimes all it takes is throwing some color on the canvas for the mood to set." Tilting my head, I looked down at her and watched her stare back. "What?"

"Get changed."

She blinked.

"I know that isn't what you wear when you paint, so go change," I told her again. It wasn't a suggestion. I knew what she got messy in, and it wasn't her school clothes. The black jeans she wore now were destressed, showing a lot of skin through the tears, and I knew her father would have hated it. He'd made comments on the style before. She never wore things like that because of it. I was glad to see her do her own thing, even if I agreed too much was exposed.

It made me snort.

"What's so funny?"

I waved her off. "Change."

She mumbled, "bossy" under her breath as she walked into her room, closing the door behind her.

Ramsay ran over to the door and pawed at it, making me shake my head. The rodent loved her, that much was easy to tell. He was usually happy to see me when I got home, but the day she'd dropped him off I came home to find a puddle of piss he left in the kitchen since she decided not to share her TV tip with me in the note she left. Guess that was payback for me being a dick. Then again, I liked to think the dog was being loyal to her by making a mess, his way of telling me I was an asshole.

Guess what, rodent? I already know that.

When she was ready, paint-covered overall shorts covering her body and hair in a messy updo, she eyed me where I still stood in the kitchen. "Are you going to watch me paint?"

It wouldn't be the first time. "Did you eat yet? Figured I could make dinner while you worked."

"I'm not that hungry."

"Della."

Her shoulders tensed. "I mean it. I ate this afternoon, but I just don't have an appetite tonight. I've been stressed."

I knew I was partially to blame for that stress, so I felt obligated to help her. "Go work. I'll make sure the dog, and you, are fed. Don't think about fighting me."

The last part was directed at her parted lips that held a retort, but no words passed them. Whatever she mumbled was lost on me as we went our separate ways—her to the spare room where she painted and me to the cabinet where I grabbed the dog dish and food.

"Animal Planet," I murmured as I squatted down to give the dog its dinner. Running a hand down his furry back as he dove into the kibble, I chuckled. "You're one spoiled rodent, huh?"

"I can hear you!" Della called from across the hall. The door was cracked open and I knew sound traveled, so it didn't surprise me. I'd been caught giving Ramsay extra treats, letting him on any furniture he wanted, and Della made sure to point it out with those knowing eyes of hers, like she found it amusing I secretly spoiled him.

It wasn't something I necessarily hid. I just didn't advertise it.

The apartment fell to silence as I cooked us dinner. Ramsay had laid down outside the spare bedroom door after he was finished eating. I bumped it open with my hip carrying two plates of eggs and toast inside. When I saw Della sitting cross-legged on the floor in the middle of the room staring into space, I nudged her leg until she finally looked up at me.

Her fingers wrapped around the plate I offered and blinked down at the food. "Thanks."

"Eat up."

She eyed me and uncrossed her legs. "Are we eating in the living room? There's probably something on the television we could watch. I won't even subject you to murder mysteries. Remember that cooking show we watched before? I set up a bunch to record."

Sitting on the edge of the desk off to the side, I picked up a piece of toast. I might not have understood why she liked those shows, but I enjoyed watching them with her simply because it was time together. "You said you wanted to work. We can eat in here."

"So...you do want to watch?"

That was a loaded question. Instead of answering it, I bit into the toasted bread and looked at the canvas. There were tints of pinks and purple taking up the upper half of the canvas, looking like it was forming some sort of circle with rougher edges. That was what I liked about Della's work. They were always colorful, emotional, whatever they turned out to be. "I like watching you lose yourself in your work. It reminds me of better times."

Her eyes remained on her plate. "You mean with Mariska? I know she spent a lot of time in the studio."

I hadn't meant my ex-wife. Della had always been interested in art. When she was younger, she'd constantly draw pictures for everybody and expect them to be hung on the walls, refrigerator, or anywhere people could see. I still had a collection of her crayoned originals stored away in my office that she'd gifted me over the years, not that she knew.

"Of you," I simply stated. "Eat, Della."

"Stop telling me what to do."

Setting my plate on the cluttered desktop, I crossed my arms over my chest and ignored her feeble demand. "There was a picture framed in Mariska's studio that she'd always look at whenever she was stuck. Do you remember what it said?"

Her head bobbed. "It was a Pablo Picasso quote that said, 'Art is a lie that makes us realize the truth.' She said it was one of her favorites."

"She told me once that she'd wanted it close by to remind her why she started painting in the first place." Mariska was always passionate about her art and insisted that no creation was good enough unless there were pieces of truth in each one. "What's your truth, Della? What do you have to say that the world doesn't already know?"

The last time we'd had this conversation, I was sure she'd shut down. But the wheels were turning as she glanced up at me and stared. Unlike then, I had an idea of what she was thinking now, and I knew it'd be smart if I walked out.

But I didn't.

"Who's asking?" she asked quietly. "Is it the Theo West that used to push me on my bike with the training wheels off or the one who barged into my apartment and kissed me like a starved man?"

Throat bobbing, I tried ignoring the hardening cock pressing against the zipper of my pants. "The one who cares about you."

Her head tilted. "Wouldn't that be a combination of the two then?"

A shoulder lifted. "It's a combination of a lot of things. For an artist, you only seem to see in black and white. It's not that simple though."

"What are you saying exactly?"

What wasn't I saying? Abandoning my food, I squatted down beside her, so we were eye level. "I'm saying that I care for you in a number of ways, like I always have."

She swallows. "Oh."

Chuckling, I said, "Yeah. Oh."

She wet her bottom lip. "My professor talked to me before I came home. It made me think about...a lot of things. Art. What inspires me." Her pause was hearty as she stared into oblivion for a moment. "Did you kiss me to make me feel something for my art? Or was that really because you wanted to?"

Closing my eyes, I shook my head and stiffened

when I felt a palm flatten against my cheek. When I dared to look, Della was already pinning me with pleading eyes that I couldn't ignore. "We both know the answer to that."

"But I want to hear you say it, Theo."

I said nothing.

"Please." Her voice cracked.

Keeping her hand pressed against my cheek with my own, I blew out a breath and settled into her warmth. "The night I showed up here drunk, I'd gotten into it with somebody your father was working closely with. The asshole...well, it doesn't matter. I lost my temper. Drank to forget my anger and wound up at the one place I knew I needed to be that would make it better." Her sharp inhale of breath had me locking eyes with hers. "The things that I want to do with you, *to you*, go beyond kissing, Adele. But that doesn't make it right."

"Right?" The dry laugh that escaped her made me draw back slightly. "What about either of our lives have been right lately? And who's to say what you're talking about isn't?"

I blinked. Then blinked again. "There are a lot of factors that society would pit against us in this situation."

"You keep telling me to ignore what they say, so why are you so enthralled by what judgement would come from them?"

"I raised you —"

"Because you care."

187

"Which people," I cut her off, "might think differently about. Imagine if the roles were reversed."

"Then I'd be some cougar. Big deal."

"Exactly. People would probably say shit but not to the extent of an older man going after a much younger woman, especially one he helped take care of. That's…"

"Bullshit."

I gaped.

"What? You're not the only one who's allowed to call me out. I'm not saying that whatever this is isn't complicated, but don't you think it's worth exploring? No matter how hard it is? We've always had each other's backs. You told me that. Who cares if you're older than me? It isn't by all that much. What they say, according to you, shouldn't matter."

"And I meant it."

"So?"

Our stare intensified. Suddenly my eyes dipped to her lips and I thought about the strawberry scent that wafted from them because of her Chapstick addiction. It matched the shampoo she loved using that she insisted she always wanted as a present when I asked what she'd like for her birthday or Christmas.

"What if I just want you?" Two years ago, that question had sparked whatever was still going on between us, feeding my head with every bad idea that said I needed to do something about it. Instead, Della got shampoo, body wash, and Chapstick. All strawberry. And the thing was, she smiled like I'd given her gold jewelry.

Putting her plate on the ground, she rose on her knees and put her palms on my shoulders. The familiar scent wrapped around us, mixed with the paint fumes and food that was clearly going to be wasted if this continued.

"What are you doing?" I all but whispered as she ran one of her hands up my neck and over my jaw until her thumb brushed my bottom lip.

"Being spontaneous and making the first move for once," was all I got before she tenderly pressed her lips to mine, one of her arms looping around the back of my neck as she parted my lips and coaxed her tongue into my mouth until it touched mine.

Groaning, my hands found her waist and tugged her body closer to me. My arms wound around the small of her back and kept her pressed against me as the kiss became more demanding. She took lead and I let her as I adjusted her legs, so they straddled me on the floor. Her hips rolled over my erection, making her shiver in my hold as her tongue twisted with mine.

Pressing her to me so she felt how hard I was for her, I asked, "Is this really want you want?" I knew what she'd say, but I needed to know before I buried myself inside her like I'd been thinking about doing for too long now, especially since the night I showed up half-cocked from the booze and fully cocked because of the skimpy pajamas she had on.

She pulled back, face flushed, and looked me straight in the eye. "Don't ask stupid questions, Theo. We both know you're smarter than that."

That made me chuckle as I pecked her lips, nipping her bottom one and drawing it into my mouth to suck on. My hands traveled up her body, finding the straps of her overalls and working them down her arms until they were both off and the top half of the stained denim fell to reveal the thin shirt she had on underneath. The outline of her perky breasts made it obvious she wasn't wearing a bra, and I wasn't sure if I wanted to growl at her or take it to my advantage.

I chose the latter. Dipping down, I drew her pebbled nipple into my mouth and reveled in the way her back arched to fill my mouth with more. Dragging my tongue over the clothed bud, my palms went to her ass cheeks and kneaded them, setting a pace as she rocked against me until her labored breath hitched. One of her hands went into my short hair, keeping my mouth on her chest, while the other squeezed my arm until her fingernails stung my skin as her core found the friction it needed to get her closer to the edge.

Moving to her other nipple, I managed to lay her down and roll my hips into her to keep her building, panting—needing more from me. I bit down lightly and listened to her moan as I worked the overalls down her body until they were peeled off and forgotten some-where behind us. It wasn't until I moved our inter-twined hands above her head as I ground into her core covered only by a scrap of white lace when I realized I'd laid her in paint. Green and blue coated the back of her hair, and black coated our arms.

Her eyes were closed as she rubbed against my

cock, seemingly not realizing the mess I was making of her body or choosing not to care. Then I got an idea.

Dragging her tank up and over her head until only her panties remained, I dipped my fingers in some of the paint and began circling her bare nipples. Swirling them with a mixture of red and yellow, I found her lips and kissed her hard the same moment I pinched her sensitive buds.

"Theo," she cried out, wrapping her arms around me. I was sure black paint from her skin was on my shirt and I didn't give a shit. She worked the small buttons until they were all undone, helping me peel the shirt off and toss it on the floor. The clang of the fork falling from her plate made me realize we'd need to do some serious cleaning after this, but I didn't give a fuck in the moment because I needed this.

I wanted to dirty her, taint her, and paint her body with my skilled hands until she forgot why she ever hated herself to begin with.

My lips trailed down her clean stomach, over the slightly raised skin where the pink scar rested just below her belly button, until the tip of my tongue caressed the top of her panty line. She moved her hips eagerly as I glided further down, my nose taking in the smell of her arousal that I was sure dripped because of me. The corners of my lips tipped up, and any reason not to do this disappeared from my conscience with the thought of burying myself deep inside her until she was officially mine.

"What do you want me to do, Della?" My voice was

husky, needy, but I wanted her to tell me exactly what she expected. "Use your big girl words."

Her hands fisted at her sides. "I want you to touch me."

"With?"

She struggled out, "Everything."

I cursed and nuzzled my nose against the seam of her lips, feeling how wet she was. My hands grazed her sides, smearing paint on the way down the slight curves of her waist until they met her underwear.

"Be specific, sweetheart."

She writhed. "I want your mouth on my pussy, Theo."

If I thought my cock was hard before, it was steel now. It took me less than a second to rip her panties off and dispose of the ruined material before she was bare to me. I looked up to see my handprints everywhere, her breasts, her sides, her stomach. I worked her tits again, massaging them with my stained palms, grabbing more paint and marking the tops of her thighs as I spread them and I trailed my tongue along the apex before meeting where she wanted me most.

"Please," she breathed.

It took that one little word before I all but dove to taste her for the very first time, and that one taste of sweetness that matched the rest of her was instantly the end of my resolve. I ate her with abandon until she panted my name and dug her fingers into my skull as I sucked her clit between my lips hard and fast. Her hips shifted upward to ride my face as I dipped down and circled her entrance before probing it until she yelled out a curse.

I chuckled against her and worked her until she was saying my name like a prayer, except I was no god. If anything, I'd be banished to hell once this was over and I'd enter freely with the knowledge of what Della Saint James sounded like when she begged me to lick her cunt. And the sound of her coming made me nearly explode before I could so much as unbutton my own pants. I gripped her hips as she rode the wave of her orgasm, her legs tightening around my head until they unlatched and landed with a thump on the floor as I licked her cream from my lips.

I rose over her and looked at the masterpiece sated on the floor in front of me. "You're beautiful, Della."

She blinked at me with pinkened cheeks like she'd never been told that before. I watched as she narrowed in on every movement I made as I slowly popped the button of my pants and unzipped them. Her eyes trailed over my hands as I pushed down my pants and boxer briefs at the same time, pupils dilating when she got a glimpse of my freed length.

"You may have days where you fight to remember that, but I'll happily be there to remind you what you do to me." Grabbing a fistful of my cock, I started working it, letting her watch me jack off as hunger rose in her gaze. Her thighs squeezed together as a bead of precum escaped my tip when I tightened my grip and twisted in the perfect place, while imaging her hand was doing the work.

"Tell me you believe it," I demanded of her, panting, and twitching in my palm.

She sat up on her elbows, eyes still trained where I touched myself. "I know I'm beautiful, Theo. I've worked a long time to get to that point. And I think…I think there's a lot of work to be done that I may need help with, but that doesn't mean it's because I can't believe it on my own."

"You should be proud." I bent down and captured her lips again, grazing our tongues and drinking her in as I built up closer to my orgasm the quicker I jerked myself. "I need to be inside you so fucking bad, sweetheart, but I need to clean myself up first."

She squirmed, wrapping an arm around my neck, and pulling me down on top of her. "I want you now."

Groaning, I stopped her. "I'm covered in paint and I want to feel what it's like to have your pussy vice grip my cock. Are you still on birth control?"

If she wasn't flushed before, she was now. I remembered the day she went on them because she asked Mariska to take her to the doctor when she admitted to me her cramps were bad. If I thought she'd be comfortable, I would have driven her to the doctor myself, but the situation didn't call for my assistance at the time.

"Yes."

I pecked her lips. "Come on." Standing up, I reached down for her hand. Her eyes traveled over her skin as she bit her lip, fingers dancing over the paint splotches covering her. I couldn't help but grin. "Don't suppose you could just snap a few pictures of yourself and submit that as your project, huh?"

Her laugh was light as she smacked my chest, the blush still blooming over the apples of her cheeks. "You want my professor to see me naked? Really?"

Hearing that aloud made me pause. "I hope I'm the only one who gets to see you naked." Backing her out of the room, I nipped her bottom lip and guided her carefully to the bathroom down the hall. My hands found the light switch as hers palmed my chest and grazed down my stomach, fingering the trail of hair leading to the part of me that was screaming to bend her over and thrust into her until I bottomed out.

She looked between me and the shower, grinning before stepping away from me and changing direction to the vanity on the opposite wall. Hanging above it was a large mirror that I instantly noticed her eyes avoided as she wet a washcloth under the faucet.

"Della—" Before I could say anything, she was in front of me with her back turned to her reflection and her hand wrapped around my cock gently washing it off. Hissing over the soft strokes, I bucked into her, burying my face into the crook of her neck, and biting down trying not to shoot my load as she worked me. "Fuck, that feels good."

Kissing up her neck and jaw, I backed her up until her ass hit the edge of the counter. Grabbing the cloth from her, I checked myself over before wiping my hands and tossing it on the ground, moving hair out of her face.

"Turn around."

Her eyes widened.

"Face the mirror."

Her throat bobbed. "Theo, I—"

"You want my cock, Della?" I asked, palming between her legs. I teased her entrance, circling where her wetness seeped then moved my fingers around her clit until her eyes fluttered closed. "Want my hard dick in there instead of my fingers, sweetheart?" The more I talked, the crazier with need I became. *I'd* wanted those things and it was the very first time I admitted as much. If Anthony were alive, if he were free and around to know my thoughts, he'd happily go to prison if it meant putting me six feet under because of what I wanted to do to his daughter. I wouldn't have stopped him either.

Her moan was soft as she nodded. Words were beyond her—the need was too strong, and I wanted to happily indulge in everything she fantasized about in that pretty head of hers.

Grazing her ear with my lips until shivers racked her spine, I said, "Then look in the mirror and watch me while I fuck you."

Her fingernails dug into the countertop until they turned white, but the squirm of her hips and the parting of her lips told she wanted to watch me pleasure her.

"Please," I whispered, grazing her cheek with my lips. Intertwining our hands, I peppered kisses down her jaw and nipped at the skin of her neck until she gave me more access to taste the salt on her skin not covered in paint.

Hesitantly she turned, her ass brushing against my dick, feeling how hard it was. It jerked, causing her to suck in a gasp as she bent with the help of my guiding palm.

"That's it," I praised, kissing her shoulder blade. One of my palms massaged her ass cheeks, spreading her and letting my finger dip down the seam until I found her puckered hole. "I can't wait to play with all of you."

She shuddered, causing me to grin against her skin as I moved downward to insert a finger into her entrance. Bucking, she said, "Theo. Please. No more teasing."

I kissed her back again and palmed my dick. "Look at your reflection and tell me what you see, Della."

Her head lifted and met her eyes in the mirror. They flashed with lust when she saw me standing behind her, her body bent over the counter ready for me. Paint still covered most of the top half of her, my handprints evident in the mess, fingerprints dipping down until they disappeared past what the mirror showed. "I see my father's best friend about to finish what he started a year ago," she panted.

That was all it took before I bit into her shoulder and exchanged my fingers for my cock at the tight hole beckoning me. "Way too long," I told her, parting her legs and filling her in one hard thrust. The sound she made went straight to my dick as I pulled out and greedily pushed back in. "I've wanted this for too long and I don't give a fuck what that says about me right now."

I held onto her hips as I entered her over and over, jackknifing until the sound of our skin slapping and her arousal fueled me to wrap one arm around her waist and another in her hair. Twisting slightly, I tilted her head back until her eyes locked on the way my hips thrusted faster into her from behind. "What do you see, Della?"

"You," she breathed, eyelids fluttering.

"And?"

She swallowed, her breathing becoming faster as she met my hips every time, fucking me with as much need as she could. The way she squeezed me had my cock demanding more, fighting to reach the climax that would happen way too soon if I kept thinking about the hundreds of different ways I'd fuck her now that I had her. "I see me. I see...*fuck, Theo.* I-I see somebody worthy. Beautiful. Is that what you want to hear?"

I bit into her shoulder again until I was sure a mark would be left and fuck if that didn't turn me on more. "I want the truth. What's your truth? What do you see of yourself right now?"

Her jaw quivered as she fought to keep her eyes open, knowing I'd force her to look again if they drifted closed. I picked up the pace and rolled my hips into her, finding that perfect place to hit every single time until she struggled to make coherent sentences. "I see a grown woman w-who faced a lot of battles and won most of them. Somebody who wears warpaint in the fform of—" She mewled when I moved a hand to her front and pinched her clit between my fingers. "—stretchmarks and scars."

Letting go of her hair, she rested the back of her head against my chest and said my name, panting it, praising it, begging me to do more to her. I flattened my palm against the scar on her torso and listened to every plead she moaned out between pants.

Faster.

Harder.

More. More. More.

It fueled me, but not as much as her words did, because every single one she spoke was the truth. Her body was a shrine that encompassed something ethereal —a soul pure no matter how much the world tried tainting it, and a love so deep she offered it to every-body who needed a piece of the goodness inside her.

And it was mine.

It was always mine in some way.

"So fucking beautiful," I said against the back of her head as I circled her clit again until she clenched my dick in a grip that was almost painful.

"Theo. Oh God. *Oh God.* Please." She repeated that again and again until I fucked her so hard, I nearly put a fist through the mirror when she came on my cock and milked me of my own orgasm. Spilling inside of her, I buried myself so deep I wasn't sure I'd come out—if I even wanted to. My face stayed in the crook of her neck as her body went limp in my arms that held her to me before we collapsed against the countertop.

When I pulled out, I whispered, "I see two people who have a lot of exploring left to do, sweetheart." I straightened out and helped her stand, watching my seed leak down her thigh with a shit eating grin on my face.

"Oh my God, tell me you're not grinning over *that* right now." Embarrassment filled her tone as she hid her face behind her hand in the mirror when she realized what I was looking at.

"Can't help it. That makes you mine, so I'm going to watch myself drip down your thighs whether you like it or not." To prove it, I caught some of my cum with my fingers and inserted them back inside her like I wanted to stay there planted inside her for good.

She swallowed. "I was always yours."

"Come on. Let's take a shower."

"Together?" Her voice was hopeful.

Honestly, she couldn't get rid of me if she wanted to at this point. "Yes, Della. Together."

chapter eleven

DELLA

THE ACHE between my legs was the only indication that what happened last night was real. As I stretched out my spent body, I turned in bed and examined the empty spot beside me, patting the cooled sheets and frowning.

Memories surfaced of waking up in the middle of the night together in my bed when Theo's fingers had found my core, playing with me until I writhed for more. I'd returned the favor a few hours after by tasting the part of him I'd been secretly dying to for longer than I admitted to him. The way he hissed when he woke up to my tongue grazing the side of his cock as I sucked him off had me feeling like a goddess. It was a feeling I didn't know well at all, and he only fed it as he put his hand in my hair with a groan and murmured, "You'll be the end of me. I fucking swear it."

It'd made me grin. Not as much as the faint remembrance of soft lips pressing against my temple and the words, "Anthony would fucking kill me" racking around my mind.

Thinking about my father was the last thing I wanted, but I could tell it plagued him. I didn't want it to, of course, but I didn't fault him for it. What we'd done wasn't some light thing. It was crossing a lot of lines that people would frown upon, but I didn't care. For the first time in a long time, *I didn't care what people thought*.

And that was…freeing.

Sitting up, I clutched the sheets to my naked body and glanced over at the clock on the nightstand. Swearing, I kicked my legs over the side of the bed and bolted toward the closet to grab whatever outfit was quickest to slide on. The jeans and sweatshirt weren't flattering considering everything else I owned, but it was comfortable, and I was going to be late for my exam if I didn't leave now.

Stumbling into the bathroom to run a brush through my hair, I gaped at the green dyed locks from the paint last night that didn't come out during the shower we'd taken together. Shaking my head, I threw it back into a messy bun and called it good.

It was when I reached for my bag on the kitchen counter that I saw the piece of paper with words scribbled on them next to it.

Left for work. Took the dog home.

Throat thickening, I ran the pad of my thumb over the last word. The light feeling in my chest made me breathe easier as I tucked the note into the front pocket of my jeans and threw the bag over my shoulder.

It didn't take long for me to get to campus, where I managed to slide into the last seat of the lecture hall with a look of disapproval from the professor. Sinking down, I grabbed a pen and barely had time to catch my breath from speed walking before a packet was dropped in front of me.

"Nice of you to join us, Ms. Saint James," Professor Ribbons said dryly. The elderly woman never liked me, but it'd gotten worse after things with my father hit the news. To her, I was as guilty as he was by association.

I murmured an apology and watched her white brow arch in disbelief. Staring down at the questions, I waited until she was walking back to the front of the room before expelling a breath and getting to work. I was halfway through when I realized I didn't study enough and could only hope I got a passing grade that didn't tank my overall class average too badly. I'd struggled as it was catching up in this class because political science wasn't an interest of mine, even though it probably should have been with the amount of times I'd heard my father talking about the subject matter over the years. It came with his role as governor, I supposed. That lack of interest didn't help Ribbons' expectations of me though. And flashbacks of last night, of that blissful ache nestled between my legs, certainly distracted me from the paper I should have focused on.

People left the room one by one until it was just me remaining, and my leg bounced when I felt piercing eyes on me for the better part of the period. I wanted to ask why she was staring, why she hated me when she didn't know me beyond being one of her students. But part of me knew. People like Professor Ribbons thrived on the rich getting what they deserved. She'd gone on a thirty-minute rant once during the beginning of the semester on how politicians used their money and power to get away with anything. Truthfully, I wasn't sure what I expected given her role as the political science department head—she studied politics and political scandals for years. If I didn't need the elective, I would have avoided her and her reputation at all costs given who I was related to, but I had no choice by the time class signups were available. Evidently, I didn't have the money or power to get out of it. Not anymore.

Relief filled me when I answered the final question and closed the packet. Stuffing my pen in the side pocket of my bag, I stood and walked the test up to her desk where she watched me carefully. "Finally finished?"

Teeth grinding, I nodded.

"Did you study for this?"

"Yes." I paused. "Not as much as I would have liked."

She looked at me with bored eyes.

"Can I ask you something, professor?" I was

surprised by my own inquiry, but not as much as she was considering I tended to avoid any conversation with her if I could help it. When she didn't answer, I went ahead and continued. "What did I ever do to you? Not my father. Not my family. But *me*."

She blinked slowly, her body leaning back in her chair as she tilted her head. I didn't like being studied, it made me uncomfortable, and she knew that. "You don't try."

My lips parted at the unexpected answer. "What?"

She repeated herself and added, "I've taught many people like you, Adele. Some of them worse, some of them far better. But you always folded into yourself when things got tough."

"That isn't true."

"No?" She stood, flattening her hands down the purple blouse she wore. "I gave you the benefit of the doubt given the circumstances, which I'm certainly not known to do, but I thought I saw potential in you. However, I realized you were no different than others raised privileged. People go through far worse things and still make it out on the top, so coddling you helps nobody."

"I lost my father. And —"

"Excuses."

Anger bubbled inside me. "I keep to myself because it's better that way, not because I don't care or don't try. All due respect, but you have no right to judge me as anything more than a pupil to educate."

Clearly, it was the wrong thing to say because her

lips tugged into a cocky smile. "Let me educate you then, my dear. Malik versus State. Heard of it?"

Of course, I had. George Malik was the state comptroller before my father took term as governor. They'd known each other for years, but my father insisted he didn't know what Malik was doing with funds. I believed him. I still did. And sure, maybe that made me naive, but he was still my father no matter what happened.

"I have," I answered carefully.

"Then I'm sure you know that Malik took more than just the funds he was responsible for. There was a very long list of those he hurt along the way. Sounds familiar, doesn't it? Even the court system said his crimes were true, but where is he now, Adele?"

I wasn't sure where he was because I hadn't wanted to follow the story when it was all over the news. My father would sometimes mention it, but it was rare. Instead, we focused on each other. How our days were. How classes were going. If business was successful. I loved my father, but things between us, regardless of how close we were once, were restricted. Looking back now, it made me wonder if I was subconsciously preparing myself for the inevitable. He'd been too invested in the Malik case when he did bring it up, like he knew more than most people. There were answers I didn't want, things I couldn't allow myself to know because it changed how I'd feel about the man I looked up to my entire life.

"According to social media, he's in Fiji with his wife

celebrating their thirty-eighth wedding anniversary. Sweet, isn't it?" The tone in her voice told me it was the opposite of that. "I find it strange that somebody who was so blatantly guilty could be out celebrating of his own free will. Don't you?"

Trick question. "Does it matter what I think about it, Professor Ribbons? You've made up your mind about it already."

"Are you telling me you don't find that he deserved punishment?"

Straightening, I readjusted my bag and stared her directly in the eye. "My father went to prison, *as he should have*, for the misuse of authoritative power. So, do I believe a man I don't truly know outside the media's reports of him deserved some sort of reprimanding for his ill actions? Yes. Does that mean I'm shocked he didn't? No. That's not because I believe it's okay that people could be bought off by false forgiveness and dirty money. It means that I'm aware of how faulty the system is. Don't put words in my mouth."

Interest piqued in her features, her brows raising and eyes widening in the slightest way. "I didn't put words into your mouth, nor did I place ideals in your head. We can both agree the system is skewed though, which is more than I thought I'd get from you."

"This has to do with me not trying how exactly?"

Walking around her desk, she stopped just in front of me. "What did you do when your father was incarcerated?"

Why was that any of her business? "Did what I

could to cope. Anybody would have no matter what circumstance they came from."

"That's a cop out. What did you do?"

"I…" Didn't she watch the news? "I'm sure if you saw the media—"

"I'm giving you a chance to prove me wrong, Adele. Unless you'd rather me continue with my assumptions? You see, teachers talk. You used to be quite dedicated to your education here. In fact, I heard your academics were next level, second to the scholarship you were offered, but that wasn't for your original major. What was that again?"

I said nothing.

"I believe it was business, correct?"

"If you know, why do you bother asking? I'm sure you also know it's not business anymore since you've clearly checked up on me."

"You got into this school because of your skills in dance and who your father was. Why don't you do that anymore?"

I'd gotten into Bentley University because I was a talented dancer, not because of Anthony Saint James. If that had been the only case, administration would have probably found a way to kick me out, so their reputation wasn't as tainted as my family name was. "Why do you care?"

"Who says I do?"

My eyes caught the time on the wall before I sighed, resigning to this pointless conversation. "I need to get going if I'm going to make my next class in time." Turning, I stopped and gave her one last look over my shoulder. "I stopped dancing because I couldn't look at myself in the mirror. And maybe…maybe that was for more reasons than I originally thought."

The scar on my stomach weighed heavily on me, but I fought to place my hand there. I was stupid, weak even, and the anti-depressants Ripley had put me on amplified how I felt. Did that excuse how far I let myself go? How badly I could have injured myself with those scissors, like slicing into my flesh would somehow help? No. I was ashamed, embarrassed, and a slew of other things for letting my emotions win. But I couldn't change that. I could only hope that one day I could look in the mirror for a long time and not hate the person staring back.

The tiniest grin tilted Ribbons' lips, but I couldn't decipher what it meant. Not willing to think about it, I tipped my head and walked out before she could say anything else. When the breeze hit my face as I walked outside, I replayed the odd conversation that just occurred and shook my head.

I didn't like Professor Ribbons, but I was starting to think maybe she didn't hate me as much as I thought. She'd once seen potential in me, and I wondered if she still did and masked it under tough love. Then again, I wasn't foreign to that concept and what she offered went beyond that. Her reputation didn't help me think that I had an ally in her either, so, as always, I drew back into myself and tried brushing off the conversation completely, shooting Theo a text.

A text that was left unanswered.

MY FINGER LINGERED over the dial button after a day of staring at my phone waiting for him to make the first move. I was officially *that girl.* I'd told myself I'd wait instead of making a big deal out of it, but I couldn't focus, got snapped at by more than Professor Ribbons, and nearly took out a student in the hall because I wasn't paying enough attention.

"God," I groaned, setting the phone down before I could hit the button that tempted me. Walking into my apartment, I'd hoped I'd find him and Ramsay again like the night before. No such luck. I wasn't sure if it was disappointment that I felt weighing on my chest or something else. Expectation?

Swallowing, I set my things down and walked into the spare room to assess the damage. It was no longer messy, something I hadn't noticed this morning in my rush out the door. Theo was the only one who could have cleaned it considering we were the only two who'd known about the mess.

Clicking my tongue when I saw some paint missed in the corner, I couldn't help but reach for my hair. The ghost of his touch lingered everywhere, but the dyed strands of my blonde locks made the replay that much more intense in my head. It helped ease the doubt over why he hadn't reached out once all day. He'd known I was busy, logically he was too. I couldn't overthink the reasoning, which was my body's first response no matter how hard I tried rewiring myself.

Closing the door behind me, I quickly changed into pajamas, let down my hair, and forced myself to stare at my reflection. Ribbons got into my head and she knew it. What I admitted to her wasn't something I said to many people, but maybe it was time to change that. Ripley told me at the beginning of our sessions that admitting the problem aloud was the first step in changing it.

In my reflection, I noticed some pieces of my blonde locks had faded green, others black in them. I fingered them and frowned, wondering how many washes it'd take before it was back to normal.

Gripping the edge of the counter, I bit into my bottom lip and remembered what'd happened in this very spot. Theo was proving a point, trying to get me to admit what I knew deep, *deep* down.

I was worthy.

I was beautiful.

I was not deserving of my own criticism.

But I knew that wasn't going to be enough, and that familiar feeling wiggled its way under my skin until I couldn't bare anymore face time with myself in the glass.

Eying the tips of my hair as they bounced with my steps, I grabbed my phone from the counter and hit a button with an idea that I might regret but didn't want to walk away from if I was going to try, really try, like

Theo wanted. Hell, like the world wanted according to
Ribbons.

"To possible regrets," I whispered, listening to it
ring as I bit my thumbnail.

"Hello?"

I wet my bottom lip, hesitating only for a
microsecond but refusing to chicken out. "Can you help
me with something?"

There was no hesitation, which I found comforting.
"When and where?" Blowing out a sigh of relief, I said
my address and a time and hung up, smiling to myself
with a new fluttery feeling in my stomach.

THE KNOCK at the door had me running my palms
down my thighs as I peeked through the little hole in
the door. Silver blonde was on full display, making me
unlatch and unlock the door before pulling it open.

"Swanky place," was the first thing out of Tiffany's
mouth as she walked in. Looking around, she assessed
the art-filled walls, colorful furniture, and finally me. "I
didn't think you'd ever reach out."

"Neither did I," I admitted, closing the door and
crossing my arms over my chest. Pausing for a minute, I
decided to rip off the Band-Aid. "I'm trying to get past a
lot of things, but I need to do that one step at a time."

She just nodded slowly, waiting for me to get to my
point. It wasn't a rude gesture, just who she was. We'd
seen each other a few times at yoga when I went, but I
didn't frequent the classes as much I usually did. Part of

that had to do with avoiding her so I didn't feel bad about not using her number.

"Can you do something with my hair?"

She blinked. "What?" Her eyes went to what I held up, squinting at the odd color. "What did you do to it?"

"Not important." My face heated, which meant it was probably red and I didn't want to go into details. "You used to do the other girls' hair all the time before recitals. It was what you wanted to do at one point."

Surprise flickered across her face. "I didn't know anybody remembered that."

All I did was shrug in return. I remembered a lot about those days. Just because I cut dance cold turkey didn't mean I stopped thinking about what it was like to have a routine, a set schedule, and how much I enjoyed being around some of the girls. Not that I'd ever admit it to Tiffany, but I always liked her head-strong, no bs personality.

"Why don't you just go somewhere and pay a professional to do it?" Walking over, she examined the hair and made a face. "I don't know what you did to this, but it's hideous."

Rolling my eyes, I swatted her hand away. "I know it is. It wasn't on purpose. And you offered to help me, so I thought…"

"With dance, Adele." I just stared at her with a pleading look until she groaned. "Tell me why you asked me. You have plenty of friends and probably a personal stylist like the rest of us."

Blinking, my throat got thick. "I think you're forget-

ting that personal stylists cost money." I wasn't embarrassed over my current financial standing. I worked
hard and was proud of what I had. Commissioning
some of my work, selling pieces I'd collected over the
years, and working different smaller jobs on campus
had kept me afloat. But everything else? "Listen, I'm
trying to be careful about what I spend and going out
isn't always the most comfortable for me."

"But you do it."

"For school," I reasoned.

She pointed toward the stool in the kitchen and
gave me a relenting sigh. "Fine, but you need to give me
more than that. Sit down and tell me where your scissors are. And I'm not cleaning up."

"Deal." Helping her get what she needed, I plopped
down on the chair and watched her grab a towel from
the kitchen to drape over my shoulders.

"This is because of your eating disorder, right? If it
were just about your father, you probably wouldn't even
go to school because there are a lot of people he hurt
there."

Wow. She went right for the jugular. I wasn't that
surprised, but it still didn't make me warm and fuzzy
to hear. "The haircut is for me. I always told myself
I'd keep my hair long, especially if it meant my
mother would brush and braid it before bed every
night." And Theo, but she didn't know who that was,
and I didn't feel like explaining the sordid tale. It
made me think about the note, which I realized
halfway through the day had fallen out of my pocket.

It'd put me in a sour mood, which was ridiculous. It wasn't a love note, but it still made me feel…something.

She was quiet for a moment as she ran a comb through my hair to make sure it was smooth. "Your mother was always kind to everybody. She stood out from the rest."

The familiar sting of old memories watered down my eyes. "Yeah, she did."

"Okay, so new hair for a new you," she moved on, allowing me to close my eyes and collect myself. "You don't go out a lot because of the disorder though. A haircut won't change that."

"I didn't say it would."

"Why do you want to be different then?"

"I don't want to be different, per se…" How could I explain it when I wasn't sure I got it myself? I froze momentarily when I felt the blades rise to a lock of my hair. They closed, snipping off a long chunk.

Sensing my reaction, Tiffany walked in front of me with her brows raised. "For some reason you trust me, right?"

I met her eyes. "I trust you not to make me look homeless."

She snorted. "Tit for tat. You're right about me being interested in cosmetology when I was younger. Hair, nails, you name it. I liked making people feel pretty using what they already have. So, I get it. What you're doing. It's about enhancing how you feel about yourself. Cutting your hair is like starting over, right?"

Maybe she did get it. "Right. I'm thinking about going back to my normal color too."

"Okay." Moving back around me, she carefully evened out my hair before snipping off more. The weight eased from my scalp with every passing minute and I refused to look to the floor where my hair rested. "Do you struggle with it? Your disorder?"

"Every day."

"But you haven't…?"

My throat bobbed. "Not in a while. That doesn't mean I'm not tempted. Some days it's easier to fight than others. Lately, I've been thinking about how easy it would be to just go back to what I used to do. To not eat. To…" Letting my words trail off, I shook my head.

"Do you think this will help? You said you had steps you were following. What's the endgame for you?"

What's my endgame? That was a question I hadn't asked myself in a long time. Maybe never. "Would it be wrong if I said I don't know? It isn't like I don't have goals—"

"Fine. What are they?"

I paused. "To be happy. To be…healthy. Or as healthy as I can be given what I'll be facing for the rest of my life. I just want…" Theo came to mind, making heat creep up the back of my neck. Squirming, I said, "I just want to be the best version of myself I can possibly be."

When she didn't say anything, I wondered what she was thinking. I didn't want her to pity me. That wasn't who she was. I preferred her talking smack, trying to pressure me into dancing, anything but what was possibly going through her head that sympathized with me. "What else do you want to do besides get a new 'do? Tell me the other steps."

Grateful, I smiled. "My art professor suggested that I do a figure drawing class. It'll be the most uncomfortable thing for me to do."

"Drawing naked people?"

Clearing my throat, I said, "Being the naked person people draw."

"Oh. *Oh.*" She stopped again. "Does she know about what you've been through?"

"That's why she thinks it's a good idea."

"Body positivity," she realized, almost sounding awed by the idea.

I hummed and did nothing else.

"Yoga."

My brows pinched. "What?"

Sighing, she moved on to the other side of my hair. "You have to come to yoga class every week. No skipping unless it's necessary. If you don't show up, I know where you live now. I'll drag you there myself."

"But why?"

She appeared in front of me again, a hand on her hip. "If you want to take her advice, you need balance. That means trying. Go to yoga every week, find a routine. Put yourself in the mindset with your new badass haircut and build yourself up to a point where you can be more comfortable putting yourself out there."

I licked my lips. "That sounds easier said than done."

"Nothing worthwhile comes easy. How many people have told us that growing up? I'm fairly sure I heard your own mother tell you that during practice a time or five million." My mother was full of wise advice that I held onto, so Tiffany was right. Until she added, "And you're dancing again."

My eyes bugged out. "Whoa. Wait—"

"Not for Judith or anybody else." That shut me up. Well, that and the narrowed look she gave me that told me to let her speak. "You're going to come to my private studio and we're going to dance like I originally offered, except I'm not giving you a choice this time."

"But—"

"No. Routine, remember? Yoga is a first step. A baby step if you will. It'll get your mind to calm and center your focus. Dancing will help you get back out there again and start recognizing your body for what it is. Plus, you can't tell me you've *never* danced since walking away. I wouldn't believe it."

I wasn't going to admit I'd found myself moving to old routines we'd practiced or turning on music here and moving my body to the beat, or even slow dancing at the warehouse with Theo, something I desperately wanted to repeat just for the sake of being held by him and caressed by the melody. "But I don't want to, Tiffany."

"Why?"

I said nothing.

"I'm not finishing your hair until I get a valid answer. Don't think I won't make you walk around looking like you lost a fight to a chainsaw. Feel me?"

My lips twitched.

"So?" she pressed.

I debated my options and met her eyes realizing I didn't have any. So, I admitted for the second time in one day what I'd held in for a long time. "It's the mirrors."

Her head cocked. "The mirrors?" When I nodded, she considered the answer, studying me like she was trying to figure out my tells. "Okay."

"Okay?"

"Okay. That's good."

"I'm confused."

She snickered and went back to my hair, clearly accepting my answer for what it was. "If it's just that, it's a fixable problem I can actually help with."

Again. I was silent.

"Think about it," she prompted. "Your endgame, subconsciously, is doing that drawing class as a nude model. Which, by the way, badass. That would be nerve wracking for anybody. But if you get back on that dance floor, in front of the mirrors, and work out those feelings, you'll be better for it. You'll get used to accepting your body again. It'll take time, Adele, like everything does."

It made sense, more than I wanted it to. So, for the rest of the haircut, we were silent while I considered it with a heavy conscious. It wasn't uncomfortable, but welcoming.

Eventually, she started humming like she was enjoying herself and I figured it had something to do with her victory considering I didn't argue.

After she told me to look in the mirror when she was finished, I touched the ends of my new short cut and smiled at my reflection. It lasted longer than normal. When I came back out and saw her sweeping the floor despite her protests before, I smiled wider because...

We were becoming friends.

So, I said, "The people who don't completely dislike me call me Della."

She paused, looked up at me, and tried hiding a smile. "Okay." Another pause. "People don't really call me anything other than Tiffany, Tiff, or bitch. Typically, the latter."

I snorted. "Tiff it is."

A last-minute decision had me snapping a selfie to show off my new look and sending it to Theo with no caption. I didn't need one.

My phone pinged.

Theo: *Like I always say. Beautiful.*

chapter twelve

THEO

IF I HAD LONGER HAIR, I'd have pulled it out by now. It was better than putting my fist in The Dick's face like I wanted to as soon as he showed up uninvited right before lunchtime. I was already on edge since I left Della's apartment yesterday morning and knew that the note I'd left wasn't good enough after what we'd done. She deserved more than one text after she sent me that picture—a call. A visit. I'd planned on surprising her tonight for dinner.

My mind wrapped around the feeling of her squeezing me, leaving me permanently hard all fucking day. It didn't put me in a good mood since I'd taken a cold shower while planning how to approach us now. We couldn't go back, I didn't want to, but that didn't mean moving forward would be easy. Dealing with an asshole like Pratt certainly didn't put my thoughts at ease because his eyes told me they knew. I wasn't sure how, but he did.

"You're not even listening, are you?" He wiped his mouth with a napkin before sitting back in the chair across from me. The restaurant he chose was busy and public, probably for his benefit since I was red-faced as soon as he stepped foot into my office and told me we needed to talk. Yet, we did a whole lot of bullshitting over the forty-five minutes I was stuck here with other rich pricks and businessmen. Half of them were probably making deals that went beyond the scope of their experience based on the beady fuckers at the tables closest to us.

"When you have something valuable to say, I'll listen." My voice was emotionless, something that clearly pissed him off. It was obvious he lived for people's reactions when he wasted their time with his bullshit. I bet it worked most of the time.

His scowl made me grin. "Let's get down to business then. Samantha."

I blinked. "Your daughter? What the fuck does she have to do with anything?"

His arms rested on the edge of the table, his head cocking to examine me with a glint in his eyes that I refused to react to. "I happen to know she's been hanging out with Adele Saint James, Katrina Murphy, and Gina Vandyke."

One of my brows arched, but silence remained between us because I wasn't going to offer him anything until he got to the point.

"I'm sure you're not surprised that they enjoy treating themselves to the Murphy and Vandyke stash." Anybody who was involved with their social circle knew that he was talking about drugs and fake money, but I didn't like his tone or what he was implying between the lines.

My eyes narrowed. Attention drawn, I leaned toward him with new anger boiling over inside me. "What are you getting at, Pratt?"

"What do you think, Theo?" His lips twitched at the corners—amusement obvious over my distaste for his accusation.

"Adele doesn't do that shit. Just because you let your daughter ruin her fucking life because you don't give a fuck about your family doesn't mean she's anything like that."

"Always so protective," he chuckled. "I have it on good authority that isn't the case though. The good little girl you thought you were raising is no different than Samantha."

"Bullshit."

One shoulder lifted. "Believe what you want, but the truth *will* come out. Sooner rather than later, in fact. Don't think it'll stop there either. There are things I'm sure you wouldn't want out that will affect the both of you."

His threat hit me square in the chest, setting off the need to deny or avoid it entirely. "I would watch it if I were you."

"Funny. I was going to say the same to you. Do you think you're the only person who has eyes and ears on other people? Money talks. We're both made of it. Some of us put it to good use if it means gaining something."

The only thing he was gaining is the likelihood of me smashing his face against the goddamn table. His family, and the Vandyke's, printed counterfeit bills as their main source of income these days, drugs were a new business venture over the past year. I was surprised they hadn't been caught yet. I'd like to think it was only a matter of time before their operation was discovered, but I had no leverage besides hearsay.

Rubbing my lips together, I considered my reply. If I said the wrong thing, he'd run with it because he *did* have the money and power to do something about it, even if some of that money was fake. That should have worried me, but I refused to let it. "I think you're a coward, Richard. You're trying to scare me into believing you have dirt on me because you're not getting what you want. Child's play, really."

His stare pinned me, but I held it. Did he have dirt on me? Probably. But there were things I was careful about, that I was positive nobody else knew. Things that involved just how invested I was with a certain blonde, and I knew immediately when his eyes flashed that he understood clearly where my thoughts went.

Digging into his pocket, he flattened out a small piece of paper that I identified immediately.

Left for work. Took the dog home.

I saw the way he watched me examine the note I'd left for Della, but I knew better than to show it was tied to either her or me. I hadn't signed it. The best he could do was assume.

"How do you think it would look if stories of your time with little Saint James came out? If people saw just how you looked at her? How you'd leave her little notes early in the morning after a sleepover together?" His inquiry was cocky. I said nothing, fueling him. Denying it would only make him go further, so silence was the only way to go. "Maybe you're right, Theo. Maybe I don't have anything on you. But her? Well, so long as she's around Samantha and the other girls, she's around the same corruption her father got head deep in. Would be a shame, wouldn't it? Such potential, I'm told. I'm not sure she'd be the same if the media came after her again considering her last round with them."

I was fine being threatened and taking it, but Della? She didn't deserve to be dragged into any of this. Standing, the chair scraped back as I slammed money down on the table and gripped the edge of it. "Your family has always been faced with corruption because you're weak. Adele, what she's gone through, has made her strong. Your threats will only ever be that."

The smirk he gave me told me that he didn't believe

it, which was a problem. If he was willing to act himself it was for good reason. Normally he hired other people to do his dirty work. But I couldn't go back and change my reaction to something that wasn't so telling.

He knew.

He knew that I cared about Della.

He'd use her to get what he wanted.

Fuck.

"Your business won't last if another investor drops. You may have the money to survive, but what about your reputation? How long will you make it in this city if people thought you were in too deep, just like your former partner? If you used his departure from this world to sink into his beautiful offspring like a predator?"

My teeth ground so hard I was sure I'd need to get them fixed. "So that's what you want? To save me?"

"I simply want to help."

"You want in my company, and I want to know the real reason why. It isn't to help others, that's for damn sure. But I'm not in the mood today. Today, I've had enough of you."

He laughed, drawing people's attention to our table. Their stares didn't last long once they figured out who he was. They were smart to keep to themselves, but I was sure they were listening for any details they could get so they could spread rumors even without him asking them to. "Can't say I'm surprised knowing your short temper. Just remember what I said. We'll be in touch."

"You sound sure."

He stood too, flattening his suit jacket, and shooting me a confident wink that I wanted to smack off his face. "Guess you'll have to see for yourself. Seems I know more things about your weakest points than you do. I'll leave this working relationship open for a while until you see sense."

"Don't flatter yourself."

He turned, waving down a waiter who appeared almost instantly. Paying him no attention as he handed over bills too big for what was spent on our lunches, he patted the young boy's arm. "Don't accept Mr. West's money. It'd be an insult to me considering I invited him to lunch."

Nostrils flaring, I glared. He never paid, everybody knew that. He was making a statement.

"You owe me now," was the last thing he said before turning to leave.

I wanted to yell.

To punch something.

But what did I do?

I went to the last place I should have, leaving behind the piece of paper on the table so The Dick couldn't accuse me of its ownership.

I SAW the black leather jacket first. It engulfed her small frame, but she wore it proudly. I hadn't seen it on her since the night of Anthony's funeral.

"Wow. Look who's alive," she commented, holding

the jacket around her like a barrier. The wince that came from her was subtle before she said, "Sorry. I had a bad day."

"Want to talk about it?" Honestly, all I wanted was to go inside, kiss her, make her dinner, and watch whatever the hell she put on TV. I didn't care if it had to do with aliens, mummies, horrible cooking, or animals. I just wanted to spend time with her and ignore the day, which had clearly been a rough one for both of us.

"Not really," she admitted quietly, looking around at a few bystanders. Her sigh was light as she brushed her new short hair behind her ear. "I've been fighting with myself a little. Just having one of those days."

Alert coursed through me. "Should I be worried? Do you need—"

"No." Her lips rubbed together before her palm swept across her cheek like she was wiping away exhaustion. "No, you don't need to worry. I'm not sure why I've been feeling this way, but I have been and I'm working through it. I spoke to Ripley about it earlier."

"Did she help?"

One shoulder lifted. "As much as she could, I suppose. You know Ripley. She gives me a motivation speech and reminds me not to backpedal after working so hard to get where I am now. She's right. I don't plan on failing, but…"

It was easier said than done. "I thought we could have dinner," I told her. "Maybe watch something together. I've been thinking about it all day."

We stood outside her building facing each other. It looked like she was leaving, but I selfishly wanted her to stay. "I really like what you've done to your hair, by the way. You look…"

"Different?"

"Beautiful." Her new cut framed her narrow jawline and high cheekbones like a masterpiece. The short style was chin-length, and it worked for her.

Her cheeks reddened. "I'm actually on my way out."

"Where?"

"To see friends."

"Pretty Boy?" I gripped the back of my neck and sighed heavily. "That's good. If you're getting out, that's great. I suppose I just wanted to talk to you about a few things. I met with somebody today that pissed me off and I wanted to see you."

She blinked. "I'm meeting with Tiffany Anderson too. I'm not sure if you remember her, but she also danced with me." There was a moment of pause between us. "If I didn't already make plans, I'd go upstairs. I'm sorry."

"I should have called," I apologized.

Her arms hugged her waist. "It's fine. Maybe we could have lunch tomorrow? I don't have any plans besides some homework."

I smiled. "If you have the time."

She walked up to me until our shoes touched, and her arms went around my waist in a tight hug. "I'd make time for you, Theo. Always."

I went rigid when I saw a couple walking past us with curious eyes, and the woman didn't look particularly thrilled over the embrace Della had me in. Swallowing, I patted her back and drew away first with a small smile.

"What?" she asked, brows pinching. I began to shake my head and tell her nothing was wrong when she saw the same couple whispering, the man not-so-subtly looking at me before shrugging at the woman. Her hand found my waist. "Theo?"

"Nothing, Della. It's just—"

"Them?" she guessed, nodding toward the couple who had passed us. My shoulders eased, giving me away. "Seriously?"

"No. Like I said, I had a shit day with somebody who got on my nerves and I'm just being cautious."

"Cautious." She blinked before laughing dryly at my bad choice of word. "You're being cautious of what exactly?"

"Della—"

Her mood shifted drastically. "We had sex!" she hissed, yanking her hand from my body, eyes watering to a glazed glare directed toward me. "I didn't imagine that. I didn't beg for it. Did I make the first move? Sure. Did you have to go through with it? Touch me? Taste me? Bend me over? No. But you did anyway. So, unless it was that bad—"

"Stop," I growled, stepping toward her. "I'm sorry for upsetting you. I didn't mean anything by it. But after today, I realized that there are going to be a lot of obstacles that we need to get through, and I don't expect you to understand my point of view."

"Try to explain it to me then."

"Things changed dramatically because of what happened between us and I wouldn't change that. But you said yourself that you were being spontaneous. It could have been a moment where you let your walls down. I wanted to be the person you needed in that moment. That doesn't mean that moments last. We both know not all of them do."

Her eyes widened. "You…" Her lips parted and then closed promptly, like she was trying to collect her thoughts. Color drained from her cheeks until she was pale. "Wow. That's how it's going to be, huh? Yeah, I get it. Moments end."

Cursing, I stepped in front of her when she gripped her bag tightly and tried sidestepping me. "I didn't mean it like that. I'm trying here, Della. I want you to be happy, but you can't honestly think this won't change us. It *has* to."

"You make it sound like such a bad thing. Enlighten me, Theo. What are you trying to say because I'm not a mind reader? I *want* things to change. I've wanted that for a long time. That doesn't mean we have to be different people though, so why are you making such a big fuss out of it?"

"We can't be who we were!" I yelled, cussing under my breath when a few people walked past us and turned in our direction. "Can we go inside and talk?"

"No."

"Della—"

"I don't want to be who we were. We'd be going two steps back. Do you think I'm stupid? Or are you worried that I'm going to start demanding more from you?"

"That isn't it."

"Then talk to me. Here and now."

Hesitation held me back, which only made her come closer to her own conclusions based on the twitch of her lips. "We can't be Theo and little Della, but in some respects, we'll always be. There are going to be memories that remind me of where we started. And no matter how much time passes, what occurs between us, that will haunt me. Not because I'm ashamed. Not because I regret finally having you as mine, because I don't and I would, *will*, do it again very soon. You're mine Della. You always have been. You're just mine in a way a lot of people will fight against."

She scoffed. "We're back to that?"

"People will threaten us." *They already have.* Pratt's face flashed in my mind, making my fists clench at my sides.

"They have no grounds!" she shot back.

"Don't they?" I questioned, shaking my head in disbelief. How many times had the public seen me out with her when she was younger holding my hand, laughing, watching me carry her on my shoulders? They saw a man helping his best friend raise his daughter when his job kept him busy. They saw somebody who was doing good for a selfless cause, but it wasn't selfless. I liked being there for Della. Watching her succeed. Seeing how she grew up into a strong woman. But if they saw what that innocent relationship grew into, it would be bad. Especially if it were The Dick who released that information like I knew he would—like he'd all but threatened.

Della gaped at me, slowly shaking her head like she couldn't believe what I was saying. Part of me couldn't either. "And what exactly have we done that warrants that kind of doubt?"

"I slept with somebody who was a ward of mine. Somebody that my longest friend trusted me with."

"Because you care about me."

I nodded. "True, but that won't mean much to a lot of people given the history we have. Trust me, Della, there are people out there who are rooting against us."

"So, I'm only allowed to be yours in private? A dirty secret you keep in your back pocket for you to play with when you see fit." Her voice wavered, splintering my heart when the hurt grew in her eyes. "I don't want to be the person you get to love in the dark, Theo. To even think that's what you might want…"

As soon as that four-letter word escaped those heart-shaped lips of hers, I was fucking gone. How many times had she told me that growing up? All innocent. All pure. Hearing that now, even indirectly, it was a possibility that struck me fucking stupid. I needed her to tell me she loved me, to know I loved her, but I wasn't sure how we could get there without serious problems with Pratt. I needed to handle him first before we explored things publicly. "You have *never* been my dirty secret."

Furiously swiping at a fallen tear on her cheek before I could, she stepped back from me with a harsh breath. "Is that why you wanted to go inside and have this discussion instead of just manning up and doing it here in public? Is that why left so early the morning after you came inside me so people wouldn't wonder why Theo West was leaving my apartment building? Did you decide this before or after I sucked you off until you shot down my throat? Or is it—"

"I get your point," I cut her off in a hard tone, fists shaking.

"But am I getting through to you?" she doubted, rubbing her temples. "Like I said, Theo, I don't want to go back to how we were. We can't. We will never be the same after what we did. It *was* a spontaneous decision. It was one I made that I was *proud* of because I got to control it. I got to do something that made me happy, something I've wanted to do for so long. And you just ruined it. So, congratulations."

"I—"

"I don't want to hear it." Holding up her hand, she took a deep breath and looked me in the eyes. "I just want you to listen to me. I've loved you my whole life as so many things and that's never going to change. What will, is how I love you from here on out. Today, tomorrow, ten years from now. Whether you like it or not, you have tattooed yourself into my life and that will never be removed even if you try convincing me that we're better off not pursuing this. Those memories you're afraid of? They're part of our story. They might even make the story we're writing. It shows that people change. Feelings change. And that it's okay for that to happen."

I didn't have a response for her that she'd accept, and she knew it. Looking at me for a moment longer, she dipped her chin and stuffed her hands in the pockets of her father's jacket.

The words I found were ones that crushed her. She didn't try to hide it. "I'm trying to protect you, Della. I've always done that. I don't expect you to understand why I'm doing this, why I'm asking you to give me some time to figure things out, but just know that I'm doing it for you. Eventually, for us."

Her throat bobbed as she blinked at me, completely silent. There was no recognition, no acceptance of my words. I wanted to beg her to believe me—in me. But I couldn't make her. I needed it to be on her own accord.

I dipped down and brushed a kiss against her cheek, then a brief one against her lips. She didn't return it. Instead, she began walking away from me with hollowed eyes.

I called out, "I haven't seen you wear that jacket in a while."

Her eyes went to the worn leather. "It comforts me when I need it most." Voice thick, but context thicker, all I could do was nod and watch her walk away.

I needed her, that much I knew.

More than she needed me, in fact.

And that was comforting—the notion an acceptance like my own leather jacket wrapped around the toughest part of me.

Della would be okay.

chapter thirteen

DELLA

SOMETHING SMELLED good when I closed the large front door behind me and heard paws *click-clacking* toward me at a fast pace. When I saw Ramsay, a huge smile came over my face. Dropping my things, I bent down and stroked his soft fur as he wiggled his back end and began licking my hand.

"In the kitchen," Theo called.

I picked up my bag and sketchpad before walking toward his voice, my mouth watering over the decadent smells coming from whatever he was cooking.

"Hey," he greeted, wiping his hands on a dish towel before walking over to me. I was surprised when he pecked my lips and grabbed my bag, setting it down on the island. "Want something to drink?"

He'd called me this morning asking if I wanted to come to his place for dinner instead of meeting for lunch. At first, I'd been disappointed. I felt bad about what had happened yesterday, but he didn't seem to be thinking about it. I, on the other hand, couldn't stop. I knew he didn't mean to upset me, that he had things he wanted to figure out, but it felt like he was asking for space and that was the last thing I wanted. It was selfish and I didn't care. I wanted Theo West. Not just for one night. For good.

"I can get something myself," I answered, walking over to the cabinet that I knew his glasses were in. I filled it with ice water and took a sip before looking around him to see what was on the stove. "Are you making Thai?"

"It's your favorite."

The flutters kicked in instantly, swarming up in my chest and doing a happy dance. I tried hiding my smile behind my glass as I drank, but he saw it and winked.

"Sweet chili Thai pork, to be specific." He lifted the lid to the large pot and let me peer into the rice, pork, onion, and bok choy combo that had a hint of soy sauce mixed in.

"Smells delicious."

"Needed to prove my skills."

I rolled my eyes as I hopped up onto the counter beside the fridge and watched him. "You said you wanted to talk yesterday."

"I want to talk about a lot of things," he said, stirring dinner before covering it again and turning to me. "But first I want to know how your day was. You sounded tired when we talked earlier."

Staring down at my water, I fingered the little droplets of condensation gliding down the side. "I didn't sleep well last night. I felt bad about our argument."

He stepped up to me, spreading my legs slightly so his body could fit between them. "You have no reason to feel bad. What you said was true."

Wetting my bottom lip, I met his eyes. "I don't want this to stop because of other people. If I'm supposed to know my self-worth, I need to know that I'm worthy of getting the things I want regardless of what others think. That means you, Theo. I want you and I want people to know that." Before he could say anything like I knew he was about to, I held up my hand. "It isn't that I don't understand where you're coming from. I'm the young naïve girl in people's eyes. You're the older man who could have anybody he wants. I may not be in your shoes, but I'd like to think we're in this together. So, if you're going to stand there and tell me that you don't think this is appropriate, that *we're* not appropriate, then you're wrong."

An eyebrow quirked. "Am I, now?"

I nodded once. "Yes. You never crossed a line when I was younger. If anything, I crossed lines. I crushed on you and made no real effort to hide it. I mean, how many times did I say I was going to marry you?" That made me blush, but it was true. My mother would always laugh when she brought it up.

"Sweet Della, I think Theo is a bit old for you, but I'm sure he wouldn't find anybody as special even if he tried."

"You were five when you said that," he noted dryly. "Not sixteen. Plenty of children are known to tell adults that. Even their parents."

"Which brings me to my next point," I cut in, smiling. He looked amused, but let me go on without interrupting. "You think because you raised me, were my father figure, that people will take notice and be appalled or something. And will some people? Sure. But not all of them. Even if they were, it wouldn't matter. All that matters is how we feel about it. We're not related. We're not doing anything illegal. You and I are two consenting adults who...are fond of each other. We like each other's company. In a way, we're getting to know each other in a new light. Not as little Della and the man who raised her. As Adele and Theo.

"And it isn't like I'm asking to broadcast it or rent a billboard or anything. I'm not asking for much at all, Theo, just that you don't shut me out. Talk to me. Tell me what's bothering me so I can try helping. I may be younger, maybe not as wise, but that doesn't mean you have to struggle through this alone. In fact, you shouldn't. Having somebody in your life who cares about you, a partner, means that they're there for you when you need them. And I want that. I want to be there for you and for you to be there for me. Okay?

Can you do that? I promise I won't even try to hold your hand in public or maul you."

His lips tipped up at the corners as he rested a palm on my leg, his thumb caressing the skin. "You've had a lot of time to think about this, haven't you?"

Sheepishly, I shrugged. "Like I said, I couldn't sleep last night. All I could think about is what you said yesterday and how you'd give me a hundred excuses as to why we couldn't continue this. That meant I had to come up with a hundred reasons why we should. I can keep going if you'd like, but I think I made my point."

His responding sigh was heavy. "For the record, I'd love to hold your hand in public and let you maul me." My eyes widened. From what I knew, he never even did the PDA thing with his ex. That had to mean something. "And there's something I need you to know."

I waited impatiently, squirming in fear of what he'd say.

"I am *more* than just fond of you, Della. In fact, what I feel for you is stronger than I know what to do with. When I think about the past, it fucks with my head. I don't want to ruin this, but I don't want to admit that I won't sometimes see the long-haired little girl who would step on my shoes and beg me to dance. And I certainly don't want people to make your life hell more than they already have because I'm a selfish bastard for wanting you."

My body heated up over those words, specifically the last sentence. I wanted him to be a selfish bastard and I liked—*loved*—that he wanted me all for himself.

"Like I said, we're here for each other if the time comes."

He looked at me with those eyes that said, *when the time comes.*

And I knew he wasn't wrong, but one of us needed to be optimistic. If he was the realist, which I had no doubt he would be in this situation, then I wanted to be the person who looked on the bright side.

"So, who were you talking to yesterday that made you so angry?" I asked when he went back to stir dinner.

His shoulders drew back. "You know what?" Looking over his shoulder, he smiled at me, but it didn't reach his eyes. "I don't want to talk about it tonight. I just want to spend time with you. Is that okay?"

Even though I could tell there was something more on his mind, something to do with why he'd shown up at my building yesterday, I let it go. "You'll tell me eventually, though?"

His head bobbed once. I accepted it and swung my legs as he grabbed a couple plates and set them on the table. "I found a show I think you'd like. It's all about King Tut and his rule over Egypt."

He turned to me with drawn eyebrows. I sighed, relenting. "Okay, so maybe you won't like it, but I will. You've never been into those kinds of TV shows which I've never understood. They're so interesting."

His chuckle made me smile. "Like I told you before. I'll watch whatever you want, Della, I just want to spend some time with you."

"And what if that time was spent *not* watching television?" I asked carefully, gauging his reaction.

When his eyes darkened with lust, I knew he was fine with that idea too. I bit my bottom lip and watched him come over to me, planting his hands on either side of my body before leaning in until his lips nearly grazed mine. "You just had to say that didn't you? Get my cock hard just before dinner to make it uncomfortable to sit through."

I exhaled shakily, feeling dampness settle between my legs. "We could skip dinner."

He groaned, kissing me lightly and then drawing my bottom lip into his mouth. I wanted the kiss to go longer, deeper, but he didn't allow it. Instead, he drew back enough to rest his forehead against mine. "You need to eat, Della. So do I. But don't think I won't lay you down on that table afterwards and eat you out for dessert."

"*Theo.*"

His laugh was husky and deep. "You asked for it, sweetheart. I'm happy to oblige. Now get that perfect ass off my counter and help finish setting the table. Quicker we eat, quicker we can get naked."

I laughed and obeyed, yelping when his hand slapped my butt as I walked past him to grab the silverware.

I liked this version of Theo.

I hoped it lasted.

. . .

My body was content as I rolled my yoga mat up after another session. Today was exceptionally relaxing, something I needed since my muscles seemed to coil over the course of the week. I didn't know why because things were…good. Almost too good, like I was waiting for the shoe to drop and ruin everything.

Dinner at Theo's last week had led to kissing, heavy petting, and eventually sex. Good sex. The kind that made my toes curl just to think about. If there was one place I didn't think I'd have Theo besides my fantasy, it was inside me. And that was where he belonged and made sure I knew it. On the table. On his couch. He'd tired me out but sated me in a way that I still felt it deep in my soul.

I loved Theo West. I really did.

I felt Tiffany's eyes on me as I stood and collected my belongings. "We start on Saturday, you dreamy-eyed bitch."

I blinked. "Uh…?"

Her eyes rolled as she propped her mat under her arm and gestured toward the door. I adjusted my bag and followed her out, waving at a few people who said goodbye. I'd found solace again in coming to these classes. I had Tiffany to thank for that since she kept her word and dragged me out twice to ensure I wouldn't ditch even though I had no plans to. "You're going to come to my place Saturday morning. Your body is more limber, but we'll do the same warmups we used to in dance before we start anything just to make sure. You're out of practice, but I'll go easy on you."

"Tiff—"

"Nope." She grinned, bouncing to a stop with a cocky look on her face. "You're opening up and making progress. And whoever got between your legs is definitely helping with your moods because I know when people get some. You're glowing." My red face must have been amusing because she snorted. "Stop being all shy, nobody here is listening. I'm just saying, I might even be a little jealous. You've been smiley all week. It's kind of gross, but I'm happy for you. And I'm not blowing smoke up your ass about the progress you've made, I'm being real. I can tell you're not in your head as much. There's something lighter in your walk. You engage with more people when we're out instead of avoiding them. That's something, Della."

I wasn't sure about that, but I did try putting aside my problems when I was with my friends. Lately, that was Ren and Tiffany. We'd meet up on campus, help each other study, or grab something to eat at the Hut or some other eating establishment close by, before heading to one of Ren's games. Turned out, Tiffany loved sports. A lot. She yelled louder than I did when he hit a homerun. Then again, maybe it was just because her thoughts about Ren were much different than mine.

With finals right around the corner, I knew I needed to get my head in the game. That meant not worrying about what Theo was thinking when it came to us. Instead, I had to focus on passing Ribbons' class since I'd gotten a C- on my exam and making sure I proved to her I was more than my last name, *and* being Tiffany's puppet since she was adamant on me dancing with her. I wasn't sure why she was so keen on getting me to start again, but she promised she wouldn't pressure me to talk to Judith. I believed her, even if a part of me was hesitant. She'd proven to be a good friend, maybe even better than I offered her considering she didn't know a lot about me, but it was something.

Blowing out a breath, I relented to her demand because I knew I wouldn't have much else of a choice otherwise. "What time?"

She beamed. "Nine too early?" We both knew we'd had earlier days when we danced together at Judith's. "You have my address still, so just come on over. My studio is in the backyard. It's a converted pool house."

I blinked, sometimes forgetting she came from money. She didn't act like most other people did when their families were well off. Then again, had she ever? She always wanted to work as a cosmetologist, and the reason she didn't was probably because of how she was raised. It made me think about Sophie's lectures to me growing up.

"You don't need to work, darling. Just look at your mother. She stopped when she met your father." But she hadn't. My mother was a well-known interior designer who did leave her job, but it was to pursue charity work with non-profits. It kept her busy, busier than when she worked for a living.

I nodded. "Fine. But—"

"Nope. I'm not going to listen to self-doubt or

boring excuses. You've got this." I glared at her as she winked. "Oh, and we're going out tonight. Thank your boy toy for that, he kept bugging me to tell you about it."

"But—"

"What did I say?" she cut me off again, making me groan loudly. "Listen, since yoga was moved to today, that means we have all tomorrow to recover from a hangover. We both need to have fun."

She must have forgotten that Sunday brunches were a thing with Sophie. Tiffany couldn't stand my aunt, a lot of people couldn't. But unlike those people, Tiff didn't hide it.

"I don't want to go out and have fun." What I wanted was to sit in my living room with my favorite popcorn and binge watch new episodes of *Mysteries at the Museum* like the nerd I was. Maybe even text Theo. Okay, I was definitely doing that, even if part of me said to hold off. I liked seeing his texts first, knowing he was thinking of me. Like the one he sent this morning of him and Ramsay. He was making a face at the camera while the dog licked him, and all the caption said was *good morning from your two favorite men.*

My heart had melted a little right there on my kitchen floor while I grabbed a protein bar from my cupboard before leaving.

"Which is your problem." Her laugh drew people's attention, making me elbow her as we started toward the sidewalk. "I'm trying to be your friend, Della. Even

Ren said you needed to get out and enjoy yourself more."

I eyed her. "Since when do you and Ren talk when I'm not around?"

She shrugged. "He annoyed me at first, but he's grown on me like a fungus. Even though he called me a bitch."

Cringing, I shot her an apologetic look. He did call her that when they first met. And what did she do? Shrugged, said she'd been called worse, pulled out an apple from her backpack, and hung out with us at the Hut while we had coffee between classes.

"Yeah, sorry about that."

Tiffany snorted. "He's honest. Not a lot of guys are. Anyway, it isn't like we paint each other's nails and trade secrets about you. We just happened to exchange numbers and he told me that we were going out because you needed it."

That was a classy way of saying Ren needed to get out and find a new toy to play with, but I didn't tell Tiffany that. If they were friends now, she'd learn it soon enough. Unless… "Are you *into* Lawrence?"

She stopped walking, giving me a twisted face, but the apples of her cheeks were red. "No! I told you we're friends. *Just* friends."

I studied her for a moment before finally nodding. What else could I do? It wasn't really my business, even if they were both my friends. Whatever they chose to do was on them. "I was curious. I get it, trust me."

"What does that mean?"

Licking my bottom lip, I shot her a timid look with my own face flushed. "Ren and I…"

Her eyes widened. "What?" It came almost like a shriek that had me blushing harder in return.

Swiping a hand through my hair, I nodded and looked around us as we walked back to my building. "Yeah. We were teenagers. Experimenting, you know? He was my first."

"Were you his?"

"He says I was, but I have my doubts." It wasn't something I dwelled on anymore, but at the time I was a little hurt by it. Ren told me he wanted to share our firsts together for a long time, which made me think he'd been serious. But I saw how he acted around other girls at school, heard the talk and gossip from them. After we had sex, it felt like I was just another notch on his bedpost. I told myself it wasn't true. But now?

"You okay?" Tiffany's voice was quiet, considerate of my once scorned teenage feelings.

I gave her my best smile. "Yeah. It was a long time ago. I don't regret what happened between us. We're obviously still close and I trust him to be a great friend. Anything else? No. No offense to him, but he's…Ren."

We both laughed at that. Even though the three of us hadn't hung out for long, it didn't take much to get to know Ren and his ways. Did that make me love him any less? No. Like Tiffany, Ren was unapologetically himself. That was probably why they got along so well.

"When am I being forced to socialize?" I asked, holding the door open for her.

"He said he'd group text us."

Ren's group texts were over the top because he knew it annoyed me. He'd blow up everyone's phones if we weren't quick enough or because he was bored. Making a face, I headed toward the stairwell off to the side. Tiffany stopped me. "Can't we take the elevator for once? I'm lazy."

"You're the thesaurus's antonym of lazy. Come on. If I'm being forced out, then you have to suck it up and walk five flights with me as punishment."

The noise she made had me grinning as she followed behind me. "I don't understand why you're so terrified of elevators. Do you know the statistics of people actually getting trapped or dying in them?"

I paused. "No. Do you?"

"No, who do you think I am? Hermione? I figured your ridiculous fear would make you able to spit out some random fact about it."

I speared her with a look before admitting, "My mom was afraid of them too. I think it's drilled in my head by default."

She blinked. "Oh."

Shrugging, I ran my hand on the stairwell railing and let the silence fill the air as we made our way up to my floor. When I unlocked the door to my apartment, Tiffany followed me in quietly and turned as soon as the lock clicked back into place.

"What was it like?" she asked, making my brows draw up.

"What was what like?"

She hopped onto the counter, her legs dangling next to where my purse and keys rested beside her. "Your life after your mother passed. It had to be hard, but it seems like you grew up okay. Until...well, you know."

"My father got arrested?"

The sympathy on her face made me embarrassed. "You mentioned that your family was always close, so I can't imagine what it was like. I always took what the media said for its word, which was stupid. Everybody knows the media purposefully bends the real story."

"Why do you want to know?" I walked over to the fridge and grabbed a bottle of water for each of us. Passing one to her, I waited for an answer.

"You don't talk about it."

"I do." *Not to you.* I didn't see Ripley as much for therapy sessions, but at least once or twice a month I would make appointments and go talk to her. Sometimes she would call to check in, but I didn't always answer. I was doing well. Or, well enough. She knew it, and she knew if I really needed to, I'd call her in case of emergency. In case I... My hand went to my stomach, knowing the scar was still there on my skin.

Tiffany watched me with pinched brows until I caved. "It was hard. My mother meant the world to me, and as far as I know, she didn't know what my father did. The evidence showed he'd been involved with the state scandal for a long time and impacted a lot of people. I mean, how could my mom not know? She was a smart woman, Tiff."

"But you don't know that for sure."

"True, but I think about it all the time."

"Maybe you shouldn't," she reasoned. "I know you love your mom, so what good would it do to think she was involved in it if it changes how you feel? You can't change what happened."

She had a point. Ripley told me the same thing once upon a time, but it didn't stop me from thinking about it.

"I know."

"Your mother was a sweet person."

"I know, Tiffany."

"So…?"

Sitting on the stool beside her, I uncapped my water and took a sip. "I can't just say I'm not going to not think about it. That only makes me want to know the truth more."

"But you won't."

"I *know*."

She eyed me. "This is exactly why we need alcohol. You won't think about it when you're filled with tequila."

My stomach churned. "No tequila."

"Boring."

"You're bor—" My phone rang, making me glance down at the screen to see Sophie's name on the screen.

"Oh." Tiffany jumped down. "I'm going to wash up and change if that's cool with you. Good luck with that." She knew I wasn't that close with my aunt, so she walked away to give me privacy.

"Hi, Sophie."

"Adele," she greeted. "I was reaching out about tomorrow. Lydia said she was going to be in town and wanted to join us for our brunch."

Lydia rarely did that, so it perked me up. Though, I wasn't sure why she was telling me. "I would love to see her. It's been a while." A while meaning my father's funeral.

"Oh. Well, I'm glad then."

Why did she sound like she wasn't? "Is there something wrong? I know you aren't close to Lydia, but —"

"Oh, stop. Who says I'm not?"

My lips parted to list the amount of times she'd made it clear that her half-sister was just that. Half. As in, not her full responsibility. Lydia and my father were the closest of the three of them because he didn't treat her different.

"You know what, don't answer that." Her voice was tight. She knew what she'd done to her sister over the years, I didn't need to tell her. "So, normal time then? There's a lot to catch up on I'm sure."

I wanted to ask her why she never tried to get along with her sister. Half or not, they shared blood. They lived together. Lydia's mother wasn't alive, so she understood my life better than anybody. Sophie? Not so much, and she never tried pretending she did.

"Same time. And Sophie?"

She hummed.

I debated on asking her what I never did about Lydia and her, but I chickened out when I saw Tiffany walk out of the bathroom with her hair down and a brow arched at me. "Never mind. I'll see you two tomorrow."

When I hung up, I frowned at my phone before setting it down.

"How's the Dictator?" Tiff asked, drinking the water I'd given her.

"I wish you'd stop calling her that," I grumbled, even if she weren't totally wrong. "She means well. Most of the time."

Tiffany was disbelieving, but she didn't say anything about it. Instead, she moved on. "I think you need another makeover. At least temporarily for the night." Making a face, I began trying to convince her otherwise when she shook her head. "It's a night out to not think. We both might as well look good doing it."

Scoffing, I said, "Like you have any trouble looking good even on your worst days. I remember when you came to dance with the flu and you still looked hot."

"I looked like Rudolph."

"A sexy Rudolph."

She laughed. "Agree to disagree. But don't act like you don't look good daily either. Just because you don't think so doesn't mean it's not true. Guys turn their heads when you walk into a room."

I frowned. "Because of what happened."

"Because you're beautiful, Della."

Lips parting, I debated my answer. Throat thick, I said, "We'll agree to disagree."

We just stared at each other.

. . .

THE FLORAL PERFUME was the first sign that both my aunts were already here. Lydia loved lavender and lilac and she always smelled like fresh-cut flowers and summertime. It was both her and my father's favorite season, and my father always admitted he loved lilac which was why I'd give him candles in that scent every year for his birthday even when people poked fun of him because of it.

I saw Sophie before my absentee aunt, her body rigid in the seat, one leg crossed over the other like how she always sat. When I walked further into the room, Lydia came into view. She was the opposite of Sophie and my father—light hair like mine, light eyes like her brother, and a fuller face unlike Sophie and my father's defined jawlines. She didn't sit with as much tightness, but casually with her hands resting on the arms of the chair whereas Sophie's were on her lap.

"You're late," Sophie stated, standing up and flattening out her dress. "The food was ready fifteen minutes ago."

Lydia looked from her sister to me, a kind smile on her face. She didn't wear much makeup, usually some light lipstick and mascara. "Hello, Della."

I walked over to her as she stood and gave her a tight hug. It was like the one she'd given me before dropping me off at home after my father's funeral. Her arms had held me as our tears soaked into the other's shoulders. I absorbed her warmth, her floral scent, and the memories we shared as I grew up. She was around a lot more when I was younger, always bringing me

255

presents and telling me stories about my father when they were my age.

"Hi, Aunt Lydia." I drew back first, squeezing her hands. "I was so happy when Sophie told me you were coming. I'm sorry I'm late." Looking at Sophie, I nodded once. "I was a bit…out of it this morning."

Out of it. Hungover. It was all the same. Tiffany made Ren and I do two rounds of lemon drop shots at the bar before ordering our own drinks. After Kat, Sam, and Gina walked into Divers and made a point to stare at me the entire night, that turned into two more drinks, one more round of tequila shots, and one glass of water that barely helped when I woke up this morning. I was tempted to go to Denny's for something greasy. I wasn't sure why, but the way Kat and Sam looked at me had me uneasy the entire night, like they were talking, plotting. I debated on saying something to Kat, asking how she was, but the last encounter we had didn't go very well and I didn't want her bringing up her departing gift. That gift that was still buried in the inside pocket of my purse.

"I heard about your outing from Monica Anderson this morning. She just loved telling me about how close you seemed with her daughter these days."

Tiffany's mother? "I wasn't aware you two talked." Last I knew, Monica and Sophie couldn't stand each other. Then again, Sophie didn't get along with most of the dance moms. Or other women. I believed my father liked to describe her as 'catty'.

"About important things."

Lydia cleared her throat. "How about we eat before the food gets cold?"

"Colder," Sophie corrected, directing her focus on me with arched brows. Disapproval was a look tattooed on her face when it came to me. It made me itch.

I followed my aunts into the dining room where food was resting in its normal spots. The selection was larger today considering Lydia was vegan, something I was sure Sophie complained about to the people preparing the menu.

After grabbing what we wanted, Lydia turned to me. "I bet you're excited to be almost done with school. How much longer do you have?"

I sipped my water. "A couple weeks of classes then a week of finals. Some of my courses are allowing students to be exempt from the exams if we have an A before finals week though."

"Then you should be set," Sophie commented.

Shifting in my seat, I admitted, "A few of my grades have dropped since...things have happened." As soon as the words left my lips, I could see Sophie's eyes widen. "But they're not bad. I'm still well over a 3.0 grade point average which is what I need to keep my scholarship."

"You mean the scholarship the school awarded you following the one you lost for dropping dance?"

Heat raised up the back of my neck like tiny pinpricks.

Lydia murmured, "Sophie."

"What?" My other aunt asked. "It was a simple

question. Adele got into that school because of her abilities, but she nearly got kicked out because she decided to stop dancing. It was a silly risk. I'm stating a fact."

"It wasn't," I argued quietly. "And I didn't almost get kicked out. I would have applied for loans if I needed to, but they offered me an alternative academic scholarship considering my grades."

Sophie dabbed her lips with a linin napkin. "I don't see why you'd need either. I told you I could help pay for school given the circumstances. Your father would have but…"

I swallowed. "Yes, well, I told you I didn't need the help. I was raised to do things on my own, which is why I denied his help too."

Sophie didn't say anything else, but Lydia smiled to herself as she poked at her food. She jumped in after a few awkward moments of silence. "I hate to bring it up, but there was a reason I wanted to come and talk to you both today."

Sophie's eyes rolled. "Shocking."

I eyed her for a moment when she wasn't looking before glancing back at Lydia with interest. Whatever was on her mind was serious because she had a sheepish look on her face.

"What is it?" I asked lightly.

Setting her fork down, she looked at both of us before sighing. "I was reached out to by a reporter from The Times. They have new information regarding your father, Della."

My heart dropped. "What?"

Sophie set her napkin down. "How on earth could they still be digging up information on him? It's done."

It's done. Those two words were so final that they hurt. I wasn't sure I wanted to believe them, even if she was partly right. It'd been months since he was buried, why would the press be reaching out to anybody? And why Lydia?

I was hesitant when I asked, "What did they want?"

Sophie shook her head. "Does it really matter, Adele? Whatever they say can't be any good, especially not for us."

Lydia disregarded her sister's comment and focused solely on me. "He said there was a list being published of the names of the people Anthony stole from. Apparently, it's extensive."

We already knew that my father had harmed a lot of people, but during the trial it was considered sealed evidence so nobody could be named publicly. Speculation buzzed in the city, in certain social circles, about something like this coming to light. But after so many months, I figured it was over.

"Why now?" I whispered, frowning.

Lydia reached over and took my hand. "I can only think that they want to give victims justice in a way that outs Anthony. I'm sorry, Della, I know how hard this has to be for you."

"For all of us!" Sophie said abruptly. "I can't believe they're going to put our name out there again. It isn't right."

How can she even say that? "What about the people

259

he hurt, Sophie?" I questioned, staring at her with unblinking eyes. She gaped at me. "It isn't fair for them."

"They were given hefty sums of money for compensation. Some more than they lost after Anthony was convicted. Why do you think they took everything from you?"

Jaw ticking, I pushed my plate away. "I don't like the thought of Dad's name being in the papers again either, but we can't ignore the people, his *victims*, that deservingly put him there."

"You act like he was a murderer," Sophie scoffed at me.

I didn't have the energy to argue with her, so I turned to Lydia. "What else did this reporter say? Did he mention when they were going to publish it?"

"Tomorrow."

I blinked. Tomorrow. That was...soon.

"We'll sue." That came from Sophie.

"We have no grounds," Lydia told her calmly, being the voice of reason that I couldn't be. "These things were bound to happen."

Angered, Sophie stood. "But why? Anthony is dead for Christ's sake! It isn't like he can hurt them any further."

Closing my eyes, I felt her words like a stab straight through the heart. Why did she have to be cruel? Even if it were true, she didn't need to be so abrupt about it.

"No," Lydia agreed, "but that doesn't mean the truth can't still come out. Plenty of people have demanded documents be made public since the trial ended."

"He wanted money, didn't he? The reporter. He must have asked for something in return to make the story go away."

I cracked my eyes open to see what Lydia's reaction was. She looked pale, sad, and a mixture of other things I could relate to. "I'm sorry, but no. He wanted me to know because of my relationship with Anthony."

"Relationship," Sophie repeated, walking away from the table with a hand on her temple like she had a headache. "So, what? He gave you a heads up out of pity? If that were the case, why didn't he call Adele or me? Hmm?"

Lydia was quiet.

I shook my head. "It doesn't matter now. These are going to come out one way or another, so why argue?"

Sophie said, "Because it's ridiculous!"

Lydia squeezed my hand.

"It's not," I whispered.

Sophie cut her gaze to me in disbelief. "I can't believe you're willing to let this family go through more shame. Between you and your father, I swear—"

I paled at her words, which caused her to stop short. The lump in my throat grew as embarrassment, shame, and a million other negative things crashed into me.

Lydia glared at her sister. "That's enough. Don't you think she's gone through a lot already? The last thing any of us needs is to create more problems. We're supposed to be supporting each other."

"That's rich coming from you," Sophie scoffed at her. "You only show up to be the bearer of bad news. When was the last time we saw you? That's right. Anthony's funeral. Convenient that you only come when you see fit." Sophie stepped toward me. "Adele, I didn't mean anything by what I said. I'm just angry." Yet, she didn't apologize. A classic Sophie move. It was like she was allergic to saying sorry or having any true semblance of guilt for anything she did.

Lydia sighed again and said, "I know this is going to be hard for *everyone* which is why we need to stick together."

I wondered how that would work since the two of them didn't exactly have a relationship in the first place. "What do you think will happen after the list is published? Those people were given their money back."

"Not all of them," Lydia admitted. "There were a few that received nothing, or very little compared to what they lost. Your father had already had a lot of assets tied up elsewhere, and the property and belongings the state sold to compensate didn't cover everything."

"Could they come after us?" Sophie wondered aloud, panic in her eyes.

I swallowed. "They can't...can they?"

Sophie held her hands up. "I'm calling my lawyer. This needs to be nipped in the bud before it gets out of hand again. We all know how the press can be and how it can...impact people."

Another reference to me and my reaction last time.

I'd lost it, but I wished she didn't bring it up, indirectly or not. It was bad enough I had to live with my breakdown, the last thing I needed was my family reminding me when they got upset.

It made me want to yell, but I knew it wouldn't do any good. Stomach hurting, I stood and ignored the food and growing headache pounding in my skull. "I think I should get going."

Lydia frowned. "You didn't eat."

"Not hungry."

Sophie glanced at me with worry etched in her eyes. "Adele, you should really try eating something. There's plenty of food."

I knew why she was pushing. "I'm not going to relapse," I told them both firmly. "So, you can drop the act."

Sophie looked doubtful, but Lydia gave me an encouraging smile and head nod. That was another difference between them. Lydia cared. It was in her nature to. But Sophie? She only cared if it benefited her.

"Perhaps you should call one of your friends," Lydia suggested. "Or Theo? You're still close, aren't you?"

I licked my lips. "He's been busy. But maybe I'll call Ren."

Sophie spoke up again. "What about one of the girls you used to be close with? Katrina and you were nearly inseparable once upon a time. Remember that?"

"We're not anymore."

"I heard —"

"You hear a lot of things," I snapped. "It doesn't make it true. Kat and I aren't friends anymore. She isn't..." Lifting a shoulder, I pushed my chair in and exhaled slowly. "Kat isn't who she used to be, and I don't want to be part of what she and the others are into."

"They've gone through a lot too," Sophie pointed out as if I didn't already know.

I did something I never had before. I let go of my anger that'd been boiling up inside me that'd been ready to blow for a long time. "Well, none of their fathers went to prison where they got beaten to death, now did they?"

Sophie gasped.

Lydia winced.

I walked out.

It was bad enough remembering that the girl I'd been close with, the one who I'd shared secrets with and planned a future with like we'd still be best friends when we were older, had changed. She didn't care that her father had almost gone to prison because he didn't. Mine did. Mine took the brunt of the fall and all the blame. Did Katrina care? Did she even reach out when news of his death went viral? No. She was too busy escaping into a world of drugs and men to be a friend. A *real* friend. So, I wanted nothing to with her, Samantha, or Gina because they were all the same.

Fake.

Every single one of them was fake.

. . .

MY FINGERNAILS WERE non-existent from biting them the following day, waiting for the news to break. Sophie had called, I'd ignored it. Lydia called too, and I *almost* considered taking it. When Theo had come by my apartment, I finally did what I kept getting scolded for —checked the peephole...then pretended I wasn't home.

I'd felt a little bad because I knew Ramsay was with him, but Theo did perfectly fine taking care of him. Ramsay preferred it. Plus, Theo couldn't come to my rescue every time I needed him. That wasn't fair to him.

I'd been confused when the rest of the week passed, and nothing happened. No online article. No breaking news alerts. The breath I'd been holding had released when Saturday came around. I knew I couldn't keep hiding in fear of what the media would say. If they weren't swarming my building, it meant something happened to the story. Maybe Lydia had been wrong. Maybe the reporter just wanted to scare us, which worked.

I showed up at the address Tiffany gave me around eight-thirty. My body was clothed in leggings and a loose workout shirt, the sleeveless gap under my arms showing off the bright sports bra underneath. I knocked on the door and waited with my leg bouncing, not sure what to expect.

Today would be the first day I danced, *really* danced, in way too long. I wasn't expecting Tiffany to go easy on me either, even if she promised to. Her version of easy and mine were two completely different things. So,

I'd only eaten half a protein bar after I woke up early following another poor night's sleep. The bags under my eyes were a dead giveaway of the insomnia I'd been experiencing since my anxiety decided to come back in full swing since Sunday brunch.

When the door opened, I was greeted by Tiffany and not somebody who worked for her family like I expected. I remembered Sophie telling me that the Anderson's used to have staff around the house often — a cook, housekeeper, and a caterer for the events they hosted. I didn't remember coming to any here, though I was sure my parents had at some point given Tiffany's father's role as a well-known judge in the city. If memory served, my father had hoped that he'd be given his case, but I was sure that would have been a conflict of interest which was why he had nothing to do with the trial.

"Are you going to come in or what?" Tiffany asked, gesturing behind her. "I can give you a tour if you want, but there's nothing exciting to see besides the basics."

I followed her inside and looked around the huge foyer. It was all neutral tones but nothing extravagant. It was…pretty. Something I could picture myself in someday, just maybe in a smaller version, this looked like it was a three-story home.

"That's okay," I told her, walking into the kitchen where she had two refillable water bottles ready on the counter.

After she passed me one, she nodded toward the back door.

"It's just us here right now, so nobody should bother us." When she pushed open the door of a much smaller building, my eyes widened. The hardwood floor was gorgeous, but it was the wall of mirrors across from us that had my full attention. "My parents agreed to renovate this place into my private studio if I kept out of trouble. It's not that hard to do considering I usually avoid most people anyway."

She set her water down by the wall and turned to me. I was still staring at the massive wall of mirrors that reflected my shell-shocked expression. Tiffany snapped her fingers in front of my face, gaining my attention back.

"We'll start easy. You look like crap today anyway." Pointing toward the center of the floor she waved me over and dropped down on the hardwood to begin stretching her legs.

Hesitating, I sat beside her and started mimicking the familiar warmup. We did it in silence for a few minutes, my eyes glancing around the white room that had a lot of natural light from the large windows. There were speakers in each corner and an expensive looking stereo off to the side.

When she said she was ready, she hopped up and rolled her neck before producing a remote from who knew where and turned some music on. It wasn't what I expected though.

"Hip hop?"

She grinned. "I never said we'd do ballet, did I?

This is way more fun. Don't tell my mother I said that though."

I made a face. "Do you do this often?"

She snorted. "Yes. Now, quit stalling and watch my feet." Before I could say anything else, she did an eight-count sidestep, her knees bouncing through each move matching the instrumental in the background until she transferred to a step and tap where her feet went out to the sides on another eight count. I studied her carefully, noticing the slide of her feet in the third move as her hands went out like she was pushing something away.

Shoulders tightening, I got beside her and watched her feet work the moves again. There were three, all on the same count, which made it easier considering I'd been used to the measure. But the moves I used to do were slower, based more on balance and flexibility. I should probably be happy she wasn't making me do ballet considering I'd barely gotten my balance back from yoga.

When I joined in with her, I managed to mess up the second move and counted wrong on the third one. She snorted when she saw my mistake, standing in front of me and counting my footwork. "No, no. And what are you doing with your arms? You look like they're tied to your sides."

I stopped moving and glared. "I'm not used to this. Judith normally—"

"I'm not Judith," she pointed out. "Come on, it's not that hard. You need to get into the music. Wait for the next chorus and then start again. Bounce each step and use your hands to clap with every count if you need to. Then, with the second one, stay on your toes instead of flattening your foot. It'll help you move faster so you don't go offbeat." She showed me what she was talking about by giving me a sideview of her sneakered feet.

The second time was better, the three moves melding together even if I was slower than the song. It was when she introduced three more moves that was supposed to build off the first set that had me frustrated over the stiffness in my body. The way she stopped me gave me flashbacks to some of my first dance classes with Judith. That woman was tough—nightmare worthy, even. I remembered some days when I begged my mother not to go because I didn't want to be yelled at. It was my mother who told me I would be fine because I was a natural.

"Ms. Judith can't scare you if you don't let her, sweet Della. You're made for this."

It was thirty minutes in when I called a water break and watched as Tiffany moved across the floor to a different song. Unlike me, she faced the mirrors and watched herself, her hips bouncing along, her booty kicking out, and her legs gliding across the hardwood with the squeak of her shoes. She had serious moves and a flawless rhythm down to the music.

I wiped off my mouth. "How long have you been doing this?"

Tiffany turned to face me, wiping off her forehead before shrugging. "A long time. I've always been interested in more contemporary dance but was always trained in classical and ballet. My obsession really started after we did Swan Lake. I saw a video online of a hip-hop version. Like a mashup, you know? I thought it looked cool, so I taught myself the steps. I never stopped after that."

"If you prefer contemporary, why not make the switch? Is it because of your parents?"

Her shoulder lifted. "Partly. It isn't like I hate ballet, I just feel more in tune with contemporary. It's like my body feeds from the energy that the moves make. Plus, it's easier not to pick fights with my mother about these things. Choose your battles and all that."

My lips twitched. "Does she know you dance to this? She'd probably be impressed if she saw the way you moved."

The noise that rose from the back of her throat told me I was wrong. "We don't all have the same kind of mother you did, Della. Mine is all about the competition just like most of the other dance moms. The more publicity, the better."

I cringed. "Publicity isn't everything." My mind went back to the article that was missing in action. It made me itch, anticipating the worst like it was coming at any second. I should have taken Lydia's calls and asked what she knew, but if she really wanted to tell me she would have left a message instead of sending Theo after me like I suspected.

Something smacked my face. I frowned at the hair tie that had bounced off me and onto the floor before looking back up at Tiffany. "You suck at paying attention today. What's up? Is it the mirrors, because I'm trying to teach you stuff that doesn't require a lot of turning. I mean, we're going to learn some songs that we'll practice in front of them but not today. Baby steps."

I shook my head. "I appreciate that, but it doesn't have to do with dance. Although, you're kicking my ass. I knew it wouldn't be easy getting back into this, but learning how to work my body to all new music is…"

Tiffany cracked a grin. "Finally, something I'm better at than you," she teased. "So, if it's not dance, then what?"

"I really don't—"

"You've avoided both Ren and me for days. I was shocked you even texted me last night confirming today. I was sure I'd have to come to your place and drag you out by your hair. Did you even go to class this week?"

I rolled my eyes and set my water back down against the wall beside hers. "It's family stuff. Things at brunch last weekend didn't go like I'd hoped. And, yes, I went to class." Well, I'd gone to Ribbons. I couldn't have her hating me more by skipping, no matter how much I had wanted to. The way she'd watched me throughout class had been unnerving, like she knew something. I'd made a run for the door as soon as time was up, and I was sure that made her day.

Tiffany's brows arched in silent inquiry. I weighed my options, going back and forth on whether to tell her what was happening. I needed to talk to somebody about it because my next appointment with Ripely wasn't for another week. I'd probably explode by then.

So, I told her what Lydia said about the reporter. How Sophie blew up. What I was worried about. Tiffany never interrupted once or even looked like she pitied me. Though her eyes softened a little when I admitted that I didn't want my name included in another smear campaign. I'd felt bad saying that out loud because it made me feel as selfish as Sophie, but it was true. I'd barely slept all week. My appetite was gone, and I had to force myself to eat what little I had. Stress was reverting me back to old habits and I felt myself slipping.

"Damn," she breathed. "That's rough, Della. But if the article didn't come out, maybe the reporter decided not to add more fuel to the fire? It's happened before."

It happened before because people were paid off. While I wouldn't be surprised if Sophie had opened her checkbook to continue the silence, I wasn't sure if that was why.

"Do you think other people have the list too or was it some exclusive with The Times?" she wondered aloud.

I shrugged. "Anything is possible, but if more than one paper had it then it probably would have been published by now. Which means…"

"Somebody influenced the guy."

I nodded.

Tiffany thought about it for a second before brushing it off. "Maybe it's better that way. It means your family doesn't have to go through more shit, right?"

Right. Except if somebody paid the reporter off, that made us no better than what Professor Ribbons and hundreds of other people thought about us already. That didn't settle well with me.

"Enough of that. Time for me to kick your ass some more. Maybe in a few months you'll actually be able to move your body without looking like something is stuck up your ass."

I eyed her. "Gee, thanks."

She winked. "Try to loosen your body up, Della. Every dance has a story behind it, right? We learned that with ballet. Those moves were focused heavily on one emotion. We need to find your story in this music."

I frowned in doubt but didn't argue with her about it when she restarted the music. By the end of the two hours we spent in the studio, I'd done a one-eighty turn with my hip out only to land face on with the mirrors.

Swallowing, I forced myself to stare, to really look at the girl whose shoulders were weighed down with the weight of the world. I wondered what story she had to tell, what could be told with my feet and music instead of my hands and paint. It wasn't until a towel smacked me in the face that I broke the stare and turned to Tiffany.

…and I laughed.

chapter fourteen

THEO

"DID YOU DO AS I ASKED?"

The dark-haired man across from me put one ankle over his opposite knee. "Have I ever let you down before? Shit, West, you padded my account for life with this job."

Scoffing, I leaned forward and rested my arms on the edge of my desk. He wasn't wrong. Dallas got a hefty sum for looking into Richard Pratt. He'd proven to be helpful when I'd asked him to do the same with other people in the past, so I knew he could be trusted.

"I could take some back, if you'd like."

Dallas grinned. "I didn't say I was miserable with

the dollar amount to my name. It definitely helps the family now that we've expanded it."

Ah. The baby. "How is Cody doing?"

"Happiest little thing I've ever seen." He seemed lost in thought, a wide smile on his face that made me stare at him a little longer than normal to figure out the emotions—contentment, peace. I couldn't see how a screaming newborn could give a man that, but he was happier than I'd seen him in all the years he's worked for me. My face twisted when he said, "You ever consider having a family of your own someday? Settling down?"

I eyed him. "We're not here to talk about me, are we?"

His chuckle was light. "No, I suppose we're not. However, we are here to talk about Richard Pratt, who just so happens to have a lot of dirt on one Adele Saint James. Seems like he's after her for a reason."

"And your point?"

Dallas raised his hands. "I'm just saying, you care about her. Adele has always been a sweet girl. It's hard not to care for somebody like her, which means it's easy to see who to go after when the time is right."

"What does he have on her?"

"More like her family," he admitted, pulling something out of his jacket pocket. "A list of names associated with the Saint James scandal."

"The people he stole from?"

A head nod.

Passing it to me, I glimpsed over the names. Some

were more familiar than others. "I should ask how you got this, but I'm not sure I care. What I want to know is what The Dick plans to do with it."

His lips twitched. "Well, I'd have to explain how I got it in order to tell you what his plans were."

I waited impatiently.

Another chuckle. "There's a reporter named Nicholas McAllister. He works for The Times and has a long-lasting relationship with some well-off families. Pratt being one of them, naturally."

Swiping my jaw, I set the list down and tapped it. "He was going to publish this." It wasn't a question. In fact, it was something Pratt would do, which was unsurprising to me.

Dallas bobbed his head once. "You remember those reports from when the trial first started? The reporter is the same one on the bylines from back then. Nick McAllister. What's convenient about those articles was that none of them painted Murphy in a bad light, or anybody else who was suspected. It was all—"

"Anthony Saint James," I concluded. Scrubbing my jaw, I sat back. "I take it the reporter is on Pratt's payroll then. Murphy and Pratt were known to be friends. Their kids practically grew up together." The Dick always put his business where it didn't belong and acted like an ally at his convenience. Knowing Adele danced with a lot of the kids of families in the same social circles made making connections easier, especially if somebody needed a fallback guy like Anthony was.

Dallas nodded along. "Yet, the Saint James family is

who is being targeted. Anthony can't be taken down any further than he already was, but Adele…"

My jaw ticked. "Why her? Why now?"

His head tilted. "I think we both know the answer to that, boss. Richard knows where your loyalty lies and it's not with him, or else you would've had him as a partner by now at IM. The more I dug into Pratt, the more I saw his investments in businesses outside his area of expertise. He's in it with Murphy, which means—"

"He paid off the reporter to make Murphy owe him," I said, rolling it around in my brain. It made sense. He all but threatened to do the same with me, except I wasn't involved in the lives that he and a few others were. Unlike Anthony, I kept my nose clean. I kept my social circle small. Non-existent. The most he had on me was my aching dick that always stood to full attention whenever Della was around these days. Not necessarily comparable in the grand scheme of drugs, money laundering, and a fuck ton more that I refused to even acknowledge given their nature.

"This reporter, McAllister, did you speak to him directly?"

Dallas rested his hands on his stomach as he got comfortable in the chair. "Persuaded him to give me the list himself, but I'd put my money on it not being the only copy."

"And what did he say about Richard?"

"Very little."

I figured as much. "Presumably, Pratt has another

copy of the list. Wouldn't be surprised if it makes the news yet. Did he say anything about other outlets getting it?"

"No. But…" Dallas shifted slightly. "I confirmed the reason he reached out to Lydia Saint James. McAllister has a soft spot for her. Apparently the two used to be cozy once upon a time, which is probably the only reason he agreed to meet me after I reached out."

My laugh was dry. "Did this asshole honestly think he had a chance? If he was going to release the list, then that would ruin any hope for him and Lydia. She loved her brother." How did they know each other anyway? Lydia didn't live in the city. She kept her distance from the lifestyle because of how people lived. I didn't blame her. Some days, I wished I'd done the same.

Shaking my head, I stood and turned to look out the window that showcased the city skyline. "Money talks more than anything else, I suppose. It's always worked that way."

"I don't think he was doing this just because of money," he commented hesitantly.

Shoving my hands in my pockets, I looked at him skeptically. "Then what? Why would a reporter who has a sweet spot for Lydia go after her niece? They might not be close, but he would have to know he'd be fucked if Lydia found out what he'd been doing behind her back. Hell, if she finds out he was part of the reason the media decided Anthony's guilt, she probably wouldn't forgive him."

His tongue swiped across his bottom lip, his eyes

not quite meeting mine. Whatever he knew, he didn't want to tell me.

"What is it, Dallas?" I growled at him.

His shoulders tensed. "He didn't outright tell me this, but I think he's afraid of Pratt. He alluded to him getting into deeper things than we knew. Everybody knows the guy blackmails people to do his dirty work, but McAllister made it seem like he'd lost control."

My body went rigid. "How so?"

"Again, this wasn't something he told me directly. I think he was too scared to—"

"Out. With. It."

"I have reason to believe that Richard Pratt was involved with the murder of Anthony." He paused to evaluate my expression, which turned cold in an instant. I straightened to full height with my jaw locked so tight it hurt. "Listen, there were a lot of phone records at Rikers Island between Anthony and his lawyer leading up to his death. It was an abnormal amount which meant they probably had a lot to talk about. Things that Richard and others might not have wanted out."

"He was going to list names of conspirators."

One of Dallas's shoulders lifted. "It's probable. Hell, word around the district attorney's office was that Saint James was never supposed to be transferred to Rikers in the first place."

My brows furrowed. "What?"

"I don't know how much truth is in it, but apparently he was supposed to go to Lincoln. The fact that he went to one of the most notorious prisons known for its brutality says a lot that backs up McAllister's fear. It was in his eyes, Theo. The man knew not to cross Pratt. Makes sense if you think about it. Pratt has a hand in just about any business you could imagine. If he went too far, he probably doesn't know how to quit and wasn't about to let Anthony talk."

I let that soak in for a moment, my anger rising higher and higher until I was sure my face was red, and steam threatened to billow out of my ears. "It was a set up," I murmured in realization, cursing, and scrubbing a palm down my face. "If Pratt hired somebody on the inside to take down Anthony so he wouldn't talk about co-conspirators in the scandal, nobody would think twice about his death because of how many fatalities the prison has in an average week."

All Dallas did was nod with a grim look on his face.

I cursed again before dropping down into my chair and exhaling heavily. "Adele can't find out about this yet. Do you understand me?"

"Yes, sir." There was a pause as I stared down at the list of names. "I've been keeping your secrets for a long time. If you don't mind me saying so…"

He captured my attention enough for me to glare at him. If he was going to threaten me, he chose a bad time to do it. But as soon as I met his eyes, I realized that wasn't what he was doing. Dallas was a good man. How many times had Della told me that? They'd talked often on their drives together. She knew more about the man than I did, and he'd been under my employment for a long ass time.

"You two have always been good together, willing to push the other. When I said that you cared for Adele, I didn't mean it in a bad way. Look at all you've done for her. Hell, you keep me on payroll to drive her around even though she rarely uses the services."

"Because she thinks you're Sophie's employee," I pointed out. That and Della hated having a driver when she could walk places. Anything that reminded her of the privilege she was born into was something she distanced herself from. I respected it, even if it pissed me off she walked on foot or called fucking Uber instead of using Dallas. "It doesn't matter what your opinion is anyway."

"No?" His brows go up. "At the risk of losing the money you gave me, I'd like to disagree with you. If my opinion favors whatever you two are doing, don't you think others will too? You're torturing yourself by thinking worst case scenario to keep her at a distance, but that's only hurting both of you."

I glowered. "What do you know?"

Amusement danced in his eyes as he stood, buttoning the jacket of his suit. "I'd say a lot considering you've paid me to keep an eye on her for all these years. She's a good girl. Smart. But she's hurting. Hurting real bad, sir. Always has been, but it's gotten worse the last couple of weeks. Not to step out of line, but she reminds me of what she was like...before. When things got tough, that is. She's a ghost of herself when I take her places, like her friend's house."

Dallas was a lot of things, and truthful was always

one. It was why I kept him on my payroll, always offering him bonuses for doing things beyond what he signed up for. Digging. Investigative work. When he signed the contract, it was to look after Adele. Drive her. Keep an eye out to ensure she was safe. Despite her not using the car much, they did form somewhat of a friendship. Normally that would have pissed me off, especially because Dallas is younger than me. Hell, he has a lot more going for him than I do married or not. But I knew better than to think Della would do anything with him because of the ring on his finger. I knew she wouldn't do anything because of me. And maybe that was the problem. I was forty. Angry. Divorced. Bitter at the world. What the fuck could I offer her other than misery and sage advice when the moment called for it? I gave her one moment to make her choice, a spontaneous decision that led to more. And I wanted even more than that.

I *needed* that night and all the fucking moments that came after.

Her scent.

Her pleas.

Her body.

Her heart.

But part of me didn't want her to know that because I was going to drag Della down with me, drowning her in the blanket of misery my mind led to even when I was happiest with her. It was inevitable. But us? Fuck. Weren't we inevitable too? Wasn't that what was building?

"Do me a favor," I told him. "Get me a meeting with McAllister. One on one. Somewhere private. He and I have a lot to discuss."

"Are you sure that's wise?" he doubted.

I stared at the list of names in front of me again before pulling out a carton of cigarettes from my desk and lighting one up between my lips. "Not at all. But I have nothing to lose."

We both knew that was a lie though.

He watched me for a moment longer before turning to the door, one hand on the knob as he hesitantly said, "I'll do it, but consider what it could mean for everyone else."

Della came to mind as I absorbed the nicotine my lungs demanded. I'd told her countless times I'd quit—that I'd try. But I also told her I'd be there for her whenever she needed me.

I was a fucking liar.

chapter fifteen

DELLA

ONE, *two, three, four, five, si*—

"Crap," I hissed, stumbling on my feet on the second turn. Sweat dripped down my forehead as I waited for the right note to drop before starting again. Without Tiffany, the stress wasn't nearly as bad, but suddenly the determination to get it right was tenfold.

My mother always used to tell me I was too strong headed for my own good. *"It's your strongest trait and your biggest downfall, sweet Della."*

How many times did she tell me it was okay not to be perfect? I knew I wasn't better than everyone, even if there were people in my life who thought I was. Lips twitching, I swiped at my skin and rested my hands on

284

my hips while trying to catch my breath. For a microsecond, I'd been glad she wasn't here to witness what I was putting myself through, but that feeling quickly diminished and was replaced with guilt, shame, and mourning.

What the hell was wrong with me?

Bending to grab my water, I startled when I saw a tall, broad figure at the doorway watching me. *Theo.*

"That was…" He leaned against the doorjamb with his hands in his pockets. "I haven't seen you move like that before. I like it."

It was hard to swallow knowing he saw me screw up. "I messed up."

I was hyperaware of my bare stomach showcasing my hideous scar. The workout pants I wore were low on my hips, which meant it was out there for anybody to see if they barged in. I'd shed my shirt an hour ago and was left in a red sports bra and black leggings. I'd noticed muscles coming back into my legs that had disappeared after I called it quits, muscles that Judith called dancers legs. They were toned but petite until I'd filled out after my stress eating, turning into my own personal nightmare.

I'd been practicing at Tiffany's when she at Judith's at least three times a week. More if I really needed to escape, whether that was at my apartment, here, or the warehouse, succumbing to the burn of my muscles and lungs as I pushed harder and harder. Today was the first time I'd watched myself in the mirror to study my footwork, and it was hard to see the hollow of my cheeks and the bags under my eyes, but they'd been expected with how many hours I'd put into getting the routine down while sleeping no more than three hours on my best nights. I knew I was going too far but I couldn't stop because the fire building in my chest had spread everywhere and it took over all the other unwanted feelings of hatred and sadness long enough for me to feel like I was halfway normal.

"How did you find me?" I reached for the towel I'd draped on the barre in front of the mirrors and wiped off my face before squatting to pick up my shirt to slide on. He'd seen me in far less, but that didn't mean I wanted him seeing me now. Not when I was vulnerable.

He pushed off the door. "Dallas."

I frowned. Dallas had offered to drive me because it was raining today. Normally, I caught a ride with Tiffany or got an Uber that way I didn't bother him. With his newborn, which he'd showed me countless photos of over the past few weeks, I wanted to make sure he had as much family time as possible. "Why are you here?" I hadn't meant to say it so rudely, but I wanted to be alone. All week, I'd wanted to stay to myself. Dance. Practice. Repeat. Get the routine down without one mistake.

He didn't step into the studio, just looked at me with watchful, curious eyes. "Want to go to Denny's and get breakfast?"

He wanted to get breakfast? My stomach rumbled to life, but I told myself to give an excuse to get out of it.

"I need to shower…" I glanced down at the way my

clothes clung to my overheated, sweaty body. I'd driven myself farther than I had since Tiffany and I started, but I almost had the entire dance down because of it. If I could get out of my head, I'd stop mis-stepping, but there was always something lurking in the back of my mind that weakened my walls.

Theo didn't relent though. "Breakfast at my house then. Ramsay misses you."

I blew out a breath. "Does he?"

There was a pause. "I miss you too, Della." His words went straight to my heart causing it to beat a little faster, a little harder, drumming to a tune that beckoned him forward.

"I don't think it's a good idea," I admitted quietly, turning off the music and gripping my water bottle.

"Since when has anything we've done been a good idea lately?" The lighthearted smirk on his lips told me he was teasing. It was a conversation we'd had before but beat around. When we'd meet up, we'd kiss, we'd touch, we'd do a lot of things, but I hadn't had sex with him since he cooked us dinner. My mind racing with thoughts of my imperfections had me lying to Theo and telling him I was on my period. He'd bought me chocolate and gave me a shoulder massage, never once pushing. I knew I needed to tell him that I couldn't find the energy even though sleeping with Theo brought my body to life in ways that had been dormant before.

I didn't want that feeling though. I wanted to be numb. My mind begged me to stay away from anything that made me feel like there was hope or else I'd be too far gone when I realized there was none.

My tongue swiped across my bottom lip in hesitation. We both knew he spoke the truth, but the allure to his words still didn't make me want to jump on the opportunity. Not like it normally would. That was when I knew...

Maybe I *already was* too far gone.

He finally took a large step into the space I occupied, one hand out of his pocket and scrubbing his jawline. "There's something I'd like to talk with you about. About your father."

Lips parting, I inhaled shakily. "What?"

Head dipping once, he said, "Come on. Pancakes, eggs, you name it. Come home with me."

Home. My stomach dropped. "So, we can talk about...my dad?" I shook my head. "I'm okay with not doing that over eggs."

"Pancakes then?"

Gnawing on the inside of my cheek, I let my shoulders ease enough for him to see me relenting. "Chocolate chip. And bacon." I walked past him into the light rain, my stomach screaming over the idea of food even though my brain yelled, *NO!* "None of that fake syrup crap, Theo. I mean it."

I heard his chuckle and promptly ignored it as Dallas's black car came into view.

When I climbed in, Dallas gave me an apologetic look from the rearview. "Sorry, Della. He insisted."

Theo climbed in beside me, not looking sorry at all.

In fact, there was anything but apology on his face. Awe, amusement, care. He looked at me like he always had, but it was more intense. Stronger. Different.

And today, I surprised him.

I danced.

It made me smile despite that haunting feeling in the back of my mind as I stared out the backseat window. I ignored the other two people in the vehicle who made small talk while I thought about what this meant, because I danced and I loved it, but I also danced because I hated myself.

I wanted that pain. The feel of my legs giving out and my lungs on their last breath. I wanted to escape into a world where I could hurt myself rather than letting everybody else do it for me.

I saw Dallas glance at me again from the rearview mirror and realized…

He saw too much.

THE FOOD WAS LEFT untouched in front of me with two sets of eyes on me for very different reasons. One of them was more intense than the other. I broke apart a piece of bacon and fed it to Ramsay while Theo watched silently across the table. He didn't like it when the dog was close by while we ate. It'd been a little while since I'd seen Ramsay, so I wanted to spoil him like I knew Theo did when I wasn't here.

"You haven't eaten," he noted.

I glanced at his plate. "Neither have you."

"It's the real maple syrup."

My lips twitched. Moving my eyes from Ramsay to Theo, I rested back in my chair and picked up my fork. Wet pieces of my hair fell against my cheek that I refused to move because they shielded part of my vision. I'd taken a much longer shower in his master bathroom than I'd intended, but the scalding water felt so good against my sore muscles. I stood under the too-hot water until my skin was red and prayed that every bad feeling I had about myself would wash away. But when I stepped out, I looked at myself in the mirror before I could grab a towel and frowned.

Frowned at my body.

Frowned at my thoughts.

I'd wanted to put my fist through the reflection that taunted me, but I didn't. I didn't want Theo to think I was losing it. That my anxiety had peeked, that the medication I was on wasn't working, and that I'd have to admit to Ripley I probably needed something different. Something stronger. Stronger medication meant the problem had peeked like the hill and valley my disorder was.

Shifting in my seat, I poked at the section of pancake that had the most chocolate chips. "I take it work has been busy?" He hadn't reached out in a few days, which was fine by me. It was easier to avoid him when he was avoiding me first. The guilt didn't eat at me that way.

"Della—"

"I get it." I smiled. "You wanted space. But you

invited me here, which means you didn't want space right now. So…how's work?"

He leaned back with his hand around his coffee cup, pulling it along the table with the black liquid threatening to slosh out the sides. "It's been busy, but it wasn't busy enough that I couldn't check up on you more often."

"I don't *need* you to check up on me." My voice was suddenly defensive, irritable. Why did he always make it sound like I was a child who needed to be monitored? "But I wouldn't have minded getting more than a text saying you hope I'm well. I mean honestly, Theo." My appetite was there, taunting me, especially after the session I had at Tiffany's. I'd burned a lot of calories and needed to eat. To refuel. In hindsight, I should have asked for eggs, or just gone to Denny's where I could have walked out easier if I decided I'd had enough. Dallas left after Theo dismissed him, which meant I'd have to wait for a lift if I walked out now before the conversation could go somewhere I didn't want it to.

There was no reason to snap at Theo when I'd been pulling away from everybody too. The texts he sent me were fine. The pictures of Ramsay he sent me were fine. Everything was *fine*. Great, even. How I wanted it to be.

"You're right." It was a smooth, quiet voice that greeted me, causing me to look up at him in surprise. What did I expect? Him to argue? To ignore me? Maybe lecture me? He'd done all those things in the past. "I'm sorry, Della. But what I wanted to talk to you about is part of the reason why I felt it was a good idea to let you live your life without me complicating it for a couple days while I figured out how to tell you."

"Who said you were complicating it?"

"You're dancing again."

I blinked. "Not much." *Lie.* "Plus, Tiffany has been making me." *Lie.* "She said it'd be good for me." That wasn't so much a lie. If it weren't for her, I would have been holed up in my apartment painting. She gave that to me like an unwrapped gift. Painting and dancing. Two forms of expression. If anything, Theo should be happy for me, not sad like he'd taken something away by always being near.

His head cocked, eyes wandering over my face for a moment too long. "Was she wrong? I saw you in there. You were lost in the music like you used to be. It was refreshing to see."

I blushed. "I was lost in my head counting the steps. Which, like I told you before, I messed up. I'm not that great at contemporary yet."

"Nobody would have noticed."

My nostrils flared as I stabbed my food and lifted it. "Everybody would have."

He let me chew and swallow before saying anything else. I didn't like his eyes on me right now. Not when my stomach was twisted with an explanation that I couldn't grasp myself. Why did I dance when Tiffany wasn't around? It seemed simple enough. To prove I could. But deep down it was more. When I looked in the mirror as I moved my feet, my hips, my arms, it was like I was watching the old version of me. The one I didn't hate so much because she still had her mom cheering her on and her family together. She was happy. Lost in a world of music because there was nothing else she had to worry about.

Then there was the other old version of me that did it because I couldn't stop myself. She won the battles more than I liked admitting, succumbing to hunger cramps that doubled her over in pain while her reflection smiled manically.

"If you'd let me, I'd like to explain," he said after silence engulfed us in an uncomfortable blanket. "It isn't going to be easy to hear, but you need to hear it from me before someone else leaks the information."

The frown was instant, but the concern weighed in my chest like an anvil was dropped dead center on my ribcage. Wasn't that what I was waiting for? Why I'd needed to escape into a world of overworked muscle and choppy breath? I thought it'd been because of the reporter who'd harassed Lydia, even though she never reached out saying he had brought it up again. It was like the story vanished into thin air, which I knew wasn't the case. It was just easier to pretend it was for a while.

"The list of names that was given to The Times is tied to a very powerful man, Della. He's looking to tarnish any reputation the Saint James family has left so people won't consider the possibility that there's truth in what could be spoken."

All I could do was stare at him. I'd figured Lydia

had told him about the list since she was keen on getting him to talk to me, but I'd never let him in until today.

"This man…" His sigh was burdened. "I know you understand the world we live in is a shitty, dark place. But what I'm about to tell you goes beyond that."

"Theo." My heart pounded so hard it hurt.

"I told you not too long ago that I'd tell you what's been going on when the time came. I was just hoping I wouldn't have to. I've had people investigate it, and it looks like your father might have had information that could have gotten his sentence reduced. Maybe even lowered to parole. He could have gotten out."

A piece of me splintered off. "He…what? They said—"

"The system was set against him, Della. It was from the beginning because there were people who chose to save themselves before him. They made him take the fall for it all. There were phone records that indicated he'd been talking with his attorney about the case, giving names of the other people involved. With that kind of information, it would have changed things for him. For all of you. Anthony…he always wanted what was best for his family. He and Elizabeth had strong values when it came to that. If he was making a deal, it was for you."

My throat tightened. Swallowing was impossible, the food in front of me no longer looked appetizing at all. Everything was crashing around me as I stared at Theo with unblinking eyes. "It doesn't matter now though. So why are you telling me this? It only hurts more." The crack in my tone had him closing his eyes for a split second and that's when I knew.

I knew what he was going to say would change everything.

And it did.

"Your father was killed to make sure the people involved wouldn't be dragged down with him. And at least one of the people is trying to hurt you and your family by ensuring that information doesn't see the light of day. If I didn't think there was a strong case against him or the others, I wouldn't have brought it up. But the chance of the case being reopened —"

I needed to get out of here. That was all I could think when I stood and moved so quickly that dizziness hit me. Stumbling, I caught myself on the chair before Theo was by my side, holding my arm to steady me.

But I didn't want him to.

"Don't," I pleaded, moving away.

"Della, I know this is hard —"

The cold, confused laugh couldn't be stopped. "Hard? You think hearing that my father was murdered because he was trying to get out of prison to be with me was *hard*? That word doesn't come close to what this situation is. It's *fucked up*, Theo. And what's worse is you thinking I needed to hear it over goddamn pancakes like it should make it all better!"

I was on a roll and couldn't be stopped. Turning to him, I tightened my hands into fists and glared past the tears that welled in my eyes. It made it difficult to see but didn't stop me from making sure he knew how I felt. "Whoever this guy is, or these people, they can't possibly taint my family any more than what's already been done. If they want to ruin me, destroy me, they can save their energy. Because this—*you*—did it for them."

The pain that sliced open his features should have made me feel guilty, but the rage, the sadness, the mixture of every feeling I never wanted to feel again was consuming me as each second passed until I was shaking. Shaking and clawing my way out of my own skin because I didn't want to be stuck in it right now. Not ever.

As I turned to the door, I grabbed ahold of the handle only for a hand to come down on the wood to prevent me from exiting. "Della, please sit down. You're not in the mindset to go anywhere right now. You look sick."

I did what I'd never done before. I shoved him. I put all my strength into the push and sent him stumbling backward because he was unprepared for it, leaving me able to throw the door open and storm out into the rain. Fitting. Clouds grayed the sky, thunder rumbled in the distance, and I thought about all those stories my mother used to tell me about Greek Gods.

"Do you really think they exist?" I'd asked her after she'd told me the story about Zeus. He'd sounded so powerful, so fearful, that I wouldn't ever want to be on his bad side. But my mother had told me every story had some lies mixed in with the truth. That maybe Zeus wasn't so

bad, just misunderstood because people with power usually were masked by it.

It made me think of my father and his friends, the men who seemed so sure of themselves out in public. When my father was indoors, he was a different man. Kind, gentle, and loving. Nowhere near the person people seemed to look up to and be intimidated by all at the same time. I'd kept hold of that when things got bad because I needed reassurance that he wasn't a bad man, just masked by his bad decisions.

"Adele!" Theo yelled after me. The rain was coming down harder, faster, but I didn't care. I let it soak me, prayed it would wash away everything I felt since the shower hadn't done it. I didn't want emotions weighing me down anymore.

I needed out.

I needed air.

A black car came into view and Dallas got out with a concerned look on his face. Why he hadn't left when he was told was beyond me. He'd always known when I needed him. It took him mere seconds before he was ushering me in the back and closing the door, gesturing toward Theo, and saying who knew what. I didn't care.

I should have but I didn't.

Because all I cared about was how I felt the loss of my father for a second time. Except, now it felt ten times worse. Before, I'd stared. I was shocked. Silent. Sophie yelled. Lydia cried. But me? I couldn't. I couldn't do any of that because I didn't know how to accept what we were being told. I'd chosen to believe it was all a sadistic prank, like he'd pop out of the bushes and laugh like it was a cruel joke. I'd known better. My father wasn't like that, but I needed to hold onto anything other than the reality that I'd never see him again.

"I'm broken," I whispered as soon as Dallas got into the driver seat. *So, so broken.*

He looked over his shoulder. "I know a lot of broken people, Della. A lot who suffered through unimaginable loss like you. You're not broken. You're human."

I closed my eyes and let the storm be the only sound I heard on the drive home. I didn't want to be human. I didn't want to be...

I didn't want to *be.*

"Can you show me the routine again?" I asked, walking into Tiffany's house the following day. She stopped what she was doing in the kitchen, making a pink shake, to stare at me.

"Hello to you too." Amusement only lasted a few seconds when she saw my face. Her brows drew up. "Uh, like right now?"

I nodded.

She glanced at her shake. "Did you want something to eat first? Maybe we could —"

"I already ate." The lie slipped off my tongue easily, and she only hesitated a moment before nodding slowly. It didn't look like she believed me, but she also didn't call me out on it.

"Okay." She finished making her shake before throwing some of the dirty dishes into the sink and turning toward the back doors that led to the studio. She was already in her usual attire.

She sipped her drink as I set my things down off to the side and began stretching. I knew she was watching but I paid her no attention. Bending in half, I reached for my foot to stretch my calf and took deep breaths.

"I didn't think we were training today," she said after dropping down beside me and stretching too. "I was about to go through some things Judith gave us to practice."

I straightened and rocked my arms to the side to warm up my obliques. I only felt a little bad I'd bombarded her last minute. "I almost have the dance down. I need a little more help to get in sync with the music. I'm always a beat or two behind."

"You're doing fine. We haven't been at this very long. Hell, it took me longer to get my first dance down."

Her compliment didn't ease the tightness in my chest that needed to be expelled before I blew. Since getting back from Theo's yesterday, I'd kept my phone turned off and my head wrapped around anything other than what he'd told me. It still nagged me, taunting, like a demon sitting on my shoulder and whispering in my ear. I painted angry black lines and red splatters and white slashes, but nothing helped in my spare room when sleep evaded me. TV didn't keep my attention. Running could only last so long in the gym located on the first floor of my building, since running outside was something I liked avoiding if I could. What I needed was to exhaust myself until I had no choice but to collapse in bed and fall victim to the abyss of unconsciousness.

We started out doing the routine fully so she could see where I was going offbeat, then twice more together before she told me exactly how to fix my mistakes. It was easy enough, but I'd messed up again. And again. And again. Twenty minutes turned into thirty. Then forty-five. By an hour, Tiffany's shake was gone and so was her shirt because it was drenched in sweat. She toweled off and paused the music, watching me still move. My back was to the mirrors, my eyes were closed, and I was busy trying to lose myself in each move even without the music.

"Della."

I didn't stop.

"Della!"

I cracked an eye open when a hand shot out and grabbed my arm during my last turn. "I was almost finished!" I snapped.

"What is with you?" She dropped her arm and shook her head. "You've been a real bitch lately, I'm not going to lie."

No answer came.

She sighed. "Whatever it is, it's got you working ten times harder than I've seen you work...ever. And that says something because you always worked your ass off in ballet. Probably more than any of us."

I shrugged, picking up my water and downing half of it in one go. "I want to be able to say I finished a routine and nailed it."

"Then what?"

"What do you mean?"

"What then? What comes after?"

There was a pause where she eyed me suspiciously while I shifted on my feet, water bottle in my hand with a white-knuckle grip around the plastic. "Then I learn a new one."

I got back into position and waited for her to turn the music on. Instead, she said, "You know, Judith asked about you the other day. She heard you were dancing again."

My stomach hurt. "So?"

"So...I confirmed you were."

I dropped my arms. "Why would you do that? She's going to think I'm coming back. It's bad enough Sophie made everybody else think that. I was hounded for weeks."

"I wasn't going to lie, Della."

Again, I chose not to say anything.

Tiffany studied me with intense eyes that I avoided as I closed mine and evened my breathing. In through the nose, out through the mouth. My heart rate came down naturally, just in time for me to raise it again if she turned the damn music on instead of interrogating a pointless matter.

"One day you're going to tell me what's bothering you," I heard her say.

Another lie slipped past my parted lips before I could stop it. "Yeah. One day."

THERE WAS a light tap on the door that told me it wasn't the man who usually showed up despite my wishes. He hadn't tried to reach out to me because he knew better. Hadn't shown up. Hadn't texted. So, it was only a matter of time before he sent somebody else.

Wiping off my hands on the overalls covering my body, I noted the way they fit even looser around the waist but ignored it. Padding over to the front door, I looked through little hole to see light hair with natural highlights similar to mine in the sunlight. The blonde tones made me blink, my hand hesitating to undo the locks before opening to find my aunt behind it.

"Lydia?"

She smiled at me, timid and small, her height an inch or two taller than me, but her features always tentative. "Hello, Della. May I come in?"

Stepping aside, I gestured for her to walk past me, closing the door behind her before turning in curiosity. "Not that I mind, but what are you doing here? You never visit."

Her lips twitched. "I know I haven't. That's some-thing I think about quite often. But that's why I wanted to see you."

"You mean, Theo asked you to come?" I walked over to the kitchen and grabbed a glass of water. "Would you like anything to drink?"

"I'm fine."

I nodded and watched her look around. Her smile grew when she saw a picture of Theo and me from my high school graduation. I was in my cap and gown with my hair curled and a face full of makeup, and Theo was in his typical dress pants and button down shirt with an arm wound around my waist, tucking me into his side. I loved that day. It meant freedom.

In hindsight, that freedom was restricted even when I thought it'd be limitless. And most of that was because of me. I'd been afraid of a lot of things, but mostly of disappointing the ghosts of my past. My mother. Even my father before I'd known the truth. Hell, even after. I was always pressuring myself to be the best, to just be...better. Not of other people. Better than myself. And I knew I was failing at it right now.

"Actually," Lydia said, "he didn't. Theo mentioned that you needed some space, but Sophie told him he was being ridiculous. Something about girls your age needing discipline not distance."

Sounded like Sophie. It made me want to roll my eyes, but I didn't. Instead, I sat down on the couch while Lydia walked to the TV and studied the frames on the entertainment center the flat screen rested on. Pictures of my parents, of the three of us as a family, one of just Theo. He looked like he always did—not quite smiling, but not scowling either. Not at me, who'd taken that picture when I told him I wanted to go to Central Park.

"Theo knows you better than anybody, so that was

why I told Sophie I'd come instead of her. We both know she'd take the wrong approach and come on too strong. I figured I was the lesser of two evils."

I winced. The last time Sophie had come here she remarked on every piece of furniture she didn't like, telling me she could buy me better things. Of course she could. Her husband let her buy whatever she wanted to get her off his back. Her taste was the opposite of mine and she knew it. The second I agreed to let her buy me new stuff, I'd lose. Sophie was family and I loved her, but I didn't want her to think she had any influence or control over me.

"I appreciate it," I told her honestly.

"You're painting," she commented, her attention going toward my overalls. "I still have one of the pictures you drew me when you were little. Do you remember? It was of me and your father. You said you wanted me to have something of us together since we didn't have many photographs of just the two of us."

I did remember that. I didn't understand why the photo album Sophie had given me didn't have many pictures of them together. Lydia might have come into their lives later, but that didn't mean she couldn't be part of family photos.

I nodded, a gentle smile forming on my face when she turned to me. "I do. You still have it? I figured all that stuff I drew would be long gone by now. They were awful."

To my surprise, she laughed. Loudly. Lydia usually only had two volumes—soft and softer. That sound was abnormal. "Oh, Della. I'm not the only one who kept them. There's a man we both know who's kept everything you gave him. Art or not."

Or not? What else had I given Theo that he could have kept? I hadn't even known he had anything I'd gifted him from back then. The drawings didn't even seem like anything worth keeping considering some of them were lines and squiggles that made no sense.

"I didn't give him anything else, Aunt Lydia. But the fact he kept those..." It made my heart thump a little faster than I wanted to admit.

Her smirk was tiny, her eyes dancing as she shook her head. "We'll agree to disagree, yes? Can I see what you were working on?"

I only paused for a moment before nodding slowly, setting my water down on the coffee table and standing. She followed close behind me as I led her to the room I'd left my latest painting, something I woke up in the middle of the night to create after a dream that was too vivid not to do something about. The sweat that'd been collecting on my brow had stayed there as I'd gotten out of bed and stormed into my spare room in nothing but a pair of panties and the oversized tee I liked sleeping in. I stayed there for four hours, until exhaustion swept over me at six in the morning and I crawled back in bed.

It took me another two hours to get it where it was now. My palms were stained a dark pink from the color I'd mixed up—a dusty rose tone that matched the tint of my cheeks when Lydia's lips parted after seeing it on the easel.

"Della," she whispered, grazing her fingertips along the edge of the canvas.

Resting in a black background with various shades of pink, peach, and purple was a lonesome girl who looked too frail, too brittle to be wearing the tutu that graced her narrow waist. The ballerina lacked the leotard that normally clung to her body, her back bare and painted in cream with the darker shadows emphasizing a sickly spine everybody would point at and whisper about because they knew it wasn't right the way her skin clung to her bones. She was bent over, as if to bow, her face hidden, her stance somber, yet screaming so many things.

Help me.

Save me.

Do something to end this.

That was what the girl in the dream did.

She begged.

I swallowed as Lydia peeled her eyes from my creation and up to me. "It's stunning. Is it...?" She dipped her chin. I knew what she was asking but all I could do was shake my head.

Another lie. *So many lies.* "It's just a girl, Aunt Lydia."

Despite my aunt not knowing me well, it was clear she didn't believe me. With good reason. She didn't call me out and I didn't offer any further information.

Maybe if I weren't scared, I could be honest with

her. I would tell her that I'd dreamt about me, the girl I *was*. I'd tell her that I saw my father being hauled off in handcuffs while being read his rights. I'd admit that I saw my mother on her deathbed, holding my father's hand and telling him to be strong.

"Be better, Anthony. For Della."

Those words plagued me. I never used to think about them as more than a plea to stop working so much and spend more time with me. We were all each other had without her. It meant we needed to be there for each other when it mattered. Now, I didn't think that was what she meant at all.

Be better.

Maybe that was why I'd repeated it to myself so often. It was like my mother had meant it for both of us even though she'd directed it at my father...at what he was doing. As morbid as it was, maybe it was better she didn't witness his demise. She'd be disappointed that he didn't listen to her last wish.

Tears stung my eyes as I inhaled a long, deep breath. It eased the pain my lungs had succumbed to at the thought that always influenced my subconscious as I slept.

The dreams were awful. If I didn't wake up right away from them, I silently pleaded to, so I didn't have to relive the torture. When I did wake up, it was always the same. I would realize it may have been a dream, but it was so very real.

My parents were dead.

The ballet dancer in me was dead.

And my mother's last wishes were ignored, leading to my father's demise.

It made me wonder how much my father really loved my mother. I knew, at one time, he loved her so much it almost felt like what he felt for me wasn't enough—like I was somehow second best to their love story. Maybe I'd gotten it wrong though. If my father's feelings were as strong as I thought they were, he would have listened. He would have *tried*.

Be better.

"Della?" My aunt's worried voice clouded the train of thoughts that left me spiraling. Sucking in a deep breath, I gave her a fake smile and stared back at the painting, trying not to give away the truth in my eyes. Our family was said to give everything away because of them. One look was all it took before the world knew...everything.

Lydia stepped away from the canvas and toward me, reaching out and taking my hand. The squeeze was what had me looking down at our joined palms, her fingers interweaving with mine. Our skin tone was almost identical, but hers was slightly darker. I remembered her tan in the summertime too. Just like my father, it didn't take long for them to get color when they went outside.

"Lydia..." I hesitated—my voice barely audible between us. "Do you think that my father was a bad person? That my parents should have been better than who they were?"

Her hold on my hand tightened. "I'm not sure it matters what I think."

"But it does."

Her head shook, kind eyes directed at me as if she were trying to tell me something without saying the words themselves. I needed to hear them though.

"Everybody has an opinion," I pointed out. "We should know that better than anyone. What I want to know is yours. You loved him."

There was no pause that time. "I did. I still do, Della, but what matters is you. You were hurt by them. And I may not know the extent of your mother's knowledge over your father's business, but I've had my own suspicions for some time. That shouldn't change anything for you, though."

How could it not? Just as I was about to argue that she hushed me. "I don't think your parents were bad people. I think they both made bad choices that they couldn't come back from. If your mother knew, she could have stopped him. If you father wanted to, if he felt he was strong enough, he would have ended his dealings. What they chose to do impacted you in an unfair way. I'm sure he held a lot of regrets over it because he loved you very, very much. Do you know that? That he loved you?"

I blinked, heart heavy over her sure words. There was no way I could tell her I believed her when I had my doubts. They'd weaseled their way into every nook and cranny and settled into my bones to taunt me when the time welcomed it.

Lydia pulled me into her, the hug not unwelcomed but taking me by surprise. She whispered, "Oh, Della. I know it may not feel like it, but it's the truth. And if...if what Theo thinks is true, then your father was trying very hard to get back to you, doing anything he could. That counts for something."

I jerked back, wide-eyed. "He told you?"

The sympathy was prominent on her face as she swept hair behind my ear. "Theo loves you too, Della. In ways that...well, it doesn't matter. But he didn't tell you to hurt you. It was something that needed to be said because there'd be a day when it got out anyway. Which would be worse? Hearing it from somebody who cares about you or from a stranger?"

I closed my eyes and buried my face in her neck. Her floral scent eased my shaken nerves as I wrapped my arms around her. There were no words that could lessen the rising guilt weaving in my conscious. I'd been awful to Theo because I was angry, but it really wasn't at him. I'd dwelled on it longer than I wanted to and acknowledged that I owed him an apology. I just didn't know how. I didn't know if he'd understand. And if he didn't? I didn't blame him. I had no right to yell—to *push* him. The last thing I wanted to do was close out the one person I had left who'd always been in my corner.

"I messed up," I whispered brokenly to my aunt. Those three words heightened the pain in my chest, and it spread throughout my body as I replayed what I'd said to Theo when all he was trying to do was be honest.

Her response was to hold me tighter, stroking my back with her free hand. "There's nothing that can't be fixed, not when it comes to you. Okay? Whatever it is, it'll work out."

Blinking back tears, I nodded.

Be better. I chanted that to myself again until it was drilled into my head like a permanent feature.

chapter sixteen

DELLA

I SMELLED the smoke before I saw the cloud lingering in the open office. The door was normally closed, so I knew he didn't have any company. He usually didn't pull a cigarette out unless he was alone so nobody could scold him or complain. Namely, me.

Instead of knocking, I stepped past the threshold and ran a palm down my jean-clad thigh. Inhaling the bitter tobacco that drifted toward me, like my lungs beckoned the torture, I watched that bulky, broad man with eyes closed and head tipped back as he leaned against his chair like he was trying to forget where he was.

Did I do that to him?

"Theo?" I whispered.

Instantly, his body tensed, straightening as he lowered the cigarette from the lips I knew all too well. Swallowing, I watched him open his eyes and take me in. Even from where I stood, I could see the dark circles under his eyes. They matched mine, and the intensity stung me. That didn't last long though as he put his cigarette out in the ashtray he kept hidden in his top right desk drawer. His entire posture changed as he stood, his face, to my surprise, softening for a moment. He took in the jeans and tee combo which was nothing special on my body, but that wasn't how his eyes reacted to the cheap clothing I'd gotten at thrift stores.

"Della." His greeting was quiet as he walked around his desk and came toward me. I was about to apologize, to tell him how stupid I was for lashing out, how sorry I was for being irrational, when his arms wrapped around me in such a tight embrace that made the words stick inside me, heavy on my tongue.

The apology was still there, but faint. All that my brain could focus on was that Theo was holding me, hugging me, his muscular arms tightening around my body as if he needed it as much as I did, like he needed me to stay right there instead of storming out again. I had a lot I wanted to say to him, but I realized it could wait for just a few more moments.

Burying my face into his chest, I inhaled the strong scent of tobacco and man that I didn't know I missed so much until now. If I tipped my head, felt his breath on more than the top of my head where his lips had pressed in a chaste kiss, I bet I'd smell Bowmore scotch or Jim Beam bourbon — one of his two favorites that he kept well stocked. He didn't often parade around his money in anything other than the clothes on his body and the liquor he drank.

Closing my eyes, I cuddled into his warmth, my arms trapped between us, and inhaled for a long moment, like it was the first time I could really breathe.

I murmured, "I'm so sorry." The speech I'd practiced all morning didn't follow the three words. They couldn't.

Because he said, "You don't need to be."

And that was that.

He nuzzled his nose against my hair, running a hand up my spine until it cupped the back of my neck. I felt his lips press against the crown of my head and stay there. We remained that way for a beat longer, my eyes clenching shut like I could pretend that we were allowed to be stuck in that moment rather than dealing with reality.

Instead, Theo pulled away, sighing heavily, like he wished he could have stayed there too. I'd wondered if he fought the urge to smoke or if it was one of those days that nicotine was essential, probably because of me.

"Theo —" I began hesitantly.

He shook his head and pressed his thumb to my bottom lip, the rough pad of his finger caressing me slightly where he'd kissed, suckled, and nipped before. "You look like you've lost weight."

My lips tilted downward, but I said nothing to disagree. I just looked at him, at his eyes that pierced mine. Those eyes...they would be the end of me if I didn't end him first. Whenever they gazed at me a little too long, it fed me hope that maybe we would survive. No matter what happened, no matter how horrible I was or how badly I'd acted out, I wanted to believe those dark blue orbs would look at me with love and reassure me that it would be okay.

Silently cursing, he stepped back and watched my frown deepen as he dropped his hand. His gaze drifted to my shirt, probably on how loosely it fit. If he'd stripped me here and now, peeling off my clothes with the skill I knew he had, he would probably see the bones of my rib cage were beginning to resemble a counting game for children who were learning numbers. *One, two, three, four bones!*

"I painted," I told him instead, ignoring his comment like he probably knew I would. Knowing him, he wanted to shake his head at me, push and argue and make a point about the transformation stress had done to my body. "It isn't much, only one piece, but Lydia said—"

"Lydia saw it?" he asked suddenly.

My throat bobbed before my head did, once in confirmation. I normally hid my pieces, too afraid of what Theo would think if they weren't perfect, like he would have judged me. Sometimes, the only way he'd see the finished product was if it were displayed elsewhere, not hidden away in the closet in my spare room or pawned off for a decent price to afford monthly bills or groceries. I hadn't wanted him to see what my mind conjured, what it begged to create.

Professor Ambrose had challenged me to paint faces, but the few times I did since her suggestion, I hated each and every one because I knew the features weren't my own. But if I had drawn the real person behind each inspiration my sleepless nights gave me, would I hate it any differently? I couldn't even look at myself in the mirror. I doubted seeing my face on a stretched canvas would be any different.

"She kind of insisted," I explained, seeing the jealousy in the pinch of his lips. They wavered for a moment, downward than up like he couldn't decide if he was upset or happy, and I wanted to kick myself for even saying anything to begin with.

Half his lips kicked up and remained that way, easing only a sliver of anxiety that bubbled in my stomach. "I'm glad, Della."

"You don't seem glad."

"What did you paint?"

I blinked, not expecting the question even if I should have. He was trying to connect, engage, and I wanted to oblige. "Just…" I paused, contemplating as I looked at him. He didn't deserve the same answer I'd given Lydia. He deserved more. "Me. I drew me."

"Can I come by today and look at it?"

My chest rose slowly, like his answer was the oxygen that my lungs needed to function, and I was gone. Gone, gone, gone and grateful I'd been given somebody like Theo in my life, like fate had played her hand and gifted me one good thing even though she'd taken everything else. "I would like that."

His lips lifted higher. "I'll bring Ramsay."

There was another pause between us, but now it was heavy as we stared at each other. It was me who broke the silence first, my timid step toward him the first sign that something was about to happen that should have been second guessed, should have been reconsidered. But when my small hand palmed his wide chest, right over his heart, all that discipline and reason escaped him with the sharp exhale of breath I was rewarded with.

"Theo?" I studied him through my lashes, our eyes locked as my palm pressed over him with firm determination. "I really am sorry, even if you say I shouldn't be. You and my father were friends too, and it wasn't fair for me to say those things to you. We both miss him. We both cared."

Placing his hand over mine, he squeezed my fingers once. "That doesn't make it any easier to accept. You don't need to apologize for how you feel, Della. I never want you to hold that in. You shouldn't have to. You of all people deserve to be angry, to lash out, to be pissed off at the world. I expect it."

One of my shoulders lifted. "I don't want to talk about that right now." Before he could tell me we needed to do, I shook my head and raised on my tiptoes. My lips brushed the bottom of his jaw, causing another small breath to escape his pressed lips.

"Della, now isn't the right time."

My hands found his waist, resting there instead of lingering like I wanted them to. My lips remained where they were, the light kiss no more than a chaste gesture that I'd done at my father's funeral. Except, the kiss between us now wasn't a kiss goodbye. His eyes closed for only a moment before his hand finally came down and cupped my cheek, moving away enough to look down at me fully.

"Theo? I need..." Swiping the tip of my tongue over my bottom lip, I exhaled heavily and fisted his shirt in my palms. "I don't know."

His thumb caressed my jaw. "What don't you know? Tell me what I can do."

My lips rubbed together before I caught his eye again. I whispered, "I don't know anything anymore." My hoarse words made him pull me back into him and rest his chin on top of my head as I curled tightly into the body he was offering me.

I heard heels behind us and figured it was his secretary, Abigail. With my back turned, I could only guess that the abrupt stop was from her seeing us like this, wrapped up in one another and not caring. Maybe we should have. I was sure Theo did since he was the one hesitant to take this step so publicly, and while I did try to understand his predicament, it didn't make it any easier to swallow.

When the heels turned and faded down the hall after a click of the door, no words spoken verbally between them, long fingers ran through my hair until I tipped my chin up to see if he was looking at me. Drawing my bottom lip into my mouth and nibbling, I felt his cock hardening in his slacks between us.

"Della…" His voice was hoarse with a warning that I didn't listen to. I could tell his defenses were down too as I rolled my hips into his length until a hearty groan rose from his throat. I wasn't sure which one of us made the move first, but eventually our lips were pressed against each other's and his tongue parted my lips as my arms wrapped around his broad shoulders and yanked him down toward me to close the height distance. He tasted like liquor and tobacco and I hated it and loved it because I loved him. So much. And I needed this even more than I needed anything else.

"Please," I said against him as his hands found my butt and gripped me as the kiss deepened. My head was tilted back as he took over, the kiss controlling but soft and slow and torturous as he started walking back-wards, my feet on his like we were dancing until he was sitting on the edge of his desk. The grip on my backside tightened as he pressed me into him, letting me feel how badly he wanted me, and I did the first thing I could think of.

I dropped to me knees.

"Fuck," he hissed as I undid his belt, popped open his dress pants, and slowly unzipped him. The bulge I was met with was impressive but not as much as when I took him out of the tight briefs that were tented. "Della, you don't have to —"

Before he could finish, the head of his cock was in

my mouth and his words were cut off by a strangled curse. His palm found my hair as I rose higher on my knees and took him further into my mouth, letting my tongue glide down the underside of him until he was cursing and panting and gripping my head until my hair stung.

"Della," he whispered breathily, head tipping back when I looked up at him. I gagged when I took him further, my eyes watering when he started thrusting into my mouth like he needed more. He was so hard, so big, that it hurt my jaw, but I loved the twinge of pain and the ache that settled between my thighs because of the way he twitched and throbbed in my mouth. "No more, baby girl. You need to stop."

I withdrew with a pop, what he called me taking me by surprise, before looking at him with pinched brows. "Did I—"

"Walk around my desk, take off your jeans, and spread your legs, sweetheart." His demand turned my blood into molten lava.

Doing as he said, I rose, toying with the snap and zipper of my own pants before walking around his desk and watching him prowl toward me with a hungry look on his face. He cupped the back of my neck and pulled me toward him in a rough kiss that had me moaning into his mouth as he trailed his hands to the denim still covering me and yanking down my jeans until they fell to the floor. I stepped out of them as one of his palms cupped over my center, feeling how hot and wet I was already from his words and presence alone.

His fingers danced over my panties, teasing me as his teeth grazed my neck and nipped just above my pulse. Flattening his tongue over the same spot as he breathed me in, I silently willed his fingers to dip under the cotton covering my core and touch me where I needed him.

"Theo," I whispered, grabbing onto his shoulders, and digging my nails into him. "Touch me, taste me, anything. Please?"

I felt his smile against my neck as he moved down my body until his mouth was over my breast, still covered by a t-shirt and flimsy bra. His free hand palmed the one his mouth wasn't latched onto as he bit into me, causing my hips to shoot forward into his hand. He palmed me slowly, one of his fingers dipping under the hem of my panties and running up and down the seam of my lips until I was begging him to do something more.

I moved one of my hands down to show him exactly what I wanted, trailing to meet his touch, and guiding one of his fingers inside of me while my thumb played with my clit. My head dropped backward as I silently moaned, trying so hard to keep quiet as he added a second finger. Opening my legs a little wider, I looked at him as he watched our hands ready me.

"Theo," I whispered, keeping his fingers in a needy rhythm until I could hear my wetness with every thrust of his digits. "I need you inside me. Taking me. Filling me. I'll do anything."

"Anything?" he repeated.

I would have done anything if it meant feeling him inside of me instead of his fingers. I nodded, helping him drag down my panties until they joined my jeans on his office floor. He picked me up and set me on his desk, spreading my legs and stepping between them. His clothes were still on save the pants that were down low enough to keep his impressive length free. He gripped it and gave it a few tugs before kissing me again like he meant it, like he was telling me everything I needed to hear without words themselves, before lining himself up and surging inside fast and hard, his breath hot and heavy on my lips as I tried matching his speed.

My fingernails sliced into the skin of his neck as his cock hit me in the perfect place with every move. He held my thighs open, spreading me wider, even though I wanted to wrap my legs around him as he drove into me over and over. This Theo was hungry, and I loved it, got lost in it, as I bit into his bottom lip as he adjusted the angle and took me deeper.

"Ohgodohgod*ohgod*," I chanted heavily when the wet sound we made together filled the room. There was no way people couldn't hear us, no matter how hard I tried keeping quiet by biting my lip. Theo changed pace suddenly, slowly rolling into me like he was trying to prove something.

I didn't like it, my protest slipping past my lips in a frustrated tone. "Faster." I was overheated and needy and couldn't stand him going so slow. I reached behind him and grabbed his toned glutes, pulling him harder into me to try building back up to what was going to make me explode around him.

He circled his hips, making me gasp loudly until speckles of white hit my eyes when he drew back and did it again.

And again.

And again.

"I want it all with you," he whispered into my neck, sucking my skin. My eyes watered from the sensation, from his words, from the sincerity in his tone as he entered me. Each thrust became harder, but slower, like he didn't want it to end. I could feel the brink of my orgasm as he rested a palm against my chest and laid me down so my back was flat against his desk. I grabbed onto anything, accidently knocking over files stacked on the side of his desk. The loud crash of them against the floor should have made me embarrassed but it didn't. All it made me was crazier for the man who listened to my whimpered pleas and started fucking me until I bit the side of my arm and came harder than I ever had before.

"You're fucking clenching me so tight," he grunted, slamming into me twice more before grabbing my hips and sliding me to him so there was no space at all between our bottom halves as he came inside of me. The feeling of him spilling into my sated body had me hotter than ever, but not as much as when he caressed my inner thigh, kissed my exposed scar from where my shirt rode up, and pulled out letting his cum drip out of me and onto his desk.

"Oh my god," I whispered, still trying to catch my breath as I stared up at the light brown ceiling.

Theo must have grabbed something because his hand was between my legs cleaning me up with something soft, making me moan when he brushed the tender bundle of nerves that were still firing.

I closed my eyes and took a deep breath before letting him help me sit up. When we were eye level, I leaned forward and kissed him softly, which he returned with fervor. Our lips and tongue and teeth played off one another in slow strokes before he pulled away and rested his forehead against mine.

"You'd do anything for me, Della?" he asked again, his breath caressing my lips.

"Yes."

I'd barely pulled away, my lips grazing his again briefly, when he said, "You need to get help, sweetheart. I'll be here for you whenever you need me, but I think you should see Ripley more often."

I tensed, feeling my face pinken for an entirely new reason other than overexertion. I'd expected a lot of things coming from his mouth, but... "You think I need help?"

"Della, I don't mean that in a bad way. You said she helped before, right? What just happened shouldn't have, even if seeing me leaking out of you makes me want to do it again. You look like you haven't slept in weeks. You're skinnier. I'm worried about you."

All I could do was stare, still feeling his cum inside

of me, still reeling in the delicious ache he'd gifted me with just moments ago.

"Whether you want to admit it or not, you've lost weight. You can tell me it's because you're dancing again and going to yoga with Tiffany, but it's more than that. I'm not stupid, Della, and I know you know that. What did I tell you before?"

Before. What he was referencing was before my father had been arrested. They'd had an intervention for me when I'd gotten home from a walk. I was embarrassed and silent the entire time they spoke to me until Theo followed me into my bedroom where I'd stalked off when I'd had enough. I'd been in skimpy pajamas heading toward the bathroom, unaware that Theo was going to follow me there too. He'd grabbed the sheet that covered the mirror and gestured at it. Making a point. Making me *see* what I refused to while I shriveled into nothing the months prior.

My father had told me he didn't know what else to do. He was a lot of things, but a quitter wasn't usually one. I should have known then that something was up with him. He'd been withdrawn, tired, easily worn out and unwilling to put in the effort it took to handle what I was going through, and I hadn't made it easy for him to understand.

He'd already been in too deep at that point, which made sense. It was only a month or so later when the feds came knocking on our front door. A door that I had answered in confusion, which morphed into more when they explained why they were there. And my father?

He let them read him his rights without assuring me anything. Maybe he couldn't.

The day they had an intervention had to have been Theo's idea. My father wasn't the same man who promised my mother to be better. He was a shell. Lost. Scared. Waiting for the inevitable. It was Theo who had been there, who had demanded I admit what I wouldn't.

"All I'm saying," he continued without me even trying to cut in, "is that you should reach out to Ripley and try making another appointment sometime soon. It'll be good for you, Della."

To that, he got a muffled scoff. "Good?" It was a win for him, I wasn't telling him no right away. Realistically, he was right. Part of me was crying for help, for something. Someone. Not an escape. A cure. But I knew even after talking to Ripley, it would always be the same because there was no cure for self-hate that the anorexia and body dysmorphia had left me with.

"What did I tell you before, Della?" he repeated, voice firmer and giving me no other choice but to answer.

With a shaky breath, I looked up at him and whispered, "You told me I'd fall and fail and break but that I wouldn't give up…"

"But you will also rise, succeed, and put yourself back together because only you can."

I remembered every word he said to me over the years, but those especially. I knew there'd be a day I needed to hear them again because what I battled wasn't a one-time thing. It was lifelong and that meant there would be fights to face when the time came. I saw my skin, my eyes, the way I held myself right now, and knew, just *knew*, I was falling. Theo knew too.

This was his second intervention.

It was the one thing he told me that day that stuck with me most. Right next to what my mother had told my father on her deathbed. I murmured, "Only I can put myself back together." I spoke it so softly, I wondered if he heard. But it hadn't been for him to hear. It was for me. Like when I said the two little words *be better* under my breath in no more than a broken whisper, like I'd been summoning the determination to honor that.

Theo didn't ask about it though because those words gave me the strength I needed. It was probably easy to see in the way I straightened my shoulders and glanced up at him like I was going to agree. I didn't though. Not verbally.

Before I could, Abigail knocked on the door again, before hesitantly calling out, "Mr. West?" There was an awkward pause, a moment where Theo and I stared at each other. "I'm sorry, Mr. West, but there's a gentleman here to see you who insists it's important. I've never seen him before or…"

Theo nodded once, his eyes not leaving mine. "Thank you, Abigail."

When she left, all I did was look up to him and say, "She prefers being called Abbie."

chapter seventeen

THEO

I DROPPED the file onto the glass desk that was too flashy for me but perfect for the egotistical asshole sitting behind it. He looked down at the manila folder in front of him for a microsecond then moved his eyes upward with an arched brow that held amusement more than confusion. For someone in his early fifties, the fucker's speckled gray hair was faker than he was, like he thought it made him look more distinguished.

"I was wondering when you'd pay me a visit," The Dick said all too casually. I didn't sit in the seat he gestured to or reply when he'd offered me a drink. I didn't want to stay longer than I needed to, and I certainly didn't want to drink whatever he handed me.

"Anthony Saint James," were the only words out of my mouth.

The other eyebrow raised to join the first as he leaned back in his chair. I didn't like the way he draped his arms on his lap or how he cocked his head to the side for me to continue without so much as a question as to why I was bringing up a dead man. We both knew the reason. He just didn't think he'd have to hear about him again. Plain and simple.

I pointed toward the document. "I don't know who's cock you had to suck to try getting those documents destroyed, but clearly you're shit at a decent blowjob since it didn't take much to collect information on what you've been up to over the years."

The moment his face turned red, I smiled. Tendons in his neck tightened and my anger grew for the bastard who acted like he didn't give a shit about anything or anyone. Least of all a man he hired somebody to get rid of. "You come into my office and—"

"It's annoying, isn't it?" I cut him off. Shrugging, I leaned my hip against his desk. "I'm curious, though. What made you think that getting Rodney Scott a new gig over in the San Fran area was going to get him to keep quiet? Was it threatening his reputation? Or his sexual orientation? Fuck, maybe it was the dirt you dug up on how his marriage was fake. Deidra Scott took that money you offered her real quick, didn't she? Can't say I blame the woman. It must have been challenging to watch your husband parading men around her all the time knowing she was the last person he was giving his dick to."

His nostrils flared. "You want to explain to me why you're bringing up Saint James's defense attorney? Seems a little pointless at this point, doesn't it?"

That made me laugh. Loud, deep, rumbling laughter escaped my previously pressed lips, only flattening his more in reaction. He loved watching people when he played the game, but he was shit at taking it. "I'm sure you'd like to think so considering the circumstances of his untimely death." His jaw ticked as I pressed on without giving him time to argue. "It's not a secret that Rikers Island is known for their unjust brutality. In fact, with the right amount of money, anybody could get away with a few crimes inside. You already know that though, so I'll skip ahead to the good stuff. Phone records. Video recordings. Oh, and one very talkative guard with an overbite. Officer Johnson? I'm sure you know the one I'm talking about because you padded his bank account with over $100,000 dollars just weeks before Anthony was beaten to death in the section he was supposed to be monitoring that night.

"Come to think of it, the video alone says plenty. But you didn't know that because the money you gave him was blood money to ensure the cameras were turned off during the attack. The phone records may not reveal a lot in the grand scheme of things because Scott wanted one on one time with Saint James without being recorded to go over their meetings, but your name was said enough to make the federal judge question why you weren't more involved in questioning during the trial. You and Henry Murphy sure were lucky all this time. Must have been a relief knowing you two could keep living your lives knowing somebody else was taking the fall."

Slowly, Pratt stood up with a deadly glare on his face. He didn't even touch the folder I dropped in front of him, much less look down to figure out what was inside. I'd wanted him to, to see what kind of evidence was stacked against him so he knew he wasn't the invincible asshole he thought he was. Money talked. Counterfeit money talked louder. Other businesses Pratt was known for, drugs, weapons, sex trafficking, practically screamed. As did the audio of Rodney Scott and Anthony Saint James discussing appeal tactics by gathering names to help prove Anthony didn't act alone. "I'm giving you ten seconds to get the fuck out of my office before I call security to escort you out themselves."

I figured he'd say that, but I didn't give up the smile I'd had since seeing his eyes glaze over with the fear he pretended not to feel. "You know George Malik, right? Real standup guy, that one. He was arrested and put on trial for stealing government funds while he was in office, remember that? Got away with it and to a lot of people's shock. There was a great writeup on it in The Times by Nicholas McAllister. From what he told me, he had a great approval rate because of that piece. Was even offered a hefty promotion that came with a raise The Times couldn't afford to pay out. Seemed fishy to me. So did the interviews with Malik that nobody else could get besides him. He said he had connections to get him on top, make sure he told the *right* story. Not the truthful one."

He picked up the phone and held it to his ear pressing one of the buttons leading out to the front desk I passed when I stormed in. "Daphne, I need you to call sec —"

"Nicholas McAllister had connections beyond you though. Slimy motherfucker was working both sides. Playing you. You don't even know that do you? Michael Flamell ring a bell?"

He dropped the phone back into the cradle with force before narrowing his eyes at me. "What game are you playing here, West? Don't think I won't play it right back. I have —"

"What?" I challenged, stepping forward and crowding his space. "What do you have on me that's as bad as first-degree murder on top of a slew of other charges which are coming your way? Whatever hold you think you have on me is worthless compared to what's in that folder right there, and the folder in Flamell's hands as we speak."

"Who the *fuck* is Flamell?"

I chuckled. "Your problem, Richard, is that you only care about power. You think the more people you control, the more money you can make, and the more authority you have over everyone else. What you forget, though, is that you'll never be able to control everybody that works under those you blackmail. People talk.

Things get out that you don't want out. Like the operation you got in the south side of the city on 10th. Or
how about the one three places down from the old
warehouse on 5th? I remember you at Anthony's
funeral looking like you actually gave a shit for about
two seconds before someone came over, whispered in
your ear, and you both left. You went to the old shoe
factory, right? Makes sense given what's made in there.
There's plenty of space, lots of filtration so the people
you hire don't die from the toxins of the drugs you have
people produce and distribute."

He paled.

"Back to your question. Michael Flamell is a friend
of a friend. A trustworthy friend, unlike the jackasses
you pretend are yours. Can't exactly be friends with the
people you blackmail into giving you control of their
businesses to use as strongholds for your dealings. That
tends to piss them off."

I'd hired Dallas for a lot of reasons, but one of the
biggest being his former background in criminal justice.
He worked for the police force upstate before moving to
the city and retiring when his wife and him decided to
expand their family. He was offered a gig working for
the NYPD because of his reputation, but he turned
them down. He'd gotten calls from the chief asking to
help with a few profiles, which was how he got into
tracking. He accepted smaller jobs along the way which
led him to me. I knew the tasks I'd given him weren't
what he was used to, but I paid him well and offered
him plenty of incentive when the situation called for it.

And the best part? He came with connections. A lot of them.

Not to mention, he cared about Della. That reason alone made me pay him more than most so he'd stick around and look after her.

"This friend told me about Flamell a while ago, said I'd be interested with the intel he had on a high-profile case right here in the city. Wasn't quite sure why the fuck I'd care, frankly, but when your name was mentioned?" I didn't hide the shit-eating grin on my face. I relished in it—relished in the fact his lips turned downward, how his face drained of color, because he knew. He knew where I was going with the story, knew who my friends were. I didn't have many, which meant targeting the ones that were around wasn't hard. Which also meant he knew who Dallas was, including his background. He had people for that too.

"Flamell wears a badge now for the feds. Made real good friends with McAllister from what I learned after our conversation. In fact, between him and McAllister, I found out you and Flamell have a lot of mutual buddies. He enjoys talking to them as well. And guess what, fuckface?" I grinned. "They like talking to him too."

"You're lying." He didn't even believe that, but it was about time he tried acting like the powerful man he made himself seem. He knew he didn't have any of his men here to get past what I was laying down. He had nobody.

"Am I?" I challenged. "If I'm lying, you wouldn't hesitate to open that folder to prove me wrong. You're a coward, Richard. Always have been and always will be. See, you may be able to scare other people into doing your bidding, but unlike the other scum you keep around, I don't get mixed up in the dark side of the city. So, you can threaten to out my feelings for Adele all you want but it won't make a difference."

He stepped up to me with hard features like he was willing to throw down. The fucker was a few inches shorter than me, leaner, and had barely any muscle because he let everybody else do the fighting for him. I could take him down with one punch, but I knew I wouldn't need to. "How do you think people would react if Adele were caught with drugs? Do you think they'd leave her alone knowing she was starting where Daddy Dearest left off? Just because you don't want anything to do with the dark side of things doesn't mean your little young pussy doesn't."

I wanted to hit him—to cave his face in with one blow. But he was expecting that. It'd look bad, even with Dallas and Flamell in my corner. They wouldn't be able to stop me from getting arrested if they knew I threw the first punch and I wasn't about to let The Dick get to me like that. "She doesn't do that. You've been talking out of your ass about her for months and have no goddamn proof, so I suggest—"

"What do you think the police will say if they knew how much time she spends in the south side? It seems convenient she's been seen there at night. What else would somebody her age, with her reputation, be doing there? All it takes is one little call, West. One."

My fists clenched. I knew everything he spouted was bullshit, like usual. The warehouse was the one place I wished Della would have stopped going to a long time ago, but the least I asked of her was to take Dallas when she decided to ignore my concern. Dallas may have liked her, but he would have told me if there was something more going on than I was aware of.

She was always by herself there. She painted. She sometimes even fucking danced—I'd seen it, watched it on more than one occasion before she even started practicing again with the Anderson girl. Della wasn't there because she was into the things her father had gotten pulled into.

That warehouse was where she felt closest to her parents. It was the only reason I didn't try arguing with her about going, even if it pissed me off. She wouldn't have listened to me if I forbid her. We both knew I didn't have that kind of power over her. I didn't want to.

"You have no proof. And even if you did, which is not fucking likely—" I stepped even closer until he could feel the anger ripple off me like radiation I hoped he burned from. "—it won't matter anyway. You tried destroying the Saint James name so no one would believe a word they said. That's exactly what's going to happen to you."

The laugh that came from him was dry and weak. False bravado like he thought he could fool me into thinking he wasn't scared. I knew better. Richard Pratt was shitting his pants because those files would put him away for a long time. Money transfers. Phone records. Witness accounts. Audio. Video. Everything he thought he could fight by blackmail was going to take him down.

When Dallas and McAllister had brought Pratt's businesses to my attention, I'd asked the question that the Saint James trial hadn't answered. It was the same one that I knew Della had wondered but refused to verbalize. *"What did Pratt have on Anthony to get him to do his bidding?"* After both men looked into it, they realized...nothing. Pratt had nothing on Anthony, but the man I'd once called my closest friend hadn't known that. He was willing to do anything for his family, even if it made him into the person he never wanted to be.

All for Elizabeth and Della.

"You've made too many enemies," I stated, my own lips quivering from the smile I'd plastered onto my face. I didn't want him seeing what I knew he'd done to Anthony, and to Della by default, make him think it changed me. He wanted it to. The Dick wanted me to be angry and lash out, but I wouldn't give him that satisfaction, even if I did want to make him bleed.

"Your girl is going down," he growled.

I didn't believe him though.

Because my girl was the strongest person I knew.

chapter eighteen

DELLA

THE HAND REACHING out to me was one I hadn't seen in years, which was why I launched myself directly toward the open arms of the softest person I knew. Right before I made contact with my mother's warmth, she said, *"I told you to be better, sweet Della"* and before I could tell her I was trying, she disappeared.

Bolting up in bed, I listened to the loud drumming of my heart as I took slow, deep breaths. I hadn't realized I was crying until I swiped my face, feeling the damp cheeks that the backs of my hands were greeted with.

Curling the comforter closer around my body, I glanced at the time on my phone screen and blew out a breath. I hadn't been asleep for more than three hours, but sleep would definitely be evading me now.

One glass of water later, I was standing at the doorway of my spare bedroom staring at the line of painted canvases that were resting against the back wall. Each one held different positions of the same ballerina slowly standing from the original bent over position I'd painted her in. I knew the easel held the final piece of the collection, a collection I named "Color Me Pretty", except the dancer was standing tall and facing forward and her features...I hadn't drawn them yet.

I walked over to examine how far I'd come the night before, when I'd decided to work on it to help me wind down after my last final, realizing shortly after I'd sat down to paint that I wasn't in the right mindset to finish the series. I was tired, spent, and focused only on what my final grades would be. If it weren't for Ribbons' class, I wouldn't have even stressed about it. But I'd barely passed the midterm exam and failed a few smaller quizzes that had come after. The paper we had to submit in person felt like a final send off between us, but I wasn't sure if the weeks of effort and research I'd put in was even worth it for somebody like her.

Potential, I'd scoffed to myself. Hadn't she told me she thought I had it once? That was worse than hearing half the things the tabloids said about me. They talked about my body and attitude, not my inability to learn or be successful as if I were hopeless altogether.

At two in the morning, I'd found myself walking

into my bedroom and digging through my closet for something that I hadn't held in my hands in a long time. Making my way back into the spare room, gripping the purple compact mirror that my mother always kept in her purse, I opened it and exhaled softly.

The girl staring back was tired, bags under her eyes, chapped lips, and flushed cheekbones. Looking from the glass to the paint I'd saved on my palette, I dipped my brush into the cream color I mixed and studied the mirror again.

It was four a.m. before I'd bit into my bottom lip and shadowed the sharp jawline and cheekbones heightened by weeks of hunger and physical activity before stepping back. I'd somehow gotten paint on my sleep shirt but didn't care as I took in the final product in front of me.

She was…beautiful. Swallowing past the lump in my throat, I grabbed my phone and lifted it to the painting before snapping a photo and texting the only person I wanted to see it.

He responded instantly.

Theo: *Almost as stunning as the real thing.*

I blushed and reread the text again before replying. *What are you doing up?*

Theo: *Running*

I double checked the time and shook my head, knowing he got up to work out early but still judging him for it. How many times had he told me he wished I would have waited and gotten more sleep? It seemed pointless to bring up how he rarely did the same.

Theo: *What are you doing up?*

I laughed at the irony of the question. *I couldn't sleep. Nightmare*

The three bubbles I expected to see pop up didn't appear at all, making me frown as I stared at the screen. A few seconds passed before I started typing something out, only to be stopped by three taps on the front door. Body locking, I stared at the door like someone was about to burst through it.

Theo: *Make sure to check the peephole*

Make sure to check the —

Grinning, I walked to the door, tossing the phone on the counter and did the exact opposite of what he told me to. When I opened it, I was met by Theo's disapproving but unsurprised scowl. "What did I just tell you?"

He didn't get to scold me any further before I was on my tiptoes and tugging his face down to mine until our lips brushed. I stepped back the same time he moved forward, closing the door behind him, and locking it without breaking the kiss. One of his arms wrapped around my waist, pulling me tighter into his body while I rested my hands on his broad shoulders.

Drawing back with a smile on my lips, I looked up at him and saw a similar curve to his own mouth. "When you said you were running, I thought you meant in your home gym."

He chuckled, smoothing hair out of my face before plucking my bottom lip with his thumb. "Found myself needing fresh air. It's quieter this time of night."

"Morning," I corrected.

"Same thing."

"Not when I'm up and you tell me that I should still be asleep," I pointed out, eyeing him with the expectation of his argument.

"What was your nightmare about?"

My lips parted for a second before closing. I didn't normally dream of my mother. At least, it wasn't the first thing my mind liked tormenting me with. And her looking at me like she'd been disappointed? It punched a hole in my heart that still ached. "My mom," I answered quietly, collecting my phone from where I'd tossed it and powering it off.

He came up behind me, gipping my shoulders with his masculine hands, massaging them until my head dipped back onto his chest. "I won't push, but if you want to talk about it, I'm here."

A hefty sigh escaped my lips. "That feels nice." Closing my eyes, I eased into his touch as he worked out the tension that had built up over the past couple of weeks. "I don't really want to talk about it. It was just... sad. It's one thing to dream about dancing or the stuff that's happened, but seeing my parents makes it harder when I wake up and they're not here."

I was sure he was nodding, but I didn't look. Instead, I absorbed the soft kiss he planted on my head before squeezing my shoulders and adding more pressure. "I get it, Della. You haven't had one about her in a while."

I'd told him about the other dreams. Not always after they happened, but he found out whenever I was extra quiet on the days we saw each other. Which, for the most part, was daily now. He'd given me some space to study for finals, but always showed up to make sure I was fed and happy. Even though I always wanted it to lead to more, it never did.

"Study," *he demanded when he saw me staring at him with my lip between my teeth and not so innocent thoughts lingering in my eyes for him to see.*

"Yes, Daddy."

I grinned thinking about the way he groaned when I called him that. Not surprisingly, he hated it. It probably would have been funnier if my father hadn't once been his best friend, or if he weren't so obsessed with the repercussions of our changing relationship. It didn't stop me from getting a rise out of him when I could, though.

"Can I see your painting?" he asked out of the blue. My eyes cracked open as I looked up at him, already seeing him watching me carefully as he waited for a reply.

I reached down and grabbed his hand, squeezing his fingers and leading him toward the room where the paint was still strong in the air. I probably shouldn't have loved the smell so much, but I did. It calmed me in a different way.

Theo didn't let go of me as he stopped and stared at the paintings along the wall, noticing how each one held something strong—an emotion in the way her arms were held high or her body was twisted. When we walked over to the easel to see the final piece, a small breath escaped him. It was hard to watch him study the most intimate thing I'd created. The woman's face was undoubtedly mine, looking pained and saddened, but freed. The cheekbones, collarbones, and narrowed waistline were the same ones I'd seen in the mirror. The light blue eyes that had darkened with every meal I missed stared back at me, but not in a taunt.

"You never cease to amaze me," he murmured, focusing on my face. "What are you planning to do with these?"

I shrugged. "I'm not sure." Truthfully, I hadn't even planned on painting so many. But the first one felt like a step in a direction I hadn't gone in some time. Then the second one happened. The third. By the fourth one, I knew the collection would have five, and the fifth would have to be the finale that I deserved. The one where I looked out into the crowd with my head held high and my body in the proper position, without flinching or breaking contact from those who stared back and judged my form.

Something broke in my chest, and a wave of ease filled the crevices that once suffocated the organs inside. "I thought about selling them, but I don't think I'm quite ready for that. So, maybe I'll keep them. For now, at least."

"The fact you painted them is powerful," he told me,

cupping my cheek with his palm before giving me a genuine smile. "You should be proud."

"You always tell me that."

"I won't stop."

Wetting my bottom lip, I try coming up with a sane response to that. The *thumping* of my heart said more than my words could because I was beyond them when Theo was like this. "Why are you always so…"

One of his brows quirked.

"Perfect?"

He grinned. "I've been called many things before, Della, but never that." Dropping his hand from my face, he looked me over from head to toe before suggesting, "Want to try getting some more sleep? I need to jump in the shower, but I can meet you in bed after."

The thought of a naked Theo West only a room away had me unsettled. It wasn't the first time he'd used my shower. Shortly after getting Ramsay, the dog had peed all over him and he had no other choice but to jump in and use my "girly soap" that made him smell like me. I didn't think he minded as much as he said because he always told me how much he loved the way I smelled like strawberries when he held me against him. Dallas had to bring him clean clothes that day, meeting me at the door with a smile on his face like he thought more was going on. I didn't correct him, didn't give him any indication one way or the other.

I hadn't wanted to.

"Want to watch a movie instead?" I bargained, uneasy about falling back asleep after the last time.

He didn't seem appreciative of that idea, eyeing me with disapproval. "I want you to try getting some rest. You look tired, Della."

I frowned. "Gee, thanks."

I swore he rolled his eyes, but I couldn't be sure because he turned on me the same time his eyes had moved. "Don't pretend you don't know I think you're beautiful regardless."

"Beauty is relative."

"Get your ass in bed, Della."

"One movie."

"Della."

"What about that action one you mentioned wanting to see? The one set in World War Two?"

He sighed.

"Please?" I added despite myself.

A palm swiped down the front of his face and I knew he was going to agree. Reluctantly, he nodded once. "Give me ten minutes."

I wrapped my arms around his waist. "I would make it twenty. You kind of smell."

He swatted my butt and grumbled something under his breath that I couldn't quite make out, but I could see the amusement dancing in his eyes when he pulled away and pointed toward the couch. "Ten," he repeated.

"Fifteen," I called out after him.

It shouldn't have surprised me that the second he was beside me on the couch, he pulled me over and rested my head on his thigh like we'd done before. With one hand in my hair, the other taking the remote from me, he turned the TV on and…

Put it on *Mysteries at the Museum.*

I'd almost told him right then and there that I loved him. I loved Theo West, and not just as little Della. I wasn't sure the love that consumed my chest and soul could be put to words in the way they deserved.

When his grip tightened on me, I wondered if he knew. If, maybe, he felt the same way. Instead of asking, instead of just ripping off the Band-Aid, I remained quiet.

We watched the show in silence.

I WAS RUFFLED awake with a pair of lips against my temple and a blanket being positioned over my body. Murmuring something, I reached out and grabbed a warm arm, cracking my eyes open as Theo slid his phone into his pocket.

"I need to get going," he told me softly.

It took me a minute to sit up and realize the apartment was bathed in sunlight. "What time is it?" He was probably late to work considering it was a Friday morning, not that it mattered since he was his own boss.

"A little after eight."

"Can't you skip work today?" I sounded pitiful and went as far as debating on giving him a puppy dog look in hopes he'd stay.

He didn't. "I'm meeting with someone in an hour and I need to get home to change."

My shoulders dropped. "Dallas?" I had no reason to fish, but he hadn't been forthcoming about the phone calls I knew he'd been exchanging with somebody. It wasn't that I didn't trust him, I just wanted to know what was going on because I didn't like being kept out of things that usually had to do with me. If they didn't, he'd tell me. Vent. Get angry. He never apologized for it and I never asked him to, even if his bad days were trying when someone at the office pissed him off.

"Not Dallas." He bent down and pecked my lips, not lingering long. "I need to go. Would you like to get dinner tonight? I could get Abigail to make reservations somewhere."

"Denny's doesn't need reservations."

He chuckled. "If you want Denny's, that's where we'll go. I can come over around seven if that works for you."

I pushed off the blanket he'd put on me and stood, stretching my sore muscles from how I'd been sleeping. I couldn't complain though. We'd fallen asleep watching television and Theo only had the corner of the couch. He had to have had a kink in his neck at the very least. "Seven works for me. Tomorrow I'm going out with Lawrence and Tiffany to celebrate finals being over." I wasn't sure why I felt the need to add that. It wasn't like we had plans. "I know we don't have anything sched-uled, but I figured—"

"It's good to know where you are," he said with a

shrug. "And I'm glad you and your friends are going out. I have something to go to tomorrow night anyway."

Gnawing on the inside of my cheek, I watched him walk around the couch. "Is it Flamell?" He stopped walking and turned to face me within a second. "The person you're meeting with today?"

He eyed me suspiciously. "How do you know Flamell?"

Squirming under his penetrating eyes, I admitted, "I don't. But his name was always showing up on your screen when your phone rang. Or I assume it's a guy."

"You *assume* it's a guy?"

Why did he look so angry all of a sudden? I hadn't meant to strike a nerve or throw an accusation. "I didn't mean anything bad by it, Theo. I'm saying that I'm not ruling out the possibility that Flamell could be a woman." Although, I really, really hoped it wasn't.

He took a large step toward me, eating up the distance between us. "And why would a woman be calling me?"

The best my stupid mind could come up with was, "Why would a man be calling you all hours of the night?" Turned out that was the wrong thing to say.

"Why would a woman be calling me, Della?" That time, his tone was hard. Offended. I wasn't sure how to respond, only making the tendons in his neck strain. "I don't even know why you'd think that. Flamell is somebody I'm working with on something important. That's all."

I sighed. "I didn't think it was a woman, I…"

He waited, jaw ticking.

My cheeks were on fire. "I don't know what to say, Theo. I swear I didn't mean to upset you, but it isn't like we've discussed this. For once, I'm using my brain by not *assuming* anything."

Again. The wrong thing to say. If steam could physically blow out of people's ears, it would definitely be coming out of Theo's. "If I didn't have somewhere to be, I'd tell you exactly what my thoughts are on what we haven't 'discussed' before now."

I blinked.

He took another step forward until there was barely any room between our bodies. "I wish you could see yourself the way I see you. How smart, kind, and beautiful you are on the inside and out. I really fucking wish..." Teeth grinding, he shook his head. "I don't have time right now. Tonight."

Tonight? "Theo, maybe we should —"

"Not now, Della."

Was he kidding me? He was about to say something that would probably change everything, and he *didn't want to talk about it now?* "What is so important you can't stay here and discuss this now with me? What's more important than finally talking about u —"

"It's complicated, Della! Christ." He swiped a palm through his hair. "Don't act like I haven't been here for you, haven't been showing you what all of this is to me. If I had women calling, I wouldn't be sleeping on your goddamn couch and waking up with a raging fucking boner and a knot in my shoulders the size of Texas."

Flinching, I knew he was right. Sort of. It wasn't like Theo ever had a lot of women calling him before. In fact, I didn't know of any that really bothered him. I wasn't naïve enough not to think that meant he didn't have…company when he needed it. That was beyond the point. He was upset, so was I. Everything I was trying to say was making it worse.

"Fine." My voice cracked as I stepped back, putting a sliver of space between us. "Fine. Okay. Go have your meeting with Flamell."

He tipped his head back and sighed at the ceiling, swiping his palms down his face. "I know I can be an asshole, but I'm not trying to be. It's not that I don't want to clear the air between us, I need to handle this first."

I nodded.

Pinning me with his eyes again, he said, "I mean it, Della. I'm not saying that this is more important than you. Understand?"

Even though I didn't like the nature of his tone, how condescending it felt, I nodded. Again. What else could I do? Theo had never lied to me before, so why would he now? He hadn't made me feel like I wasn't important before, so there was no point to assume that was what was happening. "Understood."

He watched me for too long, another sigh escaping him nearly inaudibly, before he shook his head and pulled me into his body. "I'll see you tonight, okay?" His lips pressed against the crown of my skull as my arms wrapped around his waist in a tight hug.

I wanted to ask him to stay, wanted to beg him to give me something. I did neither. I nodded into his chest, breathed in his scent, and stepped back to watch him leave.

When the door clicked closed behind him, I dropped onto the couch and stared at the blank TV screen. As soon as I turned my phone back on a few minutes later, there was a text waiting.

Theo: *I already miss you.*

DIVERS WAS loud when I entered, searching for the face that had called me in tears too early for a bar rescue. Tugging my father's leather jacket tighter around the maxi dress I'd thrown on quickly, I found the head of raven black hair sitting at the corner of the bar counter.

"Kat?" She turned her head instantly, cheeks damp and eyes bloodshot. Was she…? "I didn't mean to take so long. Are you okay?"

She blinked at me. "You came." Her voice was raspy, hoarse, like she'd been crying for a while. Taking the stool beside her, I slid down as the bartender came over with caution in his eyes.

"Of course, I did." I shook my head when the bartender asked if I wanted something to drink. Then, on second thought, said, "Water?" When he set it down in front of me, I smiled and slid it to Katrina. She murmured something, not touching the cold glass.

"What's wrong?" I asked her, hoping she'd meet my

eyes. When she didn't, I knew it was something big. "Kat?"

Her head dipped down—the bright eyeshadow painted on her lids the same extravagant color as normal but nowhere near as comforting as it should have been. She had eyeliner smudged under her bottom lashes, making my frown deepen as I examined her paled expression. "I messed up, Della. Real bad."

"How?"

When she finally looked up, there was guilt weighing down her eyes. It made me lock up, my stomach heavy like I was expecting the worst. My father gave me the same look once. It was the day he was sentenced, right before they took him away for good. Right to his death. He'd looked at me, his eyes burdened, bittersweet emotion in his rugged smile, and said, *"I love you, Adele. Remember that."*

"How, Kat?" I repeated, voice breaking, a knot of nerves hanging onto each letter that passed my lips.

Her hands drifted from her lap to the counter, fingers wrapping around the glass but not moving it an inch. "Sam." Shoulders tightening, she clenched the glass with white knuckles until I thought she'd break it. "Della, do you still have it?"

Brows pinching, I asked, "Have what?"

Her eyes looked around the room before meeting mine again. *"It.* Do you have it? What I gave you?" My lips parted for a moment before snapping closed.

"Oh my god." *Oh god*. The purse in my lap suddenly felt heavier. Much heavier. I hadn't thought a lot about what I'd kept hidden in the inner compartment since the day I'd dropped it in there.

Kat's eyes widened wider than mine. "I messed up, Della, but I'm trying to fix it. You have to believe me."

"What are you—"

"Give it to me," she whispered urgently, her hand snaking out toward my bag. I kept a firm grip on it, jerking it away. "Della, I mean it. I'm not trying to use. You can't have it."

"Are you crazy?" I hissed, getting off the stool and glaring at her. Was that why she made me come? Why she'd been crying? Because she was coming down and needed another hit? "You need help, Kat."

"I'm not going to use it—"

"Is there a problem?" The bartender looked between us again, his eyes focused on Kat and her shaky hands and red-rimmed eyes. I didn't blame him for being suspicious. She was clearly unwell. And I'd walked right into it.

"No," I told him after a moment of breathing. I didn't want to cause a scene, and certainly didn't want the cops called. "We're all right," I assured him when he didn't move. It took him a moment before he bobbed his head and walked back to the other end of the bar as an older gentleman called out a food order.

Turning to Kat, I gave her a once over again. Slowly. I was beginning to understand why people always talked about my appearance. It was easy to see when other people were falling apart, even if they hadn't experienced it firsthand. Watching Kat, her ticks, her harsh breathing, her darting eyes, I'd seen what everybody probably saw of me for so long.

A broken girl.

"You need help," I told her again, hoping she'd listen to the urgency in my own tone. I didn't want to see her break. I'd known what that was like and wanted to help. I knew Ren, Tiffany, so many people, have told me not to worry about other people's problems. I couldn't ignore it. Kat had been my friend once. We were long past that, though. Our friendship was a distant memory.

Taking a hesitant step toward her, I took a deep breath and added, "It's okay to admit. It doesn't make you weak, I promise. People will probably say it does, but you just need to surround yourself with people who will support you instead."

I swore I was getting to her when I saw her eyes soften. Then, at the last second, her jaw ticked, and she scoffed. Scoffed like she had the day I walked away from her at her place when I wouldn't join them. The day she'd given me what she was after. How could I have forgotten I'd had it? It wasn't like she'd given me counterfeit money. I had *drugs* in my purse. Drugs that I kept because I thought she'd been right at one time. I believed I'd needed that escape, that possibility of what she said it could do for my weight and energy.

How stupid was I?

She stood, pushing herself up from the counter and shaking her head adamantly. "I'm not asking for me. If you care as much as you pretend to, then listen to me. I want to help."

"And *I* want to help *you*—"

"Samantha's father is after you!" Her rushed words caught more than just my attention. A few people sitting around us looked our way with drawn brows.

"What?"

"Samantha's dad, Richard Pratt." She stepped toward me again, but I didn't move this time. "I messed up. That's what I'm trying to tell you. I can't fix it if you don't give it back."

Samantha's dad? Wasn't that who Theo had warned me about before? He hadn't liked any of the girls or their families, but he warned me with a conviction that was beyond riches and selfishness. He knew something that he wasn't telling me, and Kat knew too.

"What is he trying to do?"

I could tell how badly she pleaded for me to listen, but I needed something. Handing over what she wanted could end just as badly as not. Where would that leave me? Us? "You need to tell me something that would make me believe you're not just asking for..." I gestured toward my bag, hoping the prying eyes didn't know what was going on.

The bartender was watching us a little too carefully in between customers, and I wanted to move the conversation somewhere else but needed the comfort of a public place for protection. I wished I hadn't felt that tinge of panic in my gut, the mistrust, but it was going to save me in the long run from people like Kat.

What she said was something I hadn't expected, hadn't anticipated at all. "Everybody knows that you and Theodore West are each other's weaknesses. You love each other, Della. Richard Pratt wants to exploit that like he's done before."

I stared.

Unblinking.

Unbreathing.

"You love him," she stated. There was no question, no doubt in her thickened words. "He loves you too. Sam's dad uses people's love for those they care about against them. He'll do it to you too."

I swallowed. "You don't know that." I hadn't been talking about Sam's father.

To my surprise, she knew that and smiled. It was sad and distant but knowing. "But you do."

Closing my eyes, I counted to three and inhaled slowly. The *thump thump thump* of my heart was hard and heavy in my chest, echoing throughout my body as I reached for my bag and unzipped the top to dig out what she wanted. When I looked at her again, she'd stepped toward me, taking my hand like two friends comforting each other. That wasn't why she did it. The small baggy disappeared from my palm and into hers, her hand dropping back to her body mere seconds after getting what she wanted.

"I do," I told her thickly, staring at the floor. Theo hadn't told me he loved me, but I knew it. It was because I loved him that I couldn't fight her on this anymore. For once, I was choosing to fight my own battles. I was choosing myself.

I chose him.

"Get help, Kat." That was the last thing I told her before walking out of Divers, calling Dallas, and waiting at my apartment for the person I've loved forever.

Theo.

chapter nineteen

THEO

DALLAS WAS quiet when I opened the back door of the sleek, black tinted car and slid onto the cool leather seat. The subtle clearing of his throat over the air conditioner blowing had me eyeing him in the rearview. "What?"

"Della met with Katrina Murphy today."

Jaw hardening, I straightened in the seat, forgoing the seatbelt. "When was that?"

He pulled out onto the street, getting in line with the backed-up traffic. "An hour ago, boss. Maybe a little more. I tried asking her if she was all right, but she didn't want to talk about it. Thought you should know that it looked like she was crying."

What the hell was she doing with the Murphy girl? She'd told me months ago they weren't friends anymore, especially since the other two were being prima donna bitches to her like their fucking mothers were to everyone. "She didn't say anything?"

"No."

"You sure she was crying?" It was rare Della did that around anyone. She told me once she didn't like people seeing her weak, which was bullshit. Her mother always told her it was okay to cry. What the hell had she told Della for years when she was little? *"The sky isn't weak, is it, sweet Della? It cries too sometimes."*

Elizabeth always told Della stories about Greek mythology—how everything and everybody had a place. Della would always ask her to tell her a new one or repeat her favorites. Shit, she'd compared me and a few of Anthony's other friends to the Gods themselves. Maybe it was that day I knew that little girl owned me. Her words didn't pump my ego, they wrapped me around her finger. Either way, Zeus had been her favorite. She'd told me stories about the sky and the storms and how much she wished she were a goddess. I'd told her she was. Elizabeth would always smile and shake her head at me.

"Pretty sure."

"Fuck," I sighed, looking out the window. I'd planned on going home to change before meeting Della, but things changed. "Take me to her complex, would you?"

I saw the faintest smile in the rearview, before he'd

answered, "I already planned on it. Knew you'd want to see her once I told you."

Blinking slowly, I eyed him. "That obvious?"

"You're there for her," was all he said.

A noise rose from the back of my throat that wasn't really an answer. Dallas chuckled anyway, amused for a reason I had no interest in exploring. He could think what he wanted, I wasn't going to think about it more than I needed to.

After a moment of silence between us that was filled with cars honking, people yelling, and construction work from 3rd Avenue, I said, "Do you know if she was okay?"

That damn smile grew. "She seemed as okay as she could be. Just upset. I know she used to be friends with Katrina, but..." I waited impatiently for him to finish as he moved forward once the light ahead turned green. "Well, the girl is using. Word on the street is that she's distributing to the Pratt and Vandyke girl. A few others, too. Flamell has some pictures of them over on the south side, near the warehouse where Richard Pratt has a few businesses. The Murphy girl was with a group he couldn't identify. Dealing for him, probably."

I couldn't believe it. "You're just telling me this now? Flamell didn't say shit to me about that. If there's more evidence that Pratt is letting people like his goddamn friend's daughter distribute, then —"

Dallas sighed heavily. "I don't think it's a good idea to get involved, boss. Think about Della. Flamell knows you two are close. If you take that information and run with it, what would that do to her?"

"She was around somebody who's clearly unstable. If she's using and dealing, Della shouldn't be around her."

"I'm sure she knows that."

"Then what the fuck is the problem?"

"They were friends," he pointed out lightly, locking eyes with me in the mirror. "Even if they aren't anymore, we both know Della will always hold some sort of loyalty to people that were in her life. She wouldn't want to see Kat brought down."

Fuck me. He was right and he damn well knew it when he nodded once. Sometimes, I wanted to shake Della until sense was brought to her, but that was selfish of me. Her loyalty wasn't a bad thing. "She'd want to see her get help instead," I agreed, shaking my head.

Dallas hummed in agreement.

Cursing, I looked at my watch. "What's Flamell going to do about it then?"

There was a brief pause. "What you can't."

I stared at the back of his head until understanding sunk in. "He's going to go after the girls to get them to talk. There'd be no way for Pratt to get off with a slap on the wrist with actual witnesses testifying against him on top of the other evidence."

Again, Dallas nodded.

Sitting back, I watched the scenery pass slowly by us. Rush hour was always a pain in the ass, but it wasn't too different from any other time of day when you were in the city. It was suffocating, loud. I'd considered moving more times than I could count, but never did. I didn't want to be too far away from Della.

I spoke up again. "Everybody seems to know what Della is to me. Isn't always a good thing considering Pratt is trying to use it against me. Here I thought I was discreet."

"Do you want people to know?"

"Eventually," I murmured.

"If you don't mind me saying—" I chuckled over his cautiousness, it never stopped him from sharing his two cents. "I don't think people care as much as Pratt, or you, think they would."

"And why is that?"

A shoulder lifted as he glanced at me in the mirror again. "You two are the kind of people that others inspire to be like. They want fairytales, not ghost stories."

"Who says we're a fairytale?"

"You've loved her for a long time."

"Not like—"

"Exactly, boss. You've loved her in a thousand different ways. That kind of love is the well-rounded story people want. You don't only see her as some young girl who looks up to you. You see her for what she grew into. You're supportive and protective and willing to do anything for her, just like her parents would have wanted."

"I doubt Anthony would have been okay with what I'm doing with his daughter, Dallas," I mused dryly.

He laughed softly. "Probably not. But, not to be disrespectful, he isn't around to tell you not to. He made his bed and doesn't have a say in how you and Della make yours."

I let that sink in for a moment. "You think it really wouldn't matter to people?"

"I think hope goes a long way."

"Hope?"

A head bob. "That Adele Saint James can get her happily ever after with someone she's always had by her side. The general public knows she isn't like her family. They're rooting for her."

I found that hard to believe. Not that they'd root for her, but that they'd do the same for *us*. But maybe I was a cynic and wanted to think I didn't deserve the same ending because I was struggling to accept the story changed. The endgame seemed pointless to fight though because our narrative never drifted. The one where I've loved Della her entire life.

I was just going to love her ten times harder for the rest of mine.

"Sir?" he said cautiously. When I didn't answer, he chose to continue. "You've always been there for her, but when everything comes to light, she'll need you."

"I know, Dallas."

"All of you."

All of you.

Blowing out a quiet breath, I found myself nodding to the window. "She already has all of me."

I was met by silence.

And that fucking smile.

SEEING the lean blonde sprawled across the bed on her stomach had the tightness in my chest disappearing in a millisecond. All it took was one look at those long, tan legs and I was done. Walking around the side, I sat on the edge and moved the hair away from her face which was buried into her pillow, one arm wrapped around it while the other was somewhere under the blanket she was twisted in.

She stirred when I brushed my fingers along her cheek, letting out a little breathy moan that sounded like my name. After a few seconds, she turned her head and fluttered her tired eyes open until they found mine. "Theo?" Sitting up, she moved hair out of her face and looked at the clock on her nightstand. "I didn't mean to fall asleep."

"You must have needed it." Her bottom lip drew into her mouth. With a shrug, she swiped her eyelids with her fisted hands, and that was when I realized they were puffy. "You've been crying."

"I—"

"And don't try lying about it." Situating myself so I sat beside her with my back against her headboard, I crossed one ankle over the other and watched her. "Dallas told me."

She frowned. "He's such a tattletale."

I chuckled. "He's doing his job."

"So, you're finally admitting it?"

I quirked my brow.

"You've insisted for years that I should use him to get around the city, even though you made it seem like he was hired by Sophie." She rolled her eyes and slid backward to mimic my position, crossing her arms over her chest. I hadn't told her Sophie hired him I just hadn't denied it when she'd asked me as much. "I always suspected he was watching after me a little too much for him to be Sophie's employee."

"Why would you say that?" It wasn't like Sophie had anything against Della. She was too headstrong about how she wanted her niece to live, but she loved her.

"She's Sophie," came the response I wasn't surprised about. "She usually doesn't do anything without it being in her best interest."

I could have tried arguing, but I didn't. "I hired Dallas years ago. Wanted to make sure you were looked after when I wasn't around."

"Is that how you see me?"

I was silent, confused as I watched her face twist in horror.

"As your responsibility? Because that kind of sucks to think about, Theo. I don't want to be treated like some ward—"

"Stop." Shifting, I moved the blanket away from her and readjusted myself, so my body was fully turned toward hers. "I was more than willing to have this conversation over dinner, but now works too."

I refused to let her say anything before I got out what I had to say first. It was clear she wanted to inter-ject, but after our conversation that morning, I wasn't about to let her imagination run wild over what was going on here.

"When I told you that I didn't want to go back to what we were, I meant it. It's impossible to be who we were when you were just little Della and I was only your dad's friend. You were never my responsibility even if I wanted to believe you were. When you got older, when you started walking and talking with a newfound sass that made people laugh and turn their heads, I wished you were only that. Honest to God, Della, I wish sometimes I looked at you like I did then. As this adorable little girl who looked at the world with such innocence and hope. That meant that I didn't fail you and your family by letting corruption sink in.

"And before you tell me I wouldn't have been able to stop it from happening, I know. I've thought about it countless times and drove myself fucking crazy. You know what I realized after drinking myself into a fucking stupor over it?"

Slowly, she shook her head.

I took her hand and draped it on my thigh, squeezing it. Maybe a little too tightly, a little too aggressively, but she didn't pull away. "You wouldn't have been the person you are today if it hadn't been for everyone else's choices. I'm not saying I don't wish your father would have taken a different path, or that I wouldn't go back in time and change anything if I could. But you wouldn't be the amazing woman sitting here beside me if he hadn't fucked up." Ignoring her flinch over the blunt statement, I weaved our fingers together. "I don't how many times you need me to tell you that you're beautiful, inspiring, and the exact kind of woman I need to ground me, for you to understand, but I'll tell you over and over again until you get it.

"The truth of the matter is you don't need me to. You don't need me to tell you that you're anything because you already know it. You wouldn't have gone back to school, painted those paintings, or let your friend convince you to dance if you didn't know you were a strong woman, worthy of the kind of love I'm going to give you for a long fucking time. Not because I'm obligated to, but because I wouldn't know what else to do with myself if I couldn't."

I didn't miss the way her lips parted, how that breathy little exhale escaped them, or how her fingers gripped mine like she couldn't quite believe what I'd said.

I swallowed. "We're going to have bad days, Della. The both of us. It's not only you, sweetheart. We'll have to figure out how to navigate them together."

She blinked. "Because…"

I raised her hand to my lips and pressed a kiss against her warm skin. "I love you, Della. Plain and simple." Her eyes closed when I pressed another kiss against her ring finger, making a point. "Think you can stick with me while we figure this out? It's not going to be easy. There's a lot between us that people may or may not understand. I don't want them to dictate what we do, to make their opinions part of the relationship I want to explore with you."

Every day since the first time Anthony and Elizabeth asked me to watch Della, I'd been wrapped around her finger. Every day was a new adventure—something to learn. Her quirks, the things she hated, the things she liked. When she asked me to dance with her, I danced. When she asked me to hang up her pictures, I hung them up. Shit, how many hours of YouTube tutorials did I watch to learn how to braid hair because she wanted me to braid hers? There was nothing I wasn't willing to do to keep a smile on her face, and that hadn't changed. If anything, the need to make her happy grew into something all-consuming.

"You're an idiot." I froze at her words, keeping a firm hold on her hand as I watched her eyes flutter closed for a moment before cracking back open to study me carefully. "You're such an idiot, Theodore West. Do you know how long I've loved you? How many times I've said it as something more than your friend's daughter who looked up to you? If you can promise me that you'll be by my side during my worst days, then how could I not be there for you during yours?"

My throat bobbed as she rose on her knees and swung one leg over my lap, straddling me. Sinking down, she sat there and stared like she was afraid I'd change my mind and leave. If she thought that, then *she* was the idiot.

She ran a palm across my jaw, thumbing my bottom lip before leaning in, hovering over them with hers. "I know people won't understand right away, but they'll see."

"And what is it they'll see?"

Her lips brushed mine as she said, "That I love you too much to let you go."

Pressing her closer into me, I wrapped an arm around her waist as my other hand cupped the back of her head to deepen the kiss. She parted my lips and slipped her tongue inside, but it was me who took it farther. Rolling my hips upward, I listened to her tell-tale moan before flipping us over, so she was on her back with her bare legs spread for my body to slip between.

When her arms snaked around my neck to pull me closer, my cell rang. Ignoring it, I bit her bottom lip. Trailing my mouth down her neck and nipping it as I moved my hands to the oversized tee she wore to strip it off her, the phone pinged in my pocket.

"Fuck."

"You should check that."

"It's probably Dallas. He's outside waiting for us." Momentarily, I'd forgotten about our dinner plans. I liked the thought of spreading her legs and eating her out instead.

Her face reddened like she knew what I was thinking. "He's waiting for us?"

"I can send him off."

For a moment, it looked like she was going to nod. Then, in a quiet voice, she admitted, "I am kind of hungry." My cock throbbed with a need to be inside her, but I ignored it. It wasn't every day Della admitted something like that. Most people would consider the statement mundane, but I knew better.

Standing up, I offered her my hand, trying to pretend I didn't see the way her eyes roamed down to the large bulge that was tenting my pants. "Come on then, Della. Let's grab something to eat. We can continue this later."

She bit into her lip again, eyes sparkling with mischief. "Is that a promise?"

I bent down and kissed her again, groaning when her tongue swiped mine. "If I don't come inside you at least once tonight, I'll probably die, sweetheart. That would be a real shame, wouldn't it?"

"You can't say things like that to me," she all but groaned, pulling a pillow over her face.

I laughed and yanked it away. "Can't help it. The thought of me inside of you, maybe even planting something there someday, drives me fucking nuts."

Her sharp inhale wasn't lost on me. "You would want that?"

Did she not? I could remember all the times she would share her elaborate future, family and white picket fence included. She'd never described a high-rise penthouse where her children couldn't go outside and play without the risk of crime around. It was always some place remote, quiet, and peaceful. A house surrounded by grass and trees and close friends and family.

"If you do," I told her honestly, brushing her face with my knuckles. "Until then, practice makes perfect."

She rolled her eyes and smiled. "You would make a really great father, Theo."

The thought of her with a swollen belly only made my cock that much harder. "I need to get you out of here before I lock us inside your bedroom and have my way with you in every position humanly possible to try making that happen sooner than we both want."

"Theo!"

I swatted her ass. "Come on. Time to go."

She just laughed.

chapter twenty

DELLA

I HADN'T WANTED to go to Divers after the celebration dinner Ren, Tiffany, and I went to for the end of school. It was my annoying best friend who insisted we needed to go, which meant there was somebody there he wanted to see.

Tiffany nudged me at the table we'd secured off to the side. "What's up?" She was on drink number three, four if you counted the shot she took, and watched me carefully with the tiny straw in her mouth. She barely looked buzzed but the glaze in her eyes told me she was going to feel it soon enough.

Ren had disappeared shortly after we'd arrived, talking up some redhead who looked oddly like Rupert

Grint, which made sense considering Lawrence watched the Harry Potter movies at least four times a year. Tiffany had rolled her eyes, ordered us drinks, and watched him work over the guy who had to be our age if not a little older.

"Nothing." I faked a smile. I wanted to ask her the same thing after seeing the frown she was fighting all night. "I guess Ren and Ben stopped seeing each other for good."

All I got was a shrug.

As if he knew we were talking about him, he squeezed the Rupert lookalike's arm and walked over to us with a grin. "Ladies. Miss me?" He directed the last question to Tiffany, bumping her with his shoulder. When she recoiled, his grin disappeared.

"I was asking Della what was wrong," she told him, finishing off her drink before putting the glass down a little too hard on the table. One of my brows raised.

Ren turned to me slowly. "What's up?"

I couldn't explain the bottomless pit in my stomach where a mixture of flutters and firecrackers went off. I wanted Theo here, taking me away, telling me we were going to spend time together tonight. But he knew where I was. He'd encouraged the night out, saying, *"I'll be here when you get back, baby girl."* That term melted me in a puddle at his feet and he knew it.

"Like I told her. Nothing." Eyeing Tiffany, I noticed she was doing her best to avoid looking in Ren's direction.

"You're mopey," she accused.

Ren laughed. "She's probably moping still about the grade she got in Ribbons' class. Her final dropped it."

I frowned at the reminder. "I didn't deserve a C on that paper. It was well mapped out and researched. I spent way too long making sure she'd have no reason to critique it."

Tiffany snorted. "You're upset about school? It's over. Isn't that why we're celebrating tonight? You shouldn't even be thinking about anything other than alcohol, which begs the question of how many drinks have you had because it's clearly not enough."

I rolled my eyes and sipped at the one I'd been nursing for half an hour. It was warm and too sweet, but I didn't want to give them an excuse to order another. "Ribbons hates me, so I wanted to prove to her that I could talk about topics related to my father and do it in a professional, well thought out manner. And she *still* nearly flunked me on it."

The paper had been on political scandals in New York City. I'd even referenced Malik's case that she was so willing to bring up during our one strange conversation, which was where I discovered that her late husband had been put out of work after he was accused of stealing the money George Malik was responsible for taking. Apparently, their life had been swept up in the scandals she'd long since studied, making her hate the situation more. I wasn't sure how her husband had died, but a few articles I came across had mentioned suicide, and in that moment I'd felt sorry for Professor Ribbons. Nobody deserved to lose people they loved and cared about. I knew that all too well.

The more I'd researched George Malik and other cases similar to his, I'd cringed at the implications found in the thousands of reports online and pushed past the suggestions reporters and police had made that everything he stood for was no different than my father when his time in court had surfaced. And as if all that work I'd done to collect information about Malik hadn't been cringeworthy enough, I'd even included pieces from my father's case because of the current nature of it. Just to prove to Ribbons I wasn't shying away from right and wrong because I was a Saint James.

All I could picture during it was my father being carted away too many times. I watched him get guided out of our old house, court rooms, visitation rooms, and eventually, the funeral home. How many times did I need to relive that torture, that emotional discord, just to get other people to see that I was a victim too?

When I saw that C in the corner of the paper in bold red ink and a circle around it, I felt defeated. Shattered. Maybe I should have talked to her, tried arguing for a better grade or asking why she'd given me that one at the very least because it wasn't like I took an approach that was questioning her belief system. If anything, I was agreeing with her about how screwed up our justice system worked. I couldn't though. I was tired of chasing after people for answers.

Logically, I knew the paper was thought out and researched and edited so many times the facts were drilled into my brain. Ribbons didn't like me, and whatever potential she said I had was gone. Maybe it was non-existent to begin with. And when Theo had woken up in the middle of the night to find me working on the paper in the living room, he'd told me something that I'd only agreed with after getting the paper back. *"Why bother obsessing over impressing her, Della? You should never waste your time on people who are set on misunderstanding you."*

He'd been right. Again. I didn't tell him that though and told him to go back to bed instead. Theo, of course, didn't listen. He sat on the opposite end of the couch with his feet propped on the coffee table, the TV on the lowest volume, and Ramsay curled on his chest. He'd fallen asleep keeping me company while I finished proofreading the paper.

It was Ren who pointed out, "You still got a B- in that class. I know people on the team who took it and walked out with Cs and Ds despite studying their asses off. Tommy, you remember him right? He was the guy who…" He winced. Tommy had been the guy at the frat house who'd noticed I was acting off. After being drugged, presumably. "Anyway, he's a political science major and said all her classes were tough."

"Doesn't Ribbons hate everyone?" That came from Tiffany, who wasn't completely wrong. It seemed like she disliked me more thanks to my bloodline.

"Yeah, well…" I shook it off, brushing a hand down my face and curling hair behind my ear. "It doesn't matter. I care about my grades and doing well." *And making everybody like you even though it's humanly impossible.*

"You're such a nerd," Ren chuckled when he saw my disgruntled expression. He downed his last drink and looked around as a few women eyed him from the table over.

Tiffany noticed too, making a face at him like she couldn't believe he was even giving them his bedroom eyes. "What's going on with you and what's his face? You guys aren't tickling each other's fancies anymore?"

I smiled at her pretending she didn't know Ben's name but hid it behind my glass when she eyed me with a narrowed gaze in warning.

Ren flashed her a sultry smile. "It wasn't our fancies we were tickling on each other, baby. Why, are you jealous?"

The gagging came instantly from both me and Tiffany, but mostly from her. I wasn't sure what to think about them. They'd become fast friends but flirted more times than I think they realized. It was cute…and maybe a little weird. Only because Tiffany was insistent that she and Ren were nothing more than friends and never would be. And Ren…well, he hadn't offered me his opinion on what he thought about Tiffany, which left a lot to interpretation.

"You wish, Lawrence. I'm not keen on catching an STD anytime soon, but thanks."

A palm flew to his chest. "Ouch."

I shook my head at both their theatrics, focusing on Ren again. "So, is that guy over there the new flavor?"

I'd felt bad for asking in front of Tiffany, but I think she wanted to know even if she wouldn't admit it.

"Maybe." He shrugged. "Decided redheads were my thing."

My lips twitched. "Not shocking. Weren't the actors who played the Weasley twins your first real crushes?"

"Wasn't yours an anime character?" he shot back defensively.

I laughed. "I wasn't being mean I was pointing out that it's no surprise."

Tiffany grumbled out something about another drink before heading toward the bar.

"What's her deal?" he asked, leaning against the spot she'd been at.

"You're so stupid."

He had the nerve to look offended.

"She likes you, Ren."

The noise he made sounded like a cross between a grunt and dying chicken. "What the hell are you talking about?"

We both looked over at where Tiffany waited by the bar. A few guys had also been staring, one of them walking over to her and leaning down to say something that she didn't seem to appreciate based on the scowl. "It's pretty obvious. Then again, you're always busy scoping out other people to notice."

"She's..." He frowned, looking back at me with something that resembled sympathy. "I just don't think she's my type. She makes a great friend. It's not like I don't like her."

"You just don't like her like that," I said, nodding sadly. "I get it. We can't force ourselves to like people if the spark isn't there."

"Sounds like you've tried, Del."

I nibbled on my bottom lip, fighting off a small smile. "I mean, I did sleep with you."

The laugh that burst from him caught way more attention than I wanted. "Oh, shit. Shots fired." He downed the rest of his drink and shook his head. "So, it's really him, huh?"

I knew who he meant. "Do you wish it'd been you?" I also knew that wasn't what he was implying.

His sigh was lighthearted. "Nah. If I wasn't such an asshole maybe I would have tried winning you over, but we both know it wouldn't have worked because I'm a man whore and that guard dog of yours has always been territorial."

"I love him, Ren."

"Yeah. I know you do."

"What are you going to tell Tiffany?" It wasn't fair to make her think there was a chance if he knew there wasn't.

A shoulder lifted. "Nothing. She'll figure it out. It's better than outright saying I'm not interested and hurting her feelings."

"Is it?"

He hesitated. "We'll be doing our own thing soon enough anyway. We only hung out at school for the most part, you know?"

That had me raising my brows. "Does that mean

you have no intention of sticking around or keeping in touch with your friends?"

The exasperated look on his face made me smile faintly, but it grew when he drew me into him in a tight hug. "Don't be stupid. You know I'm always going to bug you. Plus, I can't see myself leaving the city. Can't say the same about you, though."

"Me?"

Tiffany joined us again, a new drink in her hand identical to the last one. "What are we talking about other than the likelihood of Lawrence's penis falling off from disease in the near future?"

I gave him a pointed look as if to say *see, moron?* "Ren is implying that I won't stick around the city now that school is over with."

Her brows arched. "Will you?" My shoulders dropped at her question. "What is there for you here, Della? I mean, it's not like I don't want you to stay. But even I'm going to be coming and going. I'll be performing across the country with a ballet company based out of California. Judith set it up for me."

"What? That's amazing!" I rounded the table to hug her, smiling when I drew back. "How am I just now hearing about this?"

"I wasn't sure if..." When her words faded, the smile dropped from my face and was replaced quickly by a frown.

"Tiffany, I'm so happy for you. You know I'm not doing that sort of dance anymore. I won't be. And after what Ripley said at our last appointment..." My shrug was casual, a period to the sentence. "It doesn't matter about me. What matters is that you're doing something amazing. I'm sure Judith and your family are proud."

To my surprise, her cheeks pinkened. "I guess. They want to host a going away party next month. That's when I leave. You guys should both come. It'll make it less awkward when my parents are trying to brag about me like they know anything about my life outside of dance."

I hugged her again. "Seriously, that's amazing. I'll be there. Have you told them about contemporary dance yet or considered doing something with that?"

She snorted like that was unbelievable, pulling back to sip her drink. "Not all of us get to decide what's best for us and still be loved by people."

My brows pinched. "Tiff—"

"Seriously, Della, it's not a big deal. I love ballet too. This opportunity will be huge for me, so I'm excited. And have you considered what you'll do now? You don't have to be in the city to paint and sell your art."

"Why do you guys think I'm going to ditch the only place I've ever known?"

It was Ren who said, "Why wouldn't you? She's right. This place has become a hellhole for you, and if what you told us about Sam and her dad is true, then it'll only get worse. You don't need to be around to see that."

I went to argue but couldn't find the words. Were they right? I didn't want to see the downfall of another trial, even if a new one showed my father wasn't all that bad compared to the people who pinned it on him. Had he been involved in the crime he was charged for? Yes. It wasn't only him though, and he didn't deserve to be killed so he wouldn't name anyone else.

I stared down at my hands. "I don't know what I'm going to do," I admitted in a whisper. I never thought about what it'd be like to leave because I never thought it'd be possible. My family and friends were here. Theo. His business.

Swallowing, I sighed and looked up as Sam and Gina were approaching. Chills crept down my spine as I held off from frowning. After what Kat told me, I didn't want to be anywhere near Sam, and Gina was no better. She was the yes woman, doing anything Kat and Sam told her to without thinking.

I thought I heard Ren curse under his breath and get in front of me like he was going to use himself for a shield if it came to that.

"What do you want?" Tiffany asked Sam.

Sam ignored her and kept her cold eyes directly on me. We were never close. We hung out because she was friends with Kat, but I had no reason to believe she hadn't liked me until the day I'd gone to Kat's house all those weeks ago. Why would she when I did nothing to her? "Have you seen Kat?"

I peeked around Ren's body some more to get a better view of her deadpanned expression. "No. Why?" Looking around the room like she'd be there, I shook my head slowly before seeing Gina standing off to the side biting nails that already looked rugged and torn.

"What's wrong with her?" I already knew the answer. She was acting like Kat was when I met her here, the sickly tone to her skin and eyes being a dead giveaway.

Gina was the one who was snorting the coke and not caring who was around to see it when I'd hung out with them. It made my stomach hurt.

"Don't worry about her," Sam snapped at me, stepping closer. "I know for a fact Kat was seen here with you yesterday. Where did she go after?"

"How am I supposed to know?" Stepping around Ren, I crossed my arms over my chest. Ren stayed close by my side and Tiffany even came closer. "I left before she did, Sam. I told her to get help. Just like I'll tell you and Gina. You all—"

"I don't care. I need to know where Kat is. If you don't know then I'm out of here." She grabbed Gina's arm and yanked her away, shoving past a few girls huddled in their path while Gina protested.

Ren and Tiffany looked at me. It was Tiffany who asked, "You saw Kat yesterday? Why didn't you tell me?"

"Us," Ren corrected skeptically. The disapproval was thick in his tone and I didn't appreciate it. "You said Kat told you shit about Sam and her family, but I thought you meant over the phone. You two used to talk for hours that way when we were younger."

What was I going to tell them? I wasn't about to admit what I'd kept in my purse, or how I'd gone home crying until I fell asleep because I was upset over how bad Kat had been. It didn't matter that I walked away freely, willingly, or that I handed her the drugs without much of a fight. It still hurt.

"We got into a fight. Sort of. I don't know where she went afterwards. The bartender that was working isn't here today, and I doubt he would even know." I could try calling her, but if she wasn't picking up for Sam and Gina, the girls that were closer to her than me, then I doubted she'd answer my call.

"I'm sure she's okay." Ren pulled me into him, squeezing my arm. "She's almost as scary as Lauren. Determined, too. I'd be more willing to fight her though. Like Sam."

"Yeah, what was that?" Tiffany snorted, setting her drink down. "No offense, but you're not really built to fight."

Ren did take offense to that. "For the right people, I would."

She didn't reply. Or blink. I knew how she took it the second her face drained of any expression. He hurt her feelings. Again. "Ren is protective of all his friends if he needs to be," I tried telling her.

"Friends," she murmured, downing her drink in one long gulp. "I think I'm going to head home. My mother is bringing a few new trainers by to help get me ready for the tour."

"Tiff, wait. We can go together."

She waved me off. "I'll get a cab. Don't worry about it. You and Ren have fun and try not to think about Ribbons or any other professor. You don't need to anymore. While you're at it, screw Kat and those other bitches. Trust me, girl. They're not worth your time."

I frowned when she weaved through people without looking back. When she disappeared out the front door, I smacked Ren until he whined and rubbed his arm while looking back at me. "Really?"

"What the hell did I do?"

"You upset her!"

"You're the one who emphasized the friend thing, not me." He dropped into a seat again and sighed. "She'll be fine. She's hard-headed."

"Doesn't mean I can't worry."

"Only you," he mused. "I know you're not supposed to think about school, but I'm curious, and this has nothing to do with Ribbons. What ever happened to that project you said Ambrose had offered you? You never brought it up again after you mentioned it a while ago. It was about that class that starts this summer, right?"

That class. The one where she wanted me to model naked in front of a bunch of strangers I didn't know, who probably knew me through newspapers and TV reports casted from the trial since they decided to televise the event. I hadn't told anybody but Tiffany about it because I was worried about what they'd say. Not even Theo knew more than the basics.

"I met with her a couple days ago, but she wants to speak with me again soon." She needed a final response, but I couldn't make up my mind.

"Are you still taking the class?"

My throat was dry. "Yes." I paused. "I think so? To be honest, a lot has changed. I'd be stupid not to." *But was I ready to take a robe off in front of everybody and let them draw every flaw on my body?*

Ren reached over and grabbed my hand, giving me a comforting smile. "You should do it, Della. What do you have to lose?"

I didn't want to think about that.

Hadn't I lost enough?

chapter twenty-one

THEO

SMOOTH LIPS PEPPERED kisses down my bare chest as small hands pulled the comforter down. Eyes cracking open as those bow-shaped lips wrapped around my bare cock had me groaning loudly, my hand finding the back of her head.

"Christ, Della." Feeling the hot, wet heat of her mouth glide up and down my length, flattening her tongue on the underside of my thickness, had me awake in a flash. My free hand gripped the sheets beside me, still warm from her body. Cursing as she took me deeper, I tipped my head back and thrusted my hips up.

Her gag had me smoothing my fingers through her hair as she worked to the rhythm my hips were setting, one of her hands gripping the base of my cock and jerking me while her other fondled my balls.

"Fuck," I rasped. Sentences were beyond me as she quickened the pace, her head bobbing up and down, making wet fuck-me noises, as the sunlight filtered through the blinds of my bedroom window. When I asked her to stay the night, I'd wanted to do every dirty thing my mind could conjure, but she'd fallen asleep watching some Disney movie with an old man in a floating balloon house, and fuck if I could wake her from looking so goddamn peaceful. Even the dog was curled up beside her on the couch until I carried her to bed.

The sounds her mouth was making against me was enough for me to fucking blow, but I didn't want to. "Sweetheart, I'm going to come if you don't stop." Though the thought of her taking all of me in her mouth and swallowing was tempting, I liked filling her a different way. It was a primal need that only made me harder for her as she sucked on the head that I knew was leaking. "Get on top of me, Della."

She didn't listen. Instead, she did everything she could to get me to come instead. When her hands squeezed me tighter and her teeth lightly grazed me as she deep throated, I was fucking done for. Her free hand massaged my balls as my hand tangled in the strands of her hair and pulled her into me instead of away like I'd demanded.

I thickened in her mouth, arching up, and came. Fast. Hard. And fucking came some more.

The sweet blonde between my legs took it all, looking up at me through her lashes as she swallowed and slowly withdrew, some of my cum on the corner of her lips that she licked away with her tongue.

She gasped as I yanked her toward me until she straddled my hips. With a bruising kiss, I rocked her into me, my cock already hardening again from the semi that I had even after the best fucking blowjob I'd ever gotten. The tangy taste of me on her tongue should have been a turnoff, but all it made me want to do was worship her until she got the same treatment I did.

My fingers found her panties under the shirt she borrowed from me the night before and moved the material aside to find her already soaking wet. "Jesus fuck," I groaned, drawing my finger through her arousal and toward the bundle of nerves. She wiggled on me, kissing my jaw, cheek, and trailing her lips to my ear where she sucked the lobe into her mouth as I pinched and tweaked and rubbed her clit until her breathing grew heavy.

When I dipped a finger inside her and hooked it, the strangled noise I was greeted with had me grinning against her neck as I suckled the skin above her pulse. The second finger entered and stretched her, causing her to grind down on me until she was panting. "That's it, baby girl. Ride my hand just like that."

Her hips lifted and dropped down as she circled her hips, and when I entered a third finger she tipped her head back and moaned my name.

"That feels so good, Theo," she whispered, kissing

me again. Her hands held my face to hers as she sucked my tongue and got my cock twitching against her. She kept riding my hand until my thumb put pressure on her clit again as I scissored my fingers inside her. I could feel her tightening around me, her legs locking on either side of me as she cried out and came, biting into my bottom lip so hard I could taste blood. It didn't matter. Della Saint James could mark me however she wanted to show the world I was hers.

Using the wetness gathered on my fingers, I pulled out of her and slid my fingers to her backside, teasing the tight bud I hadn't played with yet. "So many things I want to do to you," I murmured, kissing her lips as I probed her hole. "So many things that I know you'd let me do to your tight little body."

She shivered and froze as my wet fingertip entered her ass, her fingernails digging into my shoulders until my skin stung. "T-Theo. I…" It wasn't a scared hesitation or warning. She closed her eyes as I kept my finger there, letting her slowly adjust to the intrusion.

"One day I'm going to fuck your ass."

She swallowed, wiggling again until she gasped when it made my finger go deeper. "But not today?"

I kissed her slowly, letting my tongue tangle with hers as our breaths mixed and our teeth nipped, before drawing back. "Not today. I'll get you used to me first. This morning I want to show you how much I love you."

With that, I withdrew my finger and maneuvered us so I could slide down her panties and dispose of them across the room. The shirt came off next. When I positioned her on top of me, I kissed her neck, her jaw, until I grazed her lips with mine and said, "Take what you need from me, Della. Anything and everything."

She exhaled softly before kissing me again, one of her hands guiding my cock to her entrance before she slowly slid onto me. We both breathed heavily as she took me inch by inch until she bottomed out. Her arms hugged me close to her for a moment before she lifted herself up and slid back down again. She repeated the motion again and again until she needed more, my cock living for how tight she was around me.

That time when I kissed her, it was with a purpose. It was slow and needy and hungry and tortured. Every graze told her how much I cared, every nip how much I wanted her, and every suckle how much I didn't give a fuck what anybody else thought.

The spell of her hips rising and grinding and riding me was broken when my cell went off on the nightstand. Nobody bothered me early unless it was necessary, but I couldn't make myself care. Not when I had Della's pussy squeezing me so tight it felt like she was trying to milk me of cum every time she lowered down in frantic movements.

It rang again.

Gripping her hip, I kept her moving against me, our skin slapping, the wet sounds between us loud and telling, as I lifted the phone to my ear and pistoling inside of her. "Somebody better be fucking dead, Flamell."

Della didn't stop like I thought she would. If anything, the hand I kept on her only made her wilder for more as we worked each other's bodies to the brink. She started circling her hips and biting her lip to be quiet, but she rode me harder, faster, until sweat covered both of us.

"That's it, baby," I cooed, "just like that."

"It's Katrina Murphy," he told me.

I let out a breathy groan as Della changed position and took me deeper. I jackknifed upward, filling her the same time she moved down, causing her to tighten around me again and I knew she was close. "What about her?"

There was no doubt in my mind he knew what I was doing right now, and with who because I was all but grunting as Della fucked herself with my dick at the pace she set. But I didn't give a shit. I needed Della to come, to let me drive into her until I couldn't hold back and come so fucking deep inside her cunt that she'd never get rid of me.

Della was so lost in the moment I don't think she even registered the phone. "Theo," she cried out. "I need you to come inside of me. Please."

The same moment Flamell opened his mouth, Della threw her head back and came like she knew my thoughts, her mouth parted in a silent scream as she gripped me so hard I couldn't help but follow behind her, holding her down while I emptied myself in spurts inside of her. "She was found dead over on the south side. Overdosed. Police were called an hour ago. Coroner just took her body away."

I was coming down from my high with Della tucked close into my sweaty body when I tensed under her. Her arms tightened around my shoulders, seemingly unknowing of what Flamell had told me.

"West?" he asked.

"I'm here," I murmured, words thick.

"Tell Della that I'm sorry," was what he ended it with before hanging up.

I dropped the phone onto the bed beside me and wrapped my arms around Della, keeping her close to me. My softening dick was still inside her as we caught our breath.

"Baby," I whispered into the crook of her neck where I kissed her softly.

She hummed.

"There's something I need to tell you."

chapter twenty-two

DELLA

DEAD. There was no way that could be true. It'd been hours since he told me, and I still didn't believe him. It hadn't sunk in until I asked Dallas to drop me off at my apartment. I knew Theo had things he needed to do, even though he offered to stay with me. I didn't want him to.

How could she be dead?

Rationally, I knew how. I knew why. I'd told myself if she didn't get help that overdosing was a likely possibility. I didn't want it to be true. I didn't want…

Throat thick, I stared at the fluffball Theo sent home with me, his gentle licks on my shins not as comforting as I was sure he'd hoped for. I picked up

Ramsay and cuddled him on the couch, in a daze as I repeated those words in my head.

"I'm so sorry, Della. So sorry."

Exhaling roughly, I squeezed my eyes shut to fight off the onslaught of tears that burned them. Theo might not have liked Kat, Sam, or Gina, but he'd meant what he said. Whether he'd been sorry for me or for her, I wasn't sure. Maybe both. All I knew was that *I'd* been sorrier than he could have known.

Kat had overdosed.

Overdosed after I'd given her...

Ramsay barked when I made a choking noise and curled into myself. He jumped off my lap and onto the floor, head cocked, and eyes focused on me. The tears poured down my cheeks over the guilt that surfaced hard and heavy in my chest.

Reaching for my phone, I dialed the first person I could think of that wouldn't look differently at me if I admitted what I'd done with details I'd held back. "I need you to come over."

Instantly, my best friend said, "On my way, Del."

I wasn't sure how long it took, but the knock on my door had me shakily walk over and look through the peephole to see my best friend's short hair and worried eyes. I opened the door and was instantly wrapped in two arms and the lemon drop scent that was all Lawrence McKinley.

Blowing out a breath into his chest, he guided us inside and kicked the door shut behind him. As soon as he asked those three little words, I broke all over again. "Are you okay?"

I wasn't. I was far from it. I couldn't get those words out as I cried into him. He shushed me, rubbing my back, brushing a hand through my hair as he walked us over to the couch and held me close to his side when I drowned his cotton tee with my tears.

It felt like forever had passed before I was able to collect myself enough to speak. I spoke the words into his chest, feeling his arm tighten around me in comfort. "It's my fault."

He brushed hair out of my face. "What's your fault?" Gently, he moved me away to look me in the eyes, examining my puffy, red face with a frown before swiping his thumbs over my cheeks. "Hey. Talk to me."

Trying to swallow the emotion rising in me, I blinked away the tears until I was able to see him clearer. "Kat is dead, Ren. She was…" His eyes widened as I drew in a breath. "She overdosed sometime this morning."

"Holy sh—" He shook his head and hugged me again, letting us stay like that for a few long beats. From over my shoulder, he murmured, "I don't see how that's your fault. Just because you saw her and argued doesn't mean anything. Okay?"

My hands fell from where they rested on his back. "I gave her the drugs."

His entire body jerked away from me, surprise flickering all over his face. Lips parting, he blinked once, twice, a third time. "Come again?"

I palmed my eyes, drawing my knees up to my chest and burying my face into them. Taking a deep breath, I did my best to explain. He'd understand. He wouldn't judge me or bullshit me if he knew I messed up. "Kat called me crying, so I went to Divers where she was at the bar. The bartender kept looking at her weird and I could see why. Her eyes, Ren, they were so red and puffy and off, she wasn't acting right."

"She was high."

"Or withdrawing."

Ren frowned.

Daring to look at him again, I sat back on the cushion and squeezed my legs. "A while back, she'd invited me to her place. Sam and Gina were there too. They'd all been drinking. Then one of them pulled out something from their purse and it was pretty obvious what it was. Gina made a line on the coffee table and started...snorting it, and Sam and Kat were trying to get me to let loose." His jaw ticked before he opened his mouth to ask the obvious question on his mind, but I shook my head. "I didn't do it. I told them I was leaving because I didn't want to be part of that. Kat wasn't herself then, saying she'd done it a few times before and that I'd like it. That I'd...lose weight if I did it.

"She gave me some and I kept it. I don't know why I did it, Ren, but I did. Maybe even thought about using it a few times. Until I forgot. Until I found other ways to cope when I was having bad days and wanted to... It doesn't matter. Anyway, she kept asking me about it when I met her at Divers and that was when I realized it was still in my purse. I didn't have to give it back to her, but I did."

Ren swore again. Something he didn't do often unless it was justified. If now wasn't one of the times I wasn't sure what was. "You can't think that giving her that led to—"

"How can I not? She's *dead*."

Ren scrubbed his palms over his face, his silence thickening the tension in the room. I stood and started pacing, Ramsay near me with each anxious step I took. "I practically killed her! I handed her the weapon that took her life."

Ren stood too, face red and eyes full of exasperation. "You didn't kill her. Jesus, Della. I get that this must be hard for you, I really can't imagine. But you didn't hand her a gun or anything else that prompted her to end her life. That was her choice. *She* killed herself. And you don't even know if she overdosed using the shit you gave her. If she was using before, it could have been anybody's supply. Feel me?"

I didn't *feel* him. I felt too much. Her death was a weight dropping on me from the Empire State Building. It crushed me. It'd end me. And maybe it should have because I'd never know for sure if I handed her the final dose that took her or not.

Stopping in the middle of the room, I hastily scrubbed the tears from my face. "I told her to get help. That was what I wanted. She s-said she wouldn't use it. I wanted to believe she meant it."

Ren walked over and gently grabbed my upper

arms, squeezing them. "Thinking about what happened isn't going to help anybody. You can't go back and fix it."

What he said sent chills through my body as I thought of Kat's words to me. *"I messed up, Della, but I'm trying to fix it."*

Sniffling back tears, I moved out of Ren's hold. I wanted him here, but I wasn't sure what I needed from him. He wasn't wrong. There was no way I could blame myself solely for what happened to her, but that didn't make it any easier knowing Katrina Murphy, one of my oldest friends, had died today.

Died.

Vanished from existence.

"I'm going to be sick," I groaned, bolting to the bathroom. I heard Ren close behind me as I bent over the toilet and emptied my stomach and what little was inside it. He was at the sink, running water, and came over when I sat back against the wall behind me.

"Here." He squatted down and handed me a wet washcloth, watching as I cleaned off my face and then flushing the toilet while I stared off at nothing in particular. "I don't know what to say to make you feel better. But I'll do whatever you need. Call somebody. Have you talked to your guard—*Theo* about this?"

His correction should have made me warm and fuzzy, but those feelings were buried under grief and mourning. "No. I didn't tell him about any of it."

"Della…"

"I don't want him to look at me differently or be put into the middle of it if something goes wrong."

His nose scrunched. "What could possibly go wrong?"

"I gave her drugs," I reminded him dryly, not bothering to look at his face which I'm sure was staring at me with an argumentative look. "If she had it on her, my fingerprints would be on them. People would say they saw us together and she was acting strange. I could be—"

"Stop. Stop right there. If you think that anything is going to happen to you, then you're an idiot. Not when you've got somebody like Theo in your life who'd rip the head off anybody who came close to trying to hurt you. I'd know, I was on the receiving end a time or two. He's protected you for this long. He'll do it for as long as it takes."

I parted my lips to disagree, but...didn't.

"You know I'm right," he whispered, sitting beside me on the floor. He draped an arm over one of his knees and bumped my closest knee with his. "I may not like the guy all that much, but that doesn't mean I don't think he's good for you. I'd just like to think you're too good for him."

I wanted to smile, the temptation was there, but I couldn't. Instead, I stood up and felt his eyes on me as I dropped the dirty washcloth into the hamper and walked over to the sink to splash cold water onto my warm face and brush my teeth. Hands gripping the edge of the counter, I stared at my reflection, at the deep frown and the pale skin and the distant eyes.

The longer I stared, the more I felt the resemblance of hate growing in my chest. I swore the girl staring back grinned like she knew it was happening, like she was beckoning the negative feelings as if I deserved them.

I didn't.

I didn't deserve it.

I raised my hand.

And punched the glass.

"Holy fucking—" Instantly, I was being jerked away from the shards of sharp glass everywhere, my fist aching and bleeding and my bare feet being stabbed by the little pieces that strayed from the mess I'd made — from the reflection of the girl who'd tormented me for so many years.

"*Are you insane?*" Ren barked, quickly lifting my hand and examining the damage I'd done. I didn't even look to see what was there, just felt the blood dripping down my wrist and arm until it dropped to the floor. "Goddamn, motherfucking shit. Your feet." Flustered, Ren told me to stay there as he went back into the bathroom and opened the cabinet the first aid kit was in.

When he didn't come back right away, I stared down at the droplets of blood next to me on the light hardwood and I heard, "You need to get to Della's. Now. Yeah, yeah. I'm not your number one fan either, buddy. Just do it." There was murmured grumbling before he was back by my side. "You're crazy. Absolutely nuts. But I've also decided that I never want to fight you because that was one mean right hook and would probably hurt if it'd been a human on the other side of the blow."

He shook his head and rambled on as he cleaned me up. The sting of the spray and wipes he used had me hissing, but he ignored them. I deserved it, I realized. The pain.

But I found myself smiling slightly knowing I couldn't see that girl again. Not for a long time. And when Theo arrived...I was crying for an entirely new reason.

chapter twenty-three

THEO

SHE WAS lucky she didn't need stitches. She was even luckier that I wasn't around when she decided to put her fist through a mirror because I would have lost it. I wasn't planning on braiding best friend bracelets with Pretty Boy, or even use his name like she continued to ask of me, but I was grateful for him—that he'd been there for her.

Which begged the question, "Why didn't you tell me, Della?" Her friend had left hours ago after helping me clean up her bathroom. The dog was fed and curled in a ball on Della's lap as they sat on the couch, not willing to leave her side when I stepped away to do something. Her hand was wrapped with gauze, her feet bandaged and socked because of the small cuts she'd gotten, but it was her spirit that was burdened. And I understood it. In a way.

"I would have been there," I continued, setting a plate of food in front of her. Pancakes, eggs, and three pieces of bacon, so she could feed one to the dog despite me scolding her for it. "I told you I would have stayed." I put the syrup, the *real* kind, beside the plate to let her put as much as she wanted onto the stack.

"I know you would have," was the only reply I got in a quiet tone as she stared at the food in front of her.

"Then why didn't you tell me?" I didn't expect much from her. Honesty was never hard to come by when it came to Della because she'd lived too long in the dark from her father's lies. Which was why hearing about Katrina from Pretty Boy made the sting of not being told firsthand from her feel like a punch to the gut. And the little frat fucker knew by the smile on his face when he delivered the news.

Her hand reached for Ramsay, stroking his fur until he dropped to his side for her to scratch his stomach like he loved. "I was afraid to admit I'd done something stupid. I was hoping Ren would...I don't know. Tell me I did? Tell me I made a mistake?"

"Like punching a mirror wasn't stupid?"

Her lips twitched upward. "That wasn't the dumbest thing I've done lately, but it wasn't the best choice." She gazed at her hand. "I could have stopped her, Theo. If Flamell or somebody finds out—"

"Flamell isn't going after you," I told her with the

kind of hardness in my tone that drowned the room. Even if he suggested using her in any way to bear witness to Murphy's actions, I wouldn't allow it. I told him as much.

"Whatever the fuck happens, keep Adele out of it. I don't want her facing any of the assholes her father got caught up in."

"And if she'd be key to stopping those assholes from inflicting more damage?" he'd countered with a brow raised.

My retort was quick. "She's been through enough, don't you think?"

Thankfully, he agreed. Reluctantly.

"The things you've had to deal with in your lifetime have been unfair and unjust, but you've survived. We've been through this. I won't let you suffer anymore." The frown I was met with had me sitting beside her, brushing her arm. "Hey. What'd I tell you before? It's not going to be easy, but we'll get through it."

"Not easy," she repeated dully. "My childhood best friend overdosed on drugs that I may or may not have given her. When you said things wouldn't be easy, I thought you meant between us. With people's opinions. Not...this. Not Kat. None of it."

"Flamell is going to take care of it." When she met me with a doubtful stare, I had to come clean fully. About everything—every detail I'd held back, every picture Flamell had against Richard Pratt, and the shit that Henry Murphy was caught up in because of him. And now, according to Flamell's talk with the officers investigating Katrina Murphy's tragic death, there was little doubt about who was responsible. It wasn't Della. It all came back to the same man.

Richard Pratt.

Weaving our fingers together, I brushed my thumb across the back of her hand and said, "I wanted to talk to you about this when things were settled. Flamell had every intention of making an arrest by the week's end. Katrina's death almost seems like the last nail in the coffin for Pratt."

"What does that mean?"

"It means that he and the people he blackmails won't be able to get away with the shit they've done. The others might get off with less punishment compared to Pratt, but they'll still be convicted. The NYPD has been after the people responsible for illegal activity in this city for a long time, Della. It was a shame that people had to die for them to get what they needed, but it's over."

She visibly swallowed, meeting my eyes at last before wetting her bottom lip. "And Sam? Gina? They're using too, Theo. What if they end up like Kat?"

"They won't." Not if Flamell was moving forward with his plan. I wasn't going to tell her what he intended to do. The girls were one of the biggest pieces of Kat's death, of Pratt's hand in the drug distribution in the city, and we knew that it was only a matter of time before the other people associated with him started singing like canaries to get plea deals and lessen their own sentences.

"They'll get help, Della." I'd bet a lot of money that

they wouldn't get another option. That didn't mean they'd stay clean if they were forced into a rehabilitation facility and released after a court allotted sentence. That was up to them, like Katrina's choice to take the drugs that'd ended her life. Whether Della believed it or not, she wasn't responsible, and holding onto guilt, onto what-if, would only send her under.

"You can't put blame on yourself for what she decided to do. Understand me?" I could tell she didn't, but she nodded. "Look at me. I'm not going to let you do that to yourself. Whatever happens from here on out is up to you. To *us*."

She blinked, looking at me but not really seeing. It was like the thoughts in her head blinded her. "What if we left?"

That took me by surprise. "Left?"

She withdrew her hand. "What if we left the city? Left it all behind. The drama. The past. The things people know me for. Could it be that easy, Theo? I don't think I could survive another trial. The press, the tabloids, I don't want to be put through that again if my father is brought up."

"Is that what you want?" My business was here, but I could do things remotely. Hire somebody to deal with things at the office. Fuck. I could sell if I wanted to. If it meant walking away with the girl, making her happy, I would.

"I want..." She paused, staring off again like she was lost in thought. Whatever was on her mind, it consumed her because I doubted the picture frame of us at her graduation was that interesting to look at right now. "I want you. I want seclusion. Quiet. Distance. Maybe it's selfish, but I want to escape this place. Not the way Kat wanted me to or Sam or Gina. I want to be me, and I don't think I can be that here. Not anymore." Licking her bottom lip, she lifted a shoulder. "I don't think I was ever me because nobody allowed me to figure out who that was."

"I think that sounds good," I admitted. Better than good, but I didn't want to scare her with how much I wanted to kiss her and tell her we could leave tonight if she wanted to. I knew she wouldn't.

Her brows lifted. "You do?"

"I love you, Della. If you want to leave, we'll leave. I've thought about it for a long time and there was only one person who kept me here." I smiled. "It wasn't Dallas, sweetheart."

The smallest smile curved her lips as she leaned into me, her forehead resting against my shoulder as she exhaled. "I need to talk to Sophie and Lydia. And...do you think it'd be a bad idea if I went to Kat's funeral if she's having one?"

I kissed her head. "I don't think that'd be a bad idea at all. I'll go with you. We'll keep an ear out for a service, okay?"

"You hated her."

"I hated her family and what they made her into. Not the same thing. Even if it were, I'd still go to be there for you." Her lips brushed my collarbone.

"Doesn't matter the situation, you need me, and I'll be there."

"What if I always need you?"

"You're stronger that."

"Why don't I feel it then?" she doubted, moving closer to me. I wrapped her up and hauled her into my lap. Ramsay barked from the floor and watched me embrace Della on the couch. "He's angry he's not the one being held by you. Fairly sure he's in love with you."

I chuckled at that. "He'll have to deal with being second."

"Let me guess, Dallas is the first?"

The second I snorted, I heard a soft laugh against my chest. Her body loosened as I shifted us again, my back against the cushion with her side pressed against my front and her legs stretched across the cushion beside us. "You're a smartass, you know that?"

"But you love me?" she asked.

"On a scale from one to Dallas?" I mused, kissing her head again as she leaned into me. "I can honestly say my life wouldn't be the same without you in it. Now, you need to try eating something. Don't let what happened throw off the progress you've made. Wouldn't want Ripley to get after you again."

She groaned, probably thinking about all the pamphlets her therapist had sent home with her after her last session a few days ago. "I know going to a group isn't the worst idea, but it feels like sitting around a circle and exchanging stories about how we starved ourselves or made ourselves vomit is a bad idea. Like it'll give us reason to start again."

"It's for support," I reminded her, a conversation we had when she'd let herself into my office after the appointment and went on a thirty-five minute rant about how Ripley had wanted her to join a recovery group focused solely on eating disorders. I hadn't gotten a word in edge wise the entire time she told me about it, only nodding so she knew I was listening. When she'd finally taken a breath, sat in the chair across from me, and politely declined Abigail's offer to get her some-thing drink, I said, *"It might not be such a bad idea."*

She hadn't said anything about it since.

"She cares about you, Della. It's not a bad thing to have an army behind you. If we do choose to go some-where else, imagine what it'll be like to not have her in your life."

I reached forward carefully and grabbed the plate, handing it to her. She wrapped her fingers around the edges and rested it on her lap, giving me a heavy sigh in return. "I appreciate everything she's done for me. I'll admit, I'm not sure what it'd be like not talking to her about life after so long. Do you think we'd go far? I mean, Sophie is still here. I know she's a grown woman, but she and Lydia are the only family I have left."

I rubbed her arm as she picked up the fork and sliced into the pancake stack after putting her syrup on them. "I think Sophie needs to accept you're also a grown woman who can make her own decisions. Including where you want to live. Truthfully, I think getting out of the city is exactly what you need. What both of us need."

She got quiet. Too quiet as she slowly ate a few bites of her food. If I could see her face, I'd bet she was staring off into the distance, or looking down at her plate but not really seeing what was there. I wondered if her tongue was poking out past her lips in concentration, or if her nose was scrunched over her thoughts.

Finally, she broke the silence. "What do you think Sophie is going to say when she finds out about us?"

Well, I knew she wouldn't throw a party, but I wasn't going to tell her that. Della was probably assuming the worst. "I'm sure it'll be an adjustment for both her and Lydia. For a lot of people once they know."

She squirmed slightly. "I think Lydia suspects. She told me..." Her faded words made me rest my chin on her shoulder in wait. "Did you save the artwork I'd given you when I was younger? The stuff that I drew on scrap pieces of paper."

I smiled. "They're in my office."

Another pause. "Really?"

"Really."

"Lydia knew that. She made it seem like she knew there was more to the story than I did. So, I don't think she'd be all that surprised once we admit we're doing this."

"Because I kept your artwork?"

She turned her head slightly toward me, an amused

smile on her face. "Well, they were pretty bad. I know my mother threw some of them out over the years."

In Elizabeth's defense, there wasn't a lot of room left anywhere. She needed to make some room for the new pieces Della gifted her parents. "I kept them because they made me happy. Even if I didn't know what the hell they were supposed to be half the time. I'd gone through a lot of rough patches that you helped me get through back then. Imagine what we'll get through now."

"All because of my pictures?" The disbelief in her tone was limited, awe taking over the faint inquiry.

"All because of you," I answered honestly. She wiggled closer and picked at her food again, picking up a piece of bacon and, as I knew she would, threw it to the dog. "Wish you'd stop doing that."

"I wish you'd stop telling me that like it'll change. Don't think I haven't noticed you feeding him scraps when you think I'm not looking."

Grinning, I pecked her cheek. "The damn dog is spoiled."

All she did was hum out a reply and continue eating, until every piece was gone while I peppered kisses over the back of her head, her temple, her jaw, anywhere I could reach.

Eventually, she asked, "What happened the night you came here and kissed me for the first time? You said you were angry with somebody my father knew."

I hadn't thought about that in a while because I'd had the real thing right in front of me. I didn't need to jack off to thoughts of that night like I had too many times to count. "It was shortly after the first time Richard Pratt had come to my office and started insisting we become partners. Interactive Marketing was doing well. We'd gotten new investors after a few others had dropped when the scandal made the news. Pratt made it sound like he could make others drop, which would have been a huge financial loss for IM and me.

"I started drinking in my office after Abigail left for the day. Drank myself stupid, honestly, letting that jack-ass's words get to me. I believed him. And, after a while, people were pulling away from IM with their money. Looking back now, it wouldn't surprise me if Pratt told them to. Gave them money in order to take the loss that partnering with me meant. He wanted in to do God knows what. It wasn't like I had big operations like some of the other businesses he took control of."

"And you came to me?"

I wanted to ask, *where else would I go?* I didn't though. "Yeah, sweetheart, I came to you. Even then I knew what I wanted but told myself I didn't deserve it. Convinced myself the world would be against us because it wasn't right I claimed you when you and your father were going through hell. It wasn't the right time."

She shook her head. "Would it have ever been? If my father didn't...if he hadn't been killed, would you have even done anything with me? You always fought it."

"I wanted to believe there was somebody better out there for you," I admitted, sighing over how much time I'd lost by being an ass. Whenever I got pissed at the idea of Della falling for somebody, I told myself I had no right. It didn't stop me from turning green and smoking, drinking, or trying to fuck it out. But I didn't want another woman. I'd wanted Della.

"I don't want anyone else, Theo."

"I know that." I kissed her cheek. "I'm glad. Probably wouldn't end well. I'd chase them off like that asshole who kept asking you to study for that history class you took last year. The douchebag with the dyed hair."

She gasped. "Ray? I thought he stood me up when I finally agreed to meet with him at the Hut!"

I knew she did. She'd called me complaining and I offered to hang out with her to get her mind off it. I'd bought her favorite drink from a local café, ordered us dinner, and told her we could watch whatever she wanted.

I hadn't felt bad at all.

"You kind of suck, Theo." She didn't sound upset, more amused than anything. "Ray. Huh. I wasn't going out with him. I was helping him study."

I eyed her. "That wasn't what he wanted, and I knew it. Couldn't let him try making a move. And don't get me started on Pretty Boy. Watching him flirt with you makes me want to vomit and throat punch him."

Now she was laughing. "Ren knows I'm not interested, and he isn't into me. We're friends and nothing will ever change that."

I hugged her into me. "I wouldn't ask you to change that. Nobody that truly loves you would ask you to stop being part of other people's lives for them."

She was quiet for a moment. "I know."

"I know you do."

I KNEW where Sophie was from the strong scent of her expensive perfume that drifted from the parlor. She was talking with somebody on the phone when she saw me, her brows lifting when I stopped at the doorway.

She hung up a moment later, dropping the phone onto a small plant table. "You're the last person I expect to see in my home, especially when Adele isn't here."

"You know—" I walked toward the window that overlooked the extensive garden I knew she didn't keep up herself, "—she prefers being called Della. Don't you think it's time you started calling her that?"

"Her name is Adele. Why on earth would I call her something different? Especially something as childish as Della."

Patience, I reminded myself. "She's meeting with a professor of hers. Figured now would be a good time to talk."

Sophie sat at her usual spot by the opposite window that rested beside her pianoforte. For somebody who pushed Della so hard to learn, she never played herself. I knew she could, had seen it a time or two, but all it did

416

was collect dust. "I don't see what we could possibly have to talk about."

That amused me. "Take your pick. It could be about the ten thousand dollars you offered Nicholas McAllister to make the article disappear and get the hell out of the city before Richard Pratt could turn on him, or it could be about the money you threw around different law agencies that your husband wasn't associated with in case things got bad in the media. I'm sure he loved that when word got back to him."

"I don't know what you're talking about," was her defense instantly. Not that I expected any different.

"Luckily for you, I don't give a fuck what you do with your money. Or, in this case, your husband's money. Have at it. I'm here to talk to you about Della."

She straightened. "What about her?" Her eyes studied mine a little too carefully as I walked from the window to the seat across from her. Something clouded her vision. "Jesus. You finally did it, didn't you?"

"Excuse me?"

Sophie pulled a cigarette out of a box that she'd always kept in the crevice of the seat cushion, using the lighter from the small table beside her and lighting it up. "Lydia always told me there'd come a day when you went through with it. I told her that she was crazy. There was no way you'd do such an idiotic thing as go after your only true friend's daughter. Especially with the age difference and circumstance."

I dropped into the seat and leisurely draped an ankle over one of my knees. "That's why I'm here." One of her brows quirked. "We both know Della is the type of person who cares deeply about what people think about her and the choices she makes. The last thing I want is for you to say something that makes her feel guilty over doing something that makes her happy because you disapprove."

She blew out a cloud of smoke. "You think I can be told what to do by you? Adele is too easily influenced by people which only proves my point. She's only latching onto you because you were there for her during the worst. What happens when she meets a boy her own age and falls in love?"

Grinding my teeth together over the thought, I gripped the arms of her uncomfortable chair. "We'll cross that bridge if we get there, but something tells me it won't be a necessary worry. My concern is you."

"Me?"

I cock my head. "You give little fucks about anybody other than yourself. If you try telling me that you paid off the reporter for the sake of the entire Saint James family name, I'll call you out on your bullshit. You're selfish, egotistical, and controlling. The thought of your niece doing anything remotely unethical by your standards puts your reputation at risk. That's what I am to you. Unethical. The wrong choice."

"Well, you're hardly the right one for her. She's an impressionable twenty-two-year-old who only just graduated college, Theodore. If you think anyone will think this is by any means all right, you're mistaken."

"Don't be bitter, Sophie. It shows your age." Her

lips parted. The grip on her cigarette loosened and she almost dropped it on herself. Couldn't say I wanted to explain to Della how her aunt caught herself on fire because of a conversation I had with her. "You don't like the fact that I would never go for somebody like you. I rejected you and you never got over it. I'm only the wrong choice for her because you believe in that twisted, miserable head of yours that you're the right one for me.

"And you know what? There wouldn't be a day on this earth that I would ever touch you. Not just because you're a married woman, but because I have better taste and judgement in character than your husband did. So, if you say something to dissuade Della from pursuing a path that's going to make her happy for a change, don't think I won't ruin you. Because Sophie?"

Her nostrils flared.

"I'll do it with a smile."

"How dare you!" She narrowed her eyes at me and huffed as she put her cigarette out in the glass ashtray she probably spent hundreds on.

I stood, straightened my shirt, and smiled like I didn't threaten her. Then again, that was why my lips tipped. She was scowling at me, trying to look scary. And failing. "I suggest when we come back together to announce the news, you say something positive. If not, I'll happily share the reason you're not supportive is because I wouldn't sleep with you in my office the day you came to see me."

She said nothing, but her jaw was locked tight as

she glared. I simply nodded and began walking away, remembering another piece she needed to know. "Someday soon, we'll be leaving the city. I don't know where or when, but I'm sure she'll bring it up."

The shriek she gave was ear piercing. "I take it that was your doing. Are you trying to separate us and get her to stop talking to me?"

Scoffing, I turned to face her. "I would never tell her to stop talking to you. We both know Della isn't the person to cut people out of her life. She cares too much. She loves you. But it would be better if she said goodbye to the only place she's known for something fresh. A place where people can't make her miserable. If you had any sanity, you'd do the same."

"Leave New York?"

I shrugged. "Admit it, Sophie. You hate it here. You hate your husband and the life you live, so you bury it by buying pointless things. Leave your fucking husband and get a life. Take a page out of Della's book and find happiness."

There was a moment of hesitation before, "You honestly think you could make her happy?"

Nothing was guaranteed, but I was sure as fuck going to try. "Think about what I said, Sophie." She didn't stop me from leaving.

chapter twenty-four

DELLA

PROFESSOR AMBROSE ACCEPTED the coffee from the cashier with her typical wide smile stretched across her face, thanking the young man before turning to me as we scoped out the café for a free table. I hadn't been to the small brick establishment, but Ambrose said it was her favorite place to go.

"I'm hoping this meeting means good news, Della. I've been asked a few times if the new model had given her answer yet."

The word *model* in relation to me almost had me laughing. Almost. Mostly, I'd wanted to cringe. My art always reflected the conventions of beauty that often weren't seen in the public eye as traditional. The kinds of men and women that were fuller figured, too skinny, scarred, and rarely flawless. I'd wanted my work to be realistic, not some fantasy I was trying to escape into, even if I found art to be just that—a step out of my own life and into somebody else's.

Once we sat tucked into the farthest corner of the café, I gave her an apologetic smile. I'd thought long and hard about this, debating on whether to ask Theo, and choosing to make up my mind without anybody else's influence or opinion. It was long overdue for that to happen. "Actually, that's what I wanted to talk to you about. The opportunity is amazing and would make a point to a lot of people that might suffer the same trials as me. But I'm not the right person to represent them. It's not because I don't think I'm strong enough or that my story or struggles aren't worthy of being shown, but I don't think I'm ready."

There hadn't been much I was able to control in my lifetime, but I was taking that back. Professor Ambrose would always be my favorite instructor. She was kind and gentle-hearted with everybody's best interest in the forefront of her mind. However, I knew my best interest wasn't the same. I'd acknowledged it, thought about it, and knew I couldn't accept.

"I would love to be able to still attend the class because I think I'd learn a lot and improve my ability to draw people of all kinds, but I'd prefer doing that from my stool and sketchpad. Maybe one day I'll be able to let people stare at me and draw what they see, but I know me, and right now I know I won't be able to handle that."

She reached across the table and placed her hand over mine. "I won't say I'm not a little sad to see you skipping out, but I understand why. The reason is the best you could have given me, and I'm glad. Truly."

I smiled back at her. "Your advice helped me a lot, you know. You told me to be spontaneous."

Her knowing eyes sparked. "I take it being spontaneous worked in your favor in more than one way?"

My traitorous cheeks heated. "It did. I have him to thank for a lot, not that he'd ever let me. Theo is...a very stubborn man."

"Fitting for one of the most stubborn women I know." She squeezed my hand before sitting back in her seat and lifting her coffee cup. "You deserve so much, Adele. I'm glad you're realizing that as well. So, tell me. What comes next now that you're finished with school?"

All I could think about was Theo.

Of leaving.

I gave her a loose shrug. "I'm planning on painting. Selling my work. I think my next big step is to get away from here. Maybe not forever, but for a while. Too much has happened and even though this is the only home I've ever had, I'm ready to try finding another one where I can reinvent myself without old ghosts lingering."

She nodded along. "Sounds like you've got a well thought out plan. Just remember that you don't have to change yourself. It's others who need to change their perspective."

It took a moment, but I found myself agreeing with her. "I know. I'm a work in progress."

"We all are, dear."

After we said our goodbyes, I called Theo with a relieved smile across my face to let him know I was on my way home. While that was split between our two places, I knew anywhere he was, was as good as home as any.

When I walked into my apartment, I saw Ramsay and Theo on the couch together, our favorite cooking show on the television, and a Denny's takeout bag sitting unopened on the coffee table.

I stopped and stared, taking a mental picture, and wanting to bring it to life on a canvas full of color. Full of hope. It was the exact image that I would display on my wall and show off to the world because it was mine. A life deserving to be bragged about and shared.

"Theo?"

He looked over his shoulder and smiled, one hand curled around Ramsay's back. "I got your favorite for dinner. Didn't think you'd mind. Come sit with me?"

Kicking off my shoes, I sat on my knees facing him, my eyes freely scoping him out while he watched me with a lopsided grin.

"What are you looking at?" he asked gently, leaning in for a brief kiss and trying not to disrupt the pup.

It might have been cheesy, but the words slipped

right off my tongue like they begged to be spoken. "My future."

His grin widened. "Yeah?"

"Don't ask stupid questions, Theo," I teased, leaning in again and grazing his lips in a kiss that lasted too long for Ramsay's liking. He stirred and barked, causing me to roll my eyes and sit back.

I focused on getting the food out of the bag and splitting it between us. "I was thinking about seeing Sophie tomorrow. I texted Lydia and asked if she could meet us. She was free, so..." I paused, passing him a napkin. "Unless you have other plans. I should have checked."

"I'm free," was all he gave me.

"You're not worried about, Sophie?" It shouldn't have surprised me that he wasn't. Theo seemed fearless, and not even somebody like Sophie could get under his skin. She'd tried.

His hand came up and brushed my jaw, something in his eyes that was light and amused at the same time. "No, sweetheart. I'm not scared of her at all."

epilogue

DELLA

THE SUMMER CAME with a brutal heat wave that matched the growing tensions portrayed when Richard Pratt's trial was scheduled for late August after his arrest by NYPD and Federal Agents for first-degree murder, and drug, weapon, and counterfeit money manufacturing. Special Agent Michael Flamell assured me during a short meeting at the beginning of June that I wouldn't be needed in the trial and that Pratt wouldn't be getting off.

Thankfully, I escaped the city by July when Theo set up appointments with real estate agents in upstate New York, far enough from the city where the spectacle of Pratt wouldn't find me but close enough that day trips weren't impossible. It'd taken only a week to find a home that I always pictured living in, a space perfect for two people and a dog with plenty of room to run around and be comfortable without the luxuries or complications that the city came with. The house was set back from the rest that surrounded it with more acreage than we needed and held a serenity foreign to me. On the first night, it'd been too quiet to sleep, so Theo had stayed up with me watching TV even after unpacking and setting up his new home office all day. While he'd need to go to the city occasionally, we both knew we'd never truly escape the Big Apple. When he went in for work, I went to see Sophie, Ren, and Tiffany before she'd left for her newest adventure with the Los Angeles Ballet Company.

My biggest obstacle had been telling Sophie and Lydia that I was in love with Theo and had every intention of leaving with him before the new trial began. The sweat that had collected on my forehead and the clamminess of my palms seemed overexaggerated when Theo took my hand and led me into Sophie's parlor as if he had no care in the world anymore. Lydia had hugged me with a knowing smile and said she was happy as long as I was, and Sophie had told me, *"I suppose you could do worse, Adele"* with a tight curve to her lips. I'd expected a fight, a heated exchange of words that Theo would need to reassure me of when we'd left.

I'd gotten closure. A new beginning where my chest was light and the butterflies in my stomach were free to flutter all because of the man who held me in public and kissed me in crowds and hugged me with a purpose no matter who stared. And some people did. But neither of us paid them attention, even if they'd had smiles on their faces from our public affections.

Saying goodbye to the city wasn't as hard as I wanted it to be knowing my parents were buried there, but I knew deep in my gut I had to go if I wanted to survive the frenzy of a media trial. Ren had gotten me a present and told me not to open it until I'd moved into the new house (Viagra that Theo didn't find funny), Tiffany told me my present was being delivered there at the end of the week (a new mirror she told me to try to not break), and my aunts had hosted a small dinner with my friends to celebrate both graduation because I chose not to walk across the stage, and moving to my clean slate. Even though I could tell Sophie had wanted to say something, she held her tongue. That night, I'd walked up to my aunt, wrapped my arms around her lightly because I knew she wasn't a hugger, and said, *"I'll miss you."*

She'd been tense, but eventually hugged me back, rested her chin on my shoulder like I'd done to her, and replied, *"I'll miss you too." There was a small pause. "Della."*

Unlike my father's trial, Pratt's was over fast. With evidence stacked against him, they didn't want to drag it out longer than it needed to be. He was found guilty for the premediated first-degree murder of Anthony Saint James and sentenced to life without parole, with twenty additional years added for each manufacturing charge. I was cooking dinner for Theo and myself when the sentencing was announced on every news channel known to man, with reporters mentioning the lack of commentary I'd made since Pratt's arrest.

It wasn't for the news' lack of trying. Reporters had called and emailed, but I refused to talk. Sophie and Lydia were both targeted, and agreed it was better not to speak on the matter, even though Sophie had made it known she had thoughts on what she wanted Richard Pratt to know regarding her brother's death. I wasn't sure how Lydia talked her down from it, but nobody had gotten one word from any Saint James family member.

Thankfully, nobody had found my new address, which meant my lawn wasn't littered with men and women holding cameras and microphones. There were no pictures surfacing of me or judgmental comments if I was out wearing leggings and baggy shirts, or old shoes, or any articles on my fluctuating weight from the time I'd moved to the time I'd settled into my new life, to the time Pratt's trial ended. The anxiety of waiting for something bad to happen had made the first few weeks in the new house tough while news updates on the trial went viral, but nobody had ever pulled me in like I feared. I'd eaten. I'd painted. Sometimes, I'd join Theo in the gym he'd hired people to help set up in the large basement of our four-bedroom home.

It was four days after Richard Pratt was escorted to Rikers Island when I got a call from the prison's rep telling me about a settlement I'd be getting for the death of my father by negligence of the prison guards. I'd all but dropped my paint palette on myself when they told me how much it was for.

Now, I was squeezing the much larger hand tucked in mine and staring at the blueprints of the old warehouse where my parents had fallen in love, before they began construction. The settlement had been more money than I knew what to do with, and I'd seen what high dollar amounts did to people, so I chose to put it to use. The place my parents loved was being turned into a recreational center for disadvantaged youth, where there would be classes for anything you could imagine. Painting. Dancing. Swimming. Thanks to Ripley, the center would host various groups for addiction, alcoholism, and eating disorders every week for those who needed help—the people like Kat, and the people like me, and the hundreds of others that hadn't found the support they needed.

Even though Theo had asked multiple times if I was sure I wanted to put all the money into the project, there wasn't any question. It was the only other thing, besides loving him, that I was sure about in my entire life.

When the Anthony and Elizabeth Saint James Recreation Center opened, it had garnered the kind of attention that put hope back into the Saint James name that had long since dissolved after my father's arrest.

I was no longer Adele, daughter of the former corrupt New York State governor.

I was Della.

Lover of Theodore West.

Painter of human reality.

And everyday fighter.

There was always going to be somebody who had something negative to say about the way I lived, but I was learning to cope with the acceptance that it was impossible to please everyone. Like the Lauren's of the world who'd publicly spoken out about how her family, who was evidently also Evan Wallace's, had never gotten the justice from my father. They received no payout compensation for his wrongdoings then, and received nothing from the Pratt scandal, seeking anything after the settlement I'd received had made national news.

I'd chosen not to follow the story, focusing solely on the future. If I thought about Evan drugging my drink because he was angry, or Lauren seeking restitution by bringing me down, I wouldn't get to experience life away from the world I'd stepped out of. I hoped them the best, that Evan would sober up, that Lauren would be successful, and that their family found peace in any way they could. Like I had.

The bubble that had surrounded Theo and I in our new home was impenetrable. And when he'd said those four little words to me after finding me in my make-shift art studio, where my "Color Me Pretty" pictures hung with pride across the wall, I knew I'd be spending the rest of my life with him without one doubt in my mind, always dancing atop his shoes, watching TV that he may or may not have hated, and feeding him every recipe I taught myself.

"Do you want Denny's?"

Want another father's best friend romance from B. Celeste? Read Ollie and Charlie's story in Kindle Unlimited!

Check out:
The Truth about Tomorrow
The Truth about Us

ACKNOWLEDGMENTS

Four drafts later and we have my eighth book release, and I'm so thankful for the people who are always there to help me make it my best yet.

Micalea Smeltzer is the Kris to my Kim and has reminded me countless times never to get lost in my head when it comes to writing. Shout out to the best Momager a girl could ask for. We'll talk about that 10%.

Jessica Roessler, you always pull through when I need you. Thank you for dealing with my crazy ass, reading Color Me Pretty, sending me novel-long emails with your thoughts, and running my teams so I can focus on writing.

Melissa Millman and Ashlee Little, you ladies rock! Betas are so important to the process and you both made this book the best it could be. I appreciate all your help on this.

Letitia Hasser has done every one of my book covers, and Color Me Pretty's is by far a favorite of mine. Everything about it screams beauty, pain, and hope just as I wanted it to. You're a true queen and I'm so lucky to work with you on bringing my baby's to life.

My readers. Every single one of you. Thank you. I love you. I appreciate you.

All the best,
    B

About the author

B. Celeste's obsession with all things forbidden and taboo enabled her to pave a path into a new world of raw, real, emotional romance.

Her debut novel is The Truth about Heartbreak.

Made in the USA
Monee, IL
27 July 2024

62761465R10260